Breathe for Me
Brittany Ann

All rights reserved

No part of this book may be reproduced, or stored in a retrieval system, or transmitted in any form or by any means electronic, mechanical, photocopying, recording or otherwise, without express written permission of the publisher.

The characters and events portrayed in this book are fictitious. Any similarity to real persons, living or dead is coincidental and not intended by the author.

Cover Design: Brittany Ann

Editing & Proofreading: The Fiction Fix

Formatting: Sam Penrod

Print ISBN: 979-8-9865620-5-6

Contents

Trigger Warnings	VI
Playlist	VII
	VIII
Prologue	1
Chapter One	4
Chapter Two	9
Chapter Three	20
Chapter Four	26
Chapter Five	36
Chapter Six	41
Chapter Seven	51
Chapter Eight	59
Chapter Nine	65
Chapter Ten	72
Chapter Eleven	83
Chapter Twelve	96
Chapter Thirteen	101
Chapter Fourteen	112
Chapter Fifteen	118
Chapter Sixteen	127

Chapter Seventeen	140
Chapter Eighteen	144
Chapter Nineteen	152
Chapter Twenty	164
Chapter Twenty-One	172
Chapter Twenty-Two	182
Chapter Twenty- Three	190
Chapter Twenty-Four	197
Chapter Twenty-Five	205
Chapter Twenty-Six	216
Chapter Twenty-Seven	227
Chapter Twenty-Eight	239
Chapter Twenty-Nine	248
Chapter Thirty	257
Chapter Thirty-One	268
Chapter Thirty-Two	285
Chapter Thirty-Three	292
Chapter Thirty-Four	307
Chapter Thirty-Five	313
Chapter Thirty-Six	320
Chapter Thirty-Seven	330
Chapter Thirty-Eight	339
Chapter Thirty-Nine	344
Chapter Forty	351
Chapter Forty-One	358
Chapter Forty-Two	367

Epilogue	374
Author's Note	383
Titles	385
About the Author	386

Trigger Warnings

This book contains graphic and violent scenes. Sex. Sexual assault. Murder.

Characters in this book were victims of mental, physical, and emotional abuse. Mental Health issues
such as: PTSD, anxiety, suicidal thoughts, and depression are present in this story. Child loss and death are mentioned in this story.
If you have an issue with any of these topics, please proceed with caution.

Playlist

Sleeping on the Blacktop by Colter Wall *(Hallow Ranch Theme song)*
Hurt No More by Pecos & The Rooftops
Never Leave by Bailey Zimmerman
Like a Cowboy by Parker McCollum
Hurt by Johnny Cash *(Denver's song)*
Leave Me Alone by Logan Micheal
Fire Away by Chris Stapleton
I Run to You by Lady A *(Valerie's song)*
This Damn Song by Pecos & The Rooftops

To the ones who try to save everyone but themselves.
Remember that you are just as important
as the person beside you.
Remember to live.

Prologue

Eleven years ago

"Hey there, handsome," a female voice purred.

I didn't bother looking at her and brought my beer bottle to my lips, taking a long swig. The bartender eyed me, then the female who decided to take a seat next to me. When his eyes landed back on me, he shook his head and that's when I knew.

This woman was trouble.

I took another sip of my beer, suddenly craving something stronger. A hand touched my arm and every inch of me stiffened, my body going on high alert.

"I'm talking to you," the woman said softly. I slammed my beer on the countertop and yanked my arm away from her. I turned and glared, baring my teeth.

"I heard you," I clipped. The woman didn't seem to mind my rudeness, she breezed right past it. She looked up at me with big brown eyes, batting her fake eyelashes at me.

"You seemed stressed, big boy. Wanna get out of here?" she asked, suggestion lacing her tone.

It had been six months since I got to bury my cock in something warm. She was pretty, not a knockout by any means, but pretty. She wasn't my type either. Her hair was fake blonde, her tits just as manufactured. She wore too much makeup and aside from her fake tits, she had no curves, nothing for me to hold on to.

Still, she had a cunt and I needed to fuck something.

I stood, pulling out my wallet, slapping some bills on the counter. I grabbed her arm and yanked her up from her seat. "Let's go."

Excitement flashed in her eyes, and she followed me out like a lost fucking puppy. I didn't bother holding the door open for her.

She was a means to an end, nothing more.

Ten minutes later, we were on the gravel road leading to my home, Hallow Ranch. I'd only been home for twelve hours. My brother was at a rodeo in the town over, and my father wasn't speaking to me. I came home thinking I would get a warm welcome, but apparently, no one gave a shit.

Mason wasn't even answering his phone. Then again, he never answered my letters either.

Pop was still pissed at me for enlisting. That was five years ago. I served my fucking country, and my father resented me for it. The asshole didn't even bother to be grateful I'd come home in one fucking piece.

The blonde next to me was chatting away about God knows what, but I wasn't listening. My eyes were on the road, my cock twitching at the thought of a hard fuck, my mind on the ranch.

Once I pulled up, she hopped out and looked at the house for a moment. Then her eyes landed on me. "You live here?"

"It's mine. So yeah, I live here," I answered, grabbing her arm again. I dragged her up the steps and through the front door. My father was in the living room, standing by the fire. It was in the middle of July and the man had a fire going. He looked at me first, and then his eyes drifted to the woman beside me.

Normally, I wouldn't bring a girl like this home. Normally, I would just get a hotel room and fuck her until she passed out, then leave.

This time, all the fucks I had to give were gone.

"Pop," I greeted, with a nod. He ignored me, staring at the woman for a bit longer before blinking and turning his back to us. Apparently, she wasn't all that offended, but when I looked at her, she was smiling at me.

"You ready, big boy?"

Two hours later, I was balls deep, filling the condom inside her average pussy up. This was our fifth round; she didn't mind being used. I groaned, my head falling back. Her legs were shaking but I didn't give a shit, I pulled out and left to take care of the mess. Once I cleaned myself up, I pulled on a pair of sweats and reemerged to find the woman had made herself comfortable.

I shook my head, walking across the room to my phone. "Gonna call you a cab. You can wait downstairs."

Her dull brown eyes went wide, astonished. "What?"

I turned to her, my face expressionless. She was in my bed, and I didn't like the look of her there. "It's time for you to leave."

Suddenly, the bedroom door busted open with a crash and my head snapped to the side. My brother stood there, fuming, as his eyes met mine and then landed onto the woman in my bed.

"You fucking shitting me?" he growled.

I tipped my chin to him in greeting. "What's up?"

I hadn't seen the man in over five years, and this is how he greets me?

He huffed a laugh before snarling. "You fucking shitting me?" he yelled again. Guess he wasn't going to answer my question.

The woman flinched before she opened her mouth.

That's when the lies began. That's when the betrayal took over, seeping into the already damaged bond my brother and I shared, destroying it completely.

That's when I lost my brother.

The woman I'd just fucked like a whore was my brother's fiancé.

Chapter One

Valerie

Present Day

"Are you sure you're going to be okay?"

"Val, honey, I'm a grown woman," my mother argued as she sat down on her bed. We were on FaceTime, the first of many, while I was on this business trip.

I was currently at Denver International Airport waiting on my rental car. The rental agency said they were limited on vehicles, so it would be an hour wait. Not wanting to wait in the lobby, I found a coffee shop, got out my laptop and AirPods, and called my mom. After that, it would be a quiet, three-hour drive to Hayden, Colorado.

"I know that Mom, but this is the longest business trip I've taken—"

"And I told you I would be fine. I don't have treatment for another few days," she explained, cutting me off while trying to reassure me. As much as she tried, nothing would stop me from worrying about her. She's all that I have and if I lost her…I would have no one.

Mom had stage three lung cancer.

We found out a few years ago, right before I graduated college with a pointless degree and a ton of debt. I was home for Christmas when I found Mom passed out on the kitchen floor. After way too long in the hospital, we finally were given a diagnosis. At the time, the cancer was only at stage two and wasn't as aggressive.

She was almost at stage four now. Her new treatment plan was expensive, and unfortunately, insurance barely covered the costs, resulting in me paying thousands of dollars a month in medical bills.

The plan—the original Valerie Cross Life Plan—was to become a lawyer, then open my own firm in Dallas. I planned on having a kickass, high-rise apartment and a dog. I hadn't decided on the breed yet, but I would've gotten to that later. Included in that plan was falling in love with a sweet man, a kind man. One who wanted children, who wouldn't leave when they entered the world.

I planned on having a big family. I wanted to eventually move out of said kickass, high-rise apartment and move to Rockwell, into a big, warm, loving home my husband and I would've built. I planned on having a chaotic house filled with messes and laughter, because I grew up in a quiet house, filled with longing and sadness.

I'm not saying my mother wasn't a good mom. She was and is the best mother to me, her only child. My father—her high school sweetheart, the star quarterback—ran for the hills six months after I was born. My parents had a *Friday Nights Lights* love story and five years after graduation, that story came to an end. He told my mom he would see her after work. She told him that she was making his favorite for dinner, fried chicken. He gave her a kiss and walked out the door.

He never came back.

My mom thought he'd had been killed in a car accident or ran off the road. Hell, she even considered that he'd been kidnapped by the next Jeffery Dahmer. She even filed a missing person's report, and the whole community stepped up to help find him.

They found him.

One year, two months, and thirteen days later.

On a beach in Florida, with a woman on his arm. Photos were taken and the case was closed. David Nathanial Cross was alive and well, living his second life in Florida with some woman named Monica.

Fuck. Monica. Fuck. David.

After that discovery, my mom slipped into a deep depression. I was too young to remember it, but her neighbor, Allie, told me all about it when I was sixteen and hellbent on knowing my father. Allie Holden was my mom's best friend of twenty-two years. She was living next door to us when my parents were still married, but six years ago, she got into a car accident. Killed by a drunk driver.

Then it was just me and my mom again.

We made it, though. It was her and I against the world. She owned a flower shop in Greenville, Texas and was the one who made everyone corsages at my high school prom. She was a successful small business owner, so the news of her lung cancer shocked the community.

The kicker? My mom didn't even smoke. How shitty was that?

"Val, are you listening to me?"

My mind snapped back to the present and I looked at my mom on the screen. She had a silk, baby pink scarf tied around her head, and she was in her navy bathrobe, her pajamas underneath.

"Sorry, I spaced out," I admitted, taking a sip of my coffee.

"Are you nervous about your proposal?"

I nodded solemnly. "It's a huge opportunity."

She nodded—in agreement, looking down at her lap. She didn't like the type of work I was doing. If I was honest with myself, I didn't either. Unfortunately, it was the only job that could cover all our mounting bills.

Whenever I wasn't travelling for work, about one week out of the month, I lived with my mom. When her cancer took a turn for the worse, she turned the flower shop over to her partner, Lynn. Lynn wasn't like family to me, but she was a good friend to Mom. Lynn runs the shop, but we still get forty percent of the revenue. That forty percent doesn't even begin to cover her medical expenses.

"I hate doing this," I sighed.

I hated my job, but I was damn good at it. I had a gift. I could negotiate better than anyone I'd ever met. It was why I wanted to be a lawyer, in the first place. I had a way with people. This was something I learned when I was twelve years old and negotiated with my science teacher about my project grade. He'd given me a B and I deserved an A.

I got that fucking A.

"I know you do," she said, looking back at me.

"It pays the bills, Mom. You know that. It's shitty, but sometimes you have to make a deal with the devil to survive," I said, holding her eyes.

Mom's eyes—green like mine—were filled with regret, and I knew she was about to start her, "Don't Waste Your Life Working to Pay for Me to Live" speech. I hated that speech. She usually gives it once a year and every year, I give her the same response—*You are my life, Mom.*

It was true.

My mother was my only friend, my only family. My grandparents were dead, and my father's family wanted nothing to do with me. *Figures.* No friends, no family aside from my mom, and no boyfriend. Hell, I couldn't even tell you the last time I went on a date. Everything before my mother's cancer diagnosis is a little fuzzy.

So here I was, in my late twenties, sitting alone at an airport on FaceTime with my mom—my only friend. I didn't have co-worker friends, per-se. I was rarely in the office, in Dallas, due to my constant travels. The chance to make work friends was rare and, in the end, I knew I wouldn't have time. I had bills to pay.

In school, I just wanted to learn. Something about consuming knowledge that excited me, and I did it quickly. When I was four, I wanted to know about the stars. When I was five, I wanted to know about animals. When I was six, I wanted to know about the oceans. When I was ten, I wanted to know about money. When I was fourteen, I wanted to know why it was called *To Kill a Mockingbird*. When I was sixteen, I wanted to know about chemical reactions. When I was eighteen, I wanted to know everything about law. When I was twenty-one, I wanted to know how to open a law firm.

When I was twenty-three, I wanted to know how to cure cancer.

Fast forward to now, at twenty-seven years old. Now, I wanted to learn how I could convince a rancher named Denver Langston to sell his land to Moonie Pipelines, the company I worked for. No, I needed to know how I could convince him.

Why?

Because if I landed the Hallow Ranch account, my commission would cover two years of my mom's medical bills.

Two more years with my mom on this Earth.

Yeah. That's all I needed to know: how to convince Denver Langston to sell his ranch to me.

Chapter Two

Denver

"Caleb," I called from the front porch.

My little boy turned to me, his dark hair flowing in the wind. He needed a haircut. We would do that this weekend.

"Yeah, Dad?"

"Good luck on your science test," I said, giving him a smile. My son was the only person who got a smile out of me. Then again, he was the only person who fucking deserved it. My boy smiled back at me before getting into his mother's car. Her fake blonde hair was in a ratty bun on top of her head, and her fake tits were hanging out, as usual. She tipped her chin to me as she got in her car.

I didn't move an inch.

Not a wave.

Not a smile.

The only thing that woman got from me was coldness. I watched them drive away just as my cell phone rang.

"Yeah?" I answered.

"The bitch gone yet? We got a problem in pasture four," one of my cowboys, Beau said on the other end.

"She's gone. What's the issue?" I asked, putting on my hat and jogging down the steps.

"You gotta see this for yourself." He hung up before I could answer.

"Fuck," I sighed as I sprinted down the hill to the barn. My horse, Ranger, was already saddled and ready to go.

Hallow Ranch has been in my family for generations, passed down from my great grandfather. All to first born sons. This ranch wasn't just a business, or a lifestyle. It was a legacy.

A legacy that came with a curse.

"Let's go," I said to Ranger as I swung my leg over his back.

A second later, we were flying out of the barn, galloping through the field in front of us, heading West to pasture four. The ranch encompassed ten thousand acres of pure, untouched beauty. Mountains stretched around us, surrounding my ranch, other ranches, and the town of Hayden in a valley.

Home.

Every year, Hallow Ranch makes six figures in grass fed cattle profit. We, my five ranch hands and I, work day in and day out to ensure our cattle are healthy, protected, and thriving. It was nearly time for the heifers to start birthing to their calves, the next generation, and my cowboy calling me out to pasture four due to a problem meant something was up.

Something fucking bad.

Rounding a patch of trees, I approached the lush green grass of pasture four. I whistled at Beau, who was about ten yards away, sitting on his horse, watching the herd. This herd was one of two; in total, Hallow Ranch had about six hundred cattle. This was just half of them.

I slowed Ranger as we got closer. Beau was leaning forward on his saddle, facing the herd and my eyes followed suit. Jigs, Beau's father and a good friend of my late father, was at the head of the herd. Lance and Lawson, the twins who had been with the ranch for about three years, and at the back was Mags, a former Marine, like me, who wanted a simple life after coming home

"What's going on?"

"Dead calf. Other end of the pasture by that tree," Beau answered, tipping his head to the left.

"Shit," I muttered.

"Yep."

"Come on." I clicked my tongue at Ranger to get him to move towards the calf.

"Right behind you," Beau answered.

I bit out a curse as I got closer to the scene. The stench was something I was used to, but that didn't mean that it wasn't foul. A newborn calf, still covered in blood and fluid was lying in the grass. My stomach dropped; not just because it was a new life we had just lost, but because a few things can cause a miscarriage to occur like that in a cow.

One of those was brucellosis, a disease that can be transmitted to humans through the consumption of cattle.

"It's not," Beau said, reading my thoughts.

I turned my head to him, waiting for him to explain. He pointed to the right, and my eyes followed. A heifer was on the ground, panting hard. "Mags wanted to end her, but Dad wanted you to see it first."

Ranger trotted over to the heifer, and I dismounted ten feet away. After I handed the reins to Beau, I walked over to her. "It's alright," I cooed, "It's alright, momma."

I walked around her slowly so I wouldn't frighten her. Kneeling down behind her, I placed my hand on her neck, only for her to jump a groan. "Hey, hey. Shhh. It's alright, momma. It's okay," I said softly, my eyes scanning her body. When I found it, I cursed.

Fuck.

Fuck. There, on the side of the heifer's head was a gash. Blood was oozing from it, and flies had started to make their claim. I looked to Beau, leaning forward on his horse, chewing his gum. That fucker always had a piece of gum in his mouth, a trick to keep him away from chewing tobacco. I jerked my head to the herd and the rest of the cowboys.

"I gotta put her down. Go tell Jigs," I called.

He nodded once and trotted off on his horse, Ranger beside him.

I looked back down to the animal, rubbing her thick neck. "It's alright, momma. It's over," I said, pulling out my pistol. I stood and pointed the gun at her head. "Sorry, girl."

I fired.

The gunshot echoed across the valley and like I expected, it spooked the herd. Thankfully, my boys had that handled. I found myself staring down at the animal, wondering what the fuck happened. It could have been wolves. She was heavily pregnant and that made her an easy target. She could have run into a tree or been taken to the ground. Who the hell knows.

Nature doesn't show mercy, even to the ones creating life.

No one is safe from nature's wrath.

I shoved my gun back into the holster and Beau came back with Ranger. Once I was mounted, he asked, "What do you think happened?"

My jaw tightened and I looked over at the dead calf. "Wolves would be my guess."

"We hunting?"

I pondered his question, my mind drifting back to when my father would send me and Mason out to scout for wolves. Hundreds of nights, it was just us two, under the stars, protecting Hallow Ranch.

That was the way Pop wanted it.

Unfortunately for him, not everyone gets what they want.

"Yeah, I'll put the twins on it tonight," I answered.

"You're the boss," Beau replied. "The bitch gone?"

A small smirk formed on my lips. My cowboys hated Caleb's mother and for a good reason, too. She was the one who nearly destroyed this ranch over a decade ago. That woman is vile and the only good thing she ever gave anyone was Caleb.

Our son was born from toxicity.

My boys say it's a miracle he has a good soul. That boy's soul was made of rainwater, pure, untouched, directly from heaven above.

"Yeah, she is," I answered, adjusting my hat.

"Thank fuck for that," he muttered, sitting up on his saddle.

I didn't comment. There was no need. Any words spoken about Cathy were usually a waste of breath unless my son was involved.

"Let's get the herd moved," I ordered, kicking my feet as Ranger took off. The rest of the morning was spent bringing this half of the herd down to the pens.

The afternoon sun was not letting up.

Again, no mercy.

Especially for a cowboy like me.

Hours later, I was putting my hat on as I stepped out of the barn when a hunter green Dodge Ram barreled down the drive stretching between here and the house. I pulled out my bandana from my jeans and wiped the sweat from my neck as the driver hopped out from the vehicle.

It was Carson, the owner of the ranch next to mine. I lifted my chin to the man in greeting.

"Howdy," he called out to me. He was wearing a black pearl snap and blue jeans with a cream gallon hat—new from the looks of it. A smile was plastered on his face that made my stomach twist.

Something was up.

Carson Waters never just stopped by unannounced, and he sure as shit didn't do it wearing a new hat. He stopped about two feet from me, looking around at the pens and my barn.

"New paint job?" he asked, gesturing to the barn behind me.

Had it painted last summer. Red, with black metal roof.

I nodded, knowing the man in front of me wasn't here to discuss paint choices.

"Yep," I answered, moving to the stack of hay bales that needed to be brought in.

"Looks real good, Denver."

I ground my teeth, bending down to heave a bale over my shoulder. These fuckers were heavy to some, but not to me. "Appreciate that, Waters." I lifted up and placed it on my shoulder.

My eyes caught Mags riding up to the barn on his black mare. Even though he was wearing sunglasses, his tight shoulders and thinned lips told me everything I needed to know.

He didn't like that Carson Waters was here either.

I turned back to the man in question. His eyes went to the hay bale and then back to me. "Jesus, Den, you load your own hay?"

My jaw tightened. *What fucking rancher didn't?*

"How can I help you, Carson?" I asked, no longer in the fucking mood to entertain him.

"I just wanted to let you know I'm thinking of selling."

He was selling his ranch. His ranch ran along the south side of mine, about a thousand acres or so. Most of that land was flat pastures, good for grazing.

"How much are you wanting for it?" I asked. I felt Mags walk up behind me.

Carson looked shocked. "Uh, actually..." he trailed off, drawing his brows together in confusion.

I let out a heavy sigh through my nose—*I didn't have time for this bullshit*—and took the hay bale into the barn, dropping it in the storage area just inside. When I reemerged, the man was looking at me funny.

I didn't like that either.

It made me want to punch him in the fucking jaw.

"Carson, I don't have all fucking day," I started.

"I'm selling it to the state."

I blinked.

There was only one reason he was selling it to the state. He was in debt and needed to cut ties. Pity curled inside my stomach, but I squashed that shit as quick as it came. I didn't have time to pity anyone.

"Let me guess; they wanted you to come out here and see if I would follow suit," I deadpanned.

"No. No—Denver that's not it," he stammered.

"What's happening to your livestock?" Mags asked as he came out of the barn.

"That's why I'm here," Carson said, gesturing to my cowboy.

"Six of your cows dropped dead last month," I said. I'd heard about it at the livestock exchange last week.

"Yes but—"

"You're dumber than you look if you came over here to sell your sick herd to me," I growled, taking a step towards him. I was pissed now.

That was the thing about the Waters ranch; they' been cutting corners and ignoring laws for decades. No doubt those cattle had probably dropped dead from brucellosis. If one was infected, then the whole herd needed to be put down.

Humans could catch that shit.

However, a man like Carson Waters didn't play by those rules. He just wanted his money at the end of the day.

I pulled my gun out of its holster and opened the chamber as I spoke. "You know, I'm not a dumb man, Waters. My ranch is the most profitable in three counties. That's because my cattle has three generations of good genes in them, healthy and strong. You were in debt and sold your ranch to the state. No doubt there'll be a new development on it soon. A shopping mall or a fucking movie theater."

I stopped and looked up at him. His eyes were wide, trained on my gun. I closed the chamber and loaded a bullet. "You came down here to sell your cattle for a quick buck, thinking you could get away with two quick profits—"

"Listen, Den—"

"You shut the fuck up when I am speaking to you. Don't you dare interrupt me," I growled. "You got balls coming out here to my land, trying to sell me sick cattle."

His skin paled. "I—"

I raised my gun at him. "What the fuck did I just say?"

"Denver." That was Mags, a warning in his tone. I ignored it.

Carson Waters drove his new truck onto my land with the intention of bringing sickness into my herds. Thank fuck there was a mountain separating our ranches.

"You came onto my land and presented a threat to Hallow Ranch, Waters. I don't take that shit lightly," I clipped.

He was shaking his head now, backing up to his truck slowly.

"You got five seconds to get in that truck and off my ranch. Then, you have thirty minutes to report those dead cows to the livestock officer. After that, you have two days to get the fuck out of this state. Go. Retire to Florida, find a tan, blonde bimbo willing to suck that limp cock of yours."

He stared at me in shock and disbelief.

"Five. Four. Three—"

He was in the truck and speeding away by the time I got to five. Sighing, I put my gun away and turned to get back to work, only to find Mags staring at me.

"Brother—"

"Don't. Let's get these hay bales loaded."

His lips thinned under the show of his hat, but he nodded.

Mags was a retired Marine, like me. We never served together but a year after Pop died, Mags wandered into the barn. He had been a drifter at the time, nowhere to go, no place to call home. One look at him and I knew. There were demons in his eyes, demons he needed to fight or let go of. The only way for a man like him to do that was peaceful work.

I offered him a space in the bunkhouse and a job, and the rest is history. Over the years, I've tried to keep him out of shadows that Hallow Ranch possesses but eventually he wanted to know the truth. I'm not one to bullshit, so I gave it to him.

I promised Pop I would do anything to protect this ranch, even if it meant spilling blood where it was due.

Twenty-five years ago

"Boys."

I didn't want to look at Pop, not right now. My hand tightened around Mason's. He was only eight. He didn't need to see this. I was over the age of ten, nearly eleven. Pop said that's when little boys start turning into men.

I didn't think I was ready to be a man yet.

"Boys, I need you to look at me," Pop's gruff voice commanded. It was filled with sadness.

I lifted my eyes and Mason did the same. I looked over at my little brother, he had been crying a lot today. That was okay. Little boys were allowed to cry.

I wasn't.

"We're going to find them." Pop's promise held something scary in it.

Them.

The men who killed Momma.

Momma died three days ago.

She got trapped in a forest fire on the edge of the ranch. Pop said she wasn't supposed to be out there. That's where Momma liked to go to think. Her stream was out there.

Pop said there were hunters on our ranch, looking for bison. He said bison were free animals, that could come and go on our land as they pleased. Like the deer. Like wolves. Like birds. The only animals that belonged to us were the cattle. Pop said bison meat is worth a lot of money.

These hunters were on our land to kill bison, camped on our land and didn't put out their campfire.

At least, that's what Pop told me.

Pop said that during the summer, the land gets real dry and fire can claim it if it gets too hot. Those hunters brought their own fire and Momma died. Pop's cowboy, Jigs, said he spotted the hunters this morning on the east side of the ranch.

We were going after them.

I squeezed Mason's hand. I was the big brother. I was supposed to protect him. It was my job. Momma told me so...

Four days later, my body was ready to give up. Pop wasn't.

We had been tracking these men for four days.

Mason and I hadn't spoken a word in four days.

Mason hasn't been in his bed in four days. He hasn't showered. He needed a shower. Momma said that little boys need to shower every night.

I grabbed his hand again as we sat on a rock. It was night and the hunters' campfire was starting to die. Jigs had one of the men tied up on the ground, and Pop had the other. The look in Pop's eyes scared me.

"Boys, this is what happens to people when they hurt the ones you love or hurt the ranch," Pop growled, his voice angry.

I didn't want Mason to see it.

"Boys, close your eyes. Denver cover Mason's ears."

I got up on my knees and covered his ears with my palms. Pop looked up at me. "Close your eyes," he clipped. I did as I was told.

There was no one there to cover my ears.

I heard every scream.

After that night, Pop sat Mase and I both down, made us promise him we would dedicate our lives to Hallow Ranch.

I kept my promise.

Mason didn't.

Mason hasn't stepped foot on this ranch in ten fucking years.

All because of Cathy.

Chapter Three

Valerie

Holy.

This place was beautiful.

I stared up in awe at the large iron entrance of Hallow Ranch through the windshield of my rental car.

I had been up since the crack of dawn, prepping for today. I called my mom before leaving, just to check in. She didn't have treatment today, which meant she had some energy. She told me her in-home nurse, Jackie, was going to take her outside, to the backyard. My mom's garden was back there—although technically, it was mine, since I'd been the one tending to it these last few months.

At the beginning of spring, Mom said she wanted a garden, something to focus on, to get her mind off all the depressing things that hovered around her. Her doctor thought that was an excellent idea.

So, taking the money I'd earned from my last commission, I went to Home Depot and bought her the supplies. We built flower boxes together and planted some pumpkin and cucumber. In the beginning, I doubted the seeds would even grow. Green thumbs weren't a family trait that I particularly possessed. Every plant I had died. Thankfully, though, nature was on our side—or Mom's side. We had three pumpkins and five cucumbers growing strong. Mom said that when the pumpkins were ready, she would make a pie. It gave her something to look forward to, another reason to keep fighting.

Even if it was something as small as a pie.

After our call, I logged into my company laptop and answered some emails. There was a deal I'd closed last month on a ranch in West Texas. Moonie Pipelines was putting in a small pipeline across four counties. The owner of the ranch was in his late seventies, running the ranch on his own. He had no children, no wife, nothing. He was the one who contacted us. He'd been trying to sell it for months. It was an easy deal, with minimum negotiation and a quick turnaround.

He got his check within the week.

My eyes scanned the patch of trees up ahead. The road cut straight through them. The drive to Hayden from Denver was mesmerizing, but the drive from Hayden to Hallow Ranch felt I had died and gone to heaven.

Colorado was beautiful.

It made Dallas look like a dump.

I took a deep breath and continued forward. The gravel road went on for about a mile, surrounded by thick, dark green trees before emptying into clearing.

When I reached it, I sucked in a breath at the beauty before me. Hallow Ranch was nestled in the same valley as Hayden but on the far north side of it. The sun wasn't shining today, and the sky wasn't clear and blue. It was overcast, which was my favorite type of weather. Breathtaking. My foot eased off the gas as I took in the beauty of Hallow Ranch.

Up and to the left I could see a large—*huge*—red barn with a black metal roof. Off to the side was a smaller structure, red like the barn. Up and to the right, sitting on a small hill, was a house.

Not just any house.

The house every woman dreams off.

A house filled with memories.

A house that needed to be filled with children and laughter.

A house that would be warm and welcoming in the dead of winter, with a Christmas tree glowing in the front window.

A house of love.

It was a large, white two-story structure with a roof that matched the barn. It had three large, brick steps leading up to the wrap around porch. The porch even had a swing, which in my opinion, made it a masterpiece.

I took a deep breath and straightened my spine before pressing on.

"You got this, Val."

My boss had sent me the file on Hallow Ranch three days ago. I read over it twice when I got it but last night, I made sure to memorize every word.

Hallow Ranch has been around for generations. It was the largest ranch in over three counties, and it produced well over six figures in annual profit, which comes from their grass-fed cattle. Denver Langston was the current owner of the ranch and had been for the last ten years. Hallow Ranch had five employees, five cowboys. I assumed that's what that extra building beside the barn was for—the bunkhouse.

It was early morning still, and I knew no one would be inside. Cowboys rose before the sun. I didn't even bother parking by the house, continuing down to the barn. When I got out, I was greeted by the cool morning air. I wanted to get here early to get a feel of the place. In my line of work, it took some convincing to get men to sell their ranches.

This wouldn't be my last time on Hallow Ranch.

There was beauty here. Peace. That was going to take a lot of convincing to sell.

My stomach twisted at the thought of bulldozers and smoke taking over this beauty, ruining the land, tarnishing it for the pipeline. I hated my job.

But I loved my mom more.

I rounded the car, gravel crunching underneath my sandaled wedges. It was a miracle I hadn't faceplanted yet. That was another thing that came with this job—the dress code. I had to dress to impress, despite the terrain. Over the years, I'd gotten quite good at it.

Even though I was from Texas, I was a city girl. I never knew anything about country life before this. Did I hate the outdoors? No, absolutely not. In fact, I loved being outside. I guess that was one perk. My office was outside. Back in Dallas, I dreaded going into the actual office. Boring, dull colors, lifeless smiles, and fluorescent lighting…it was soul sucking.

I made my way to the open, barn doors and peeked inside. Not a sound.

"Hello?" I called.

Nothing, not even a neigh from a horse.

I stepped further into the space and noticed that all the stalls were empty. Spinning on my heel, I decided to round the barn. Maybe there was someone on the other side. I moved my tablet to my right hand and pressed my left to the red siding, dragging it behind me as my eyes scanned for another human.

This was weird.

Usually, there was always at least one cowboy hanging out by the barn, cleaning stalls and doing random tasks during the day. That's how all the other ranches I'd been to have been.

"Hello?" I called again to no one in particular as I came around the back of the barn. I looked up and stopped short. There was a giant, black "H" painted on the back side. Jesus. That was huge. Who in the hell painted that?

Who in the hell got that high up with a bucket of paint and a brush?

After taking a second to admire its beauty, I rounded the last corner of the barn, coming up on the other side, an open door in the middle of the siding. Butterflies swarmed my stomach as I prepared to face the human who may or may not be inside. I had my fake smile locked and loaded, ready to plaster on a second's notice. The gravel crunched underneath my heels and in the distance, I heard the faint mooing of cows.

"Hello?" I called again as I got closer to the door.

Denver

Who in the fuck—

I stepped out of the bunkhouse, hand on my gun as my eyes scanned the property. First, I noticed a bright red sedan in front of the barn. Next, I noticed the driver of the said vehicle.

The third thing I noticed—*which pissed me off the most*—was that my cock twitched at the sight of her. She was gorgeous. Tall and curvy. A fucking vision.

Christ.

She was walking along the side of the barn, in heels, dragging her hand over the siding. She was too fucking pretty to be in a place like this, that was for sure. Grabbing the bandana from my back pocket, I dusted my hands off, as I watched her. Her steps slowed as neared the side door of the barn and I moved, seeing red.

The last woman who set foot on this property, the only one who had in the last ten years, shattered the bond between my brother and me. I lost the only family I had left because of some average pussy.

This woman had her back to me, her dark hair flowing down her back in waves that stopped at her waist, the overcast sky making it look even more striking. She was a city girl, that much was clear, dressed in a tight pencil skirt that covered every fucking inch of her perfect, round ass and a dark green silk blouse.

A woman like that had no business being out here.

A woman like that didn't come to ranches for shits and giggles.

A woman like that was a threat to Hallow Ranch.

I closed the distance between us, grabbing her elbow, spinning her around and shoving her against the side of the barn, with my forearm against her neck.

Her eyes were wide with shock and fear as she looked up at me.

Christ.

Those fucking eyes.

Green.

Forest green.

Eyes a man could get lost in.

Eyes that *made* a man want to get lost in.

Something clattered down to the gravel beside my boots, and then her hands were on my forearm. I wasn't pressing hard. She could still breathe. She just couldn't get away from me.

That's exactly where she needed to be.

The fuck away from me.

"What the fuck are you doing?" I hissed, baring my teeth at the beautiful woman.

Chapter Four

Valerie

Gray.

I was surrounded by gray smoke, holding me against the barn with unrelenting strength as it slipped into my throat, choking me.

"What the fuck are you doing here?" Smoke asked, his gravelly voice breaking the intoxicating spell of his gray eyes.

A woman could get lost in those eyes.

I wanted to get lost in those eyes.

This was the most gorgeous man that I'd ever seen.

He was big—huge. He was taller than me, and that's saying something, because I was in heels. From the age of seven, I had been the tallest person in my class, and it remained that way until the second half of senior year when a boy named Donny finally hit his growth spurt.

He had an inch on me.

My piece of shit father was tall. My mother was, too. Just not as tall as me. I ended up in the middle, and I hated it

I had never been with a man who was taller than me.

How pathetic is that?

The men in my life just liked short women. There was nothing wrong with that, but it was hard out here for a tall girl.

"You gonna speak or you just gonna keep starin'?"

I blinked at the tall—*huge*—man. He had on a black cowboy hat and it looked damn good on him, made his smoke gray eyes stand out. Judging by his dark, short beard, his hair was also dark, maybe black. His skin was tan, evidence of years spent working under the hot sun.

His face—*God*.

His jaw line wasn't hidden underneath that beard. It was sharp and strong. His nose looked like it had been broken in the past, but it only added to his fierceness. He was in a brown Carhart jacket, and the shirt underneath was a cream color. It was dusty, proof he had been working.

Was he a ranch hand?

"City Girl, I'm fucking talking to you."

I blinked again, shaking my head. "Hi," I squeaked.

It was his turn to stare. "This is private property. Get the fuck off it," he ordered, releasing me. Without another word, he turned and stomped through the side door.

Val? Your job? Remember that?

Shit.

I unpeeled myself from the barn, ignoring the tingles and heat that spread throughout from the cowboy's hold.

"Excuse me?" I asked, following him. Shit. My tablet. I spun back around and bent down, scooping up the device. When I stood again, I felt heat at my back.

His heat.

"That wasn't an invitation to follow me," the cowboy growled, his voice low. I felt his breath flowing over the top of my head.

"I—"

A hand landed on my elbow again and then we were moving. He all but dragged me across the gravel, his hand holding a firm—but not painful—grip on my elbow.

"Hey!" I protested. "Let me go!"

"You and your long legs with your fancy shoes and your fancy fuckin' hair need to the hell off this property," he barked back at me.

We got to the front of the barn, and he spun me around. My back was against my rental car and his arms were on either side of me, caging me in. We were both taller than the vehicle, but he made me feel tiny against it as he towered over me.

Seriously? How tall was this cowboy?

"The answer is no, City Girl. Go on back to your paved roads and dirty air. Whatever you're selling, we don't want it. The answer will always be no. Go back to your city. Go get your suit wearing boyfriend to lay you down and fuck you until you fake it. Then, in a year or so, he'll put a ring on your finger and a baby in your belly. You'll be a stay-at-home wife. You'll go to yoga and hire a nanny. You'll be living off his money, so you won't have to deal with men like me."

I was stunned, but only for a second. *Then,* I was a fucking angry.

My hands found the center of his broad chest, and I pushed with all my might. He staggered back a step or two, his thick brows raising a fraction of an inch in surprise.

"Who in the hell do you think that you are?" I snapped.

He stared for a second and then, he was on me again. He bared his teeth—*white, straight, and perfect*—at me. The next words out of his mouth were spoken in a tone that should have scared me away. Instead, it sent tingles flying across my body.

"The owner of the ranch your fancy ass is standing on. Get *the fuck* off my property," he clipped.

The man in front of me was Denver Langston.

This was Denver Langston?

He was nothing like I expected.

Then again, he was nothing like any of the other ranchers I had done business with. Most ranchers would be working, and I would come across a ranch hand. They would direct me to the house and then from there, I would be greeted by a member of the family—except for the rancher in West Texas. I had found him drinking whiskey on his porch at nine in the morning. Nevertheless, everyone was kind—*at first*. After they learned who I was, half of them would seem interested and the other half would just blow me off.

Denver Langston didn't seem interested at all.

He was blowing me off from the start.

"Sir, I'm here as a representative of Moo—"

"Bitch," he quipped.

I flinched at his harshness.

I have been called a lot of names in the past, *bitch* being one of them. Usually, I was able to shrug it off, but the man in front of me? The one towering over me with his smoke gray eyes and strong jaw. I didn't like hearing that word from him. I didn't like that it was directed at me.

This man just called me a bitch and it stung.

A stranger just hurt my feelings. The last stranger to hurt my feelings was my mother's doctor the day he told me she had cancer.

"Whatever you have to say, I don't want to fucking hear it," he growled.

"Sir, please," I whispered. His features were hard—cold. "I just need a moment of your time."

"I don't have a moment and even if I fucking did, darlin', I wouldn't be givin' it to you."

I had no words.

He continued staring at me, the smoke of his eyes swirling around me, leaking toxic hatred.

This man didn't even know me.

I didn't know him.

Yet, he was treating me like I was the scum under his left boot.

I sucked in a breath, my chest rising and falling between us.

He wasn't breathing. He was just staring at me, those eyes filled with hatred. Swallowing the lump in my throat and biting the inside of my lip to keep it from quivering, I pushed him back again. He didn't move this time.

I looked to my feet. "Mr. Langston, if you would like to me leave, then I need you to please move."

He grunted and pushed off the car. When I looked up, he was walking away, heading back into the barn. With his back to me, I let my lip tremble. I got in the car, checked my mirrors, put in the directions to my hotel and I took off.

On the ride back into town, I didn't take in the beauty of the land around me. I didn't have a smile on my face, and the hope I had yesterday deflated in my chest. I had failed.

I failed the company—which I didn't really care about. Honestly, they could kick rocks, but it paid the bills, and I needed those taken care of.

I failed my mom.

Without the Langston deal, the future was murky.

I only had enough money to pay for another five months of treatment.

I failed in getting the Hallow Ranch.

Therefore, I was failing at keeping my mom alive.

Tears flooded my vision and I had to pull over on the side of the road. I think I was outside of that awful man's property, but even if I wasn't, he could kick rocks too. It was dangerous to cry while driving.

I put the car in park and buried my face in my hands. Then, I let it out. Every few weeks or so, I would do this.

I called it, *emptying the emotion tank.*

You can only bottle stuff up for so long and there was no point in trying to convince yourself otherwise. Your body would expel that negativity one way or another.

So, once a month, I would cry. Ugly cry. I'm talking ruin your make-up that you spent two hours on to empress the owner of a ranch kind of cry.

I cried for my mom.

I cried because she had to have someone help her get to her garden in the back yard.

I cried for the life that she was missing out on.

I cried for the flower shop she had to give up.

I cried for the children I would have someday who would never get to see their grandma.

I cried because I was a stupid woman who didn't have what it took to stand up to a man like Denver Langston.

I cried because he called me a bitch.

Then, I cried because I *let that get to me.* Stuff like that never got to me.

I cried because I was going to have to tell my boss the Hallow Ranch project would have to be put on hold.

I cried because I knew I would probably be fired over this. I knew this because a girl named Lacy, who had been with Moonie Pipelines for ten years and sold a lot of ranches, was fired after her first refusal. Mr. Moonie doesn't take no for an answer. He fired her and sent someone else. Someone better. *Me.*

I cried because I really needed a fucking coffee. There was only one coffee shop in Hayden, and it was closed for renovations.

I cried because the hotel coffee sucked.

I cried because my mom might not see Christmas this year.

I cried because after mom died, I would be all alone.

"Hey, Mom," I said, smiling at the screen.

She looked good today. Being out in the sun did wonders for her. It was currently eight in the evening her time. She was dressed for bed with a purple silk wrap around her head. Her green eyes had a sparkle in them, one that she used to have all the time.

"Hey, honey. How'd it go today?" she asked.

There was an underlying hint of hope in her voice that was like a dagger piercing straight through my heart.

I looked at her for a moment, soaking in how healthy she looked today, how her skin glowed, how she was sitting a little taller in the reading chair in her room. Once upon a time, that chair had been mine. I would always come home and find her sitting in it, listening to her music or reading a book. So, I moved it into her room. She said it was comfortable, and I wasn't about to deny my mom the gift of comfort.

My spine stiffened at her question. I knew it was coming, and I thought I had a way to avoid it, but that would mean lying to my mom. I never lied to my mom. If it was bad news, we gave it to each other straight, with the promise that we would figure the rest out later.

"Not good, Mom," I admitted, my shoulders sagging. I had been hiding in my hotel room all day. I hadn't eaten—unless you count the bag of peanuts from the airplane I found in my purse. I ate those on the way back here.

After I cried in the car for twenty minutes outside of Hallow Ranch, I came back here and laid on the bed for two hours, staring at the ceiling. I called Mom around lunch, but it was brief. She didn't ask me about it then because she was out in the garden, instead telling me about the pumpkins.

I could listen to my mom talk about that damn garden for the rest of my life if it meant that she would never be taken from me.

"What happened?"

I shook my head, biting my lip. Her features softened and her eyes assessed me. "Valerie Cross, have you been crying?"

I ran a hand through my hair. "Yeah, Mom. I've been crying," I sighed.

"Honey, was it that bad?"

"Let's just say I couldn't even introduce myself."

Her face twisted in confusion. "What do you mean? Was the cowboy there?"

Oh, he was there alright. He was a force of nature, knocking the wind out of me and filling my lungs with his smoke.

"He called me a bitch and told me to get off of his property."

My mother flinched and her hand drifted up to her chest. "That's very rude. Why on Earth—"

"It doesn't matter. He told me no and that's that. I have a phone call in thirty minutes with my boss."

After I stared at the hotel ceiling for two hours, I'd gotten off my ass, and sent an email to my boss, letting him know that Hallow Ranch turned us down.

That I had failed.

"What for?" she asked, confusion lacing her voice. I looked away from her and stared at my luggage on the far side of the room.

"To schedule a flight home and—"

"Valerie Cross." I looked back at her. She was shaking her head in disbelief. "I know I wasn't the perfect mother—"

"Mom—"

"—but I did not raise my daughter to give up," she finished, cutting off my protests.

"He said 'no'."

"You said you didn't even get to introduce yourself, right?"

"Yeah, that's right," I sighed.

"Then he doesn't even know what he is saying 'no' to, Valerie."

"Mom—"

"I'm sorry he was rude to you, but I don't know why you let that man get to you. None of the others have affected you like this," she noted. Like I said, I'm straight with my mom and she's straight with me. She knows about all the rude encounters I have had; not because I liked ranting about those things to my mom, but because she was my only friend.

The truth was, I didn't understand why Denver Langston's words got to me. I hated it. I was off my game, because of him. He threw me off my game the second he pinned me against his barn...

"There's a lot riding on this account, Mom," I said softly, looking at my lap.

The shadow over our lives leeched into the conversation, and even though the phone, both of us could feel it. I swallowed the lump in my throat.

"Vallie," she whispered, "You don't have to do this. You can come home, and work at the flower shop. Be with me—"

I looked at her. "For how long, Mom? Huh? A month? Two at the most after I run out of money for your treatment?" I snapped.

"Vallie..."

"I will not sit at home and pretend to be happy while I watch you die," I hissed, clenching my teeth, my eyes burning. I shook my head. "I will not, Mom."

"You don't have to waste your life for me, baby girl. I've lived a good life. I had a successful business, and I raised a beautiful, strong daughter. You on the other hand...honey, your twenties have passed you by."

"I'm twenty-seven, mom," I returned, pulling my hair over my shoulder.

"Twenty-seven," she said, nodding. "You have no friends, besides *me*. You don't go out. You have a job—one you're working for *me*, to pay *my* bills—that takes you to the most beautiful places in the country but that you don't experience. Then, you come home and take care of me. That's not the life I wanted you to live, Valerie."

"The only life I want is one where you're in it, Mom," I whispered, my voice shaking. Tears streamed down my cheeks, landing on my blue sweatshirt. I got it in a Christmas gift basket from the company. The logo, Moonie Pipelines, was etched on the front in bold lettering. I didn't wear it because it was my company's. I wore it because it was the only thing that could keep me warm at night.

"I love you," she said after a moment of silence. "But I will not sit here and watch you cry over me."

I looked up at her and she pressed on. "You are a beautiful woman, Vallie. You have your whole life ahead of you, but I'm not going to argue about this with you anymore. So, the way I see it, you've got two options..."

My lips tugged up, forming a small smile. She used to always give me two options when I was kid.

"Option one, you call it quits, drop that stupid company, forget all about that cowboy, and come home to me. Option two, you wipe those tears, tell your boss you would like another chance, go back to that cowboy, and try again."

I stared at her, smiling.

She shook her head, smiling back at me. "We both know option two is your choice. So, let's cut the shit."

I nodded and crossed my legs. "Tell me about the pumpkins again."

An hour later, I hung up with my boss, my jaw on the floor.

They were giving me another chance, but not before Mr. Moonie himself spoke to me. In person. *Tomorrow*. There was a charter airstrip just outside of Hayden, and there would be a plane tomorrow morning I was supposed to be on. It would fly me back to Denver, where Mr. Moonie was, and we would be having lunch.

All because Denver Langston told me no.

Chapter Five

Denver

"What the hell did you say to that pretty woman to make her cry like that?" Beau asked from behind me.

I grunted in response, not taking my eyes off the security feed playing on the screen in front of me. We were in my office, in my house. Two years ago, I spent a shit ton of money on a security system. There had been a group of idiots going to different ranches and stealing supplies. The boys and I got tired of taking watchman shifts, it wasn't doing anyone any good if we were missing sleep.

There were cameras posted at the front entry, the house, all sides of the barn and the bunk house. Cost me a pretty fucking penny, because all the lines ran underground, but it was worth it.

Now, sitting here after a hard day in the fields, watching that beautiful woman cry in her car, it didn't seem worth it anymore to me. My jaw tightened as I watched her bury her face in her hands, her shoulders shaking. The red rental was parked outside the property line, and it should have pissed me off. I'd told her to leave.

Instead, her crying caused my chest to tighten.

I didn't like that.

She was hunched over for more than twenty minutes, crying into her hands. Her dark hair fell around her, shielding her face from my view.

She took my words to heart, and she was crying over them.

Ignoring the tightening in my chest, I thought; *good.*

That means she won't come back. This was good. I didn't need some city girl on my land, representing some company—*most likely a fucking pipeline*—on my fucking land.

Not a chance in hell.

They were smart though, I'd give them that, sending in a beautiful woman first.

Except she wasn't just a beautiful woman. No.

She was the most enchanting thing I'd ever seen.

Which meant she was dangerous.

A threat.

To me.

To my son.

To Hallow Ranch and its future.

"Boss?"

I blinked and looked to Beau, who was leaning against the doorframe. Mags was looking out the window. Jigs, Beau's father, was sitting in the chair across from my desk. Caleb's chair. He liked to sit in here with his old man while I did the books and ordered supplies. The twins, Lance and Lawson, were in town, getting everyone dinner from Ching's.

I didn't eat with my cowboys often, but every few weeks or so, I would send someone into town to pick up dinner, on me. Every Sunday, I would cook them breakfast in the bunkhouse.

"If she comes back, what do you want us to do?" Beau asked.

"Tell her to get the fuck off the ranch."

"And if she keeps coming back?" That came from Mags.

"Then call Sheriff Bowen," I spat, closing the laptop. I took a seat, my lower back aching from breaking in that horse last week. I winced, shifting in my seat.

"Your back?" Jigs asked.

I nodded, taking off my hat and setting it on the desk. "That fucking mustang from last week." The room filled with low chuckles.

"That beast put you in your place, Denver," Mags said, his voice low.

"I could have done it for you, or one of the twins," Beau chastised me.

I scoffed. "Then one of the twins would be in the fucking hospital, and you would still be out there trying to break in the damn horse."

His father laughed, throwing his head back. I shook my head, smirking as Beau glared at me. "Bastard," he muttered under his breath.

"Where are the boys? I'm fucking starving," I said, leaning back in the chair.

When they got here, we would all migrate downstairs to the dining room. The eight-seater table used to be filled with food every night, surrounded by warmth and laughter every holiday, now, it was occasionally occupied by a bunch of cowboys with broken souls.

"The rodeo is in town. Tonight's the last night. They're probably trying to fuck a buckle bunny or two," Beau said. Mags scoffed, folding his arms over his chest while Jigs chuckled again.

My jaw tightened, and I looked over to the wall. There was a huge painted canvas, done by a local artist, of the ranch. It was beautiful, a wedding gift for my parents. After my mother died, my father didn't have the heart to see it hanging in the living room anymore, so, he moved it up here. This room used to be her studio.

My mother was a photographer. Pop transformed this room into a darkroom for her a few years before her passing.

It remained untouched until after I got back from my deployment. Mason didn't even want to come in here. When we were kids, he said he could feel her in here.

I didn't feel her in here.

I felt her out *there*, on the ranch. She was in the wind, the rain, the dirt, and sunshine.

Anyways, I found the painting and hung it there. Conveniently, it also served as a hiding place for my safe where I kept about twenty grand in cash, a few of Pop's old guns, and all of Mason's newspaper clippings.

My brother, Mason Langston, was the top professional bull rider in the world. Ever since we were kids, that fucker wanted to be on the back of something that could kill him. I never knew what he was chasing. The thrill. The adrenaline? Maybe, it was the pussy that it attracted.

Hell, I never knew but I never stopped supporting him.

Not once.

Even when he spat in my face and told me he hated me. Even when he turned his back on me and this ranch. I never stopped. His biggest sponsor is Evergreen Feed. That's just a cover name for Hallow Ranch.

I was his biggest sponsor, and he would never know. His manager knew, but I made him sign an NDA.

My brother hated me, but I would love him from a distance.

Headlights in the distance drew my attention away from the painting.

All of us stood, hungry and ready for a hot meal, then a shower and fucking sleep. I was the last one to head down the stairs, stopping to poke my head into Caleb's room. His bed was made, and his toys were put away. He was such a clean kid. I had a gut feeling he inherited some of my OCD.

He was nothing like his slut of a mother, thank fuck for that.

Cathy was blonde—dyed more now due to her the gray coming in—and her brown eyes were now dull. She was waitress at the local titty bar, Tinkles. She was too ugly and old to get on that stage, not to mention that she had fucked half of the fucking town.

No, I don't approve of my son's mother being the biggest slut in town or working at a titty bar, but it was the only job she could get. She only got to see Caleb one week out of the month during the school year. During the summer, I tried to give him more freedom to choose where he wanted to stay, since he was getting older. Cathy lived in a two-bedroom apartment on the far side of Hayden. The furniture in

Caleb's room was mine, the toys in his room were mine and the clothes on his back were provided by me.

Cathy was too poor to raise a son.

All the money she had was spent on cigarettes and cheap hair dye.

He will be back here tomorrow morning. He had a science test at school yesterday, and we would need to go over that. School was ending in a few weeks, and then he would be out for the summer.

I quickly closed his bedroom door and went downstairs.

I expected to find my cowboys already digging into their food at the dining room table. What I found instead was my cowboys standing around the butcher block island in my kitchen, looking pissed.

My body instantly went on alert, noting the look of violence in Mags eyes.

What the fuck?

There was a knock on the front door that I turned to answer. I looked at the twins, and Lawson lifted his chin while Lance was looking at the counter, lost in thought.

Sheriff Bowen was standing on my front porch, *not in uniform*.

Fuck me.

I swung the screen door open.

"Chase," I greeted. His badge was on the waistband of his jeans. He looked me in the eye, his baby blues telling me something was wrong. I stepped aside to let him in.

He went into the kitchen, facing my boys. I came up beside him and leaned my shoulder against the fridge, folding my arms over my chest.

"What's going on, Sheriff?" I asked.

He looked at each of us for a moment before he started.

"Got some news, boys…"

Chapter Six

Valerie

"It's a pleasure to finally meet the famous Valerie Cross in person."

A large, cold hand engulfed mine.

"It's a pleasure to meet you, Mr. Moonie."

I stared up at my boss. The boss of all bosses.

Mr. Tim Moonie, the son of the late, Charles Moonie.

Tim took over the company years ago when his father passed. He had sandy blonde hair and dull blue eyes. He was about my height and could only be just a few years older than me. There was something off about him though, something that had the hair on the back of my neck on end.

When he smiled at me, my stomach twisted.

There was a look in his eyes I didn't like. He was hungry, greedy, he didn't like hearing the word no.

We were in a fancy restaurant—*that I wouldn't remember the name of due to my nerves*—in downtown Denver. He offered his arm and after I took it, we were escorted to our table.

Once we were seated, he took a good long look at me. I wore my hair up, twisted into a bun, secured by a big clip. I wore eyeliner, something I never did, but Mom said it would make my eyes look less puffy from crying. She also told me to wear the gray pant suit I'd gotten on clearance at Macy's last season.

So here I was, hair up, in a pantsuit, paying to the good Lord above that I didn't throw up on my boss.

He smiled. "You're different. Far different than I expected," he noted. There was an underlying message in his voice I couldn't quite make out, but my gut was telling me not to trust this man.

I gave him a tight smile in return.

He chuckled, picking up his menu as our server approached. "Take that as a compliment, Ms. Cross."

He turned to the waiter and ordered a whiskey for himself. I got water.

No way in hell I was drinking in front of him.

"Did you have a good flight here, sir?" I asked, opening the floor for conversation.

He nodded. "I did. Thank you for asking."

"That's wonderful to hear."

"How is Hayden?" he asked, looking at the menu. I had yet to pick mine up, keeping my hands folded tightly in my lap.

"It's a relatively small town, nestled in a valley. The population is min—"

"Ms. Cross," he chuckled. "If I wanted general facts, I would have Googled it."

"Right, sorry, sir." I looked down at the table.

"Nervous?" His voice was gentle and *that* caused me to look up. He was smiling at me like we were old friends catching up. I didn't know why but I didn't trust it. I wouldn't allow myself to trust it, but I could play along.

"Yes," I breathed, faking it.

"There is no need to be nervous, Ms. Cross. Honestly, I was surprised you asked for an extension. You aren't the first to be turned down by Denver Langston."

"But I will be the last," I declared.

A slow, slick smile spread across Tim Moonie's face. "That's exactly right."

I ignored the red alert signal going off in my head. I was doing this for my mom. No one else.

My mom was the only one who mattered to me.

Over the next hour, he told me that Moonie Pipelines wasn't the first to approach Hallow Ranch. Companies had been eyeing that land for more than forty years, but the owners have held strong, turning down every offer that thrown way. Mr. Moonie explained that the land is vital because of its location at the end of the valley, something about the dirt. I don't know, I kind of tuned it all out after Mr. Moonie said that Denver's father had two sons. He told me that it was public record Mason Langston signed over his rights to Hallow Ranch ten years ago, making Denver Langston the sole owner.

Was that why he was so grumpy?

His brother walked away from the ranch?

I was an only child. I never had a sibling to bond with, but I'd dreamed of it. How wonderful it must have been to grow up with sibling, having a playmate, someone you could share all your secrets with, get into trouble with...

"So, when you go back to Hallow Ranch, here's the offer," Mr. Moonie said, snapping me out of my thoughts.

I nodded, focusing on him. At this point, the meal was done, and he was on his second whiskey.

"Ten million for the ranch and staff payout. Jobs and benefits will be provided to those who want them within the company. They will be offered to work on the pipeline crew, competitive salary and benefits," he explained. "Janet, my assistant you spoke with last night, will forward all of this to you via email, along with the contract for Mr. Langston to sign. Once he does, I will fly out to Hayden personally to deliver the check, take a few press shots. I assume their local paper will want to do a piece, and that's fine. Your name will be in it, of course, since you will be the one closing the deal. Is that alright with you, Ms. Cross?"

I blinked; my mouth open as I gaped at him. "I'm sorry, sir...You said ten millio—"

"Million dollars, yes. Yes, I did." He stared at me for a moment, tilting his head. To men like him, ten million dollars was pocket change. Of course, he didn't find it shocking.

"You must understand that the Hallow Ranch would be the company's biggest account and the profit it would make from the pipeline is staggering. So, yes, Ms. Cross. Ten million dollars."

I nodded. "Ten million dollars."

He smiled. "Once you close this deal, I may bring you down to Houston. You are a valuable asset and this company thanks you."

Ten million fucking dollars.

The next day, I showed up at Hallow Ranch at eight in the morning. I rounded the hood on my rental car and planted my butt on it. I was wearing something similar to the outfit from my first visit, a black pencil skirt and gray blouse. I had my tablet propped on my arm and began reading over the contract while I waited for the grumpy cowboy to show his face.

Yesterday afternoon, after lunch, I flew back to Hayden.

Then I locked myself in my hotel room and studied everything that Janet sent me. I gave myself a pep talk in the mirror. I went down into town and ordered some fried rice from Ching's, a local Asian restaurant.

It was the best fried rice I'd ever put in my mouth. I came back to the hotel and called my mom. I took a hot bath and then went to bed.

Fast forward to this morning—here I was, leaning against the hood of my rental on one of the prettiest pieces of land I have ever been on, waiting on that asshole to come out of the barn.

A few minutes later, he did just that.

I tried to ignore the way my heart skipped a beat when he stepped out in a flannel, jeans that hugged his massive thighs, and that damn black cowboy hat. I tried to ignore my heart again when his smoke gray eyes drunk me in and then again when his hand balled into a fist by his thigh.

"You got a death wish?" he barked once he was just a few feet from me. I beamed at him, plan in place, ready to fight. Crossing my legs and perching my tablet on my thigh, I greeted him. "Good morning, Mr. Langston."

He didn't stop charging towards me, not until I was leaning back, his hands planted on the hood beside my hips. I tried to ignore the tingles in my thighs and the heat radiating from his massive body.

"Thought I told you to leave," he all but growled down at me.

"You did," I said firmly. "But that was yesterday."

He blinked and then stared at me like I'd lost my damn mind.

Maybe I had.

I was here, wasn't I?

I smiled up at him again before getting down to business. "I'm here, representing Moonie Pipelines. Mr. Tim Moonie has an offer for you and your ranch. Now, I understand that you may have some concerns—"

"That man doesn't know shit," he hissed, cutting me off. He pushed off the hood and took two steps back before gesturing to me. "This ain't going to work, sweetheart."

"I—"

"You sittin' on the hood of this car with your long legs crossed ain't going to get me to change my mind about shit," he continued, venom in his voice.

I remained silent, letting him get it all out before I continued. He closed the distance between us again. I had to tip my head back to look into those smokey eyes of his.

I ignored that I liked having to tip my head back to look into his eyes.

"My dick ain't on a fucking leash," he sneered, his jaw muscle jumping underneath his short, trimmed beard.

My brain short-circuited at the mention of his dick. I should not be thinking of this man's body, at all, let alone his dick. Heat crawled up my cheeks as his smoke began to surround me once more, just like it did the other day. The tablet slipped out of my hands and landed on the gravel as he leaned down closer to me, getting in my space. Way in my space.

So close, I could smell him.

And, dammit, this cowboy smelled good, like pine and mint, not like sweat and dirt. No. *Of course not.* The infuriating, rude, handsome, taller than me, cowboy had to smell good. The universe had no plans of being benevolent today.

"You women are all the same. Let me clue you in, City Girl. Seducing me ain't going to work. Get off my land," he sneered.

I stared at him in disbelief, my chest brushing against his with every quick breath. His smoke drifted away as he bent down to pick up my tablet. He didn't hand it to me. No, he tossed on the hood of the car next to me like it was a piece of trash. He looked me up and down once more.

"They need to do better than *that* if seduction is their play," he said, looking at the pasture.

Pain sliced through me at his words, digging deeper than when he called me a bitch. It was like a hot poker was shoved into my gut. I knew I wasn't the skinniest woman in the world, and I was not small by any means. Still, I tried my hardest not to let my height and weight define me. I was curvy and tall, that wasn't a crime.

I sucked in a breath. He didn't hear it, though, because he was already walking away from me. Again.

Ten million dollars.

I sat there for a few more minutes, watching the barn waiting to see if he would return. He did, but this time, he was mounted on a beautiful brown horse, flying out to the pastures.

Denver Langston didn't even cast me a second glance.

That's okay.

He would tomorrow.

The next day, I got there around the same time, ready to fight. Yesterday, after I left the ranch, I went back to the hotel and changed into jeans.

Then I explored the town of Hayden.

I walked downtown, taking in the peaceful, little town with a smile on my face. This town really was lovely, a place where, maybe in a different life, my mom's flower shop could have been, nestled across the street from the bakery between the grocery store and the police station.

I shopped, I ate, I walked until the late afternoon. Then I went back to the hotel and called Mom. She was having treatment this morning and I wouldn't be able to talk to her until this afternoon. She liked to take a nap after treatment.

Last night, I told her all about Mr. Moonie's email he had sent me after I got back from exploring the town. He said he would be in Denver for a few more days and that I should keep him updated.

Mom said he was persistent. I told her he was just greedy.

This morning, I got up and dressed quickly before going down to the diner I found yesterday. They had good coffee. It wasn't Starbucks or my favorite spot in Dallas, but it was better than the hotel coffee. This diner though, had the best waffles on the planet.

My stomach was full, caffeine searing through my blood, and I was ready to take on the world. *Or at least a grumpy, stubborn cowboy.*

I was perched on my usual spot, the hood of the rental, reading through the latest email Mr. Moonie sent me at five this morning.

Geez, did the man ever sleep?

I heard a horse neighing and my head snapped up just in time to see a man step out of the barn. He was leading a horse to the pile of hay in by the fence. I watched as he tied the horse's reins to the metal bar, patted its neck and then turned to me.

The man who approached me was *not* Denver Langston, in any way, shape, or form. That should have thrilled me because of Mr. Langston's harsh behavior, but it didn't. Instead, a sour feeling settled in my chest.

Where was my grumpy cowboy?

"Good morning, darlin'," the man drawled. His presence was powerful, but it wasn't like Mr. Langston.

That man's presence sucks the air out of your lungs and fills them with his smoke.

"Good morning, sir," I said with a smile, hopping off the hood and stepping up to him. This cowboy was brighter than Denver Langston, with his bright blue eyes, kind smile, and blonde hair peeking out from underneath his cream cowboy hat. I held out my hand to him.

"I'm Valerie Cross. I represent Moonie Pipelines."

The man grinned at me, which was surprising.

Then again, it was surprising that I was standing on Hallow Ranch and even got to introduce myself. Denver Langston didn't even know my name yet.

The man's grin grew wider as his bright blue eyes assessed me, looking me up and down slowly. "You sure are pretty, ma'am, but I don't shake hands with my enemies."

My smile didn't falter. *This* I could deal with. This was the type of cowboy I was trained to negotiate with. Nothing could have prepared me for Denver Langston, but I was prepared for this man, that's for damn sure.

"Is Mr. Langston around? I would like to speak with him."

"He's eating breakfast," the blonde cowboy answered, jerking his head to the gorgeous house I wanted to pick up and move back to Texas with me. I would have dreams about that house until the day I died, and I hadn't even been inside it. My eyes lingered—not on the house, but on the silver Mercedes parked next to the beat up, red, Chevy.

Hm.

I shook it off and returned my attention back to the man in front of me. "He'll be down soon, right?"

The man grinned again, like a cat who had gotten his cream, giving me another view of his perfect teeth, just like Mr. Langston's. "Persistent, aren't you?"

"That's the job," I said. "You never gave me your name…"

"I know," he returned, shutting that window firmly closed.

"Don't give your name to your enemies either, I take it?"

"Smart girl," he murmured, his eyes dropping down the length of me once more.

A loud bang had both of our heads turning up to the house. A short haired, skinny, blonde woman, in a red dress, stomped down the porch steps.

"Looks like Denver is done with breakfast," the cowboy said with a chuckle. I flinched, something foreign sparking inside me, something that felt a lot like jealousy.

I ignored it.

We both watched in silence as the woman drove away, dirt flying behind her car. Was he seeing her? Did he like how she looked? Maybe he just preferred blondes…

Heaven's sake, Val, get a grip.

When the vehicle was out of sight, I turned back to him. "Would you like a pamphlet?" I asked sweetly.

He stared at me for a beat before he threw his head back in a laugh, rich and deep. A good laugh, one that would bring a woman to her knees. The man in front of me, just like the grumpy one who just finished *breakfast*, was hot.

"God damn, girl. You're funny," he smirked, picking up his hat and readjusting it.

My eyes met his and he gave me a wink. "You have a good day now. Boss told us that if you came back, we were supposed to tell you to leave and ignore you."

I lifted my chin, holding his stare.

"You're going to be hard to ignore, pretty girl."

With that, he tipped his hat to me and walked away. He was right about one thing; I was going to be impossible to ignore.

Chapter Seven

Denver

She came back.

That beautiful, enchanting, tall, curvy, green-eyed woman came back.

Fuck.

I couldn't fucking keep her away. I was staring at her through the window in my kitchen. Her dark hair was high up in a ponytail today, and my hand ached to wrap it around my fist and yank that pretty fucking head back as I—

"Fucking hell," I muttered, draining the last of my coffee. I didn't need this shit today. I didn't need this shit any day, really, but definitely not today.

"Hey, Dad?"

I looked to find my boy sitting on the stairs, an open book sitting on his knees.

"Yeah, bud?"

"Do you think Lawson could play catch with me later?" he asked. My brow furrowed.

Why in the fuck couldn't I play catch with him later?

"Uh, bud, is there a reason you don't want to play catch with me?" I returned, turning away from the window and away from *that fucking woman.* She had been talking to Beau and no doubt that fucker was flirting with her.

Fuck, how could he not?

She was wearing that navy dress like a second goddamn skin, clinging to her curves in just the right fucking way.

Moonie was good. Too fucking good.

"He played baseball in college," my son deadpanned.

"You saying he can throw a ball better than me?" I tilted my head, a smile playing on my lips.

"Uhh..."

The little shit.

"Go," I ordered, tipping my chin to the door.

He was staying at Dan's place for the day. Dan was a good buddy of mine who lived just down the road from the ranch. He wasn't a rancher, but he had a nice piece of land with a pond stocked with fish. He also was the father of Caleb's best friend, Adam. I called Dan this morning, when Diana—*my lawyer*—was here, to tell him about Moonie.

I didn't want Caleb around this shit.

I felt bad since he just got back from his mom's, but he was excited to see his little buddy. Dan, being the good man he was, welcomed my son with open arms.

After yesterday, after that woman—*I didn't even know her name*—left, I finished my work with the second half of the herd and went up to the house to research Moonie Pipelines.

Needless to say, I did *not* like what I found.

This was a nasty company, run by slippery, greedy men—who took from the land, instead of nourishing it. All for money. *That woman* down there, was one of the foot soldiers.

"Bye, Dad!" he called. I made my way to the door and down the front steps quickly so I could pull him in for a hug.

"Have fun, be safe, don't do no stupid shit," I said into his hair.

"I won't!" he said, turning and running to Dan's Dodge. He lifted his hand, and I lifted mine as Caleb clamored into the back seat with his little buddy. After watching them drive away, I turned toward the barn. Moonie's soldier was sitting on the hood of that stupid rental, reading something on her tablet, waiting for me.

Might as well get this shit over with. Apparently, making her cry wasn't the way to go.

Once I was only a few feet from her, she looked up from that stupid tablet. Probably looking at other ranches to take, food supplies to cut down, souls to fucking reap. All in the name of money—so she could go buy a new pair of shoes and a purse.

The woman—*beautiful as ever*—smiled at me, a smile so fucking *breathtaking* that I had to suppress a growl. *Fucking woman.* The little minx. My eyes wanted to trail down that tight dress of hers and see if her curves were as luscious as they seem. Her boss probably told her to step it up today.

Anything for money, right?

She didn't have any respect for herself, that much was clear.

"Good morning, Mr. Lang—"

"Get the fuck off my property," I snapped at her as I headed into the barn.

I saddled Ranger and walked him out. Usually, one of the boys would saddle my horse for me, but lately, I didn't mind the extra work, the familiar process. It calmed me in a way. Plus, I got to spend time with Ranger.

When we came out of the barn, his hoofs clacking against the wood panels on the pathway, she was still sitting there, her eyes on me. I hated how much I wanted to like that.

My jaw tightened, and I ripped my eyes from her. She didn't know how to listen.

Ignoring her, I mounted Ranger, and we headed out. We were putting up new fencing in pasture four today. Whatever spooked that momma cow the other day came back. There was a struggle, and one of the posts was damaged.

Mags and I discussed it and we decided to replace the whole side—*a mile of fencing.* The twins had gotten out there early, needing to clear their minds from the other night.

It wasn't every day that the sheriff came to Hallow Ranch for something other than a decent game of poker. He showed up in jeans and a plain shirt, his badge on his hip. When he came for poker, he never brought his badge. When the badge came out, that meant trouble.

He never wore his full uniform to Hallow Ranch.

The sheriffs before him didn't either.

There was a problem in our town, a toxic, sinister problem—nothing like the one currently perched on the hood of her rental car.

No, this problem was a man, one who thinks he can take want he wants.

Not in my god damn town.

Sheriff Bowen came to my house to make sure justice would be served, that the problem would cease. He knew that a man like me had no issues with blood. He also knew my cowboys didn't either.

He would also look the other way.

It was an unspoken agreement.

Hallow Ranch protects him, and he defends it.

After our discussion, I walked him out and asked about Moonie Pipelines. Usually, pipelines had to go through local governments. Chase told me Moonie was a private company, and that usually the states were calling him, not the other way around.

That made sense.

The state had been after Hallow Ranch for the last decade—but we weren't the only ones taking the heat. There were other ranchers, like Carson Waters, who just wanted out. Ranching was not for the faint of the heart, and neither was farming.

They wouldn't get my ranch—not on my fucking life.

Shaking the thoughts of pipelines, blood, and green eyes out of my head, I focused on work.

By the time the sun was low in the sky, the fence was as done as we were. We were making our way back to the barn, Beau beside me on his horse. Keeping my gaze ahead, I asked, "What did she say to you?"

"Pretty girl?" he drawled.

I remained silent, not willing to entertain his bullshit today.

"She introduced herself and told me who she worked for," he said as the ranch came into view. I was lucky to have grown up in a place like this. Though my memories were dark, light surrounded my home. I would die trying to keep that light around it.

"What did you say?"

He scoffed. "I took one of her stupid pamphlets and said I would give her a call when I convinced you to sell this piece of heaven to that greasy pipeline."

"Heavy on the sarcasm there, aren't you, son?" Jigs, his father called out over his shoulder. Mags, who was beside him, chuckled.

"Fucking asshats," I muttered.

"I haven't seen her yet," Lawson noted from beside Beau. "She really pretty?"

Beau whistled low. "Yeah, man. She is."

That *right there* is why she couldn't be trusted.

She had only been here a handful of times and already they were drooling over her.

I couldn't blame them.

She was new pussy.

This town didn't have a lot to choose from. The twins usually went to Denver one weekend out of the month to get their dicks wet. Sometimes, Beau tagged along, sometimes he didn't. Jigs didn't bother chasing pussy anymore; he was chasing peace instead.

Then, there was Mags.

He never left the ranch, not once since the day I took him on. If he needed something, he would order it. The boys always invited him, and he always declined.

I understood him, though. That man was fighting demons, like me.

"Maybe she'll be back tomorrow," Lance said as we approached the barn. My eyes drifted to the spot where she had been parking, her tire marks deep in the dirt and gravel.

For my sanity's sake, I hoped not.

She was *back.*

She was back in her usual spot, and today, the twins got to see her for the first time. My men *looked* at her.

Again, how could they resist?

Just one look and she would have you hooked.

Green eyes had been plaguing my thoughts for the last few nights and sleep was a distant memory. I stayed up watching recordings of the rodeo, my eyes glued to my little brother as he held on for eight seconds.

Every. Single. Fucking. Time.

No matter how big the bull was, my brother didn't let go. Mason held on. When the buzzer sounded and the crowd roared, he would look up and smile, taking off his hat before bowing.

No one saw it, the hatred in his grey eyes.

Hatred for me.

That's what fueled his fire.

Yet, I watched.

I watched every single recording until the early hours of dawn. Then, I would go start breakfast for Caleb and me. I would take him to school, come back and she would be there, sitting on that damn car.

That's how it went for the next week.

My cowboys, though they ignored her—for the most part—they still looked. I didn't bother telling them what they could or couldn't do with her. If they wanted to fuck her, they could.

The thought of their hands on her made my stomach churn.

What the fucking hell?

I didn't give a shit about her.

I just wanted her gone.

She wasn't gone.

She kept coming back, every single day.

On the fourth week, school was out, and Caleb was here.

She kept coming every fucking day, persistent as ever.

A month.

One fucking month of this shit. I should've had her ass arrested by now, but Diana told me that would bring unwanted attention to Hallow Ranch. She was right, Moonie Pipelines would take advantage of that shit. So, the fucking enchanting woman came every morning and by the time the day was done, she would be gone.

Today, like all the others, I just walked by her, ignoring her presence. Today was Thursday, and I guess that meant City Girl got to be bold. She hopped off the hood of her car and followed me. Before she entered the barn, I whirled around to snap at her, but there was a pamphlet in my face.

Moonie Pipelines—the right choice for your land.

Just like acid is good for your balls.

I took at the paper, ripped in half, handed it back to her and told her to fuck off.

Newsflash: she didn't fuck off.

On the fifth week, Caleb was getting cabin fever, but I told him to stay in the house. He hated it, and I did even more. The kid liked being out in the sun, but I didn't want him anywhere near this woman. He already had one leech in his life; he didn't need another.

I ignored her. My cowboys ignored her. Yet, she persisted.

By the time week six rolled around I was done with this shit. I contemplated calling the sheriff, despite Diana's advice. Knowing Chase, he would laugh at me for not being able to handle a woman.

So, I ignored her again, but Beau didn't.

I shoved away the anger that flared in my chest as I watched him make her laugh. She tossed her head back, her long dark hair flowing down the back of her cream top in waves. I couldn't hear her laugh. I was too far away and inside the house.

It pissed me off that Beau got to hear it.

It pissed me off that Beau was the one to make her laugh.

Why in the fuck was it pissing me off?

That night, after the green-eyed leech was long gone, Chase returned. Once again, not in uniform. I called the boys up from the bunk house and we gathered on my porch.

Caleb was inside, upstairs in his room, reading Harry Potter.

Sheriff Bowman gave us the go ahead, after weeks of gathering evidence. It would be taken care of. The twins, Beau and Jigs would go into town and bring the problem back here.

Then we would eliminate the problem.

Chapter Eight

Valerie

"How are things going?"

I was on the phone with Mr. Moonie at ten at night, and I was exhausted, but he called anyways.

"Mr. Langston is about as stubborn as a bull, sir," I admitted. A bull I have been trying to talk to for *weeks*. I had been in Colorado for a little over a month. I didn't think that this trip would be over a month long. After two weeks, human resources booked me an extended stay at the town's hotel. I just wanted to go home and see my mom. She told me she was doing fine, that Jackie was good with staying with her until I returned, but that meant owing more money.

"Mr. Moonie?"

Silence.

He didn't like that answer. Unease washed over me.

"But I have been making progress with one of his ranch hands," I stammered.

A moment of silence and then, "Oh?" There was a terrifying angry tone in his voice, like he was trying to control his fury.

"Yes, sir," I said, trying to calm my breathing.

"Maybe this cowboy could talk some sense into yours…" he trailed off, hoping I would catch on.

I did.

"That's the plan, sir. I drafted a packet of information, going off the pamphlet, but in a little more detail—"

"Was there something wrong with the pamphlet?" he asked slowly.

Nope. Besides Denver Langston ripping it in half. "No, sir. I just wanted to try a different approach."

"I see."

"Was there anything else that you needed, sir?" I asked, after another stretch of silence.

"Get the ranch hand to listen to you. Then call me and the three of us can have lunch in Denver."

He hung up.

I let out a shaky breath before burying my face in my hands. This was a disaster. Earlier, when I called my mom, she gave me that look—the one from before when she told me to quit and come home.

There was no point in going home if I had to put her in the ground.

Bile rose in my throat.

After she had gone to bed, Jackie called me. She told me my mom was having her lawyer come by the house next week—to update her will.

Her fucking will.

Of course, I panicked, because I feared my mom was losing her fight. She didn't want to fight anymore, and that was on me. I was never home and when I was, I was diving headfirst into work, looking for another ranch. I couldn't afford a minute of calm and quiet. I couldn't afford to take the time off. Working ensured my mother's treatment was paid for and that was the only thing that mattered to me.

Yet, she was updating her will.

Once I'd gotten off that phone call, I could feel it coming: the panic, ready to chew me up and spit me out, leaving me in a ball of worthless anxiety on the floor. I didn't have the time for that, so I jumped in the shower, scrubbing every inch of my body three times while counting to a thousand.

Finally, it dissipated, slithering back into its dark crevasse.

By the time I was dressed and ready for sleep, Mr. Moonie called.

Once that was over, I found myself staring at the ceiling, my thoughts drifting away from the stress and pressure to something else.

Something gray.

Smoke.

Intoxicating smoke that surrounded a man I had no business thinking about, not this late at night, not while lying in bed. Yet, here I was, closing my eyes and picturing his face.

His dark beard, tan skin, gray eyes. I wanted to suffocate in them. My mind wandered even deeper, going back to the first day I'd met him, the day he pinned me against a wall with his forearm. The skin on my neck prickled as I remembered the way he stared down at me, holding me captive—

What the hell was wrong with me?

I sat up and rubbed my eyes.

Nope.

I was just tired. That's all this was: lack of sleep on a crappy bed in a state I'd never been to. That's all this was.

Yet, when I fell asleep, I was surrounded by gray smoke...

Rain.

It was raining.

More like the sky had opened and decided to dump its entire water supply directly over Hayden. Thunder had woken me up hours ago, but anxiety kept me awake.

I worked for an hour or so before getting a cup of that nasty hotel coffee. Then I went back to work for another hour. Once I finally got ready, I took my time as I tried to calm my mind. The rain helped with that, actually.

Summer was here and the heat was on its way, or so I thought.

When I got ready, I liked to have the TV on and turned to the weather channel, and today was no different. I was curling my eyelashes when the weatherwoman announced that the storm had brought in a strange, drastic cold front.

Well, shit.

I finished my make-up and headed to the window to pull open the curtains. The sun was supposed to greet me, but a gray cloud that reminded me of a certain cowboy's eyes, was in its place. I touched my hand to the glass.

The temperature was dropping.

Suddenly, my mind was on the Hallow Ranch, and other ranches in the storm. Temperature drops like this were unusual in Texas, but I didn't know about Colorado. Were the cows okay?

Oh, now you care?

Shut up, conscience.

Bite me.

Sighing, I turned away from the window and went in search for my umbrella. A few minutes later, when I was set and ready to go deal with the grumpy cowboy, I called Mom.

"Hi, honey."

"Hey, how are you this morning?" I asked while making the bed.

"The pumpkins are getting bigger!"

I smiled. "That's great, Mom!

"They're still really tiny, but I have high hopes," she beamed. I could hear the smile in her voice. I wanted to bring up her will but decided against it.

"What's your plans for today?"

"I found a really good book series yesterday."

"Oh?"

Damn, I missed reading. I missed a lot of things. Reading and painting were two hobbies I had to put on the backburner when mom's life changed.

"It's a historical romance," she sighed.

"Those are your favorite," I noted.

"You going to see The Grump again today?"

The Grump.

What a nickname.

"Everyday. Mr. Moonie called me again last night," I said, plopping down on the edge of the now—made bed.

"This must be really important to him, if the CEO has a direct line of contact with you," she noted.

I swallowed the lump in my throat and the dread from last night filled my stomach. "He wants to me to try and convince one of the ranch hands...."

"He wants you to play dirty."

I sighed. "It would seem that way."

"Life is too short to be working for men like that," she declared.

"I know, Mom."

"So quit."

I picked at the fuzz on the comforter. "You know I can't do that."

She sighed, sounding defeated. "It's too early in the day to fight with my daughter."

The corner of my mouth turned up. "Then go relax and read your books. Let your daughter take care of you."

We exchanged our goodbyes, and I headed out. Once I was in the rental, the dread in my chest only intensified. Mr. Moonie wanted me to play the snake and turn Mr. Langston's cowboys against him. He told me to bribe them with the promise of a good salary and benefits...

I wasn't a snake.

I was just a girl trying to save her mom.

Chapter Nine

Denver

Thunder clapped outside my window and my eyes flew open.

I looked to my alarm clock: it was only four in the morning.

I had to be up in an hour. Wind howled outside as the rain pelted the metal roof above me. The weather didn't call for rain today.

I got out of bed and went to check on Caleb. Of course, the kid was still passed out. The little shit could sleep through a goddamn tornado. I headed back to my room and swiped my phone off the nightstand.

"Sir," Jigs answered.

"Everything alright?" I asked, turning on my TV to the weather channel. Shit.

A fucking cold front.

In the beginning of summer.

"Yup. We've been up for the last hour."

"This freak storm took us by surprise. We got moms and calves out there."

Those calves were still new to this world and weren't prepared for low temps just yet. I had a secondary barn in pasture two. It was huge, bigger than the barn here. I purchased it two summers ago because we were in for a bad winter. Thank fuck I did, or we would have lost half of the herd, like the ranches around me did. That was a hard season.

"We'll get on it."

"I'll be down there in a few. Saddle up Ranger, would you?"

"Yes, sir."

I hung up and looked back to my bed. My dreams were of her again, green eyes, dark brown hair, and a laugh I couldn't hear. I scratched my bearded jaw.

What the fuck was wrong with me?

Why was this woman stuck in my fucking head?

I still didn't even know her name. Beau did but I refused to ask. The last thing I needed was for my cowboys to think I was interested in her.

After leaving Caleb a note, I went downstairs, made a quick breakfast scramble for him, and left it in the microwave. I didn't know how long I would be gone. On the way out, I grabbed an apple for myself. When the cows were safe, then I would make everyone breakfast in the bunkhouse.

Caleb would come, too. That boy eats more than a grown man.

On the porch, I was greeted with cold rain and harsh winds.

Fucking hell.

Good morning, Hallow Ranch.

"Good Lord son, you eat more than your father did when he was your age," Jigs said through a chuckle.

"I'm just hungry, Jigs," my son answered between bites.

It was mid-morning. The cows were safe, and breakfast was almost done. The storm hadn't let up yet, and it wouldn't until tonight. No telling what the farmers in the county over were going to do. It was currently forty degrees outside, and the temperature was continuing to drop.

Bacon was frying, pancakes were done, and there was a new pot of coffee brewing. Everyone was at the table except for Beau and me; he was standing at the window, a cup of untouched coffee in his hand, staring out at the rain.

"Beau, get your ass to the table," his father ordered. I shot a look at Mags, who had his chair tipped back, his face buried in a book. *Dracula*. How fitting. Lance and Lawson were bullshitting back and forth, Caleb was sitting next to Jigs.

My father died before Caleb was born. Jigs has been a part of this ranch since my father ran it. He knew my secrets. He helped me bury a body when I was a boy. When Caleb was born, I saw him as a blessing. I didn't resent my son for what his mother did to Mason and me. Caleb wasn't at fault.

But when he was born, I was alone.

Jigs was the only hand I'd had at the ranch at the time, Mags didn't show until Caleb was almost a year old. Beau was off at college. Mason was *gone*. No amount of phone calls that I made, or rodeos that I showed up to would've made him come home. It was just Caleb and I. Cathy went off to try and find Mason after Caleb's birth, in an effort to win him back.

I never hated her more.

I was angry. I was hurting. I was scared.

Scared I wouldn't be a good father. Scared I would fuck everything up. Then, Jigs stepped in. He was like a grandfather to Caleb, and I owed him my life for it. I looked over to Beau, noting the worry in his features, then his face hardening as the sky cracked open with lightning.

"Something's wrong," Beau said, his voice low.

"What do you mean?" Lawson asked.

My eyes darted to where Beau was looking—where *she* parked. It was almost ten in the morning, and she hadn't arrived yet.

"Maybe she stayed in because of the storm," Jigs said casually. The twins nodded. Mags lowered his book and raised a brow at me.

"Nah. Something is wrong, Den. That woman is stubborn," Beau said, turning to me.

My stomach dropped as unease sat heavy on my shoulders.

He was right.

She *was* stubborn. She had been here every single fucking day for the last six weeks. She would have come out rain or shine.

Fuck.

"Caleb, stay in the bunkhouse," I ordered, grabbing my hat and keys, moving without a second thought. *Was she hurt? Had she gotten into a wreck?*

The nearest hospital was in the next county over...

Images of her dark hair and greens eyes flashed before my eyes.

"Dad?"

"Stay here, bud," I said, ripping the bunkhouse door open.

Then I was gone, running through the freezing rain to my truck, while my mind played images of her hurt or dead in a ditch somewhere over and over. I shouldn't be giving a shit about her. I wanted her gone.

You wanted her gone, Denver. Not hurt or worse...

I put the truck in reverse and spun away, rain and gravel flying behind me as I headed down the long drive of Hallow Ranch. I turned onto the main road that led into town and floored it. My truck fish tailed, but I righted it quickly. I tossed my hat onto the seat beside me, wondering if she would look good sitting there. Fuck. Fuck. *Fuck.* The rain came down harder, Mother Nature reminding me she was in control.

Not today.

My eyes scanned the road for that stupid little red car. Headlights passed me, muted in the thick grey waterfall around us.

A truck.

Son of a bitch.

Where are you, City Girl?

Thunder clapped outside and I regretted being a dick to her.

Fuck.

Valerie

So cold.

It was freezing cold outside and raining.

Just my fucking luck. I'd been stuck in this ditch for over an hour. I had no cell service. I was stuck on a country road outside of a town that I barely knew, that led to a ranch where I wasn't wanted, and my boss was most likely going to fire me.

Here I was, standing in the rain, staring at the back wheels of my rental, which were sinking into a muddy ditch. I'd hydroplaned and spun out. Pretty sure I hit my head on the steering wheel, but I was too jazzed to worry about that.

Cold.

So damn cold.

The sweater I brought with me was soaked and my umbrella broke about five minutes ago. Then, lightning struck in the field next to me and I was grateful that my umbrella broke. I wasn't grateful for my phone being out of service though. I hadn't seen a car for the last hour. Everyone was inside, safe from this storm. Smart people.

I should've waited until the storm passed. I should have called Mr. Moonie and told him to shove it. He wanted me to be a snake.

I couldn't be a snake.

I wasn't that kind of woman. I was better than that.

Are you? You buy out ranches for a company that destroys the land.

I didn't want to destroy Hallow Ranch. I didn't want to push my grumpy cowboy. I didn't want any of this.

I just wanted my mom to survive.

My bottom lip trembled as I continued to stare at my pitiful rental. Suddenly, headlights in the distance caught my attention. My heart pounded in my chest. They were coming right for me, driving in the middle of the road.

Oh, thank God. Maybe they could help me.

I squinted as the vehicle got closer.

As it came into view my stomach dropped, and my luck got worse.

It was a red Chevy.

Denver Langston's Chevy.

If I wasn't so cold, I would have stomped my foot like a toddler—today was *not* a good day. I watched, arms wrapped around my waist, as the truck swerved over to the side, parking a few feet from my car. I watched as the mountain of a man got out of the vehicle—cowboy hat all— and he stalked towards me.

He looked good.

Even in the rain, the smoke was beautiful.

"Are you fuckin' crazy?"

Denver

Fucking Christ.

She was even more beautiful in the rain.

Her dark hair was stuck to her pale cheeks, her neck, her limbs were shaking, and her clothes were soaked. She was dressed for summer, not this shit. The cream blouse looked like it was painted on her body, clinging to her breasts and torso, showing the slight curve of her belly. Her makeup was running down her face, down the sides of her cheeks.

Jesus.

This woman.

"Wh-what are you d-doing here?" she stammered, wrapping her arms tighter around herself. She was fucking freezing. I stared at her as her question sunk into my head.

The answer: I didn't fucking know. I just needed her to be warm.

Chapter Ten

Valerie

His smoke surrounded me again, not diminishing as the rain pelted down around us.

"Mr. Langston, I—"

"Get in the God damn truck," he ordered, his deep voice on the edge of pissed as it carried across the distance between us.

"I have a tow truck coming," I called back, lying through my fucking teeth. I waved him off, not wanting him to see me like this.

Not when I was freezing and miserable.

Not when I was down on my luck, when he could beat me down more with his harsh words while staring at me with his beautiful eyes.

The last thing I needed was for Denver Langston to see me like this.

Today was a bad day.

I couldn't pretend to be strong on days like today, and I needed to appear strong to the man who'd been plaguing my mind since he pinned me against his barn.

"That's not what I fuckin' said," the cowboy barked.

He was less than a foot away from me now, a sheet of rain falling between us. I could see those gray eyes under the rim of his black cowboy hat. I could see them on me—*feel* them on me. He was everywhere again, his smoke crowding around me, seeping into my skin. I closed my eyes, wishing that he would go away.

I didn't want him here, not when I felt like a failure.

I was failing Mr. Moonie. I was failing Hallow Ranch because I was trying to take it away from the man in front of me. I was failing my mom.

God—*my mom.*

When I opened my eyes again, he was still there, fuming., his smoke all around me, wrapping me in it...

Maybe his smoke would warm me up.

He pointed back to his Chevy. "Get in the truck!"

His smoke was in my lungs, and I couldn't breathe. It was so damn cold, all I could focus on was him—*his presence, his eyes*—the way he looked at me, like he wanted me to be safe, to be warm.

Like he wanted me to *breathe.*

Denver Langston's smoke was thick, heavy, and mesmerizing as it swirled in his eyes. He was so close to me now, I had to tilt my head back to look at those eyes.

"Smoke," I whispered.

He bit off a curse, then he was gone. Suddenly, I was flying, flying next to something warm and solid.

I liked warm and solid.

Then, I wasn't flying anymore, and the rain had stopped. Now, warmth was all around me, but I still shivered. I was on something soft, my head resting against it. I felt heat run over my shoulder, down my torso and then a faint click. Then a slam.

He put me in the truck.

I was in the truck.

His truck.

I shivered again as I heard another door slam. I rolled my head to the side. He was there, his dark presence taking up most of the cab. I blinked, shaking my head.

He was staring at me, studying me closely. He was wet.

I didn't like that he was wet.

"No," I croaked out. I felt weird. I was still cold.

"No, what?" he snapped.

I lifted my hand—or tried to. *Why did I want to touch that beard?*

He needed to be warm.

"You're wet," I rasped.

He stared.

My throat hurt now. Today was a bad day.

"Don't want you wet and cold..." I trailed off as another shiver rolled through me.

Then, we were moving. "Flying again," I said, closing my eyes.

"Come on, City Girl. Stay with me. Let me see those pretty eyes," a deep, velvet voice rumbled.

Cold.

So damn cold.

But my eyes were pretty.

Everything faded away and I was back in my mom's flower shop...

My eyes opened and I was back in my hotel room.

It was all a dream, a horrible, embarrassing dream.

My body ached, and my throat was still scratchy. I was so tired, my brain convinced me that this hotel bed was *actually comfortable*. It hadn't been comfortable the last however many weeks I'd slept in it.

I rolled over, groaning in frustration. I pulled the pillow under me, wrapping my arm around it and resting my head on top. Even the pillows were comfortable again.

The pillows also smelled good—like pine and mint.

Like—

I sat up, gasping and throwing the pillow off the bed.

This wasn't the hotel.

Blinking quickly, I took a second to look around me. I was in a room—a man's room.

I was in a man's *bed*.

The room was large, a window to the left of me, the dark grey curtains still open, letting the moonlight come through. I sat in the middle of a large bed, surrounded by hunter green sheets, blankets, and pillows. The walls were painted a dark gray, the hardwoods a rich, deep brown. The furniture was wooden, stained dark, and looked handmade.

I swung my legs over the bed and stood.

I wasn't wearing pants.

Looking down, I found a Marines shirt on my body, draping down over my butt and stopping just below my cheeks.

This was Mr. Langston's room.

My heart seized at the revelation.

Holy shit, I was in his room—

Wait.

Why was I in his room?

I fell back, sitting down on the edge of the very comfortable, very gorgeous, very large bed. My mind wanted to know how many women had been in this bed. My heart was in denial.

He's a very large man. That's why he has such a big bed.

My mind drifted back to a few days ago, when that blonde woman hurried out of this house. *Had she been in his bed?*

Had she worn this shirt?

I gulped, my stomach turning. Denver Langston was a beautiful man, carved from the earth and built like a strong pine. Only a fool would think that the man didn't have women.

Oh, this cowboy had women.

Probably a slew of them.

On speed dial.

Categorized by a number.

One for every day of the week.

That was his prerogative.

So why was I jealous?

Shaking my head, I glanced at the clock on the bedside table. It was nine at night. How long had I been out? How did I—

Oh, no.

Memories from this morning came rushing back, not slowing, not allowing me to brace for impact.

I was standing in the rain, surrounded by his smoke.

Then, I was in his truck, not wanting him to be cold.

My brow furrowed as I stared at my bare legs, my hands braced on the bed beside my thighs. Then…

Warmth. Strength. Pine, mint, and smoke. Grumbles, like thunder against my skin. Sheltered.

Held.

I was held.

My hand drifted to the shirt on my body. My clothes were gone. Had I been hypothermic? My heart was racing now, hurtling towards a finish line that I feared would never come.

Did Denver Langston…*hold me?*

The thought alone was pure madness. A man like that, holding a woman like me? A woman he hated. A woman he insulted. A woman who was trying to take everything from him.

He held me. He warmed me.

He *saved* me.

"Don't think about it, Val," I whispered to myself as I looked down at the shirt once more. At least his shirt fit me. Being tall and plus sized, it was rare to find a man larger than me. My stomach was hidden under the cotton fabric, loose and drowning me.

Denver Langston was indeed a large man.

A bear of a man.

My mind wanted to think about the fact that he was a Marine. Images of him fighting for our country flitting through my head, the things he must have seen...the terrors he must've endured, all to protect innocent people. Hell, even people *that* he hated—like me.

Maybe that's where he got his attitude from—because to him, I wasn't worth it.

He saved you today, didn't he?

There was a bathroom in front of me, and I padded over to it. After taking care of myself, I braved a look in the mirror.

My eyes widened. I didn't recognize the woman standing in front of me.

"Holy shit, Val. You look like death."

My skin was paler than usual, my hair frizzy and in knots. Dried mascara stuck to my cheeks. My eyes were sunken in, probably due to the stress and exhaustion. I looked like a frumpy, homeless person. After I washed my hands, I combed my hair with my fingers, and rinsed my face. I did all this knowing I was in a house I didn't know, and I needed to call my mom.

Panic set in then.

I hadn't called my mom today, aside from our phone call this morning. I braced my hand against the counter, my head falling between my shoulders as panic began to consume me.

I didn't know where my phone was.

Was it in the rental?

Did Mr. Langston take it?

Was Mom okay?

Did Jackie take care of everything? Surely, she was worried about me.

I didn't need her worrying about me. Worry caused stress which caused her body to panic. She was in the middle of a bloody, violent war with cancer. The stress of worrying about me would distract her from fighting it. It would make her weak...

I would lose her all together.

"I gotta find my phone—my phone," I breathed out, black spots dotting my vision. I closed my eyes and inhaled a deep breath. I needed to ground myself.

I heard a bang somewhere in the house, causing me to jump, distracting me from the panic that coursed through me. He was here. I needed to ask him—then I would call mom. I poked my head out of the bathroom, expecting to see my grumpy cowboy, but the room was empty.

"Mr. Langston?" I called; my voice shaky.

Why are you being so formal? You are in his shirt with no pants.

I waited a few more minutes, waiting to see if there was another sound. Nothing. Zip. Maybe he was down at the barn.

Maybe he's staying the hell away from you because you're trying to take his home away.

Shoving down my thoughts with a sigh, I went to his chest of drawers and opened the top one. Boxers and socks. I scanned the room for my clothes once more, and they were missing too. No phone. No clothes. I sighed and grabbed a pair of black boxers, sliding them on over my underwear before I padded out of the room.

The stairs were in front of me. There were three rooms, two across from me and one beside Mr. Langston's room. The bedroom directly across from me, over the stairs was open and I saw a toy chest.

My spine straightened.

Maybe that woman from the other day was his wife. That was a child's room. I walked around the stairs and peaked inside. No signs of life. The room was tidy, and I could tell it belonged to a boy.

A little boy.

He was definitely under the age of twelve.

His twin bed was pushed up against the wall, the window across from it. I took a closer look at the toys in the bins—bulls and cowboys. I smiled at the thought of Mr. Langston's little boy following in his footsteps.

The little cowboy...

Until you get his ranch taken away and Moonie digs up the dirt under this house.

I shook my head and made my way downstairs. The stairs ended in the foyer, a beautiful hunter green front door standing proudly in front of me. To the left of me was a living room.

I poked my head in there as well and called, "Hello?"

Nothing.

The large flat screen TV mounted above the wall above the fireplace was off. There was a navy-blue blanket thrown over the back of a cream sectional, a book—*Harry Potter*—resting on the round, dark, wooden, coffee table, a Pokémon bookmark sticking out of it. Mr. Langston's son was about halfway through it. Again, no signs of life. There was a hallway that led to the back of the house, but it was dark.

Something told me not to go down there. Instead, I spun on my heel, crossing the foyer while wrapping my arms around myself as a shiver ran through me.

My breath caught as I came to a huge kitchen.

A—*stunning*—kitchen.

The kitchen every person dreams of. It was a kitchen that needed to be filled with happy memories and delicious smells.

It was L-shaped, with a huge island in the middle. The cabinets were a sage green, the countertops butcher block. There was a gas range stove, double ovens and a massive fridge. The countertops were empty, save for a few stray coffee mugs, and beer bottles.

There were three stools on my side of the island, one of them pulled out sightly, the place mat on the counter above littered with crumbs and a half empty cup of red juice.

Maybe they went into town.

I approached the farm sink, my eyes on the photo frame in the windowsill. The smiling face of a little boy, around seven years old or so was looking back at me. My heart strings tugged.

If the little boy had been standing alone in the photo, I would have assumed it was a childhood photo of Mr. Langston, who was standing beside the boy, looking down at him. His side profile was showing under the brim of his black cowboy hat, a small smile playing on his lips.

He was absolutely *beautiful*.

His eyes were concealed in the shadow beneath the hat. The two of them stood side by side in front of a creek, dark green trees in the background, a tackle box beside Mr. Langston's boot. His son was holding a fishing pole in one hand, a fish in the other. He was beaming, his little crooked smile warming my soul.

The smile I was wearing slowly faded away as I looked back around me, taking in the beautiful home.

Where was momma?

Pow

My entire body jolted at the sound, and fear latched onto me.

That was a *gunshot*.

Holy—*that was a gunshot!*

Suddenly, I was moving, darting around the island and running into the foyer. On bare feet, I pulled the front door open, my heart beating out of my chest as I scanned the front porch.

Mr. Langston's truck was right there, where he usually parked it.

All was quiet.

I stepped out and closed the door quietly behind me.

Maybe he saw a bear or something.

Be quiet. Just in case, Valerie.

Pow

A second gunshot rang out through the night, and my head snapped down to the barn. Logic deserted me as I ran down the steps and down the hill. My bare feet pounded against the cool, damp ground. When I hit gravel, I didn't even notice the pain.

I was too afraid.

I was afraid for myself.

I was afraid for the little boy with the sunshine smile.

I was afraid my grumpy cowboy would be hurt.

I didn't know what the hell I was doing, I just needed to know Denver was okay.

Now he's Denver? What happened to Mr. Langston?

My speed picked up going down the hill, and I headed straight for the back of the barn, retracing my steps from memory. I stopped about halfway back and pressed against the cool, red wood of the barn.

"Please. Please, be okay," I whispered.

I didn't have a phone—I didn't even know where my phone was. There was a landline in that gorgeous kitchen, by the fridge. Dread pooled in my stomach.

I really hoped I didn't have to run back up that hill to use that phone.

Shaking my head, I willed myself to focus and moved again. My feet were going to hurt in the morning. One of them might be bleeding. I suppressed a wince as I slowly walked the rest of the way. Once I was at the corner, I poked my head around, just as third shot rang out.

I slapped my palm over my mouth, swallowing my scream.

Three gunshots.

Oh God, *oh God.*

There was no one at the back of the barn, but there was bright light illuminating the other side of the bunkhouse. I quickly scanned the area in front of me and darted across space.

Then, I heard a pain-filled grunt—that was a man.

Oh God, oh God.

My feet were moving faster, and I rounded the corner of the bunkhouse. I came to an abrupt halt at the sight in front of me.

My heart imploded.

My stomach dropped to the floor.

Suddenly, I was very, very afraid—for *myself.*

There was a clean-cut man, dressed in a blue suit. He'd fallen to his knees, blood dripping from his mouth. He coughed violently, blood and spit spraying the dirt below him. His eyes drifted up to the man standing in front of him before he fell completely, his face smashing into ground with a heavy thud.

His head landed at pair of cowboy boots.

My eyes dared to move up, over the backs of thick, jean covered legs, to a dark coat that held broad shoulders underneath. Sitting on top of those shoulders was a head of dark hair.

That head turned to me.

That head had a handsome, bearded face.

That head had a black cowboy hat on top of it.

That head also had gray eyes.

Those eyes— they were on *me*.

Smoke filled my lungs, holding me captive.

Gray smoke.

My smoke.

I whimpered, bringing my palm to my mouth.

My cowboy.

Chapter Eleven

Denver

Fuck.

She ran, but I didn't. I didn't move my feet, only my torso as I twisted back and faced my boys. There was nothing around this ranch for miles—town was ten miles down the road. It was dark. She had nowhere to go. Only a person with a death wish would try to survive a night like this on foot after a storm.

My city girl knew better.

She was smart.

Jigs' eyes met mine in question. None of them gave a shit she'd just witnessed our hit. The dead man at my feet deserved what he got.

He was lucky we didn't torture him first.

Tilting my chin up, I answered his silent question. "Burn it."

"Yes, boss," he said with a nod.

Beau pushed off the bunkhouse, taking a long drag of the cigarette between his lips. Beau only smoked on nights like this, the nights blood was spilled. He looked to the dead man and then in the direction she ran, his blue eyes flashing with something that pissed me off. It shouldn't have, but it did.

"We have a problem with her?" That was Lawson.

I shook my head. "Nope."

He grunted. His brother was already putting on gloves, ready to get this night over with.

"Hopefully by tomorrow, I'll be able to call the sheriff," I said. The boys nodded and I turned away from them. There was nothing else that needed to be said. Tonight, wasn't a night for beers and shooting the shit.

My boots crunched over the gravel as I stared ahead. Why had she run down here? Why—for a spilt second—had there been *worry* in her eyes?

Worry for me?

The night was quiet, and my house on the hill was eerie similar.

This was good, I thought.

At least she wasn't screaming her fucking head off.

What she'd just witnessed wasn't a good reason to be screaming.

I had other ways to make a woman like her scream, ways we would both enjoy.

Once I was in front of the barn, my steps slowed. I didn't bother looking at the entrance, keeping my gaze on the house.

"You could have stopped her," I muttered.

"I could've," Mags answered behind me.

"Why didn't you?"

"Because she'll never come back here after tonight," he said, his voice cold. Mags didn't like her being here either. Hallow Ranch was his home, his safe haven. He was right. This would likely chase her away, leaving my ranch behind untouched by greed. My chest ached at the thought of never seeing her again.

Shake it off. She's the fucking enemy.

I sighed and adjusted my hat. "Guess I'll go deal with that."

He chuckled. "I'm sure you will."

There was something in his tone that had me twisting my neck to look at him. He was leaning against the open barn door, his arms crossed over his chest, ankles crossed, looking unbothered. Tonight's events hardly ever bothered Mags. He'd spilled blood long before he stepped foot on Hallow Ranch.

I stared at him.

He stared back at me, reading me.

Then he said calmly, "She's beautiful."

"And?" I clipped.

"When's the last time a beautiful woman was in that house?"

"When my mother was breathing," I snapped.

That woman may be beautiful, but she had a toxic heart. She was the fucking enemy. She was here to convince me to sell my land to her greedy, snake of a boss.

He nodded and looked down at the dirt. "Uh huh."

"She works for a fucking pipeline."

"And you just put three bullets in a man," he returned.

What happened to him wanting her gone?

He didn't give me a chance to bite his fucking head off, because he turned and walked into the darkened barn. Cursing under my breath, I made my way back up to the house. It was still chilly, but the weatherman said the temperature will be back up tomorrow.

Normal summer weather would recommence.

City Girl had been out all day—*in my bed.*

After getting her into the truck this morning, soaked and freezing—borderline hypothermic, I raced back to Hallow Ranch. She was out of it, drifting in and out of consciousness. When I pulled up to the house, Beau and Lawson were on the porch. It was still pouring rain, but they came and got her out of the car.

We rushed her upstairs into my bathroom.

"We need to get her warm," Lawson hissed, putting his hand on her forehead. I didn't like that. I didn't understand why I didn't like that.

"I know," I said, yanking off my shirt while she was passed out in Beau's arms. I lifted my chin. "Set her on the bed and get out."

"Get out?"

"Yes, out. I have to undress her. She doesn't need all these eyes on her body without her knowing," I snapped. Beau glared at me but set her on the bed.

Once they were out of my room, I shrugged off my jeans then set to work on getting her out of those clothes.

The woman I'd held for four hours against my chest was now sitting on the front porch of my house, the landline in her shaking hands. I slowed my steps and watched her, shoving my hands in the pockets of my Carhartt to keep myself from touching her.

Fuck, I really fucking wanted to.

Images of her body pressed against mine came rushing back, her hands gripping my arms in her sleep, as she mumbled something that I couldn't make out. She felt so damn good against me, in my arms—

Shut that shit down, Den.

She was crying now, a normal reaction from a person who had never witnessed a murder before. She was still in my Marines shirt, and I noticed she slipped on a pair of my boxers.

Fuck, even in distress, she was a work of art.

Her hands were shaking, and she dialed 911. She put the phone to her ear, and I knew she got a busy tone. She whimpered and tried again, over and over.

"Phone tower is down, City Girl," I said.

Her head snapped up as she let out a gasp, and those green eyes scanned the darkness for me. She raised a shaking hand. "Stay away from me."

Damn.

Her sweet voice was more unsteady than her hands.

I didn't like that.

Why did I give a fuck?

"You going to sit out here all night?" I asked as she looked up from her lap to me. "Or are you going to get inside?"

She continued to stare up at me, a single tear rolling from her eye and descending down her reddened cheek. Still, she remained silent.

"Do what you want, but you go hypothermic again, I ain't saving you."

Nothing.

My stomach tightened.

I didn't give a shit about what she just witnessed. She just got a firsthand look at the monster inside me. The monster—*my monster*—was a permanent resident in my soul. It was branded on my skin. That would never change.

I wouldn't give a shit if the phone towers weren't down, and she did manage to call 911. She didn't know the full story. She would never get the full story. No matter what she did, I would never see the inside of a prison cell, not before taking down some very powerful people with me.

For some reason, though, I gave a shit if I scared her.

Fuck me.

I lifted my chin. "Get inside. It's cold."

"You just killed an innocent man," she breathed, looking at me with fear in her eyes.

I chuckled darkly, pulling my hand from my coat and getting down on my haunches so we were eye level. "That man, City Girl, was anything but innocent. Get inside."

"You killed hi—"

I stood and put my boot on the first step. "Get inside," I ordered.

"I would like to leave."

"Believe me, I would love nothing more than to watch you go," I sneered.

That was a lie, but she would never know that. "But the phone towers are down and the creek that runs under the Little Pine Bridge on the way into town is flooded. Not to mention, your fucking rental is still in that ditch."

"So," she sputtered. "I'm just trapped here?"

I smiled and gestured to the darkness behind me. "You wanna leave, get lost, and die in these mountains? Be my fucking guest." I gestured to my clothes hanging loosely on her curvy body, hiding from me. "But you ain't doing that in my clothes."

"I would like to have my clothes and phone back please," she whimpered.

I tilted my head. "Your clothes are in the dryer. Your phone is most likely in that rental. You didn't have it on you while you were standing in the fucking street in the middle of a fucking storm," I snapped, angry at her for being so foolish. Something could have happened to her. She could have been seriously hurt.

She moved one of her legs and winced. "Ah." At her whimper, I looked down to her feet.

Her. Bare. Feet.

She'd been running on gravel.

Fuck.

They were bleeding. I clenched my jaw and looked back at her face. "You ran down there without any fucking shoes?"

She looked away from me. "I would like to leave, please."

"Get inside," I barked. Jesus. This woman ran on gravel...*why?* I pushed that thought to the back of my mind.

"No," she snapped, looking back up at me. She stood, mostly likely ignoring the pain in her feet, and glared at me with those devasting green eyes. "I would like to leave. Now."

I blinked once. Then I moved, ducking and throwing her over my shoulder. She yelped in surprise as I wrapped my arm around the backs of her thighs, ignoring the way her skin on mine felt like fire.

She was pounding her fists into my back and kicking her legs. I paid her no mind as I opened the front door and marched up the stairs with her still over my shoulder. My eyes focused on her feet.

Fucking hell.

I made it into my room, noting that one of my pillows was on the floor. After I dropped her on the bed, I'd intended to go into the bathroom and get the first aid kit. City Girl, however, had other plans.

She pushed off the bed and tried to run. With a growl, I caught her by the waist and yanked her to me. She was still fighting me as I looked to the ceiling, my patience wearing thin.

Whatever man she had back in her city wasn't doing his job right.

I stepped forward, pressing her against the bedroom wall, her back—*her fucking ass*—pressed against me.

"Do you ever shut up?" I hissed in her ear. She tried to push off the wall, but I snatched her wrists, pinning them above her head with one hand. She wiggled and bucked against me, her perfect, round ass grinding against my crotch.

My cock noticed. My cock liked it, maybe a little too much. Another growl ripped from my throat as thrusted my hips into her, pinning her against the wall further, my erection digging into her cheeks. "Stop."

She froze, her body stiffening, her breathing labored. I squeezed her wrists and brought my other hand to her hip. "Yeah. You feel that. Don't you, City Girl?"

No words. Just soft, quick breaths.

I chuckled in her ear. "Be a good girl or I'll *fuck* you into one."

She gasped, the sound going straight to my cock. I wanted to hear that sound again. I wanted to hear it while she was on her back, spread open for me, watching as I sunk my dick into her.

Slowly, I dropped my hands, letting her arms fall to her sides. Then she shocked me.

"Thought I wasn't good enough for seduction?" she snapped. Clearly my words had gotten to her. I smiled, turning my head away from her.

"You aren't," I said, stepping back away from her. "You need to rest. Get some sleep. Your rental will be here in the morning. Then, you can leave and never come back."

Before she could respond, I was out the door, shutting it behind me and locking it. I headed downstairs to grab some cleaning supplies.

There was blood on my front porch and Caleb didn't need to see that when he came home in the morning.

Today was nothing like I had planned.

That storm fucked everything up, but it did bring out that piece of shit who was probably burning to a crisp right now. The twins went into town earlier, got him drunk, and promised him some good whores. He came willingly.

I also lied to City Girl. The creek wasn't flooded. I just didn't want her to leave tonight. I pushed open the front door and immediately knew Mags was there. He was sitting on the swing, looking out into the night.

"She quiet?" he asked.

"Yeah," I clipped. "I told you I had it under control."

"Just wanted to make sure. Everyone in the bunk house could hear her screaming."

I grunted in response as I scrubbed the blood on the steps. I felt him watching me as the blood mixed in with the cleaner, running down the brick and into the dirt below.

"How quiet is she?" he mused. I looked up to find him staring at the mess, his eyes guarded.

"I don't hurt women, Mags," I grumbled. "She ran across the fucking rocks barefoot."

"Saw that."

"And yet, you didn't stop her."

He sat back in his seat, looking out at the night. "She going to be a problem?"

"Are you going to make her one?" I shot back, tossing the rag into the bucket.

He chuckled. "Yeah, she's going to be a problem."

"She was already a problem," I growled.

He looked at me as I stood, his cowboy hat in hand. "Let me ask you something, Kings, where is she sleeping?"

Kings was my call sign in the Marines. I stared at him.

He answered for me when I didn't. "She's in your bed. That's the first woman to be in your bed since Cathy," he said, putting his hat on.

"It ain't like that, Mags," I hissed.

He chuckled again, and the sound made me want to break his jaw. "Woman is in your bed, Kings. You have other bedrooms up there."

He stood, clapping a hand on my shoulder. "Think on that."

He left me there, calling out over his shoulder. "See you in the morning."

When did Mags become an expert at life? The fucker never left the ranch. He was my best friend though, so I couldn't kill him. I was pissed off and speechless.

Speechless because he was right.

Pissed off because I wanted her in my bed.

I didn't even know her name. I sighed and looked down at the wet spot on the steps. She was still bleeding, and she was in pain.

"Fuck me," I growled, pinching the bridge of my nose.

When I returned, I unlocked the bedroom door and braced for impact. I was shocked to find her not in my bed, but in the bathroom. She was sitting on the toilet—still in my clothes—trying to clean her wounds.

"You gonna let me help you now or you gonna start screaming again?" I asked when she glared at me.

"I don't need your help, Mr. Langston."

I fought back a laugh. My dick was just pressed against her ass, and she still called me that. I wanted to hear my name on her lips, my first name. I wanted to know hers. I stepped forward, taking off my hat and hanging it on the hook. Then I joined her in the bathroom and snatched the cloth out of her hand.

"Hey—"

"Hush," I ordered as I got down on my haunches and held out my hand. "Lift your leg."

Her green eyes held mine, fear still lingering behind them. "You don't—"

"You're tracking blood all through my home, City Girl. I would very much appreciate it if that stopped," I said, grabbing her ankle and pulling her foot towards me.

The bottoms of her feet were bloody, several lacerations on her heel and toes. "Gotta clean these, and then I have some ointment to help with the pain. And the healing process," I explained.

She remained silent, her hands gripping the edge of my shirt she was still wearing. A semi-comfortable silence stretched between us as I set to cleaning her wounds. Her other foot was in the same condition. I had to hand it to her, though; these wounds were pretty nasty, and I knew this shit hurt. Yet, she didn't make a sound. She just stared at me. After I finished wrapping her right foot, I gently eased it down and lifted the left one.

"You know, not a lot of people would get away with staring at me like you are right now, City Girl."

Silence.

"I couldn't get you to shut up this last week and now you don't have anything to say?"

She cleared her throat. "Why are you doing this?"

I looked at her for a second, then back at her feet. "Because you're tracking blood through my house."

"But—"

"And I've dealt with injuries worse than this," I continued.

"Are you going kill me?" she whispered. I looked up at her, lowering her foot slightly.

I laughed. "No, City Girl. I ain't gonna kill ya."

"What if I go to the police?" she dared.

I gestured to the door. "Have at it."

She gaped at me, like she couldn't believe what I was saying. Then again, if I was in her position, maybe I would be the same. I just killed a man in front of her. It wasn't my first time taking a life, and it wouldn't be my last.

"You are going to let me go?"

"This isn't some fucked up version of Beauty and the Beast," I retorted, putting my focus back on her wounds. She tried to pull her leg away from me, but my hand clamped down on her bare thigh. I looked up to her again, baring my teeth.

"You can leave in the morning. Now, stay fucking still so I can get this wrapped," I ordered.

Those green eyes flashed with anger. "You are the worst man I have ever met," she snapped.

"City Girl, you saying that to a man on his knees in front of you, cleaning your feet and wrapping your wounds, makes me think you aren't a good judge of character."

She gasped. "I am an excellent judge of charac—"

"Right. Who do you work for again?" I asked.

Her mouth snapped shut.

We remained silent until I was finished, until I went downstairs and got her clothes. When I returned to my room, she was still on the toilet. After tossing her clothes on the chair in the corner of the bedroom, I joined her.

She quickly wiped her face, but I knew she'd been crying. I also knew that I didn't like her crying, but I ignored the twinge in my chest. She would be gone tomorrow, and all of this would be over.

Hallow Ranch would be untouched.

Moonie pipelines would move on to a different ranch, she would be the leech to suck the poor sucker dry, and I would be here.

Thinking about her.

"Come on," I said softly, bending down to scoop her into my arms. She didn't fight it. Her green eyes were empty as she looked up at me, her arms around my neck as I held her bridal style.

Fuck, she smelled good, like cherries.

Fucking cherries.

"Are you going to hurt me?" she whispered.

"No."

"Are you—"

"City Girl, I'm laying you down on my bed. Then, I'm going into the guest room. It's late. You need to rest and heal. I have a ranch to run. We both need to sleep," I said, laying her down gently. I pulled the sheets over her wrapped feet and bare legs.

She looked up at me again, her dark hair splayed out over my pillows. The hunter green sheets made her eyes seem brighter and her lips pinker.

Did she taste like cherries too?

I shook my head, turning away from her. "Beau will bring your car 'round in the morning."

Then, I was gone.

I didn't go to the spare bedroom. No, I went downstairs into the living room. I sat on the couch and looked to the rock chair in the back corner. It was out of the way, hidden. You couldn't see it until you came into the center of the room.

That's why Mason liked it so much. He used to hide there when we were kids, behind the chair, Momma's chair. She nursed us in that chair. She rocked us to sleep in that chair. She sang in that chair. That chair was meant for the next woman in this house. Pop told Mason and I that the chair was meant for our wives.

Cathy never got to see this chair. I never let her.

Until the sun came up, I stared at the chair, and I didn't move until I heard steps coming down the stairs.

I shot up, my eyes darting to the front window. Her car was here, parked beside my truck. When I got to the foyer, she was halfway down the stairs.

City Girl was dressed in her day-old clothes, wearing her heels, and biting back a wince every step.

"You shouldn't be wearing those," I murmured, my voice low and rough from no sleep. My eyes were on her feet, still wrapped from the night before.

Once she was in front of me, she spoke. "I'll manage."

Then she stuck out her hand to me. "Mr. Langston, I would like to thank you for helping me yesterday. You and I have not gotten along but you still brought me into your home and for that—"

"What the fuck are you doing?" I folded my arms across my chest and glared down at her. She was a tall woman, coming up nearly to my shoulder, so I didn't have to look down far. Her emerald eyes flashed.

"I was trying to be professional," she stammered.

"Woman, you saw me kill a man yesterday. I think we're well past that," I deadpanned. She flinched but recovered quickly.

"Goodbye, Mr. Langston."

Chapter Twelve

Valerie

"You alright, Val?"

I jumped and twisted around to see the light cowboy coming towards me. The blonde one. The one who approached me. The friendly one.

The one who was standing behind the man Denver Langston murdered last night.

He was dressed in jeans and a blue flannel, his cream cowboy hat on his over a friendly, tentative smile. I pressed my back against the door of my rental.

"Please," I said, holding up my hand. It was shaking. Shit.

Beau's eyes darkened as his brow furrowed. "Valerie, I'm not going to hurt you."

"Please, just leave me alone. I'm leaving now. You won't ever have to see me again," I stammered. I just wanted to find my phone and call my mom. Then I wanted to call Mr. Moonie and quit my job.

I wanted to go home and forget Hallow Ranch and its owner's smoke gray eyes.

"Leave her be, Beau."

That voice. That deep, rough, intoxicating voice washed over me. I turned my head to see my dark cowboy, standing on the porch, leaning against the railing, a cup of coffee in his hand.

His smoke was coming for me once more.

This time, I looked away.

Beau was staring at me, his blue eyes pleading for something I didn't have the strength to give. "Never judge a cowboy for his sins, sweetheart. Ask who wronged him first."

He left me with that, turning away and heading back to the barn. I blinked.

"This is crazy," I whispered. Then, I spun to get into the car but something—*someone*—caught my eye. Mr. Langston was now at the bottom of the steps, coffee forgotten, staring at me.

"Drive safe, will ya, City Girl?"

I didn't answer him.

When I pulled out into the drive, though, I looked back.

I shouldn't have looked back.

Because his smoke followed.

"Mom? Momma?" I called, my voice trembling as my hand gripped my cell phone tighter.

"Valerie? My god, honey—"

"Are you okay? Please tell me you're okay. I am so sorry, Mom. Momma, I am so sorry," I cried into the phone, my head falling.

"What in the world are you apologizing for? Val, what's going on?"

"Where are you?" I asked, wiping my tears away. "Are you okay? Did Jackie get you to your treatment?"

"Valerie Cross. Breathe. Now." My mom's voice was stern.

I nodded and took a deep breath.

"Tell me what in the world is going on?"

"There was a storm," I croaked, pulling my feet up on the hotel bed. They were still wrapped, but they weren't hurting. Whatever ointment Mr. Langston gave me last night worked its magic.

Denver. We're calling him Denver, remember?

I shoved all thoughts of him to the back of my mind.

"Val, I know. It was all over the news."

"What?" I breathed, sitting up slightly.

"Yeah, some weird weather phenomenon," she answered. "I was worried about you. You didn't call or answer me but, then I figured it was due to the weather. Did you make through all right?"

"Yeah, I did," I lied.

No, I didn't. *I witnessed a murder by a man I can't get out of my head.*

What's worse is that I believed him. Mr. Langston said that man wasn't innocent, and *I believed him.*

What the hell was wrong with me?

I needed to get out of this town and away from Hallow Ranch.

For the next ten minutes, I proceeded to tell her everything, aside from the murder and my feet getting hurt. By the time I finished, I was exhausted. I didn't sleep at all last night.

I had laid in a murderer's bed, thinking about how good his touch felt, how good it was to be taken care of, despite everything that I'd witnessed.

Then, this morning, when I walked down those stairs, I was mentally ready to give myself a clean break. I would be professional and leave. Unfortunately, Denver Langston didn't give me the chance to do that.

Woman, you saw me kill a man yesterday. I think we're well past that.

His words rang in my head over and over, etched into it. Along with the memory of his touch. The memory of being lifted into his arms. The memory of being pinned against the wall by him, his smoke and strength surrounding me as he pressed himself into me.

My nipples hardened at the thought.

"Valerie, what in the hell is wrong with you?" I asked aloud, falling back onto the crappy hotel pillows. Maybe I just need therapy.

No, you need sleep. You're delusional.

I set my phone on the charger and got what I needed. Sleep. When I woke up, I would deal with everything, but right now. I just needed to sleep.

Hayden, CO. Tinkles Bar.

The bar was nearly empty.

There was one stripper on stage, swinging her body around the pole for a married man in the booth in front of her. There were two more men sitting at the bar, drowning their mistakes and sins in liquor.

Behind the bar was a woman.

She was in her mid-thirties but looked fifteen years older.

Her blonde hair was fake as well as her tits. She wore too much makeup that looked like it was purchased from the drug store. She chewed gum like a fucking animal.

A new man came into the bar, dressed in a navy pinstriped suit. He had blonde hair, slicked back and wore a red tie.

Mr. Tim Moonie.

His greedy eyes scanned the titty bar quickly before landing on the blonde behind the counter. He approached her, an oily smile spreading across his face.

"Hey, beautiful," he greeted.

Under normal circumstances, the woman behind the bar would tell a man to get lost. She didn't talk to poor men, but Tim Moonie wasn't a poor man, and she could tell. She looked up and down with her dull brown eyes, the wheels turning in her head.

"Well, hey there, big boy," she purred.

It was unattractive, but Mr. Moonie didn't show it. In fact, he overlooked it.

He was tired of waiting. Ms. Cross was moving too slowly for him. While he admired her skills, he knew Denver Langston would be a tough cowboy to crack.

Thus, he used his money to his advantage, by doing some digging.

He found what he needed.

He sweet talked the woman named Cathy, the mother of Denver Langston's son. She was also the former fiancé of Mason Langston, the second son of the Langston family. Mason Langston was a professional bull rider and wanted nothing to do with Hallow Ranch.

That worked for Mr. Moonie just fine. One less brother to deal with.

Hallow Ranch would be his soon enough.

Cathy was a dumb woman. She thought her pussy could give her the world and Mr. Moonie was fine with letting her think that.

The two spoke quietly together at the end of the bar.

Then, thirty minutes later, Mr. Moonie's cock was in her mouth. He fucked her face violently, stroking her tear-stained cheeks as she looked up at him. He praised her and promised her the world as he released down her throat, and then he gave her two hundred bucks.

Not for the blowjob.

She had another job to do now.

Then Mr. Moonie called Valerie Cross and fired her.

Chapter Thirteen

Denver

Three days.

Three days had passed since she left, and yet, my sheets still smelled like cherries.

It was driving me insane, laying down in bed every single night, smelling her sweet scent and getting a raging fucking hard on from it. I tried to ignore the urge, but then I would be lying in bed and looking at the spot on the wall where I'd pressed against her, and my control would snap.

I've fisted my cock seven times since she left, thinking about those gasps and her green eyes as I came.

It was fucking ridiculous and pissed me off to no end.

I glared at the spot where she used to park her car, then looked up to where it was parked by my truck the morning she left.

Son of a fucking—

"You looking for that woman, Dad?"

I turned around to find Caleb sitting on his stool. Narrowing my eyes at him, I took a long sip of my water. "Who are you talking about, son?"

Caleb blinked and then shrugged. "The pretty one who pisses you off?"

My eyebrows rose. "Who in the—"

"The guys are talking about her in the bunkhouse," my son continued as he brought his sandwich to his mouth. I watched as he took a bite, gulping it down with that red juice he likes so much.

"Number one, who taught you that word? Number two, you don't need to be listening in on their conversations, son," I scolded.

"Answer to number one, you did. You cuss all the time. I have ears. That leads to number two; the guys in the bunkhouse talk loud," he said, taking another bite.

I found myself looking at the ceiling.

Jesus fucking Christ.

"Son—"

"Who is she?" he asked. He was curious, that's all this was. The only woman he'd been around was his mother, unfortunately for him. He'd never known a good woman, and I knew his classmates had good women in their lives. My son was at the age where he realized he was missing out.

I hated it.

"No one important, son."

"Is she the one you went out in the storm for?" he asked.

I would go out into any storm for her. *Rain or hellfire.*

Fuck me.

I looked out the window again. "Yes, son."

"I'm glad you were there for her, Dad. Not a lot of people get to be saved by a man like you," he said, beaming at me.

Not a lot of people are killed by a man like me either, son.

I set my cup in the sink, grabbing my hat, as I went to my boy. "Alright, bud. Shit to do. You coming or staying?" I asked, putting my hand on his head.

"Can I ride Ranger?" he asked, pushing my hand off and giggling.

"Saddle him up, yes. Man needs to learn how to saddle his own horse."

"Mags saddles your horse for you," he pointed out.

"I know how to saddle my horse, smartass," I said, putting him in a soft headlock. "I also own this place and give that man a home."

"Yeah, yeah! Okay, okay!" he laughed in my hold, trying to get out of it.

"That's what I thought," I said, chuckling. "Let's head out."

We walked down to the barn, saddled Ranger, and trotted right past the spot where I killed a man who decided to take what he wanted without asking for it.

His ashes had been spread in the stream near where Pop found my mother's body.

Hours later, Caleb and I were riding back to the house for some lunch.

The sun was high, its warmth erasing any evidence of the storm. The herd was being moved to a different pasture while the fence was being mended. We decided to replace more than the mile we originally planned. The work was being done, my boy was with me, the cows were healthy, the storm had passed, and *she* hadn't come back.

"Faster!" Caleb cried as we rounded the bend, clearing the wall of pines as our home came into view. It was a flat stretch from where we were to the barn. Ranger was excited. Caleb was excited.

My boys needed this. I needed this. I needed to feel the wind around me, the thumping of Ranger's hooves against the earth, Caleb crying out in glee.

"Let's go, boy!" I commanded, kicking my heel.

Ranger sped up as Caleb laughed and brought a hand up to hold his hat—one Jigs got him for Christmas last year, because every cowboy needs a decent hat. The barn was coming up fast, the field passing by in a blur, the clouds above racing us.

Life was good.

Life was back to normal.

Normal was good in my book.

Normal was running this ranch on my own.

Normal was watching my brother achieve his dreams on a screen—refusing to come home.

Normal was having my boy with me, learning from me.

Normal was shooting the shit with the boys in the bunkhouse after a long day.

Normal was drinking a glass of whiskey on the front porch, alone.

Normal was going to bed alone.

Normal was travelling to a different state once a quarter to fuck some woman in a bar and leave right after without learning her name.

Normal was *her* being gone.

I didn't want normal anymore. She invaded my life weeks ago, and I wanted her to stay in it. I wanted to keep telling her "no" and get her to shout "yes" while she was under me in my bed. I wanted that stupid rental car back. I wanted those green eyes back on me.

I wanted her to tell me what "Smoke" meant.

I wanted to know why she didn't want me to be cold.

I wanted to know why she let me take care of her.

I wanted to know why she ran *to* the bunkhouse after hearing those gunshots and not away from it.

I wanted to know her fucking name.

"Dad?"

I gripped the reigns and eased Ranger to a walk as my son brought me away from my thoughts.

"Mom is here," he said, disappointment lacing his voice. That snapped me out of thoughts of things that never would be. My head jerked up to the house and found her car sitting next to my truck.

That wasn't the car I wanted here. That car—that woman—is the reason I lost my brother. That woman was the reason I couldn't trust any other woman.

That woman ruined me at the same time she gave me a son. I loved Caleb more than anything in the world. The way I got a son caused my brother a world of pain I couldn't control.

We made it to the barn, and I instructed Caleb to get Ranger settled.

"Can he have some carrots?" he asked while brushing his coat. I put my hand on his shoulder.

"Yeah, bud, give him some carrots. I'm going to talk to your mom and then you and I are going fishing," I said softly. No way in hell Cathy was taking him today. Summers were meant to be spent at the ranch, not cooped up in some crappy apartment.

Leaving him be, I walked up to the house. Cathy wasn't standing by the car anymore. She was sitting in the porch swing like she was destined to be there, the wind blowing through her horrid blonde hair.

Maybe a decade ago, she could have been here, if she had chosen not to fuck over Mason and me.

"Cellphones are a wonderful thing, ya know?" I called, heading up the front steps.

"Just wanted to make sure everything was okay with Caleb after that storm," she mused, pushing her chest out a bit. Wasn't interested in her chest a decade ago, and I wasn't interested now. I withheld my sigh. She was in one of her moods.

That mood was her getting a wild hair and wanting us to be "a family again."

We were never a fucking family. She was the toxin that destroyed one and by the grace of God, Caleb was born out of it. A good, wholesome little boy was born from betrayal. I would never be able to wrap my head around it. I was just grateful for my boy. He was kind, thoughtful, gentle, and so fucking intelligent that it scared me sometimes.

Every single time Cathy would try to seduce me again, I would tell her to fuck off and threaten to take her ass to court. That usually shut her shit down. She knew I would get full custody of Caleb if I needed to. She didn't have a case.

Caleb was in her life because she, despite being a vile bitch, was his mom. She loved our son, that much was clear, but she knew she shouldn't be sitting on my fucking porch, wind in her hair, staring out at Hallow Ranch like it was hers.

In another life, it could have been.

Caleb would have been Mason's. Cathy would be Mason's, and maybe—just fucking maybe—I would've be happy in that life.

I hadn't been happy in ten years—apart from being with Caleb. Unfortunately, there's more to life than fatherhood, and I was unhappy in every other way.

"What do you want, Cathy?" I asked, folding my arms over my chest.

"Is the ranch alright? Cattle okay?"

I barked a laugh, shaking my head. "Don't pretend to give a single shit about Hallow Ranch. We both know you're a terrible actress."

Her brown eyes flared. "I wasn't a terrible actress ten years ago, Denver," she spat.

My blood ran cold. I didn't like talking about that night and I sure as shit didn't like talking to her about it. My eyes flicked up to the barn. Caleb was still inside it. I moved then, leaning over her and caging her in.

"You weren't anything to me, Cathy. I needed a warm hole to bury my dick in, and you were more than willing to spread your legs as well as your fucking lies," I growled.

Her face paled. "Den—"

"You don't get to come here and sit on my fucking porch like you own it. Your ass only belongs in that swing if my brother's ring was still on your fucking finger. It isn't. That shit was ripped off of you like he was ripped from me. So. Get. The. Fuck. Off. My. Porch."

She nodded. "Den, I didn't mean anything by it. I just..."

"What?" I clipped, pushing back and stepping away from her. "You got another wild hair to make us a family?"

She shook her head. "You made it perfectly clear you never want that, Den."

I bared my teeth, coming at her again, my boots stomping on the wood below me. "You don't get to use my nickname, Cathy."

She looked away and nodded. "Sorry. I just..."

"Cathy, I swear to Christ if you don't just spit it out," I hissed.

"I wanted to see if Caleb wanted to have lunch with me," she blurted.

That was a lie.

She wasn't here for that.

She was here for something else, and she was afraid to move further because I shut that shit down.

"Caleb is here with me. Summers he will be here."

"No kid wants to be on a ranch all summer," she retorted, standing up.

"My kid does. This will be his one day. All of it will be his," I said, gesturing out to the land around us. The glory. The beauty.

"I know that."

"His, Cathy. Not yours," I clipped.

She huffed. "I know that. I just wanted to take my son into town—"

"He is coming fishing with me this afternoon. After a storm, the creek is usually higher. My boy wants to fish. He doesn't want to go have lunch and then go back to your apartment. All he is going to do there anyways is watch TV while you smoke on the balcony."

She winced.

"Anything else you wanna try today or is that it?" I asked, leaning against the house.

"I guess not," she spat.

I unfolded an arm and waved. "Then get off my porch."

"You are such an asshole."

I winked. "Says the whore who made me one."

"Holy! Dad!"

"Keep reeling, buddy. That's it!" I said, standing behind my boy as he reeled the line back in. He was struggling but didn't want my help. He told me on the way up here that he wanted to reel in his own fish.

My boy was becoming a man. I had to step back and let him do that.

"It's a big one!" he yelled, his voice echoing through the woods around us. I chuckled and looked down the stream before focusing back on him. The fish cleared the water and we both stepped back. Caleb handed me his pole and bent to get the fish.

It was a good size trout; bigger than the others we'd caught. For the last three hours, I'd spent time with Caleb, laughing and joking with him. We talked about life and how next year school would be different for him.

He was going to be in advanced placement classes—*in every single subject.*

He also wanted to go out for the kid's football team. He told me this as we were baiting our hooks for the first time. His voice was shy and timid. When I asked him why he was being shy about it, he said, "Because football isn't the ranch, dad."

To which I replied, "Football is football. If you decide football is your dream, then you have my support."

Would I love for him to take over the day he gets back from college? Absolutely, but I wasn't going to hold my kid back from chasing his dreams. My dream was Hallow Ranch. Mason's was PBR. Caleb's could be football.

"You going to throw it back or keep it, bud?" I asked, watching him marvel at his catch.

"Can you cook this one?"

"I can," I answered, smiling.

"Then I guess we got dinner!"

"I guess we do."

The sun was setting by the time we got back. The herd was gazing, the fence mended. The workday was done, and my son was happy. We got back to the house, and after unloading everything, he went upstairs to grab his book.

He was reading *Harry Potter* and didn't fail to give me a play by play while I cleaned the fish. We moved outside to the back porch where my grill was. The sun was nearly gone, casting a red orange glow over the valley. Caleb was in a rocking chair, his legs crisscrossed as he read aloud to me.

Dinner was nearly done when Lawson walked up to the side of the house.

"Hey, boss."

"Yo," I greeted, tipping my beer to him. "Everything alright?"

He looked from Caleb to me and then back to Caleb. *Fuck.* I twisted and looked at my son. "Hey, bud. Fetch me another beer, would ya?"

"Sure thing, Dad!"

Once he was inside the house, Lawson spoke.

"Cathy is coming up the drive."

"Son of a bit—"

"She's hammered and swerving all over the place," he said, cutting me off.

I looked up at the sky. "Jesus—keep bud inside, would ya?" I asked.

Lawson nodded once and headed inside. I turned the grill down and walked around the house. Cathy's car was pulled off the gravel, by the oak tree. She was walking towards me—barely. Her hair was greasy, like she'd been sweating and didn't take a fucking shower. She was wearing a skintight shirt, and her fake tits were falling out. She had on tight jeans with a suspicious stain on them.

"Dennnveerr," she slurred, raising her arm and pointing it at me.

"Fucking Christ," I muttered. I looked to the bunkhouse to see the boys emerging. This wasn't the first time this bitch has made a scene.

I got about two feet from her and stopped, planting my boots. "What are you doing here, Cathy?"

"We gotta talk," she said slowly.

"You driving drunk?"

She shook her head. "No. I want Caleb to come home with me tonight," she said, wobbling on her feet.

"You aren't getting anywhere near my son with that much alcohol in your system," I said. Mags and Jigs were coming up the hill now and Cathy's focus shifted from me to Mags.

"Hey, big boy," she purred.

"Rather fuck a cactus, sugar," Mags said before looking at me. "She drive here like this?"

I nodded once.

"Cathy, you need to leave," Jigs said softly. Part of me wanted to hate him for treating her so nicely, but a few years back, I brought it up. He told me she was the mother of Pop's grandchild, that because of her, the family grew, and for that, she would be treated with respect—even if she didn't deserve it.

"I want my boy," she spat, ignoring Jigs' kindness.

"No," I growled.

"I want my boy!"

"You are three sheets to the fucking wind, Cathy! Jesus fucking Christ," I barked and threw a hand out to her car. "It's a miracle you even made it out this far."

"I have things to discuss with my son," she slurred.

I adjusted my hat. "Two options, woman. Number one, you let Jigs take you home. Number two, I'll call the sheriff. He'll nail your ass for drunk driving and then you'll lose custody of Caleb."

She snapped her cheap lipstick covered mouth shut, glaring at me.

"Don't test me," I clipped.

"It's Saturday night, Denver," she stated, as if that was reason enough to be hammered and driving.

"Don't give a shit what day it is, Cathy. Jigs will drive you home."

"I hate you," she spat at me.

I closed the space in between us, glaring down at her, venom sinking into my blood. "Good, bitch. I fucking hate you, too."

"That's enough," Jigs said, putting his old, weathered hand on Cathy's arm. "Come on. I'll take you home."

My nostrils flared as I watched them walk away.

"That woman is a snake."

Mags.

I turned to him, finding his dark eyes on Cathy.

"No shit," I deadpanned, looking back to the house, wondering how in the fuck something so good came out of a woman like that.

"Kings."

I looked back to Mags. Even though we didn't serve together, we were both Marines. That made us brothers. We had shared a lot over whiskey and campfires since he came to Hallow Ranch, war stories and such. I trusted this man with my life. So, when he held my eyes and said, "Something isn't right."

My gut believed him.

Something wasn't right.

Cathy came to the ranch twice in one day. It reeked of desperation and something else.

"You're getting that feeling, aren't you?"

He nodded. "I don't like it, Kings."

"I don't either, Mags."

Chapter Fourteen

Valerie

Three days after I left Hallow Ranch, I got the courage to go back again. I didn't tell Mr. Moonie about the murder I'd witnessed. I didn't tell him about my feet getting cut up.

I told him about the storm and how Mr. Langston helped me. I also told him I think I got through to him and I had high hopes for the Hallow Ranch account.

Then I got fired.

Fired.

By Mr. Moonie himself.

Over the phone.

"Valerie, while I appreciate your efforts to obtain the Hallow Ranch account, I have decided to go in a different direction," he said through the phone.

My gut twisted. "Sir, please, give me more time."

"Moonie Pipelines doesn't have the time. Denver Langston is a hard one to crack, and rest assured that he will, just not by you. By me."

My throat was thick, and tears stung my eyes. "What does that mean for me, sir?"

A soft chuckle and then, "Ms. Cross, you have been an asset to this company for years. However, you failed to do your job. Normally, you would have the contract signed by the owners and be home by now."

"Yes sir, but—"

"You don't have the contract. Mr. Langston isn't budging," *he stated, his voice void of any human emotion. He sounded like a robot.*

"What does that mean for me, sir?" *I asked, repeating myself as the panic set in, my mom's face flashing before my eyes.*

"Your severance package will be sent out within the week."

Then he hung up.

That bastard hung up on me.

Forty-five minutes later, in the middle of my breakdown, his assistant emailed me the details of my termination. I had to sign the exit paperwork. They weren't even paying for my flight home, and I was expected to check out of the hotel tomorrow morning.

I didn't call my mom.

I didn't book a flight.

I didn't pack my bags.

In fact, I did the one thing I probably shouldn't have done. I put on some dark blue jeans, high heeled booties that I got on sale two years ago, curled my hair, put on make-up and left.

I left that shitty hotel room in the middle of Colorado after getting fired to do something I'd never done in my twenty-seven years of life.

Get drunk.

Fast forward two hours, and here I was, sitting on a bar stool in Hayden's watering hole, drinking a rum and coke. Jack Sparrow drinks rum and he always looks like he is having a good time. So, I decided on rum.

I was going to get drunk tonight. Then, I was going back to my hotel room, getting naked and playing with myself while imagining smoke gray eyes and strong arms.

That's what I was going to do.

Part of me wondered if I'd just told Mr. Moonie about what I'd witnessed, if my job would've been safe. The Hallow Ranch would have been taken away from the Langston family, ending generations of hard work and glory. Moonie Pipelines would have swept in after my admission, using my trauma as a tactic. Why should a madman, a murderer, keep a ranch? That would have been their angle.

I would have kept my job and gotten paid.

Mom would've been set for the next two years and maybe I could've been able to breathe easy again.

No, you wouldn't have, Val.

Because Denver would have been rotting in prison and your guilt would eat you alive.

Why?

That man killed someone in front of me.

He was a murderer.

He was rude.

He was arrogant.

So why didn't I rat him out?

He told me I could run to the sheriff if I wanted. He didn't care. He had power here, in this town, in this state, but what about everywhere else? I could go to the FBI. A man was murdered three days ago, and nobody was doing anything about it.

The town buzzed with its usual calmness. No one was thinking twice about a man not being seen in three days. Was he a local? Was he just passing through? Is that why no one was talking about it?

"You need a refill?"

I looked from the TV above to the handsome, young bartender standing in front of me. He was cute, in a boyish sort of way, no older than twenty-three.

"Yes, please," I answered.

His eyes took me in slowly, looking me up and down. "Sure thing, doll," he said with a wink. Great. Now I was getting hit on by young men.

I wasn't old, but I was closer to thirty. He didn't have a mortgage to pay. He probably worked his shifts here at the local bar and did what he wanted. Fucked who he wanted to fuck. Slept in. Went on trips. Hung out with his friends.

As he walked back to me, I studied him. He looked like a man with a lot of friends.

I didn't have any friends.

I was twenty-seven, drunk for the first time ever, realizing my life was lame. I had no great stories to tell. I had nothing to brag about. I had no one to kiss me and tell me I looked pretty. I had no one in my bed at night.

"Here you go, doll."

The drink slid in front of me as he leaned in, bracing his forearms on the wooden bar top. He was tall, probably only an inch or two taller than me. He was lean, though, skinnier than me.

Despite being tall, he didn't have the ability to make me feel small, not like Denver did.

Don't go there, Val.

"You're new here," the bartender stated. I looked up from his arms and into his eyes. They were hazel, pretty, but not intoxicating.

Not like my cowboy's smoke.

Wow, I was drunk.

"Just passing through," I answered.

"Seen you around. Saw you a week ago, doll," he stated.

I remained silent.

"Been waiting for you to come in here," he said softly.

He was definitely flirting.

"You have?"

"Woman like you in a town like this? Yeah, doll. I have," he murmured as his eyes dropped to my cleavage. I lost interest, and I did it at the right time because he was called away.

For the next hour, I was left alone. He brought me another drink, winking at me again. I gave him a polite smile because it was a nice thing to do. Just when I was ready to close out, someone sat in the stool beside me.

His cologne made me want to vomit.

"Hey there," he said. I turned to look at him, just my head, keeping my body straight forward. He was older than me, maybe by a year or two, dressed in a cheap suit that hung too loose on his body. His hair had too much gel in it, and there was a line of sweat over his brow.

He was trying too hard.

I said nothing.

"How you doing?" he asked, giving me a slimy smile that made the urge to vomit intensify.

How original.

"Fine," I answered, keeping it short in the hopes he would leave me alone.

He didn't.

For the next few minutes, the man peppered me with questions while his eyes got their fill of my body. He leaned in a little too close, pushed a little too hard. It made me uncomfortable—and suddenly, I felt more sober.

The bartender noticed.

"Everything good here, doll?" he asked me, his hazel eyes on the man beside me.

The man scoffed, putting his hand on my knee. "She's doing just fine."

I looked to the bartender, my eyes pleading. "Can you close me out?" I asked.

Those hazel eyes bounced from me to the man and back to me. "Sure thing."

"You going somewhere?" the man asked.

"It's getting late," I answered, sweeping his hand from my body. I stood quickly, putting the stool between us.

"You need a ride?"

"No, thank you."

The bartender came back. "Here you go, doll."

I paid my tab quickly and headed for the door, ignoring the creepy man. The hotel was just half a block down the way...

Chapter Fifteen

Denver

Caleb and I were on the couch, watching the Yankees game. A player named Dean Connors was up to bat, making his first appearance in five years.

"Jesus, where in the hell has that guy been?" I mumbled, watching the blonde haired, tattooed player spin his bat while smiling up at the crowd. Last I heard, he played for the Chicago Cubs—five years ago.

"Who is that, Dad?"

I took a sip of my water. I usually cut myself off after my second beer until Caleb went to bed. Then I'd have a glass of whiskey on the porch. I looked down at my boy.

"That's a damn good baseball player, son. One of the best of this generation."

"So, he's like Uncle Mason but for baseball," he stated.

That felt like a punch in the gut.

I pushed past it.

"Yeah, bud." I ignored the burning in my stomach and looked back at the TV, just in time for Connors to swing. He hit the ball out into left field and broke into a run. The bases had been loaded. He got to third base safely.

Pounding on the door had me ripping my eyes away from the TV.

"What the hell?"

"What's going on, Dad?"

"Stay here, bud," I answered, setting my drink on the coffee table. When I got to the door and swung it open, Jigs was standing there, looking winded.

"Jigs, what the hel—"

"Pretty girl is in trouble," he breathed, his eyes panicked. I looked over at living room. Caleb was watching TV. I stepped out and closed the door.

"What are you talking about?" I hissed.

"Green eyes, Denver. She's in trouble."

My spine stiffened and my blood ran cold. "Where?"

"In town. You need to get there fast. She went into David's."

"David's is a bar, Jigs."

"*His* friend followed her inside."

I was moving. "Take Caleb to the bunkhouse tonight. Keep him safe. Tell Mags to be on standby," I ordered, running down to my truck.

For the second time, I was running after my green-eyed woman. For the first time, I was actually scared shitless.

The drive into town was a blur. The only thing I could focus on was the sound of my heart pumping in my ears and the ice-cold panic crawling up my spine. I pulled into David's, parking right up front. David's had been David's since I was kid, but it was owned by a woman named Martha.

She was a good woman, and she hated a man named David. So, she named the bar after him so people could drink their lives away like he did. At least, that's what Pop's told Mason and I when we were kids.

I barreled out of the truck, ready to storm inside and raise hell when I heard, "Leave me alone!" It came from my right, in the direction of the hotel.

Fuck.

I ran. Boots to the fucking ground, I ran. My pistol was in the waistband of my jeans, and I knew there was a very strong chance I might have to kill a man tonight, especially if that man touched her.

No one was allowed to touch her.

Except me.

I heard a muffed scream from the small alley way behind the local diner. I came to a halt when I rounded the corner.

Green eyes.

Green eyes were staring back at me, pleading with me.

Pleading *for* me.

She was pressed against the wall, front first, a man's hand in her hair, his other hand was trying to push down her jeans. "Denver!" she cried.

I saw red.

Blood.

Fucking.

Red.

The man noticed me and paled. He immediately let go of her and tried to back up, but I was *there*. My fist slammed into his jaw as the other grabbed his hair. I walked us backwards until his back hit the wall, I pinned him there as I punched him until I heard the crunch of bones and pain radiated from my fist.

I didn't care.

He touched her.

I spun him around, holding him still by the hair, and with my free, bloodied hand, I shoved the back of his loose pants down. "How do you like it, huh?"

He was crying. The little pussy.

"Please! Please—"

"Shut the fuck up," I hissed, getting my pistol out. I spread his legs by kicking them open with my boot. "You like that?" I taunted, my jaw tightening to the point of pain as I pressed the gun to his limp, poor excuse of a dick from behind.

"Please! Oh, God," he cried. "I'm sorry!"

"Men like you don't deserve to have dicks," I hissed, yanking his hair back further. "Men like you get raped in prison. You ready to be someone's little bitch boy?"

The man was shaking now.

"You don't touch *my* woman. You don't look at *my* woman. You don't think about her green eyes. You don't think about her pretty hair. You don't think about her enchanting face."

"Okay! Okay! Please!"

I leaned in close to his ear. "Ya boy got three bullets in his body before I burned it," I said, my voice low. He stiffened, and I chuckled. "One in the dick, one in the chest, and one in the stomach. Bam. Bam. *Bam*."

"I'll do anything—"

"You'll stick around," I ordered.

"But—"

I cut off his whimpering. "You'll stick around, or when I find you—and I will—I'll rape you with barbed wire."

After a moment, he nodded, still shaking. I released him with a growl and stepped back as the man pulled his pants up.

Then he made a grave mistake.

He twisted around and looked *directly at her.*

His eyes took in her body and decided *to claim it as his.*

I told him not to look or think about her.

He disobeyed.

I looked to the dark sky above and adjusted my hat. Then, I looked back at her. She was trembling, her arms wrapped around herself.

Her green eyes met mine and I said, "Baby, close those eyes for me."

"Den—"

"Close 'em, baby," I demanded gently. When she did, I fired my gun, staring at her as I did it. She let out a yelp with each shot.

One.

Two.

Three.

The gunshots echoed out through the night. It was late, and even though it was Saturday, this town was a quiet one. I looked back at the man, who was now slumped against the brick wall, blood trickling from his mouth. His eyes were still open, staring at her. I hated knowing that the last thing he ever saw on this Earth was her beauty. Men like him didn't deserve to see beauty like hers.

"Fucking hell."

I didn't move. I knew that was Beau. He must've followed me into town, his father probably called him because he knew I would need backup.

That old man knew blood would be spilled tonight.

"Jesus, boss—"

"Burn it," I ordered, looking over at him.

He stood at the end of the alley in jeans, a Carhart jacket, and his cowboy hat. Even though I couldn't see in the shadows, I knew his blue eyes were on her. He had been kind to her, spoke to her, made her fucking laugh. All I'd done was scared her and insult her. She still had her eyes closed; her head bent in fear and submission.

"Call the twins and *burn* it," I said, my voice low as he walked closer. I could see him now, his eyes on the body of the man who touched something he shouldn't have.

Beau's jaw tightened as he looked away from the body. "Got it."

"Get it done. I'll call the sheriff," I said, holding his stare.

"He isn't going to like this," Beau noted.

"Don't give a shit. It's one less problem we gotta worry about and his hands stay clean," I bit out. He nodded and got to work.

I moved to her, ignoring the sounds of the dead weight being shifted behind me. Her shirt was crooked, her hair everywhere, and her jeans were unbuttoned. Her face was red, cheeks wet with tears.

"Look at me," I demanded. My body was humming with rage, and I was trying to tone it the fuck down to be gentle with her. She needed gentle. I needed more blood, more screams. I wished I could bring the fucker back to life and take my time, torture him, make him scream like he wanted to make her scream.

Her head snapped up, green eyes on me.

"Stay lookin' at me."

She did as I told her, and my hands drifted down. I righted her shirt ignoring the burn that her skin left on mine, and pulled her hair over her shoulders so it was flowing down her back again. Then my hands went lower as I buttoned her jeans gently.

The whole time she kept her eyes on me. When I was done, my hands immediately dropped away.

"You got shit at the hotel?" I asked.

She nodded, confusion lingering in her green eyes.

"Let's go."

I led her to my truck, passing by Beau, who was standing on the sidewalk on his phone. He murmured something to her, but I didn't listen. I opened the passenger door for her but didn't touch her. Instead, I got in on my side and drove the short way to the hotel.

"Room key," I demanded, holding out my palm once I parked.

"I don't want to say out here alone," she said weakly.

"You aren't. I need to sweep the room before you enter it, though."

She handed me her key, from the back pocket of her jeans. I got out and moved around to open the door for her, but she was already sliding out.

I didn't like that.

I stepped forward, crowding her against the door of the truck. She was breathing heavily, her chest heaving but she didn't have fear in her eyes. No, there was something else lingering in her green.

Something I should run away from.

But I couldn't. Not now.

"You don't get out of the truck until I open the door for you, understand?" I growled.

"Denver—"

"Do you understand me?" I clipped, looking down at her.

She nodded, and I grunted and pulled back. We went inside the hotel, and the old man who ran it greeted me. "Heya, Denver."

"Bart," I greeted, heading for the elevators. Once we were inside, she punched in the floor and off we went.

"Bart's nice," she murmured, looking down at her boots.

I stayed silent.

The doors opened and I followed the signs and the numbers. Once we were in front of her door, I unlocked it. "Stay here," I ordered, before stepping inside.

My eyes scanned the small room, noting how tidy she was. The bed was made—not by hotel staff. Her laptop was on the desk, her charging cords wrapped on top of it. Her suitcase was tucked away. I stuck my head in the bathroom, expecting to find a hurricane aftermath of girly shit.

No. Everything was arranged nicely.

Tidy.

Clean.

I opened the door for her, and she stepped in. "Get your stuff together."

"I have to stay here tonight," she said.

I looked at her. "You aren't staying here tonight."

"But—"

"Pack your shit."

"I don't check out until tomorrow morning," she explained, brushing past me. I stiffened. She was leaving.

Was that why she was out and dressed like that?

She looked good.

Damn good.

Why in the hell was she leaving?

"You're leaving?" I asked, folding my arms over my chest.

She looked over at me and all of a sudden, she looked exhausted, worn down. The adrenaline from a few minutes ago must have worn off, which was surprising.

"I have to."

I didn't like that she was leaving.

I didn't like that she was leaving, and *I wouldn't have known.* *Because you already thought she was gone.*

"You didn't convince me," I returned, raising a brow.

She huffed a laugh. It wasn't pleasant; it seemed forced. I watched her as she ran a hand through her hair, looking around. "Trust me, I know I didn't do my job. I don't need you reminding me."

"So, you're just giving up?"

She shook her head, looking away from me. "No."

"Then why are you leaving?" I asked, stepping closer to her. Her eyes met mine again.

"I got fired this morning," she said, her voice monotoned, unfeeling.

I jerked. "That son of a bitch fired you because I refused to sell my ranch?"

She moved to look out the window. "Yep."

That fucking bastard.

"Was this your first assignment or something?" I pressed.

She turned to me. "No. I was very good at the job. The woman I replaced got fired after her first rejection too. I was hired, trained, and sent to the ranch that rejected her," she paused for a moment. "I had the contract signed in an hour."

"Jesus," I muttered.

She sighed and looked to her feet. "Mr. Langston, I wanted to thank you for what you've done for me," she said, her professional mask back in place. "I can never repay you. You saved my life tonight. You saved me the other day. For that, I am grateful."

I stared at her. This woman witnessed me murder two men this week and now she was talking to me like we're having a lunch meeting. *What the fuck?*

"Look at me," I demanded again.

She didn't. She just kept on. "I have to be out of the hotel by morning, and I have to book my flight tonight. I have to wake up early and drive to Denver. As much as I appreciate you helping me, I need to get some rest."

"You're in shock," I deadpanned.

She nodded, still looking anywhere but me. My stomach twisted. "That may be true, and on that matter, my lips are sealed."

I stilled. "Excuse me?"

"What happened this week will remain here."

But not you.

"You aren't staying here tonight," I said firmly, moving to grab her suitcase. I brought it to the bed and unzipped it. I ignored the red lace peeking out from beneath one of her shirts. "Pack your shit."

"Mr. Langston—"

I was moving, closing the distance between us. Without a second thought, I grabbed her chin between my fingers, and tilted her head up. Her eyes were wide as she sucked in a breath, the sound shooting straight to my groin.

"You called me Denver in that alley. You called me Denver in my truck. You will only call me Denver from now on, is that clear?"

"I—"

"Is that clear?" I asked, bending my head as my fingers tightened.

Her eyes flashed. "You don't get to tell me what to do!"

"Baby, I'll gladly take you over my knee if need be."

She froze, and I pulled back from her face. "Pack your shit. I have to make a call."

Chapter Sixteen

Valerie

It was dawn. Early dawn.

I hadn't slept.

It was early dawn, and I was at the place that got me fired, in the home of a man who refused me, rescued me, doctored me, and then saved me from something tragic.

After I'd left the bar, I knew that man had followed me. The streets were empty, which was odd, considering that it was a Saturday night. However, looking back on it now, there weren't a lot of younger people in that bar last night. The bartender might have been the youngest one there.

The man followed me, and I ducked into the alley, thinking I would be able to fend him off. He looked weak underneath that suit; I could hold my own. I was fully ready to go down fighting; at least, until he pulled out a switchblade.

He told me to face the wall, or he would cut me open.

I planned on fighting him then, too, which I did. I'd managed to step on one of his feet before he slammed my head into the brick, holding me by the hair. I closed my eyes and screamed, even though no one was outside. I had to hope someone would come.

I never expected my dark cowboy. His smoke was all around me, cloaking me, protecting me from that vile man.

When I opened my eyes, all I saw was him. I cried out for him, and he saved me.

He killed for me. He protected me.

Then he took me to the hotel and told me to pack. I didn't understand it, didn't understand the look of anger that flashed over his handsome face when I told him I was leaving. I didn't miss the hurt in the smoke of his eyes.

I was too tired to ask questions, so, I packed. He made a phone call, speaking lowly behind the bathroom door, before we headed to the lobby. From there, Denver checked me out of the hotel and made sure Moonie Pipelines was covering the cost. After that, we rode to the ranch in silence.

He put me in one of the spare bedrooms down the hall, told me to get some rest and left.

That was it.

Fast forward to now. I was sitting on the bed in my nightie, watching the sunrise from the window, wondering how in the hell I got here. This wasn't the plan for my life. None of this was in the plan.

Mom getting cancer wasn't the plan.

Me saving Mom had become the plan.

Now—

My throat thickened with pain as tears formed in my eyes, making the view of the sunrise watery.

Now, I was going to lose her. Not immediately, of course. The cancer was aggressive, but the chemo treatments had been working. However, I only had enough to pay for a few more months and depending upon the severance package from Moonie Pipelines…

I shook my head.

I was nearly raped last night in an alley, yet, I was sitting here thinking about the medical bills piling up on mom's kitchen table. I loved that table. When I was kid, she always made sure to have a fresh bouquet of flowers on it every week. As I got older, she would take me to her shop and we would make the bouquet together, letting me pick the flowers.

My bottom lip trembled, and the tears finally overflowed, falling silently down my cheeks in a downpour of sadness, hopelessness, and anger.

God, I was so angry.

Angry at myself for thinking I could do this. Angry because I convinced myself to set aside my values and morals to make money. That wasn't me.

I was angry because I didn't recognize the woman I'd become.

Was my mother even proud of me?

She told me all the time to quit this job and be happy.

I wasn't happy, not even close.

I hadn't been happy in years.

Nothing about my life was worth telling.

I wasn't some grand adventurer.

I wasn't an artist, creating something meaningful to leave behind in this world.

I wasn't a doctor or a nurse, healing the broken and sick.

I wasn't a rancher, feeding people.

I was leech.

I was a disappointment.

My head fell into my hands as a wretched, broken sob left me, my body trying to expel the pain and trauma. All I wanted to do was bottle it up. I cried until my phone rang. I took a deep breath, wiped my tears.

It was Mom.

I answered it on the third ring. "Good morning," I said.

"Good morning, darling," she said softly. She sounded tired today. "Are you alright?"

I rolled my head, stretching my neck, letting her voice wash over me. "Yeah, I'm okay."

"How are things with the Hallow Ranch?" she asked.

Oh, just wonderful. I got fired because Mr. Langston rejected me, and Mr. Moonie is impatient. Then, I went out last night to get drunk, because I have never done that before, but I ended up getting assaulted—then getting saved by Mr. Langston. Also, I've seen him kill two men. On top of that, I don't know how to tell you that I failed you and you may not see Christmas this year.

I squeezed my eyes shut and gripped my hair with my free hand. When I didn't answer, she called out for me. "Valerie?"

"I'm here," I croaked.

"Honey, what's going on?"

I had to lie. I had to pretend so she would continue to fight for me. It was selfish. It was sickening, but I needed more time with her.

I needed my momma.

"I just—I just really miss you," I whispered, picking at the blue lace of my nightie. I only had a few of these. They were old and worn, but they made me feel like I had my shit together. They made me feel I like the woman I was when I bought them. Confident. Driven. Kind.

That woman was naïve.

What I would give to be that naïve and happy again.

"I miss you, too," she replied. "Let's get your mind off of that stupid job, yeah?"

I wanted to laugh but I couldn't. All I could do was agree. "Okay, Mom."

She spent the next thirty minutes telling me about the pumpkins while I watched the sunrise over Hallow Ranch. In twenty years, when I looked back on this moment, I knew I would miss her voice the most.

It was around mid-morning when I got the guts to leave the room. I heard a movement around five, and I assumed Denver was getting up for the day.

After getting off the phone with my mother, I got ready for the day.

There was a lot to do, and I couldn't waste the day crying in a stranger's bed.

I put on a face, piled my hair into an elegant "messy" bun on the top of my head and put on a dress. I didn't pack many casual clothes, but I had a few sundresses to get me by.

This particular one was cotton, baby blue with tiny brown buttons down the front. I threw on a thin white, thin cardigan over it and my brown, strappy, heeled sandals. The outfit made me feel a little bit better, the brightness of it hiding the darkness lingering from yesterday.

I made my way downstairs, scanning for any signs of life. For some reason, I was drawn to the pale green kitchen, directly to the window above the sink. The last time I was here, I was blissfully unaware of the violence Denver Langston was capable of. I hugged myself, eyes on the bunkhouse and barn beyond.

Denver's herd of cattle was in the front pasture, grazing as the men circled them. I watched as two cowboys cornered a calf and roped it. A third man came up and held the calf down—

"Gosh, you are really pretty."

I jumped, letting out a slight yelp. I spun, hand on my chest, only to find my dark cowboy's son sitting on the bar.

Had he been there the whole time?

Jesus, he *did* look like his father.

He had dark hair, short but messy, and gray eyes. They weren't quite as intense as his father's eyes, but smoke lingered in them. He was dressed in a white T-shirt. I couldn't see the lower half of his body but no doubt, he was wearing jeans. The *Harry Potter* book I spotted on the couch the other night was in front of him, laying open on the counter.

He was nearly finished.

"I didn't mean to scare you," he said. Then, I realized I was staring at him, no doubt freaking him out.

I shook my head. "It's alright. I didn't see you when I came in," I answered.

"You have a nice voice, too," he said as he looked back down to his book. I looked around and glanced back out the window.

"Is your father around?"

Without looking up from the book, the boy answered, "He'll be back around nine for breakfast. He told me to tell you're welcome to some coffee." He lifted his arm and pointed to the coffee maker in the corner.

"Oh, thank you."

"Sure thing, ma'am," he said, turning the page.

I went up to the coffee maker to find a clean mug sitting beside it. I poured myself a cup and scanned the countertop for sugar.

"Creamer is in the fridge on the right and the sugar is in the cabinet above. Dad drinks his coffee with just a little bit of creamer, so he doesn't keep sugar on the counter," the boy explained.

I thanked him and went to the fridge. It was filled with fresh produce, dairy products, eggs and meat. I fixed my cup of coffee and noticed there was a clean spoon on the counter too.

I smiled at the thoughtfulness.

He'd set the mug and spoon out for *me*.

I turned and leaned against the counter as I took a sip. The rich taste hit my tongue, and I had to hold back a groan. This was some good coffee. "Wow, this is—"

"Dad gets his coffee from the farmer's market," the boy said, looking up at me.

"It's really good."

"I hope when I turn eighteen, coffee tastes good to me, because it tastes like dirt right now," the boy stated.

I choked on my next sip. He didn't notice and pressed on. "I don't want to drink coffee, but Mags says every man needs a cup of coffee in the morning and then a glass of whiskey at night."

"Mags?" I asked.

"Dad's best friend. He works on the ranch," he answered as he reached for his cup of red liquid.

Mags was probably the one who avoided me at all costs when I was here. I saw Beau, of course, as well as two men who looked like brothers, and an older gentleman. There was another cowboy, dark, like Denver, and I only ever saw his back.

"What's your name?" the boy asked.

That's when it dawned on me.

Denver still didn't know my name—well, I hadn't told him my name yet. Beau knew my name. Perhaps he told Denver, so he didn't bother asking.

"Valerie. My name is Valerie."

The little boy stared at me for a moment, silence stretching between us. It broke when he said, "Even your name is pretty."

I smiled into my mug. "Thank you, sweetheart. You are very kind. What's your name?"

He blinked. "I'm Caleb, but you can keep calling me sweetheart. I like that."

My lips parted to respond when we heard the front door open.

"Son."

That voice.

Denver's voice was stronger and richer than the coffee in my hands. My spine tingled as I listened to his heavy footsteps make their way into the kitchen. When he emerged, my breath caught.

Why did he have to be gorgeous?

Why couldn't the man who cost me my job be old and fat?

No, he had to be huge, taller than any man I'd ever met. He had to have dark hair and a matching beard. He just had to have intoxicating eyes.

The universe was a cruel bitch sometimes, and she had been fucking me six ways to Sunday for years.

"Good morning," he said, his deep rumble making my stomach feel funny. He looked at me for half a second before he turned to his son. "Eggs or waffles?"

Caleb looked over to me, his eyes shining as a smile broke out. "What do you want, Valerie? Eggs or waffles?"

"I—"

"Valerie."

My name left my dark cowboy's lips, and I thanked the heavens that I was leaning against the counter, or I would have fallen to my knees in a puddle.

My eyes shot to Denver to find his smoke-filled ones descending the length of me. His smoke stretched across the kitchen, over the butcher block island, wrapping around my ankles and rising between my legs, over the hem of my blue dress, up to the swell of my breasts, and finally surrounding my face. I breathed it in, inhaling deeply so it could settle in my lungs, drugging me.

"Yes," I rasped, not meaning to sound so damn...*bothered.*

His jaw tightened under that short-trimmed beard. My eyes drifted from his jaw, down to his strong, thick, tanned neck and further down to his black shirt stretching across his strong chest. The view of his chest was cut off when he turned around.

I blinked and took a sip, watching as he took off his flannel and hung it on the hook by the phone. He took off his black cowboy hat next, hanging it over the shirt.

A full head of thick, black hair. Wavy. My fingers itched to touch it.

Yes, the universe was a cruel bitch.

He turned back to us, looking at his boy. "Eggs today. Waffles tomorrow, yeah?"

Caleb had gone back to reading in the middle of my lustful episode, thank God. He looked up from his book and nodded. Denver made his way deeper into his kitchen, walking right up to me. I tipped my head back to look at him, ignoring the way my heart was racing and how close his body was to mine.

"Gotta move out of my way, Val, so I can make you and my boy breakfast."

Val.

Each one of his words sent a shot of warmth through my body, leaving me dumbfounded. Wordlessly, I slipped out and rounded the island. Denver set to work, pulling out a skillet and walking to the fridge.

I felt awkward. I felt like I was in the way. Usually, I was the one doing the work.

"You don't have make me any—"

"Sit down," he ordered, back to me. I looked down to Caleb—he wasn't a muggle right now—who could care less.

"Denver," I said, ready to protest.

"Valerie."

My body zinged and my nipples hardened in my bralette. *Fine.* I took a seat next to his son and watched him cook for me. When he started cracking the eggs, I asked if he needed any help.

He grunted and I took that as firm no.

Finally, he sat a plate of eggs, bacon, and toast in front of me with a fork on top. Caleb dug in, mumbling a thank you to his father as he inhaled the food. I watched with fascination at the speed he was eating.

"You'll get a tummy ache if you eat too fast," I found myself saying. Caleb stopped mid-bite, fork full of eggs hanging in the air.

"Gotta eat fast so I can get to work," he answered.

He was the son of a rancher, and a future cowboy, so no doubt there was work to be done. I watched as he looked from me to his fork and then back to me. "You are probably right. My tummy does hurt when I get down to the barn."

"Should take her advice then, son," Denver noted from his place in the kitchen. He was leaning against the opposite counter, ankles crossed, holding his plate with one hand and fork in the other.

A man shouldn't look *that good* eating breakfast—let alone a murderer.

A murderer who's a father and you seem to not have a problem with it.

I kept my mouth shut and continued the meal. Of course, the handsome, murdering, cowboy knew how to cook, too. That's just *great*.

Caleb finished before me, and he hopped off the stool, taking his dishes with him. I watched him as he took them to the sink, ran the water for a moment, and then went to the foyer.

"I'll be down with Beau!" he called, slamming the door behind him.

"That boy," Denver muttered softly.

I looked back to Denver and sucked in a breath. His plate and fork were gone. His hands were braced on the counter behind him by his hips, his arm muscles flexing under tan skin. He was staring at me.

"Thank you for breakfast," I said softly.

"Just eggs and some bread," he returned, still staring at me.

Panic set in. I was in *his* house, under *his* roof, he made *me* food and gave *me* a place to sleep—and I tried to tell *his son* what to do.

Valerie, you are an idiot.

"I'm sorry," I blurted. "Caleb is a growing boy, and he can eat as fast as he wants."

"You're apologizing for being kind and looking out for my boy?" he asked, tilting his head to the side.

"I—well, yes."

He didn't say anything.

"Do you have WiFi?"

He nodded once.

"Would you mind giving me the password? I have to book a flight back home."

"Where's home?" he asked, ignoring my question.

"Just outside of Dallas," I answered.

"Thought I heard an accent," he murmured, his eyes dropping to my mouth.

I did not want to be sitting in a house alone with a murderer. I did *not* need to have said murderer looking at my lips like that. I also didn't need to like it as much as I did.

"So, can I have a password?" I asked, my voice breathy.

"Why are you leaving?"

The question threw me. *Had he not been present for the last twelve hours?*

"I got fired yesterday," I returned.

He nodded as if that answer wasn't enough.

"I got assual—"

"Do not remind me of that pathetic waste of breath," he growled, "touching you."

I nodded.

"It's done. He's gone. He ain't ever going to touch you or anyone else again, you hear me?" Not only was he still growling, but now he was moving. Towards me. He stopped on the other side of the island and braced his hands on the butcher block.

Why couldn't he put the flannel and hat back on?

Why did he have to look so good all the time?

"Valerie."

"You know my name," I blurted. *What in the hell was wrong with me?*

He nodded and tipped his head to his son's stool. "Found out what it was about twenty minutes ago."

"Wait—you didn't know my name last night?"

He shook his head.

He helped me in the rain without knowing my name.

He doctored my feet without knowing my name.

He let me sleep in his bed without knowing my name.

He saved me without knowing I was Valerie.

I swallowed.

"Didn't answer my question, Val."

"I have to leave," I said.

"Why?"

"Why are you asking me that?" I asked. Why were we having this conversation? We were strangers. I didn't know him. He didn't know me. I was just the bitch who was trying to take his land.

"Moonie showed up this morning."

My spine locked as I sat up straight, and a cold rage coursed through me. "What?"

He nodded again. "Showed up at six am."

I stared at him in disbelief. Mr. Moonie told me he would be taking a different approach with the Hallow Ranch account. He was taking this head on. The CEO came directly to the source.

"He never left," I whispered, closing my eyes and shaking my head.

"What?"

I took a breath and opened my eyes again. "Mr. Moonie never left. He must have followed me back from Denver."

Something flashed within his smoke eyes. "Denver? He was in Denver?"

I nodded. "After you rejected the offer the first time, I reported it back to my boss. I guess word traveled up to him. Next thing I knew, I was on a private plane to Denver. He invited me to lunch," I explained.

He was staring at me, and I didn't like the look on his face. It was one of judgement, whether I deserved it or not.

You deserve it. You tried to take his home from him and that sweet little boy.

I looked away from him as I felt my cheeks hit with embarrassment.

"You workin' with him still?" he asked, his voice hard.

My head snapped back to him. "What? I just told you I was fired."

"You and him workin' together to try and get under my skin? Being sweet to my boy, while your boss is making plans behind the scenes?" he hissed.

He was assuming things, trying to put a puzzle together with broken pieces.

I flinched. "Denver, I was fired yesterday. I no longer represent—"

"You got fired, put on a sexy outfit and went to the bar. Then, I save you and you tell me that you only got one night in the hotel left—"

"You wanted me to come here," I spat. "I wanted to stay at my hotel, book a flight, and go home!"

"Get the fuck out of my house." His voice was cold and hard. His smoke was all around me now.

Where was this coming from?

"You're insane," I whispered, staring at him as tears threatened to form. I didn't understand this hot and cold. It was too much.

"He came here and told me he was looking forward to getting to know me better. Said he sent you on another job." He came around the island. "This your other job, baby? Getting under my skin?" His voice was mean, downright cruel and his gray eyes were cold, guarded.

He didn't trust me. I haven't given him a reason, either.

Not only was I a threat to his home, but now to his freedom. I was a *witness.*

He had no right to trust me. Perhaps this breakfast was just a set up to make me comfortable. He said Mr. Moonie was here early this morning. So maybe this was Denver's plan all along. He didn't care whether I stayed or left. He just wanted to protect his home and he thought that I was still a threat to it.

I ignored the sting of it all when I looked up at him and said, "I'll leave."

"Now," he clipped.

Chapter Seventeen

Valerie

With tears in my eyes, I turned and ran up the stairs to gather my stuff quickly. After I finished, I went downstairs. No Denver.

I was done with this state.
I was done with that stupid fucking job.
I was done with Hallow Ranch.
I was done with Denver fucking Langston.

Without taking another look at this beautiful home, I pushed through the front door and down the porch steps. I ignored the visions of that night, my feet bleeding as my body shook with fear, and headed down the gravel path. Pushing away the thoughts of Denver taking care of me after I witnessed him kill a man—*twice*—I looked up from my sandals.

I didn't have my rental.
It was back in town at the hotel.
Bags on each shoulder, I walked.
I walked and walked for what seemed like miles and when I hit the main road, I turned and headed towards town. Cars and trucks passed me but none of them stopped.

I didn't want them to.

I was done with everyone in this fucking state.

I would get my rental, drive to Denver, book my flight and *leave*.

Colorado and the Hallow Ranch would be a distant memory for me in a few months.

A red truck sped past me and screeched to a halt in front of me.

Smoke.

My footsteps slowed as I watched him get out of the truck. He was charging towards me, anger radiating off him in powerful waves.

"The fuck do you think you're doing?" he barked.

"You told me to leave!" I shouted back.

"So, you decided to walk back into town?"

"Yes!" I snapped. "What did you think I was going to do?"

He opened his mouth to talk, but then it happened. Everything I'd been bottling up overflowed and exploded.

I *exploded.*

"Do you honestly think I get off on taking land away from the people? I grew up in Texas! I know how important ranches and farms are. I know that you feed people. I know what hard work is like. I have worked my whole fucking life, Denver! Since I was *child!* My mom owned a flower shop, and I would help her in the mornings and after school to make ends meet because my father was a piece of shit. He decided one day he didn't want us anymore and *left*!"

"Val—"

"He left without a word. Said he was going to work and never came back. Mom thought he was *dead*, that something happened to him. She called the police. He was declared missing! His job didn't know where he was, or his friends. He just vanished. Mom was *devastated*. She hired a PI and you wanna know where he was?"

Denver was staring at me now. I didn't wait for him to answer.

"He was in Florida with a blonde woman! A woman that he had been having an affair with. So, it was just Mom and I against the world. We had the shop and the little house. We were gonna make it. I wanted to be a lawyer. I wanted to help people! I was going to be the best lawyer in Dallas, I made sure of it. I did well in school and focused on work. I never made any friends in high school..."

"Valerie—"

My bags fell off my shoulders onto the concrete, but I didn't care.

I kept *going*. I couldn't stop it.

"I never even had a boyfriend until I was in college. He took my virginity and dumped me shortly after. That's the last time I was with a man. That's the last time I was kissed! Then—*then* life really decided to shit on me. I was nearly there, Smoke. My dreams were just within reach, and you wanna know what happened?"

He was closer now, studying me. His smoke was reaching out to me, gentle this time, caressing me. I wanted to get lost in it, hide from this pain I'd been burying.

It was time to stop burying it.

My face crumbled as the pain broke free. "My mom got cancer."

"Christ."

I shook my head and cried, "I don't want your sympathy! I don't need you! I don't need anyone, okay? I just need my mom." My voice cracked. "I need my mom to live so I don't have to be alone!"

My knees gave out and I was prepared to hit the hot street. For some reason, I didn't. Instead, I collided with a solid, warm body. Arms around me, holding me firmly against him.

"You gotta hear the rest," I whimpered. He gripped my chin and forced me to look up at him. His gray eyes were like beckons in the shadow his hat cast, and I never wanted to look away.

"I was a dick."

"I'm just a bitch who takes homes from people. I'm not a good person, but I want you to know—no, I *need* you to know—that I wasn't always like this. I never wanted this. You have a beautiful home, and your ranch is amazing. Your son is wonderful, and I was trying to take it all away from him—*from you.*"

He stared at me as I continued, his chest rising and falling against me.

I shook my head. "I have to do this to pay for my mom's chemo. That's the only reason why I do—*did* this. That job was the only job that paid well enough to do it without having to spend years in school. I didn't have years..."

"Shit," he bit out, looking away from me, his jaw tight under that gorgeous beard. I ached to touch it, but instead, I swallowed and continued.

"I just—I needed you to know that."

He looked back down at me, the smoke in his eyes hiding something from me, something I desperately wanted to see.

"You telling me no man has had you because you dropped everything in your life to take care of your mom and made a deal with the devil to do so?" he asked.

I nodded.

His eyes flared.

I was sharing everything, and I couldn't seem to stop. He was a stranger, holding me in the street as I cried in his arms, but I couldn't stop. "So, when I came to Hallow Ranch and you pinned me against the barn, you have to know that I wasn't afraid. I was glad."

His brows drew together.

"I was glad I got see something so beautiful in my dull, sad life."

"What did you see?" he asked, his voice rough and thick.

"The smoke in your eyes."

Chapter Eighteen

Denver

The smoke in your eyes.

Jesus.

This woman. This enchanting, broken woman thought I was beautiful. I would have laughed at the thought if it didn't hurt so God damn much.

"She back?" Beau asked as he walked his horse into the barn. I looked away from the house and focused on my boots.

"Yeah," I answered, keeping it short.

"Why did she leave in the first place?"

Because I'm an asshole who can't control his fucking mouth.

Seeing her this morning, in my kitchen, holding my coffee cup, wearing that dress...*fuck*, that dress. She was a vision—a *dream*. Since I was boy, I dreamed of a woman like her standing in my kitchen the way she was this morning.

Then I learned her name.

Valerie.

Of course, her name had to be just a pretty as she was

"Why is she staying here?" Mags had joined the conversation.

I don't know.

I just knew that I didn't want her to leave.

Seeing her walk down to the street with those bags on her shoulders, her back to the ranch—*to me*—while wearing that dress...

That didn't sit well with me.

A week ago, I would have let her go.

Now, I'm not sure I ever want to.

Thought we didn't trust her?

"Den?"

Jigs.

My boys and I were in the barn, finishing up the day and putting up the horses. I looked up from my boots and focused on my horse. Ranger was chewing on an apple as I ran my hand down his neck.

"I don't trust Tim Moonie," I declared.

"No shit," Lawson said from beside me. "That guy is fucking snake."

"But *she* isn't," I finished, turning to face them. I put my hands on my hips and looked to the ceiling. Fuck, a week ago, I thought she was snake...but she turned out to be something much more fearsome.

A sweet woman.

"She's gotten under your skin," Mags noted.

"She was nearly raped last night," I spat, looking at my friend, my jaw tight.

Every one of us remained silent for a moment, our anger back in spades.

"You burn it?" I asked the group.

"Yes."

"That's the second fucking one," Landon growled.

"These city boys coming into our town to rape the women...barbaric," Jigs growled.

The man from the other night had done the same, to one of the cheerleaders at the high school. The kids were out at the diner celebrating the end of the school year, something Mason and I used to do when we were kids, and that asshole focused on a sixteen-year-old girl.

She reported the assault to her mother, her mother called the sheriff, and then he showed up at Hallow Ranch seeking the only justice there was for raping a woman—a painful death.

"Tracked down the info. You were right, him and the last one worked in the same company in Denver. They were in town on business."

"What business?" Beau asked, folding his arms over his chest.

"Development," I answered, my upper lip curling into a sneer.

"Son of a bitch," Mags muttered.

"Talked to Danny down at the feed store, said there are rumors Bart is selling the hotel to a bigger company. They're going to tear down the old one and build new," Lance informed us.

Another one bites the dust. I wasn't a man who enjoyed change, but I could bite my tongue and deal with it. There was just something about growing up in a small town and seeing everything you knew change before your eyes that stung.

The one thing that hadn't changed was Hallow Ranch.

Pop left it to me, Mason left it all together...over my dead fucking body would I let someone take this from me. That included Tim *fucking* Moonie.

"Someone go drag Bart to the bar," I muttered, pulling my hat off and running my hand through my hair. "Get him drunk and see if it's true. Danny lies out his ass sometimes."

They grunted in agreement.

"Caleb in the bunkhouse?" I asked, lifting my chin to Jigs.

The old man chuckled. "He found his birthday present."

I shook my head. "That boy. What was it?"

"The Hobbit," he answered, his eyes crinkling a bit.

That was Pop's favorite which just so happened to be my favorite. I ignored the slight twist in my stomach. "Alright boys, the work's done. Thank you. Tell that boy if he wants supper, it'll be ready in an hour," I said, turning back to Ranger and rubbing his nose. "See ya in the morning, bud."

I was halfway out of the barn when Beau stopped me. "That woman has pain, Den. I saw it the first day I met her."

I gritted my teeth.

I hated the way he spoke about her, like she had been in his bed, healing, instead of mine.

I turned my head to look over my shoulder. "I know that."

"And I know that being gentle isn't your strong suit," he spat.

"Beau," Jigs warned.

I met Beau's eyes. "I've got her."

"Hi, Mom," I heard through the crack of the spare bedroom door. I was coming up to tell Valerie about dinner but stopped on the top step.

"No, no, I'm okay," she croaked. "It's been a long day."

The pain in her voice was like a punch in the gut.

"That's not the hotel room. Val, where are you?"

Her mother. Her mother with cancer...the reason why Valerie did what she did.

I heard her sigh. I didn't think she would tell her mother where she was. How in the hell would you explain that to someone? Especially your mother?

Because moms love without judgement, my sweet Denver.

My mother's voice echoed in my head and my hand tightened on the railing. I held my breath, my eyes on the cracked door. I couldn't see her from where I was standing, but I hoped like fuck she was still wearing that blue dress.

I wanted that dress on my bedroom floor.

"I—uh—I'm at the ranch," Valerie answered.

"The ranch?"

"Yes."

"The Grump's ranch?" her mother asked, her voice raised.

The Grump. I bit a curse under my breath. She'd told her mother about me.

Of course, she did. She's all she has, dipshit.

I was the grump who insulted her looks, her job, her ambition...

"Fuck," I muttered. Without another glance, I headed downstairs. She needed her mom, not some deranged asshole cowboy. I poked my head in the living room, only to find Caleb wasn't there.

He wasn't in the kitchen either.

I pulled out my phone and found a text from Lawson.

Lawson: Kid's eating chili and playing cards with Jigs tonight.

Shaking my head, I typed back a thank you and headed into the kitchen. Chili sounded good and I knew there would be enough for me in the bunkhouse.

But what if she came down?

What if she was hungry?

Had she eaten since breakfast?

Why do I fucking care so damn much about her?

She was a stranger to me and yet I didn't leave her in the rain. I let her sleep in my bed, I let her into my home. I saw red when I thought someone was hurting her, flew into town like a bat out of hell. I killed two men in front of her.

I bared my darkest parts of my soul to this woman and yet...she thought my eyes were beautiful.

Is that was she meant by smoke?

My eyes were gray, like Pop's and Mason's. It was a Langston family trait; one I passed down to my boy. Still, Momma used to tell me mine were different from Pop's or Mason's.

My sweet boy.

My feet moved from the kitchen, and I found myself in the living room, staring at her rocking chair.

I wasn't her sweet boy anymore.

Yet, you chased after Valerie today and held her in your arms.

"I'm the only one here, Momma," I whispered, pulling my hat off. I was the only one left. When I was a kid, she used to dance in that kitchen, singing Johnny Cash while she spun Mason around in her arms. I would sit at the counter and watch her.

"One day, my boys will be dancing in this kitchen with their own women," she said, looking at me. Mason giggled and chewed on his fist.

"Girls are gross, Momma," I said.

She looked at me and smiled. "This house will be full for generations."

I didn't know what she was talking about. I just wanted her to keep singing. "Can you sing again, Momma?"

This house hadn't been full in ten years, because of me.

I was the one who broke this fucking family.

"Denver?"

I whipped around to find Valerie by the stairs, still in the blue dress, her hair down now, falling in messy waves. Her greens eyes were on me before they drifted to the chair behind me.

"Are you alright?" she asked.

She was still wearing the blue dress.

Fuck, that dress.

It was cotton, meant to be a casual dress, no doubt. But fuck, it could have been a wedding dress and I wouldn't have been able to tell the difference.

"You hungry?" I said, as I brushed past her.

Her cherry smell followed me into the kitchen as she moved with me. I turned to the fridge and stole a glance at her feet. She was barefoot.

"Your feet aright?" I asked, pulling out ingredients for dinner.

"Oh, yes. That cream you gave me really helped."

That cream was a miracle worker. "Good," I grunted, avoiding looking at her again. I turned to the stove and pulled out some pans, and I could feel her.

Fuck, I could feel her.

"Den—"

"You eat red meat?" I asked, unwrapping a steak.

"Yes," she answered. "But you don't have to—"

"Gonna make steak sandwiches. You good with that?"

She didn't answer. Instead, she moved closer, not stopping until she was beside me, in my space. "Will you look at me?" she asked, her voice shaking.

I did. *Fuck me, I did.*

All I wanted to do was kiss her. Take her pain away. The pain of her father leaving her. The pain of her mother getting fucking cancer. The pain of her giving up her dreams. The pain I caused her. I wanted to take every single ounce of pain away until she felt nothing but bliss. I wanted her to smile at me. I wanted her to laugh for me. I wanted her to moan—

"I just wanted to let you know that I'm leaving in the morning," she said.

Leaving.

Leaving in the morning.

She was still leaving.

"Leaving," I repeated, moving the sink and washing my hands. When I was done, I turned to her and leaned my hip against the counter. I folded my arms over my chest to stop myself from touching her, pushing the image of her in my arms from my mind.

She was leaving.

"Yes, leaving. I wanted to thank you for everything," she said, meeting my eyes. "I mean everything, Denver."

Everything.

In a span of two weeks, we were strangers, but we had shared a lot of everything.

"Don't mention it."

"I never will," she promised. I knew she was sincere. I didn't give a fuck if she told anyone. I had friends in high places, thanks to my father, but she didn't know that.

Here she was, promising me she wouldn't tell anyone of my sins.

One of those sins I committed for her. No one else but her. I would have no regrets over that. I wouldn't lose sleep over killing a man to protect her.

I would lose sleep over her being gone.

I hadn't even kissed this woman and I was going to lose sleep over her.

I stared at her, anger boiling up inside of me because I couldn't find a way to make her stay.

Hell, I didn't even know why I wanted her to stay.

I just know that I needed her with me.

That's all I knew.

But she was leaving.

"Anyways, that's all I needed to say," she noted, looking away from me.

Don't let her leave, my sweet boy. Don't you let this one go.

I nodded. To Valerie, not my mom's voice, and pushed off the counter. "Gotta get dinner started," I said, dismissing everything I wanted.

Her. At Hallow Ranch. In my bed.

Just...her.

Something flashed across her face, but she buried it quickly and stepped away, going to the other end of the island. Both of us sat in silence as I cooked. We sat in silence as we ate. Then she offered to do the dishes and I simply refused.

She went upstairs to pack, and I went into my office upstairs to drink.

The whiskey burned, but not as much as the image of her walking away.

Chapter Nineteen

Valerie

I was dressed for success.

I was dressed for—*hiding*. I was hiding. I was putting on a fake smile, raising my chin, and burying every single ounce of pain I let out yesterday. Valerie Cross didn't have the time to be weak.

I didn't sleep a wink last night. No, instead, I laid in that bed, wishing was in the stranger's across the hall, wrapping myself in his scent. I stared at the ceiling and tried not to think about the way he looked at me when I told him I was leaving.

I called Mom last night and admitted the truth—well almost all the truth. She knew Mr. Moonie had fired me. I lied and told her the hotel kicked me out. I hated doing it, but I did it. I did it while ignoring the look on her face and the devastation in her eyes. There was something else there, too.

Fear.

Mom was afraid to die.

Despite what she'd told me in the past, the look in her eyes confirmed all I needed to know. It was also my fault.

I was going to lose my mom, the only person in my life because I failed. I was a failure. Now I had to go home and soak up as much time as I could with her.

Jackie was trying to find a discount medical insurance program for us. However, I knew that nothing would come of it. Medicaid denies Mom every single year. Healthcare in America was jacked.

I shook those thoughts away and picked up my bags.

Today, I was leaving Hallow Ranch. For good.

I was leaving behind a handsome cowboy with smoke gray eyes and a voice that made me tremble. I would never forget that voice and the way he said my name. I took one more look in the mirror. I was in my black pencil skirt, hunter green silk blouse, and heels. My feet were nearly healed now. My body was already moving on from Denver Langston. Taking a deep breath, I opened the door and headed downstairs.

It was around mid-morning, and I knew Denver wouldn't be here. There was work to be done on the ranch. There was an airport taxi waiting for me outside—yes, that cost a pretty penny, but I don't think that I could stomach asking Denver for a ride.

The taxi would take me straight the airport. My rental would be picked up later today. That was another pretty penny. I would use some money from my severance package to pay for all of this.

Anything to avoid being alone with Denver Langston again.

I wanted him to kiss me last night.

The naïve, romance reader in me wanted him to pull me into his arms and never let me go, but that didn't happen. This wasn't a fairytale. This was the real world.

The kitchen was empty, as was the living room. Before I stepped outside, I took one more look at the rocking chair in the corner. I had found Denver staring at it last night, deep in thought. That chair was special to him. I knew it in my bones, so I took one more second to appreciate its beauty. I looked around the house, this dream house, and whispered goodbye to the walls.

Denver Langston wouldn't miss me, his kid would forget me, but the walls of this house wouldn't.

Taking a deep breathe, I stepped outside. The taxi was waiting, a young woman in a polo shirt standing by the trunk.

"Good morning, Ms. Cross," she called. She was young, no older than twenty-one. I smiled at her as I stepped down from the porch.

"Good morning."

She stepped forward and helped me with my bags. We were loading them into the trunk when I heard it.

Hooves.

Horse hooves, pounding against the earth and getting closer.

Oh, no.

No, no, no, no.

I couldn't see him.

I had to leave. *Now.*

The driver was looking down towards the barn, but I refused.

"All set," I declared with a fake smile, in the hopes she would take the hint.

She looked at me and nodded. We both turned away from the barn, away from the house. The driver got into the car, and I pulled open the back door. I had one leg in when it happened.

When my world spun.

"Valerie!"

My stomach fluttered almost as fast as my heart.

I turned to see my dark cowboy heading up the hill to me, on his horse, his body moving with his steed. From his dirty boots, blue jeans, black shirt, flannel, to that damn cowboy hat—*he was a vision*. I knew in that moment that Denver Langston would haunt me for the rest of my days.

I would never forget him.

I would never forget the fury in those gray eyes as he approached, dismounted the horse and charged towards me. His smoke blew out all around me, caging me in, holding me captive and I couldn't breathe.

"Denv—"

"Shut the fuck up," he growled, his hand going to the back of my neck. Then he did it.

He *ruined* me.

His lips crashed against mine, his huge body, shoving me against the cab, pinning me to it as he pried my lips open with his tongue. His hot, delicious, tongue. My mouth fell open, letting him in, and I was kissing him back with the same urgency. I couldn't control it. A sound ripped from him, causing my insides to quiver. It was rough, uncontrolled, dark...

Then it was over.

He pulled away, his hand still on the back of my neck. "You leave me, so help me God, baby, I will hunt you down," he clipped. "I will find you and take my anger out on that perfect, round ass of yours. You won't be able to walk for a fucking month."

I stared up at him, his taste still on my tongue.

"Denver—"

He leaned down, getting a centimeter from my face, the brim of his hat over me. "Shut. The. Fuck. Up."

His hand went down and gripped the back of my elbow, and then he pulled me away from the car. The young driver was out, staring at us with her mouth hanging open.

He pulled me to the back of the car and ordered, "Pop the trunk."

She did, without question.

Traitor.

Still holding on to me, he pulled my bags out and shut the trunk. "Thank you for your time. Ms. Cross isn't leaving today," he said to the woman, his voice like velvet. His face was set in stone, his eyes holding hers. I looked back and forth between them.

"S-sure thing," she stammered. Then. She. Left.

Yeah, she was a traitor.

I was too busy staring at her car to notice his horse until the animal decided to put his face in front of mine. He neighed and nudged my shoulder. I turned to the beast and smiled. I was about to say hi and give him a little nose rub when my cowboy interrupted.

"Hang on, Ranger," Denver said, taking a hold of his reins.

Then…he guided *both* me and his horse to the porch. He dropped my bags on the steps and let go of me. I moved to take a step back. This shouldn't be happening.

He just kissed me.

Denver Langston kissed me.

I needed to get out of here, before I let my heart take over.

"You move one fucking inch, I will take you over my knee," the cowboy threatened, not looking at me.

What in the hell was going on?

Denver tied his horse to the porch, and the beast didn't mind. He was munching on the flower bed, living his best life.

A hand wrapped around my arm again, and then my bags were lifted. He opened the front door of the house that I just said goodbye to and tossed my bags back on the floor.

His eyes found mine and I sucked in a breath.

Then my back was against the door, his body against mine, my face was in his hands.

"What are you doing?" I whispered.

"Not letting you go," he hissed, baring his white teeth.

Then he kissed me. *Again.*

It was filled with anger. His tongue pushed inside of my mouth, taking over. I was clumsy at this. I hadn't been kissed in years. He didn't seem to mind, though. In fact, he growled as I stroked my tongue with his. God, he tasted good, like mint.

My body was on fire, his smoke all around me, *in* me, taking my breath away with each punishing kiss. His teeth pulled on my lower lip, and I whimpered. Another sound left him, rumbling from his broad, hard chest. It went straight to my core. My hands finally got with the damn program and wrapped around his neck, my fingers finally getting to touch his hair. I wanted to touch all of it.

"Denver," I rasped, pulling away from him.

"Fuck, the way you say my name..."

I opened my eyes, and my world was nothing but smoke. His smoke. We were both panting, and I prayed his heart was beating as fast as mine was.

"Can you take your hat off?" I asked.

His eyes darkened. "You want my hat off, baby?" His voice was deep. *Rough.*

I bit my lip and nodded. He focused on my mouth as he slowly took off his hat and hung it on a coat hook. Then he was back on me, kissing me with abandon, hunger driving him. His hands weren't on my face anymore. Now, they were drifting down my sides, his thumbs sweeping over my breasts, and down to my hips. When they snaked around to cup my bottom, I broke away, gasping.

"Jesus, your fucking body. I don't even have you naked yet, and I know it's perfect," he whispered as he dropped his head to my neck.

My heart pounded louder and faster as his words settled over me.

I'd never been perfect, not once in my whole life.

I wrapped my arms around his shoulders as he trailed wet, hot, *scorching* kisses down my neck. His hands squeezed my ass and then his long fingers began to yank up my skirt from behind.

He growled and I heard fabric ripping.

Oh, God.

One of my hands climbed up and snaked into his hair, gripping it tightly. "Smoke," I breathed. There was another sound of ripping and then I felt the wood of the door against my ass.

This man had just ripped my skirt open from the back.

I was focused on that when he found my ear. "Nod if you want this. If you don't, I'll step away," he ordered, his breath caressing my ear.

My heart was cloud nine. He was making sure I was okay. *After everything*, he was making sure that *I* was *okay.*

I nodded, clinging to him, my breasts pressed against his hard chest. I needed less clothes and more skin, more *him.*

"You sure?"

"Denver, touch me," I begged.

I was pulled from the door, spun around, and pushed back against it. The air in my lungs left my body in a *whoosh*. He pressed against me from behind, his hand wrapping around my throat, squeezing gently. I whimpered, remembering the last time we were in the position.

"Wanted to pound into you then," he growled into my ear, somehow reading my mind. "*Fuck*, I wanted to make you scream. Fuck you until you promised to be a good girl for me." He snapped his hips, and I could feel his hard erection against my ass. "You wanted that too, didn't you?"

Yes.

I wanted it then and I wanted it now.

I tried to reach for him, but his free hand snatched my wrists and pinned them above my head.

He ground against my ass shamelessly as he continued, "Fisted my cock thinking about you, Valerie. You've been in my fucking head since the second you stepped foot on my ranch."

I pushed back against him, needed more, but he didn't move his hands—just his hips. My mind was trying to keep up with his words, so my heart could hold onto them, but my body wasn't paying attention.

"Coming on my ranch, looking like *that*, looking up at me with your big green eyes," he sneered, head pressed against mine as he continued to shamelessly hump me. "*Fuck*, I shouldn't want you."

"Honey," I whispered.

He froze and he squeezed my throat harder. "That guy who took your virginity and tossed you aside like trash, you call him that?"

"What?"

"You call any other man that?"

"No," I breathed through his grip. The hand at my wrists dropped down to my ass, his large, rough, warm palm rubbing in circles. I felt him lean back a bit, and I twisted to find his eyes on my ass.

"You call any other man that, I'll make this ass red, baby," he murmured. I gaped at him, my body trembling against the door. My eyes drifted to the kitchen, to the window above the sink. Then a chill ran down my spine.

"Denver, Caleb—"

"Boys are in pasture two for the day. Supposes to be out there with them," he explained, his voice rough.

He was missing work. He had a ranch to run.

"If you need to—"

The hand around my neck snapped up to my jaw, gripping it firmly and he leaned in, towering over my tall frame. "You were leaving," he spat, his eyes flaring.

I swallowed. "Yes."

"You feel this?" he clipped, pressing against me.

This.

That little word held so much weight, and it terrified me.

But I still found myself saying, "Yes."

That was all he needed to hear, because with the next second, after a vicious tug, my panties were on the floor and Denver's finger was sliding through my folds. The feeling of someone else's hand caused me to moan—because this wasn't my hand. This was a hand that belonged to a cowboy. A rough, rude, arrogant, dark, murdering cowboy.

My body loved it.

"Oh," I gasped.

"God damn, Enchantress. You're dripping for me," he said softly, against my ear.

Enchantress.

My hands snapped down to his arm, holding on as he sunk a digit inside of me. My head fell back against his shoulder as he brought the finger back up, rubbing it against my clit and until I was panting against him.

"This fucking cunt," he growled, shoving two fingers inside of me.

Oh, wow.

Then he started fucking me with his fingers as his other hand snaked underneath my blouse. He wasted no time, fucking me hard and fast with his digits as he pulled my bra down, freeing my breasts underneath the silk of my blouse. He was greedy. He didn't rub my nipples like I thought he would. No, he grabbed my full breast, squeezing it as he began to hump me from behind in time with his hand. He groaned in my ear, and I knew he was barely holding on.

"Smoke," I rasped, my hips moving with his.

"Fuck, yeah," he grunted. "Fuck my hand, Val."

Val.

Pleasure zinged throughout my body.

I was the only one getting pleasure in this. That didn't sit well with me. My right hand left his wrist, and I reached behind me, shoving it between us. I cupped his stiff bulge in the front of his jeans.

A dark chuckle escaped him. "You aren't ready for my dick, baby."

"I want—I want—"

My hand was pulled from between us and pinned against the door. His fingers worked me harder, *faster*. My legs began to shake, and I moaned, my eyes fluttering closed. I felt his lips quirk into a smile against my temple.

"Good girls get cock, baby."

I whimpered.

"You aren't a good girl yet," he murmured, his thumb rubbing circles against my clit. *Oh, God.*

"You said—you said you would fuck me into one."

My jaw was cupped again, and he finger-fucked me harder. The house was silent, the only sounds were my moans, his harsh breaths in my ear, and the wetness between my legs.

"You wanna be a good girl for me? Hm?" he hissed.

"Yes!" I cried, nearly there.

"Then fucking come on your cowboy's hand. Soak it."

Your cowboy.

Pleasure took over at his words, and I fell away from the world, drifting far away. I cried out as my body shook, hips thrashing, heart soaring.

"That's it, baby, that's it," he growled. "Give me all of it."

I whimpered. "Kiss me. Kiss me, please, kiss—"

His lips crashed against mine, his tongue dominating my mouth, commanding me as he stroked my pussy lightly, sending flutters of pleasure through my body. Our lips melted together in a kiss that seemed to drag on. That was fine with me. I could kiss him forever, getting lost in his smoke.

Unfortunately, all good things must come to an end. He pulled away from me, my eyes slowly opening, and my world was filled with him. Gray. Smoke. Pine. Him.

"Hi," I whispered.

He stared at me when I thought that he would smile. He didn't. Then again, I don't think a man like Denver knew how to smile.

"You aren't leaving," he said firmly.

That's when reality came crashing back—full force. "Denver, I have to…" I said, still whispering, wanting to stay in this little bubble, me half naked in his arms. He pulled his hand away from my core and turned me to face him.

"You aren't leaving," he declared. Before I could protest, I was up off the ground. He was carrying me—*me*—in his arms bridal style. My arms were around his neck as he carried me up the stairs.

I looked to the spare bedroom, and he grunted. "Never again."

He took me to his room and sat me down on his bed. Wordlessly, he turned and disappeared. I heard his boots going down the stairs. Looking around, I saw an armchair in the corner with a throw blanket. I moved to it, taking a seat and covering my lower half with the blanket.

A moment later, I heard his boots coming back up the stairs and when he emerged, he had bags. My shredded clothes were probably in the trash. He looked to where he'd sat me on the bed and then his eyes slowly lifted to where I was.

Something possessive flashed within his smoke, and I gulped.

What in the hell had I gotten myself into?

"Warning, baby. If I put you in my bed, you stay in my fucking bed," he said, his voice low.

I straightened my spine. "I would like to know what's happening here."

He tossed my luggage on the bed and came around to face me. He took a seat on the edge, bracing his elbows on his knees, those big hands hanging between them. God, he was so handsome.

"I don't know, Val. All I know is that you were walking away from me yesterday and...that was something I didn't like," he looked up at me, his eyes scanning my face. "I shouldn't want this—you. I should let you fucking leave and never come back but I can't."

His words lingered in the air between us.

"Denver, my mom—" I stopped myself. I could feel my throat getting tight and my eyes started to sting. Before coming to Colorado, I was skilled at hiding my feelings, putting on a brave face for the world. There must be something in the air here. Ever since I cried in my rental after our first encounter, I've had a difficult time keeping my emotions at bay.

My cowboy's features softened at the mention of the only other person in my life and suddenly, I knew there was a different side to Denver. I had seen bits and pieces of it, from his gentleness with me when doctoring my wounds, to when he told me to close my eyes before he took a man's life...

There was a soft side to the hardened man before me. Something happened to him. He was guarded and protected the things he loved with ruthlessness.

He and I were the same.

He protected Hallow Ranch and his son.

I protected my mom.

"Work for me," he said.

I stared at him, waiting for the punchline, because this was obviously a joke. Those gray eyes noted my posture and he spoke again. "I'm serious."

"Do I look like a ranch hand to you?" I deadpanned. I wasn't a girly-girl, but I wasn't a cowgirl either. I knew how a ranch worked, but I didn't know the first thing about maintaining one.

His lips twitched. That image would be seared into my memory for the rest of my days because that was the closest thing to a real, genuine smile he had ever given me.

"No, but you look like the woman who's going to help me stop Moonie Pipelines from getting Hallow Ranch."

Chapter Twenty

Denver

Damn it all to hell, she was even more enchanting after an orgasm.

Her eyes seemed greener, like the deep green forest that surrounded my ranch. Her dark hair was tousled, and I wanted to wrap it around my fist as I sank my cock into her tight, little pussy. Her skin was flushed, and I couldn't ignore the swell of pride that rose in my chest at the sight.

I've had my fair share of woman in my thirty-five years of life.

None of them compelled me to dry hump them. None of them had been so eager to touch me, to make sure that I got off, too. But the only thing that I wanted was to feel her come for me, to hear her cries of pleasure as that sweet cunt contracted around my fingers, trying to milk them.

It had been the best sexual experience of my life and my dick wasn't even out.

I dry-humped that gorgeous, curvy body like a fucking teenager out of pure desire. I couldn't help myself.

I'd never lost control like that before.

Then again, I kissed her.

That was a form of lost control, period.

I hadn't kissed a woman in ten years. I never gave them my mouth, just my fingers or my cock. They would never face me, and no matter how much they begged for intimacy, I wouldn't give it to them.

But when Valerie was lost in ecstasy, begging me to kiss her...

I knew then that she could ask for anything, and I would give it to her. I didn't know what the hell I was doing when it came to this woman, and I was tired of wondering.

I just wanted to want her without question, without doubt lingering over my head.

She is not Cathy, dipshit.

I swallowed.

Valerie was staring at me like I was crazy. I dropped my head and closed my eyes for a moment. I dragged her back into my house like a caveman and damn near claimed her against the door.

You didn't let her go, my sweet boy. Now convince her to stay. You know how. You're just scared. Let go of that fear, Denver.

"You want me to help you stop Mr. Moonie?" Val asked, breaking up my momma's voice in my head. I looked back up at her.

"That fucking asshole fired you because I told you no," I deadpanned, anger rising inside of me. Of course, a man like me would say no. However, there were other ranchers out there who wouldn't have. That wasn't her fault. She did all she could. That asshole was greedy, and he didn't care if he ruined lives to get what he wanted.

"I know, but—"

"Stop calling him 'Mr. Moonie.' He doesn't deserve your respect, Valerie."

She looked down at her lap, her hair moving with her, covering part of her face. I leaned forward and brushed it back, tucking it behind her ear. Green eyes met mine as a little gasp left her lips.

"Work for me," I whispered.

"You just ripped my skirt and underwear off downstairs," she reminded me. Her skirt was in the trash. Those white lace panties she had on were in the pocket of my jeans. Shredded or not, those were mine now.

"And you fucking liked it," I returned, gripping her chin and pulling her towards me.

"Maybe I shouldn't have," she murmured.

"Maybe," I agreed with her, my eyes dropping to her lips. They were usually a light pink, but right now, they were swollen and red—because of me.

My dick twitched in my jeans.

"Work for me," I repeated.

She shook her head. "Denver, I have to go home and take care of my mom."

I'll take care of her, and you. Both of you, baby. Just let me.

I didn't say that. I couldn't say that.

It was too soon.

Fuck it.

"Work for me," I repeated, softer this time.

She shook her head. "I can't work for a man who just fucked me with his fingers!"

In an instant, I was on my feet, pulling her up to me, her chest against mine. I tightened my jaw. "Baby, you aren't leaving. The second I pinned you to my barn, you felt this."

"What is this?" she cried. She looked away from me.

"This," I growled, grabbing her chin once more and forcing her to look at me, "is you and I being drawn to each other. This is me wanting you in my life, in my bed. This is you being a good daughter and fighting for your mom. This is us giving in."

"I—"

"I'm sorry for yelling at you," I stated.

Her mouth closed, her memorizing eyes flashing.

"I'm sorry I insulted you. I'm sorry I doubted you when that bastard hurt you, took away your livelihood, and then I had the audacity to assume you still worked for him...after everything that you had gone through the night before," I said, my voice gentle.

"I don't want to talk about that," she whimpered.

Neither did I. Thinking about her eyes filled with fear, being held against her will...it made me want to kill that bastard all over again, slower this time.

"Give me a week."

"A week?"

"Help me get Tim *fucking* Moonie out of Colorado."

"And after we do that?" she pressed.

I didn't get the chance to answer, because downstairs, the front door was opened and I heard Mags yell, "Kings, get your ass down here!"

I tensed, looking to the open bedroom door, and called back, "Coming!"

"Kings?"

I looked back to my enchantress, cupping her face with one hand. "My callsign."

We held each other's eyes for a moment, neither one of us willing to break it.

"Denver!" Mags roared. I broke our stare then, looking back at the door, my jaw tightening.

"God, *fuck*—if I leave, will you be here when I get back?" I asked her, growling in frustration.

"I..."

"Val, I got a man down there who needs me," I reminded her.

She nodded.

I almost smiled.

Almost.

God, I wanted her mouth again. So, I took it. My tongue swept inside her sweet mouth, and I groaned at the taste. When I broke the kiss, her eyes were hooded, her flush intensified.

Enchanting.

"Be back. Stay in the house," I ordered, leaving her in the room.

I moved downstairs, grabbed my hat, and headed out of the house. My eyes went to the barn and fuck it all to hell, the sheriff was here, talking to the twins.

Mags was leaning against the railing, petting Ranger.

"You know what you're doing with her?" Mags asked.

"Not a fucking clue," I found myself saying, putting on my hat.

"Jesus," he muttered.

Exactly.

I untied Ranger and mounted him. I looked down at my friend, being real with him. "I don't know what I'm doing, man. All I know is that I didn't like seeing her walk away from me."

"You're talking like she's yours," he said, stepping down from the porch.

I turned Ranger to face the barn and looked at Mags over my shoulder. "That's because she is."

Valerie was mine, whether she liked it or not.

She was mine.

"For the love of Christ, Denver, you can't just kill a man in the street."

"Technically, I wasn't in the street, Sheriff," I returned, calm as ever. I killed a man in the alley. Chase stared at me as I leaned against the back of the bunkhouse. He bit out a curse, put his hands on his hips and paced back and forth in front of me.

"Now is not the fucking time to be a smartass," he clipped. He looked at the fields. Half of the herd was grazing there today, moving on their own from pasture two to here. The sun was shining down on him, his badge like a fucking beckon, a reminder of what he is and who he had to be.

Clean.

Sheriff Chase Bowen had to be clean.

He left the dirty work to me.

"What's really bothering you, Chase?" I asked, folding my arms over my chest.

"That woman—the one you protected, is she *here*?"

I tilted my head. He looked at me up and down and then pinched his nose.

"You're getting in bed with Moonie."

"Valerie was fired by Moonie Pipelines days ago," I snapped.

"You sure about that? You sure she isn't just trying to get under your skin, using her good looks and pussy—"

"You lookin' to get your jaw broken today, Sheriff?" I growled, pushing off the wall.

His nostrils flared. "You get my fucking point."

I went up to him, looking down at him. The sheriff was a big man, but I was bigger. Langston genes made big boys. Mason was only an inch shorter than me, and we both towered over everyone in town. Our Pops was the same way.

"Your point is shit, Chase. That woman has no one but her mother."

"Oh, so she has a sob story."

Before I could stop it, my hand was at his throat, and I spun him back against the bunkhouse. I bared my teeth, leaning down to his shocked face.

"Disrespect her again, *Sheriff*," I warned, my voice lethal. "And you'll be the next body burning."

"Den—Denver," he rasped.

I released him, and as he gasped for air, I felt eyes on us. I turned to find Beau and Lawson standing about three feet away, Beau glaring at Chase and Lawson was chewing on chicken wing.

"Best do what he says," Beau bit out.

Lawson chuckled. "Look, Sheriff, we protect our own here, you know that. The way I see it, Denver claimed her. That means she's one of us. That means—"

"You fuck with her, you end up in pain," Beau finished for him.

There was a feeling coming alive inside of me, a feeling I used to get when I looked at Mason. I shoved it away and looked back at Chase.

"Valerie made a deal with the devil to pay for her mom's chemo. She never wanted to do this job, man. She was just a pawn. I refused to sell the ranch and Moonie fired her for it," I explained.

"Moonie is in town," he spat, his voice scratchy.

"We know," all three of us answered him.

"Dad?"

The four of us turned to the sound of my boy's voice.

Caleb poked his head around the corner of the building, his brown cowboy hat tilted too far back. "Is the pretty lady still here?"

My lips twitched. "Yeah, son."

"Cool!" With that, he took off running, probably up to the house to see her. Jigs told me this morning that the boy spent half the evening talking about her. How kind she was. How pretty she was.

My gut twisted.

Caleb has never had a gentle woman in his life. His mother was...Cathy. That's all I could say about that. His teachers were old ladies who, according to him just "wanted the kids to be quiet."

He'd never really had a woman to talk to in his life, and that was partially on me.

Lawson leaned back and watched him go. "He's out of earshot," he said after a few seconds.

"You were saying?" I prompted, looking back at my old friend.

The one you just choked because he disrespected her.

"He's snooping around town."

"That's what's up your ass?" I raised an eyebrow in question.

He looked at me. "What's up my ass is that he's sinking his greedy claws into our town. He walked into the PD this morning and wanted to introduce himself to me."

I bit out a harsh laugh. "The fucker is trying every angle he can."

"He know about the development deal?" Lawson asked, throwing the chicken bone behind him.

"With Bart?"

We nodded once. Chase shook his head. "No, but he's been at Tinkles bar every fucking night."

My spine stiffened as my blood ran cold.

Chase caught it and it was his turn to nod.

"We'll handle it," I growled.

"Try not to kill him in the street…or at all, please."

Beau chuckled darkly.

Lawson smiled.

My mind drifted to Caleb's snake of a mother.

Chapter Twenty-One

Valerie

"Mom, I can't—"

"Yes, you can, my darling girl."

I braced my hand on the counter and bent my head as tears stung the back of my eyes. Denver left about an hour ago, and I just sat there stunned, dazed, and confused. After digging in my bags, and putting on another sundress, I heard the door open.

Caleb called out for me, and my soul liked that: a child's voice echoing through this big, beautiful home calling out for me. I'd met him in the middle of the stairs, and I was stunned when his little arms wrapped around me, as much as they could. Instinctively, my hands went to the back of his head, holding him to me.

Then, he looked up and said, "Dad said you were leaving. I'm glad you didn't."

Now, I was standing in the kitchen while that precious little boy read the second *Harry Potter* book in the swing on the front porch.

"Mom—"

"You have to live, Vallie," she said softly.

My bottom lip trembled. "But not without you."

"Valerie," she breathed.

"I can't just stay here and leave you behind—that's—that's...Mom, I don't know what I'm doing."

A soft laugh came through the other end of the phone. "My prayers are being answered, that's what."

"What?" I asked, wiping my eyes and straightening.

"I've been praying for something to come along for you, something that will draw you in and hold onto you tight."

I looked out the window again. There was a breeze, the tops of the trees in the distance rustling as the mountains stood tall and proud in the background. After Caleb got settled on the porch, I got Mom on the phone and told her everything—well, almost everything.

I told her that I was set to leave, that Denver came rushing up to me on his horse and kissed me. I told her he wanted me to stay. I did not, in fact, tell her that he pressed me up against the door and made my body come alive while calling me "Enchantress."

No, *that* I would keep to myself.

"Mom..."

"*Live*, Valerie."

I didn't say anything. There was nothing to say.

"Tell me about him," she offered, a smile clear in her voice.

I shook my head. "I can't."

Because if I did, my heart would do the talking. My heart would tell her that this man was one of a kind. That this man, this cowboy, made me feel things that I never thought I would get the chance to.

"Is he old and fat?" she asked, teasing me.

I took a deep breath, shaking my head. I wish he was; then, this would be easier. She needed to know the truth; I was already lying to her enough.

"Mom, he is the single most beautiful man I have ever seen," I admitted, picking at my dress. It was a pale purple, almost lilac, but not quite.

There were no buttons down the middle. Instead, the fabric was dotted with tiny white daisies. It was cute. Feminine. I loved it.

"I knew it!" That was Jackie.

I gasped. "Am I on speaker phone?"

"Mmm, of course you are! Your momma told me about this cowboy the other day and I knew—*I knew* he had to be fine," Mom's nurse gushed. I blinked, my brain trying to process what was happening right now.

"I mean, you have been doing this job for years and not once have you met a fine cowboy...Smells like bullshit to me."

My jaw dropped and Mom was giggling.

"Now, you go and *live*, Val. I got your mom. Take the job. Whatever that man is offering, take it. He sounds fine. Too damn fine, if you ask me. A man like that running up to me on a horse, kissing me, and telling me to stay? Mmm...I like that."

I looked to the ceiling, a laugh forming in my chest. Mom laughed harder. This was the most she had laughed in years.

"Oh! I have to tell you about the pumpkins!"

A smile tugged on my lips. "Yes, the pumpkins..."

Twenty minutes later, I was hanging up and stepping through the front door.

"God damn, you are pretty."

I let out a yelp and looked up to find a cowboy, one of the twins. He was standing on the bottom step of the porch, his boot on the next step.

"Lance, you can't cuss like that in front of me," Caleb said from the porch swing. He had his feet up, the book in his lap.

"My apologies, Wizard," Lance said to the boy, a smirk playing on his lips.

Were all these men just gorgeous out here? What was in the water?

Lance was tall. He wasn't as tall as Denver, but tall. He had tan skin like all cowboys do, dressed in Wranglers, brown boots, a white t-shirt and a cream cowboy hat. His brown eyes scanned me up and down slowly.

I cleared my throat.

"Name's Lance," he said, stretching out his dirty, calloused hand to me. I stepped forward and took it.

"I'm Valerie."

"Oh, I know," he said, flashing me a smile that could bring a woman to her knees. He was young, younger than me by a few years.

"Can I help you with something?" I asked.

His eyes looked me up and down again as he held my hand. He was chewing gum, and another smile spread across his handsome face. "Nah, darlin'. Just heard from the boys you were staying. Wanted to come up and introduce myself."

Denver had been talking about me?

To his...men?

"That's very kind," I said, something catching the corner of my eye, movement on Caleb's side of the porch. I turned and immediately stiffened. There was a man, another cowboy—*the other dark cowboy*—the one who never let me see his face. He was staring at me, his head tilted, and even though I couldn't see his eyes under the brim of his hat, I could *feel* them. He looked like he didn't like what he was seeing.

"Mags," Lance warned.

Caleb looked up from his book and over the porch railing to look at Mags. "Hey! We riding to the herd?" the little boy asked.

The cowboy's eyes were still on me as he said, "Yeah, kid. Get your boots back on." Caleb closed his book and ran into the house, rushing past me. His voice was deep, and I could tell he and Denver were around the same age.

Was this the brother he had a falling out with?

I thought Denver's brother left the ranch.

"Stop staring at her," Lance growled, climbing the steps and getting in front of me. I tore my eyes from Mags and looked up to Lance. He was about three inches taller than me.

Caleb ran out and charged down the steps. "Bye, Valerie!"

"Bye, sweetheart," I found myself saying, looking at his back. I saw Mags move out of the corner of my eye and without a word to me or Lance, he turned away, following Caleb back down to the barn.

"Jesus," Lance muttered.

"Was that Denver's brother?" I asked before I could stop myself.

Lance stiffened.

I took a step away from him and a chill ran down my spine as he tilted his head. Just. Like. Mags. Did.

Me and my big mouth. Shit.

"How do you know about Den's brother?" he asked, his voice low.

I swallowed. "I, uh, it was part of my research…"

"For Moonie?" he spat.

I nodded, biting my lip. He looked away for a moment, and I decided to ramble. "I didn't mean to pry, it just slipped out. It's none of my business. I know that. I'm the enemy."

"You're Denver's, darlin'."

My heart skipped a beat, maybe two…No, at this point, it might be suffering from cardiac arrest.

You're Denver's, darlin'.

"Uh—"

He sighed. "Look, there's a story there, a story that is gonna hurt telling. It's Denver's story, not mine. So, I'm not going to tell it."

I nodded. I could respect that.

"I will tell you *that* wasn't his brother. That was Mags. He's worked for Hallow Ranch for years. He's a vet, Marines, like Denver. He is a different kind of brother to him, like all of us are."

I didn't understand that. I didn't have any siblings…or friends. Lance continued, "This needs to be said though, and I know I'm the only one with the guts to say it. None of the other boys will, even though they all agree with me."

"What's that?"

A shadow passed over his face. "Mason Langston can go fuck himself and if he ever steps foot on Hallow Ranch again, I'll kill him."

I flinched, my lips parting as my eyes went wide. Fear trickled down my spine, reminding me of the horrors I had seen.

He took a step towards me. "I know you saw us that night, darlin'. I know you witnessed Denver in the alley. What he did to protect you...any man in his right mind would've done that."

"Lance—"

"Not gonna hurt you. No one is. You aren't the enemy anymore, Moonie is. You are Denver's, which means you are family," he said, his voice soft again.

Family.

The air in my lungs left me. "I-I-you don't know me."

"Denver does," he returned, stepping away from me.

I shook my head. "We barely know each other. This is crazy."

He smiled again, stopping at the steps. "Life usually is, Valerie. Gotta live it."

"Val?"

I looked up from my laptop. I was currently on the couch in the living room, my legs tucked under me, my hair pulled back by a big clip. I had spent the rest of the afternoon doing research on my old employer, digging up anything I could find, which wasn't much.

The Moonie's were good at covering their tracks. There were whispers through the company grape vine of course, but I never really paid any attention to them. I was focused on one thing. My mom.

"Valerie."

I blinked; my thoughts of Moonie were pushed away by gray smoke. Denver was standing in the living room entryway. His dark washed Wranglers were dirty, along with his black shirt. He still had his hat on, probably just to torture me.

I looked up into his eyes and his smoke came at me in a slow, gentle, teasing crawl, like a predator stalking its prey. His bearded jaw was tight as those eyes dropped down to my chest, then to my lap.

"Been busy, baby," he murmured.

"Hi," I breathed. He stared at me for another beat, something that looked a lot like longing drifting over his face. When he looked away, his eyes went to the rocking chair in the corner. I followed his gaze, then looked back at him.

"I'm sorry," I said.

He looked back at me, confusion masking his handsome, dark features.

"I don't—I don't really…" I trailed off. What was I apologizing for?

Trying to uproot his life.

Watching him kill a man.

Having him take care of you.

Him saving you and then killing another man.

Taking me in.

Him listening to my life story in the middle of the street.

Me developing feelings for him.

"Why in the hell are you apologizing?" he asked, his voice stern. He moved closer to me, his boots pounding against the hardwood floors.

I ran my hand through my hair and looked down at my keyboard. "I don't know, really. I just felt like I should apologize."

I felt his warm, rough fingers slide underneath my chin, gripping it firmly and tilting my face up to look at him.

"If you're apologizing for not giving me a fucking kiss, then I'll accept it, but for anything else, no. There's no need to apologize, Val."

I blinked. "Kiss you?"

He cocked his head to the right, his eyes dropping to my lips. "Yeah," he whispered.

"I did kiss you—"

"Baby, I just got done with a long day of work. You sit on my couch in a pretty dress, I'm going to want a kiss." His voice was deeper now, thicker, but somehow gentle. He leaned down closer stopping when our lips were a centimeter apart.

"What are we doing, Denver?"

"Fuck if I know, but damn, it feels good."

Then he kissed me.

He tasted like pine, sunshine, and mint. My arms wrapped around his neck and his hands dropped down my waist, squeezing me. He was covered in dirt, having spent the afternoon outside sweating, and I couldn't get enough. I whimpered, sticking my tongue out, brushing his lips lightly. I didn't know what the hell I was doing, but I wanted to try to please him—*to learn.*

To live.

He groaned, and suddenly my laptop was gone, and I was up. Then, without breaking contact, he spun me, dropped down on the couch, and pulled me into his lap. My dress rode up my thighs, pooling at my hips. I put all my weight on my knees, refusing to drop fully down into his lap. He pulled away, looking up at me as one of his hands snaked into my hair.

"Want you on my lap," he commanded, his hand at my waist, trying to urge me down. Suddenly, I was nervous. My skin felt clammy, and I didn't want to be in this dress, on his lap.

I wanted to be under a blanket. Hiding from the world.

"Now," he growled, attempting to pull me down further. I put my hands on his shoulders and shook my head. His features softened. "What's going on? Am I hurting you?"

I—

He was thinking about the other night. He was making sure this was okay.

My dark cowboy wasn't so dark after all.

"No, no, it's not that," I said, my voice quiet.

"What is it, baby?" He was being gentle and soft again.

My stomach flipped as I looked away from him. "I don't—I don't want to crush you," I admitted. His hand cupped my face and turned me back to face him.

"Crush me?" he repeated in disbelief.

I gestured down to my body. "I'm not a dainty little woman. I'm—"

"I am two hundred and eighty pounds," he deadpanned. I stared as he continued, pulling off his hat and setting it down on the cushion beside us. "I'm six foot seven, baby. I'm a big man." His dark hair was messy, and my fingers itched to be in it.

"That has—"

"You enchant me," he said, cutting me off. The hand in my hair pulled me towards him and my hands slid down to his chest. "Enchantress, I can handle you. I was born to handle a woman like you, perfect for me."

My heart was soaring, high in the skies of love, and she was probably never coming back down after that comment.

"Denver," I breathed, my cheeks heating.

"My boy is going to be home in just a few minutes, and then I have to make dinner for you both. But right now, I want to kiss the fucking shit out of you with your little pussy pressed against my jeans."

I dropped into his lap and his eyes darkened. "That's my good girl."

I kissed him.

I kissed and kissed him, whimpering and moaning as his rough hands explored my body.

When they dropped down to my ass, I broke away, gasping as tingles spread through my body like fire. My lips leaving his didn't bother my cowboy. No, his head dropped to my neck, kissing and licking my sensitive skin. My body was in control now, and my hips began to move and a low, raw, growl left Denver, going straight to my core. My hand dove into his dark locks, anchoring myself.

"That's it. Rub that needy pussy on me," he ordered gruffly before he moved to my shoulder, pulling the strap of my dress down, pressing hot kisses against my skin. I ground against his erection, suddenly regretting putting on new panties earlier. His hands on my ass guided me, helping me move back and forth against him.

"Oh," I moaned. His hands came up my back and he pulled away from me. My eyes met his just as he yanked the fabric of my dress down further, exposing my breast.

"Enchantress," he whispered. Then, his mouth was on my nipple, sucking long, hard and so deep that my panties were soaked.

"Denver!"

He grunted against me and bit my flesh. I tossed my head back, my hips moving faster against him.

"Dad! Valerie!"

Both of us froze, and Denver's head flew up. I looked to the door, but it was still closed. Panic set in, and when Denver stole a glance at me, I could've sworn he was ready to smile. I scrambled off the big man and adjusted my dress. I looked over at him and to find his hand on his jeans, shamelessly adjusting as he stared at me. When he was done, his thumb stroked my cheek.

"Thanks for the kiss, baby." Then he winked—*winked*.

"Boy!" he bellowed, heading to the door. I stood in the living room, shocked, aroused, and scared as I watched Caleb burst through the front door and hug his father.

Shocked because I didn't think a man like Denver had a playful side.

Aroused because...duh.

Scared because when he walked away from me, he took my heart with him. She wasn't soaring in the skies of love anymore. She was in his hands.

Chapter Twenty-Two

Denver

"Do you need help with anything?"

I looked over my shoulder to find Valerie standing by the fridge, looking a bit lost. Her bun was tilted, her cheeks were flushed from our session on the couch.

This woman will undo me. I could feel it.

"No, baby. Don't you need to call your mom?" I asked, holding her gaze. I watched as the green of her eyes flared slightly at the mention of her mother. It wasn't with anger, though. It was something else.

"Why..." she trailed off, struggling to find the right thing to say.

"Val, you always call your mom around this time. I also know you call her in the morning, too. If you need to call, and check in, go ahead," I said, gesturing to the ingredients on the counter. "I got dinner."

"I'm not used to being taken care of like this," she blurted.

Of course, she wasn't. She'd been taking care of everyone around her for years, working in a shitty job, coming home to a sick mom for years. She put her dreams on the backburner. I nodded. "I know you aren't, Val. I'm going to change that."

She took a step forward. "I would like to help with dinner, please."

A chuckle left me. "That's cute, but no."

She stared, mainly at my mouth.

"Val, cut that shit out," I warned. She blinked and met my eyes, confusion dancing in hers. "Stop looking at my mouth like that."

"I don't think I've seen you smile before," she murmured. "You just chuckled, and I saw a bit of it, but it was gone before I could enjoy it."

Fuck.

Me.

I opened my mouth to say something but was cut off my Caleb coming in from the front porch. "Dad!" he exclaimed, waving a book in his hand. The second Harry Potter book, I think.

"What is it?"

He ran in and stopped by Val. "I finished it!"

"Already?" she asked, her brows going up.

I tipped my head to him. "Kid reads faster than anything. You got the third one ready to go, or are you taking a break?"

He looked up at me. "Did you take a break?"

No. I didn't. After my mother was murdered, I was either sleeping, working on the ranch with Pop, or reading. I never left myself alone with my thoughts, not until I was a Marine, sleeping in enemy territory. My thoughts were my only escape from the hell I was living in.

"If you have the third one, I suggest you start it quickly." Valerie's sweet voice was there, but I was already slipping away.

I traded a living hell for a haunting nightmare.

I felt my mind slipping away from the present, where my son and Enchantress were. I was back on the hard rocks, guns going off on around of me, men shouting and begging for mercy. The cries of innocent women and children rang in the distance, forced to watch the game men play, and knowing they might lose their lives in the process.

"Kings! Kings! Twelve o'clock," someone cried.

It was too late. The rounds I was firing weren't enough. Planes roared from above and suddenly, I was surrounded by fire and smoke. I looked to my left as the man next to me flew back, bullets impaling his body. I screamed, but there was no use. I disengaged and started dragging his body through the smoke.

No man gets left behind.
No man gets left behind.
Mom left you behind...
Pop left you behind...
Mason left you behind...

"Denver!" A hand touched my cheek, and my body reacted before I could process it. My hand was around their throat, and I had them pressed against the nearest wall. The man was smaller than me, flailing his arms out, but I wasn't letting this one get away.

This was one of the men who killed my mom. Their selfishness and greed killed my mom.

The man's face changed then. Now, I was looked at an enemy shoulder, a man who has been known to kill children in the streets of his city to prove a point. I squeezed harder.

The light was going out of their eyes, and then I was looking in a mirror.

Gray eyes. My gray eyes were staring back at me. I blinked.

"Jesus, Den, get a fucking grip. I was just out at the rodeo," the man said, my hand on his throat not fazing him. A cocky smile formed.

I wasn't looking in a mirror.

I was looking at my brother.

"Mason," I croaked, trying to release my hand from his throat, but he caught my wrist, forcing me to continue choking him.

"Don't stop now, Den. You already ruined my fucking life. You took my happiness from me. Don't be afraid to take my life too. We both know you want to," Mason sneered.

His eyes were changing. The gray was melting away and I swore I could see a patch of green...

"Denver!"

I was pulled from my brother and shoved away.

"Jesus, sweetheart," someone muttered.

"Denver, what the fuck?"

I blinked, but the image of Mason looking at me in terror while that bitch was in my bed was all I could see.

"You are no brother of mine. Fuck you, fuck Hallow Ranch, and fuck that cunt upstairs!"

I looked up, and Mason was still here, a few feet away, lighting a cigarette. He took a long drag of it, and as the smoke lifted into the air, he said, "Do you honestly think you deserve her?"

Blinking again, I shook my head. Who was he talking about? Cathy? I looked at him, leaning against the wall now. "Do you think that a man liked you deserves something so...*enchanting*?"

Cold washed over me.

"God fuckin'—DENVER! GET A GRIP!" That was a roar. A roar from a man who is usually quiet.

Mags.

My vision was clearing and the smoke I was lost in drifted away. Mags was in front of me, holding me against someone. Arms were encasing me from the front and behind. I shook my head.

"Come on, brother, come back to us. Leave that shit there," Mags ordered.

I got a good look at him now. His hat was gone, exposing his black hair, wild and damp. His dark eyes were wild with fear. "You here?" he clipped.

I nodded and tried to move, but the arms around me tightened.

"What's your name?" Mags asked.

"Denver Langston."

"How old are you?"

"Thirty-five."

"What's today?"

"June tenth."

"Where are you?"

I swallowed, something nasty pooling in my gut. "Hallow Ranch."

Mags looked behind me. "Let him go."

I looked around. We were outside of my home, in the front yard. Mags sighed and bent to pick up his hat. The arms around me were gone, and the twins came into view, looking at me with concern.

Fuck.

Fuck.

"What did I do?" I asked.

"You fucking choked her!"

All heads snapped up the porch. Beau was standing there, fuming, his blue eyes pinned on me.

Choked her?

Choked who—

Valerie.

I was moving then, charging up the porch steps, but my men crowded me. Beau and I were nose to nose, me looking down at him.

"Let me in my house," I growled.

"Kings—"

"She alright?" I clipped, worry settling over me in a way I'd never experienced before.

"You don't—"

"IS SHE OKAY?" I roared.

"Denver?" That was Valerie.

"Let me pass, Beau," I growled. My body was tight with rage and fear. There were so many emotions running through me right now. Beau was being the man he was—kind of man I respected—but he was blocking me from my Enchantress. That was just pissing me off. "Move, or I'll move you."

He raised his chin. "You put your hands on her," he hissed.

I ignored the stab I felt in my gut, the knife deep, piercing my organs.

The door behind Beau cracked open, and over his shoulder, I saw her step out. Her pretty dress seemed duller now. My eyes immediately went to her neck. It was red—dark red. I shoved Beau out of the way and went to her. My men where on my heels, staying close to protect her, and fuck, that made me feel good, knowing they would protect her, even from me.

She was the enemy weeks ago, but now she was family. She was mine and they knew it. My hands cupped her face in an instant, my thumbs brushing over her reddened cheeks. She wasn't crying, but there was uncertainty in her eyes.

I didn't like it, but somehow, I knew it wasn't fear.

"Are you okay?" I asked, my voice quiet and low.

Her hands came up to my forearms, her touch sending jolts of electricity throughout my body, followed by an aftershock of calm. Her eyes bore into mine, searching.

"Den," she whispered, her eyes scanning mine.

"Fuck," I groaned, pulling her to my chest. I wrapped my arms around her, holding her to me. Slowly, tentatively, her arms slide up to wrap around my shoulders. My eyes closed, and I focused on her warmth, her steady breaths.

"Dad?"

Caleb. Shit.

Did my son see the monster inside of me?

My eyes snapped open, and he was holding the door, a new book in his hand. His little brow was furrowed, and his gray eyes were on Valerie.

"Is Valerie okay?" he asked.

The woman in my arms pulled away from me. She turned to my son, and I stayed close to her. Fuck, I needed to have her near me.

"I'm okay, sweetheart."

"What happened to your neck?" Caleb asked. The men around me tensed; I was still as fucking stone.

I put my hands on her.

Fuck.

I put my God damn hands on her.

Suddenly, I wanted to chop them off. I didn't deserve to touch her, to feel her softness, my skin burning against hers. I was waiting for her to say it, to tell my son I am nothing but a monster.

A worthless man.

At least this time, she wouldn't be lying. Not like Cathy. No, Valerie would tell the truth. My son would hate me.

He would hate me for my past.

He would hate me for my nightmares.

He would hate me for my weaknesses.

"I ate a blueberry," she said.

What?

"A blueberry?"

She nodded and kneeled in front of my boy. He bent and looked at the skin on her neck as she angled her head back. Her eyes met mine as I stood over her. There was no anger. There was no judgment. There was no pain.

"It looks bad," Caleb said slowly.

She straightened her head then shook it. "I have a mild allergy. They just turn my skin red." Shrugged.

"Okay. Well, no more blueberries, okay? I don't like that," he declared.

Me either, son.

She nodded. "No more blueberries," she promised. "Is that the new book?"

He pulled it out from under his arm to show her. "Yeah, I had to dig for it in my closet. Dad bought me the whole series last year for Christmas."

"That was nice of him," she said. There was a smile in her voice, and it felt like a punch in the gut.

"Caleb, Jigs is making bacon mac n' cheese for dinner. We came to see if you wanted some?" Lawson asked, lying to my son to protect his precious innocence.

My son's eyes lit up. "Yeah! Valerie, do you want to come?"

She put her hand on his shoulder. "Your dad was going to cook me dinner, so I'm going to pass this time."

He shrugged. "That's probably best. Between Mags and I, there won't be any leftovers. Beau eats all the dessert."

"Shut up, kid," Beau said, shaking his head beside me.

"Let's go," Lance said.

The men and my son left. Then, it was just Val and me. She stood up and turned to face me.

"Are you alright?" she asked, softly.

Chapter Twenty-Three

Valerie

His smoke was around me, but not touching me.

He wasn't touching me. He could barely hold my eyes for more than a second. At that moment, he was looking towards the barn, his jaw tight as a muscle jumped in his cheek. His broad shoulders were tense, just like the rest of his body.

"Denver," I called.

"Don't," he said, his throat working. I stepped closer to him, closing the distance between us. There was only an inch between our bodies now, much like this morning, like earlier on the couch.

"Talk to me," I begged. I kept my hands at my sides even though I wanted to touch him. I didn't know if that was what he wanted. He was in a bad place. I had to stand there and watch my dark cowboy get taken away from me.

There was nothing that I could do.

I knew he was a retired Marine, but I obviously knew nothing of the horrors he faced overseas.

"Honey," I whispered.

"You were right to try and leave this morning."

Each one of his words sliced through me, my throat was getting tight, this time, it wasn't his smoke choking me. It was fear. Fear that I let myself believe I could have something good. Fear that this wasn't real, like my heart wanted it to be. Fear that my soul would never heal from this.

I could hear it in his voice. He made a mistake. He lost me in the process of battling his demons. He lost his grip on reality.

"You didn't hurt me," I assured.

"I could've killed you," he snapped.

"Do you want to talk about it?"

He looked at me then, and it felt like the wind was knocked out of me. There, in the gray smoke of his eyes, was pain. Torment. Anguish. Agony.

"I am so fucking sorry, baby," he whispered, his voice thick with emotion.

"Can I touch you?" I breathed, tears stinging my eyes.

"Valerie..."

"Come inside," I suggested. "You still have to make me dinner."

It was after dinner, which was surrounded in silence and calm smoke.

Denver made me an excellent meal, and I sat at the island, watching his every move. I studied the way his hands worked as he blended the ingredients together, the way his lips moved when he tested something, the way the tension in his shoulders left him as the process went on.

Denver was good in the kitchen. It was his sanctuary.

Watching him was like sitting in front of a masterpiece in an art museum. I would never grow bored.

Now, I was sitting on the front porch, in the swing Caleb likes to sit on. There was a blanket wrapped around my legs and I was staring out into the night, listening to the rustling of the trees, the sounds of wildlife in the distance. Denver was inside, doing something in his office. I don't know what, but I didn't want to bother him.

He went to a dark place today, and he needed to process that.

My eyes drifted to the gravel driveway.

Just this morning, he rode to me on his steed and kissed me.

Seems like it was ages ago. Days like today terrified me. They were life altering days.

My phone buzzed in my hands.

Mom FaceTime.

I answered, plastering a smile on my face. "Hi, Mom."

My neck wasn't red anymore, my skin back to normal. It was like it never happened. His hand wasn't on my throat for long, maybe ten seconds at most. The boys were coming up to invite us to dinner at the bunk house at the right moment. Beau shoved Denver off me and Mags took care of him.

"Let's cut the shit," Jackie said, poking her face in the camera. "Where is he?"

"Jackie!" Mom scolded.

Jackie got beside my mom in the frame. "Don't start. You've been wanting to see him all day."

Mom's green eyes rolled, but a smile played on her lips. They were in the living room on the couch. Mom had a purple silk wrap on her head today. Her skin was paler than normal but there was a light in her eyes I'd never seen before.

"I would like to meet the man driving my daughter crazy," Mom said with a smile.

He was driving me crazy. This was crazy.

"He's busy," I admitted.

Jackie blinked. "Cowboys don't work at night. Cowboy drink whiskey and listen to sad music at night."

A laugh bubbled up through me, and I threw my head back.

"Jackie, how in the world do you know that? You're from L.A.," Mom noted, which only made me laugh harder.

"I've seen movies, woman. I know."

I sat up and wiped my eyes. "I don't think Denver listens to sad music."

Just then the door opened, and he was there, commanding the air and energy around him. He was still in his jeans and black T-shirt, but his hat and boots were gone. His gray eyes were on me, studying me, his face set in stone.

"I think the hot cowboy just entered the chat," Jackie loudly whispered through the phone.

Denver raised a brow, and my eyes followed it up and his thick, dark locks. "She's checking him out," Jackie continued.

"Oh, for the love of—"

Jackie cut my mom off. "Val, honey, turn the phone a bit. I want to see!"

I bit my bottom lip and dropped my head.

"I'll make the introductions," Jackie decided. "Mr. Fine Cowboy, I'm Jackie, the nurse! This is Valerie's mom—stop staring at me like that—"

"We'll let you go, Val," my mom said, giggling. I looked at the screen to find her hand over Jackie's mouth.

"Thank God," I muttered, gesturing to Jackie. She shot me the death glare.

"Good evening, ladies."

Smoke was all around me, cocooning me, and somehow, I found it easier to breathe. I looked up to find him beside me. His face wasn't stone anymore. His lips were twitching slightly, and his eyes had a shadow of amusement in them.

"Hi," I whispered.

"Get ya' hand off of me, woman! Valerie Cross, if you don't let me see that man!" Jackie bellowed.

In a flash, my phone was out of my hands and in one of Denver's massive ones. He faced the screen. "Hello."

Silence.

Then, "Holy Christ on a cracker."

"MOM!" I cried, my jaw dropping. I wasn't sure if my jaw was dropping because of my mother's outburst or the fact that Denver's handsome face spread in the most addicting, spellbinding, way known in history.

Denver *smiled*.

At my mom.

"I was thinking the same thing when I saw your daughter for the first time. I'm Denver Langston," he said, his deep voice holding a light tone. I sucked in a breath at his words. He looked at me and stepped to the other end of the swing. I got the message and lifted my legs for him. He took a seat and pulled my legs into his lap.

"It's a pleasure to finally meet you. I'm Nancy," my mother said. "I've heard a lot of things about you."

"Not all of it was good, I assume," he returned. I watched as he sat back, getting comfortable—*settling in*—to talk to my mom. My chest ached because of how hard my heart was beating. His face got serious, and his eyes found mine as he spoke. "There were things I said to your daughter. I disrespected her. I misjudged her. She isn't the kind of a woman I blindly assumed she was—"

"You don't have to explain yourself to me, Mr. Langston," Mom said, cutting him off.

"We know you were just protecting your home. Val was a threat to that. You acted the way any normal person would," Jackie added.

"Nevertheless, I would still like your forgiveness for the hurt I caused," Denver said, his voice firm.

"You have it," Mom returned.

He smiled and looked back at me.

"Now, tell me about your ranch," Mom ordered.

For the next half hour, I watched my mom get to know the man who saved me. I watched my mom get to know a man who meant something to me. Twice, I had to stop myself from crying because I thought I would never get to have this.

A man meeting my mom.

"We'll talk soon," Denver promised, still chuckling at something Jackie said. He handed the phone back to me. Mom was smiling brightly, her eyes greener than before. She looked at me, communicating something to me.

He'll make sure you live, my Valerie.

I nodded. "I love you, Mom."

"I love you, too. Goodnight."

The FaceTime ended and I slowly dropped the phone back into my lap. I felt Denver's eyes on me, but I couldn't meet them. He didn't have to come out here and meet her. He could've stayed inside. He didn't have to talk to her about his home and he sure as hell didn't have to listen to her talk about her old flower shop and her pumpkins.

"Val, look at me."

I shook my head. "You didn't have to do that."

Rough, warm fingers gripped my chin. When my head was lifted, he was right there, his smoke closing in. "You are so fucking strong, Valerie Cross. You are a magnificent daughter."

My face crumbled.

"Baby," he murmured, pulling me into his lap. The swing began to move, and my face was buried in my hands, his arms wrapped around me.

Shaking my head, I looked up at him through my tears. "You didn't hurt me, Denver."

A pained look flashed over his features, and he looked away. "I shouldn't have—"

"You went to a dark place." He looked at me and I continued. "I saw it. Something triggered it, but you didn't hurt me. Your hand didn't even squeeze my neck that hard," I gently explained.

"Let me see," he whispered. I lifted my chin, and after a moment, I felt his fingers brush across my skin. "I'm sorry. I'm finding myself to be sorry about a lot of things when it comes to you."

I put my hands on his shoulders. "Do you regret it?" I asked, my heart in my throat ready to jump ship if he answered a certain way.

"What's that?"

"Me."

He was quiet for a moment, his fingers playing with the bottom of my hair. "You were the last thing I expected," he finally said, his voice rough. "I'm not a good man, Valerie."

Chapter Twenty-Four

Denver

"I'm not a good man, Valerie," I admitted. I knew I wasn't a good man. There are things my hands have done that would scare Lucifer himself. I'm not proud of it but I'll do what I have to in order to protect my home.

Including becoming a monster.

I never expected her to show up in my life.

After Cathy, I never expected to have a woman in this house again. I expected to spend the rest of my days alone, finding sex outside of my home, and I was content with that.

Now, I don't know if I could live without the Enchantress sitting in my lap.

"You are to me," she said, putting her hands on my face. I looked into those green eyes, searching for her lie, but I only saw acceptance.

"I don't deserve to touch you," I whispered, my voice hoarse as I slid my hands up her waist. The blanket was still covering her legs, thank fuck for that. My control was nearly at its breaking point.

"I don't deserve your kindness," she returned.

I shook my head. "I misjudged you, Valerie. Fuck, your mom? That's what you have been trying to protect and save?"

There was an ache in my chest. Part of me was jealous of Valerie, because her mom was still here. The other part felt sorry for her, because her mom was in pain.

My mom was in heaven.

Valerie's mom was here on Earth, fighting for her life.

"She's a wonderful woman," Valerie said, looking away from me. "She's strong and fierce. She took care of me and ran a business with a smile on her face after my father left us. Not a lot of people can do that."

I nodded, rubbing my hands up her back. "No, they can't."

"I never thought I would have tonight," she croaked. "I-I never thought I would have the chance to introduce her to a man like you."

I winced. "A few hours ago—"

"Already forgotten, Denver. You didn't hurt me. I was more worried about you than—"

In an instant, my hands were in her hair as I pulled her to me, crushing her lips to mine. Val kissed me back with the same urgency, our lips molding together in a heated frenzy.

Kissing her was an addiction I never wanted to overcome.

She whimpered as I stroked my tongue against her lush lips, begging her to let me in. When her finally lips parted, I swooped in, drinking from her, savoring her sweet taste. If her mouth tasted this good, I could only imagine what her cunt tasted like. Her hands came to my shoulders, bracing herself as I consumed her. Her breasts were against my chest as my hands snaked under the blanket to grip her ass.

She moaned, pulling back slightly to gasp.

I needed her closer.

I needed her under me, writhing for me as I finally claimed what's mine.

Mine?

Fuck, yes—she was mine.

With a growl, I pushed to my feet, holding her up. Her long legs wrapped around my waist as her arms banded around my neck. The blanket fell, and her body heat was against me. *Finally.* Her core was pressed against my crotch and all my blood seemed to rush to that spot.

"Fuck," I hissed as she bit my lip. "Valerie."

"Denver," she mewed.

That did it.

I was moving, stomping into the house with her in my arms, clinging to my body. Her lips pulled away and then they were at my neck, kissing, licking, sucking. I squeezed her ass with one hand as I yanked the door open with the other.

"Baby, you don't stop, I'm fucking you on the stairs," I warned.

She shuddered against me but didn't let up. *Naughty girl.*

"You taste so good," she said against my skin as she dragged her tongue up my neck.

When I was with other women, they never got to touch me, unless it was my cock. That was it. I didn't want their hands on me. For years, I didn't want any woman touching me. All that changed the second I saw this woman standing in the rain.

"Fucking hell," I growled. I was halfway up the steps when I lost control, slamming her against the wall with a groan. My hands flexed on her ass as she gasped, her pussy rubbing against my aching cock. No doubt it was already weeping for her.

"You drive me insane, Enchantress," I rasped, gripping her jaw and kissing her again. After a punishing kiss, I dipped my head into her neck, inhaling her cherry scent. "Been thinking about this body for *weeks*, Val." I pressed my hips into her core. Her hands were in my hair, her nails scraping against my scalp.

I wanted her nails on my back.

I wanted her marks on me.

Only me.

The thought of another man having her made my blood boil and my trigger finger itch.

"Denver," she pleaded, grinding against me, snapping me out of my caveman thoughts. Her forehead was against mine, those green eyes staring into mine. I thrust against her again savoring her little whimpers.

"You gonna scream for your cowboy when he stretches your little pussy? Hm?"

She just nodded, so I flexed my hips again, dropping my mouth to her neck.

"Tell me, baby. Use your words. You gonna scream for me?"

"Yes," she breathed.

I smiled against her skin, the front of my jeans damp from her. She was practically *leaking* for me. That motivated me to move. I didn't want to take her on the stairs for our first time. I needed room for what I planned on doing to her. When I sank my cock into her, I wanted her spread wide for me.

Pulling her away from the wall, I ascended the stairs with her clinging to me in a way no other woman has. My tongue dove in her mouth as I kicked my bedroom door open.

There was no time for fucking around. I needed to be inside of her.

I dropped her on the bed, her luscious tits bouncing for me. The left strap of her purple dress was hanging off her shoulder, teasing me. Her lips were dark and swollen, the skin around them red from my beard. Pride swelled in my chest knowing I'd marked her. I wanted to ruin her for all other men. My dick twitched as I focused on her lips, wanting to be in her mouth. My eyes took their time, memorizing this moment, the woman in my bed—an enchantress. Her dark hair was splayed against the green comforter, her green eyes standing out against the dark colors.

A fucking enchantress.

That's what she was, come to cast her spell on me.

She bent her long legs for me and slowly, her knees fell apart. My hand drifted to the front of my jeans and a low groan left me as I palmed my erection. Her eyes dropped to my crotch; those dark pink lips parting in awe as she watched me. My nostrils flared.

"This is what you've been doing to me, baby. Every *fucking* day, I woke up with fucking hard-on knowing you would be out there, waiting for *me*." I undid my belt and pants before shoving my hand into my jeans.

Valerie's chest was heaving rapidly now, her green eyes dilating as she watched me. She liked this. She liked knowing the effect she had on me.

"Had to jack off every morning and night for you," I growled. She whimpered and licked her lips, her hips moving slightly. "You like that, don't you? You like knowing that my dick gets hard for a city girl like you."

"Smoke," she breathed, meeting my eyes. *Jesus, that fucking nickname.* It was better than honey. My hand was shamelessly working my cock through my boxers now.

"Touch your tits, baby," I ordered softy. Her hands came up and cupped her breasts. I groaned at the sight, my hand working faster. Her hands weren't big enough to fully cup them.

But mine were.

She was fucking made for a man like me.

"Dad!"

Fucking hell.

Cold water washed over me and apparently her. The heat between us faded as I looked to the ceiling.

Never thought my son would be a fucking cockblock.

My jaw tightened as I pulled my hand out of my pants. After righting my jeans and fastening my belt, I looked down at her. She was sitting up now, her legs crossed, as she ran her fingers through her hair, a smile teasing her lips.

"This ain't funny," I scolded. She bit her lip and looked out the window.

"Dad! Valerie! Where are you?" Caleb called. *The little shit.*

"Coming, sweetheart!" Val answered.

I was looking at the door—*glaring at it, actually*—when her soft hand touched my face. My eyes found hers, and she stood on her toes to press a soft kiss to my lips. A zing of warmth went through my body at the contact.

"Tall girls never get to do that," she whispered under her breath, pulling away from me. A little louder she said, "Thank you."

I swallowed, wrapping my arm around her waist. "For being taller than you?" I deadpanned.

"For making me feel alive," she answered, looking into my eyes.

Fuck.

She slipped from my hold, her green eyes bright, and headed downstairs to see my son.

I stood there for a few minutes, staring at the doorway.

What the fuck have I gotten myself into?

The Hayden Hotel. Room 312.

She was attempting to be cute for the man in the chair, watching her with a fake smile. There was a whiskey in his hand and a file on the table beside him. The blonde bartender from Tinkles Bar had done what he asked of her.

Now, there was something else that needed to be done.

Destroy Denver Langston.

Tim Moonie focused on her fake tits, not her face, as he willed his dick to get hard. He would fuck her tonight, giving her the illusion he actually gave a shit.

She was stupid, like all the rest.

Years ago, there had been a woman for him. She was perfect, perhaps a little too strong-willed, but perfect, nonetheless. He has no issues breaking a woman's spirit. In fact, that was what he wanted to do to his perfect woman. Alas, she slipped through his fingers. She didn't have fake blonde hair or fake tits. No, her hair reminded him of fire. He enjoyed it.

"You look handsome tonight, sir," Cathy said, her voice raspy from years of chain smoking. His thoughts of his perfect woman drifted away as he looked up to Cathy's face. Her hair was washed, and she'd attempted to curl it. A failed attempt. She was wearing jeans, cheap high heels, and a red tank top.

She looked like a washed-up buckle bunny and perhaps that is what she was. He knew she was engaged to Mason Langston years ago, when he was just starting out in the rodeo. Now, he was a top bull rider, and Hallow Ranch was in his past.

"Thank you, darling," he drawled. He looked away from her then, setting down his whiskey. "Let's go over the story again."

She nodded and opened her mouth to speak, but Tim cut her off.

"On your fucking knees," he barked.

She did as she was told. He sighed and smiled down at her. "Good. Continue."

"Denver Langston raped me," Cathy said.

"How?"

"He got me drunk at the bar and took me back to Hallow Ranch where he punched me. Then he held me down and raped me eleven years ago."

"That's when Mason Langston came in?" Tim guessed. She nodded. "What else, Cathy?"

She looked down, and anger flared inside of Moonie. He didn't have time for remorse. He was on a deadline. Without a second thought, he decided to give her what she wanted. As much as he hated doing it, he reached out, gripped her chin and kissed her.

"Do you want Caleb to have a good life? Go to college? See the world?" Tim asked, struggling to be gentle.

Cathy nodded. "Yes."

"Then what else happened? What are you going to say to the police if Denver doesn't comply tomorrow?" he pressed.

"That Denver forced me to have his child so he could have an heir for Hallow Ranch," she said, her voice unsteady. "Mason left me in the dust to chase his dream and doesn't want anything to do with the ranch. That was Denver's plan all along. He wanted his child to have the ranch, not Mason."

A cruel, wicked smile broke out over Tim Moonie's face. "That's right." He stood and unzipped his suit pants, then jerked his chin to the table. "Go."

The woman got up and bent over the table. Tim Moonie put on a rubber and proceeded to fuck her like a back-alley whore, knowing damn well that when this was all over, her and her son would be in the ground.

Chapter Twenty-Five

Valerie

A rough hand touched my cheek, and my eyes fluttered open to find my dark cowboy standing over me. Night still blanketed the sky outside of the bedroom window. I looked up and suddenly smoke was around me. Even in the shadows, Denver's eyes stood out.

"Is everything alright?" I asked, my voice thick with sleep.

He had his hat and jacket on, and with the darkness covering him, he looked terrifying. I sat up on my elbows and then his hand snapped to the back of my neck, holding me in place as his gray eyes held mine.

"Enchantress," he growled as he bent down. His lips were on mine, hot and rough, causing my belly to flip and my core to clench. After a moment, he tried to pull away, but I wasn't done. I needed more of him. My arms wrapped around his neck and a low rumble came from him, causing my legs to squeeze together.

He kissed me back, his tongue forcing my mouth open and clashing with mine.

"Gotta get to work, baby," he said, pulling away.

"A little more," I rasped, kissing him again.

When he pulled away once more, I was panting and aroused. His eyes dropped to my chest, and even in the dim light, I knew they were dilated. Denver brought his other hand to me, cupping the side of my right breast, his thumb sliding over the silk of my nightie directly over my nipple.

It was one swipe, but it felt like I'd just been touched by fire. He did it again and I let out a gasp.

"Wanted to wake you up earlier and fuck you until you couldn't walk," he murmured. I arched into his touch as the hand on the back of my neck snaked into my hair.

"A beauty like you in my fucking bed, coming on my cock...that's a perfect morning for a cowboy like me."

"Denver."

"Christ," he bit out, then kissed me again. Lips, tongue, teeth clashed together, and soon, the blanket was ripped from my body, and I was in his lap. There was no hesitation with me now that I knew he was attracted to me. He didn't give a shit about my size or height. *He wanted me.*

It felt damn good to finally be wanted and desired.

Live, Valerie.

My hips ground down against his Wranglers, my inner thighs scraping against the rough fabric. My fingers went into his hair and then his hat was gone. I grabbed a fistful in each hand and tugged. When he groaned, I did it again, taking his lower lip between my teeth and sucking. His hands snapped to my hips, urging me to move against him. My body did as he commanded, grinding against his rigid length. We were like teenagers in those cheesy movies I used to always watch.

"God dammit," he hissed as he broke away from me.

My core was throbbing and damp. Every time I moved up and down his crotch, it got wetter. My thong was soaked, and there wasn't a doubt in my mind that he could feel it.

"Baby, am I going to go down to the bunkhouse with a wet spot on my crotch?" he asked in a teasing tone but didn't slow me down.

The friction felt too good.

My head fell back, and I pressed down hard, desperate for the release building up inside me. A part of me wanted to be embarrassed for how turned on I was and how quickly I was going to reach my peak. The other part of me didn't give a damn.

I just wanted to feel pleasure. Pleasure that my cowboy wanted to *give me.*

"That's it," he whispered. "Rub that pussy on me. Make yourself feel good."

"Oh," I moaned. He lifted his hips, and my breath escaped me. I needed more. *More.* I was nearly there. "More, please. More."

One of his hands left my hip and then my nightie was pulled down. My breasts fell free, and my nipples hardened even more as the cool air hit them. He pinched my left nipple, rolling it between his fingers. Pleasure zapped through me, causing my hands to fall to his shoulders.

"Look at you, Valerie. Look at how *desperate* you are, humping me when I've barely touched you."

I whimpered, my clit brushing against the fabric of my damp panties, his jean clad erection right underneath.

"You gonna come apart on my jeans?" he taunted, his voice rough. He pinched my nipple again before taking my breast in his hand. "Answer me."

"Yes, Smoke," I moaned, looking at him. He gripped my jaw, and his other hand went under my nightie.

"You wanna know why that is? Why you're so fucking desperate for me?"

I nodded, panting. His fingers yanked my thong back, causing the fabric to press against my clit in the most delicious way. He brought my face an inch from mine, his eyes holding me captive. His smoke was everywhere now, and I wanted to get lost in it. My hips were moving faster, chasing my climax as he held my thong tight. My body was shaking, anticipating the pleasure.

"Because you are a good little *slut*," he growled.

Good little slut.

Stars filled my vision as my head fell back, my body quaking. I cried out, his palm covering my mouth just in time. He kept moving me through my orgasm, not letting up. My legs were shaking by the time I was done, finally on my way back down to Earth, my forehead against Denver's, his lips on mine.

He kissed me like I was the air he needed to breathe.

My cowboy pulled away, nostrils flared and there was a flame within the smoke of his eyes. "God damn, Val."

I didn't have the energy to reply. The next thing I felt was my head hitting the pillow and my mind drifting to dreams of Hallow Ranch and my mom's pumpkins planted by the barn.

When my eyes finally opened again, the sun was out.

My body hummed, feeling at ease for the first time in years. I felt my lips stretch into a wide smile. I rolled over, throwing my arm across the empty side where Denver slept last night.

After Caleb had successfully "cockblocked" his father, we went downstairs to find him digging for ice cream in the freezer. He then proceeded to tell us that he didn't want to stay in the bunk house that night because, "Jigs didn't take his farting medication."

Around eleven, Denver sent Caleb to bed. I was already in the spare bedroom getting myself ready for bed when he came and leaned against the doorframe, watching me.

"What do you think you're doing?" he asked.

I stared at him, nightie in hand.

"My bed is the only one you belong in, Val."

With a smile still on my face, I got out of bed and headed to his bathroom. My shower bag was there, but my toothbrush and toothpaste were on the counter. Right beside his. My heart skipped a beat. I washed my face, brushed my teeth and got ready for the day.

It was only eight in the morning, and I wondered if Caleb was up yet. I pulled my hair into a high ponytail and went to my bags. Denver had placed them on the chair in the corner. My heart skipped another beat. I was running out of clothes to wear. When I originally packed for this trip, I only packed for two weeks. I never expected to say over a month and half.

Perhaps forever.

Last night, when we were in bed, Denver didn't touch me again. It was only after I reached out and put my hand on his chest in the dark that his arm shot out. He pulled me to him, and I rested my cheek on his chest. That's how we stayed for a long time, our thoughts drowning us. That's how I fell asleep.

I didn't get to see Denver shirtless, but I got to feel him. The muscles under his hot skin, the hair on his chest...

"Stop it, Val," I muttered, pulling out the only pair of jeans I'd packed. I'd slipped those on and one of the more casual blouses in the bag. This one was a soft cream, with capped shoulders, and tiny pink polka dots. I looked at my shoes and decided against them. The sun was shining, and summer was here. If I needed them, they would be here.

"Caleb?" I called as I came out of the bedroom. I looked across the hall into the little boy's room. His bed was made. He must already be gone.

Once I got into the kitchen, I found a note on the island.

V,

Caleb's going fishing with a friend today. He should be back by three. I'll be around the house for lunch. Coffee is already brewed. Enjoy.

Here's my number, just in case you need to call me.
D.

I smiled at the note, studying his handwriting for a moment. Denver was nothing if not straightforward. Ten minutes later, I had a cup of coffee in hand, my laptop fired up and my butt in a stool. I called my mom first, before diving into more Moonie research.

"Good morning, Mom," I chirped.

"Morning, darling," she said. She sounded tired today, so I checked the date. It was a chemo day.

"How are you feeling?" I asked, ignoring the regret pooling in my stomach. Here I was waking up happy and she was going to get chemo.

"I'm alright," she sighed. "I had the weirdest dream last night."

"About what?" I asked before taking a sip of my coffee. *Damn, this was good*. Liquid gold from the heavens above.

"You, darling. In a forest."

This gave me pause.

"A forest?" My eyes drifted to the kitchen window, focusing on the lush green at the foot of the mountains beyond the barn.

"Yes, you were running through it," she explained.

"That's it?" I wondered, raising a brow as I clicked over to MoonieP ipeline.com on my laptop.

"Yeah," she said, coughing.

I winced and listened to her struggling to breathe over a thousand miles away. Guilt washed over me. I shouldn't be here. I shouldn't be here, sitting in a gorgeous kitchen, drinking amazing coffee, and smiling at a handwritten note from a cowboy who makes me see stars.

I should be home, taking care of my mom.

I owed her that much, after everything that she'd done for me. She was all that I had. My only friend. My only family.

If I lost her, what I would have? An empty house full of memories that would only bring me pain.

"I'm coming home," I declared, ignoring my heart's cries.

"You will do no such thing, Valerie Cross," Mom snapped, her voice sounding stronger than before. I knew this game. She was putting up a front for me.

"You are getting chemo and I—"

"My daughter is finally *living*. After over two and a half decades, my baby girl is finally experiencing some of that life I promised her when she was in my womb."

I felt my eyes sting and I dropped my head, inhaling an unsteady breath. "Mom," I begged.

"You come home, I'm changing the locks," she threatened. I tried to say something but the emotion clawing up my throat was too painful. She continued, "Its chemo day, darling. I'm always a bit weaker these days, but you know Jackie will be here. That goofy woman lifts my spirits."

"That's my job," I muttered, feeling like a failure.

"Last night, you lifted my spirits, Valerie. You were laughing in the presence of that man. God, I wish I could've seen the way he was looking at you. The evidence was all over his handsome face when he took over the phone."

"You think he looks at me a certain way?"

"He'd be a fool not to," she whispered. "Now, before I go to my appointment, tell me what you've dug up about that vile man."

With that, I got to work, going over my notes from yesterday with Mom until she had to leave. Jackie said hi and that I needed to find her a cowboy. I told her she was crazy.

By the time lunch rolled around, I had my legal pad out, and it was filled with notes. Tim Moonie was not a good man, by any means. The Moonie family were based out of Houston, Texas. Tim Moonie was the star sports player at his high school, bringing in multiple championship trophies. That was the shiny glitter that covered up his darkness. After digging in the local newspapers, I found an article that made my skin crawl.

Tim Moonie and a few friends hazed a freshman on the football team. The boy was rushed to the hospital after being force-fed bleach and being beaten within an inch of his life. I tried to get into the court records, but they were sealed. Moonie and his friends got away with it, and that boy's trauma was buried. That was over twenty years ago.

My stomach growled, reminding me I haven't eaten today. I hopped off the stool and made my way to the fridge. Maybe I could make Denver lunch. He refused to let me help him with dinner, but the truth was, I enjoyed cooking. Baking more so. My eyes wandered to the green apples sitting in the basket on the far side of the counter.

An apple pie would be good...

All thoughts of food and making it vanished when I heard a car door slam outside. My blood went cold. "Moonie," I whispered. I rushed to the island and swiped my phone, ready to call for Denver when I heard it.

A woman's voice.

"Caleb! Caleb, get out here right now!"

My feet were moving and when I pulled the front door open, there was a blonde woman at the bottom of the porch steps. She was wearing cutoff blue jean shorts, black strappy heels, and a black ripped tank. Her makeup was caked on, and her hair was poorly curled.

"Who the fuck are you?" she sneered; her brown eyes glared up at me.

"I think I should be asking you that, ma'am. Can I help you?" I asked, my voice firm. I stepped up to the edge of the porch and put my hands in the back pockets of my jeans.

She studied me for a moment, and then a cruel smile spread across her face. "He fucking you? Is that it?"

I flinched at her words but covered it up well. She didn't notice, but she didn't stop, either.

"You know, the last woman he had in his bed was me," she boasted.

"You aren't in it anymore," I returned coolly.

She didn't like that. The strange woman took a step towards me, baring her teeth. "Where is my son?"

"With his father," I snapped.

"I don't have time for this," she muttered. I watched as she turned her back to me. She had her cellphone to her ear, shifting back and forth on her feet.

She was nervous.

That made the hair on the back of my neck stand up.

"Where are you?" she barked. I waited. "I need to talk to you." Another pause. "No, I will not come down to the barn. I'm in heels!" Silence. "Yeah, now!"

The woman turned to me, sporting a nasty glare. "I'll just wait on the porch for him," she huffed, brushing her hair over her shoulder.

Alarm bells went off in my head. "No, you won't," I said.

"Excuse me?" she gasped, her brown eyes going wide for a second before they narrowed. "Bitch, you don't have any idea who you're dealing with."

My spine straightened. I took a step down.

"Why don't you come show me then?"

I was on the steps, but even if I wasn't, I knew that I would tower over her. I learned how to fight when I was kid, running around the streets in my neighborhood away from the older kids. Mom taught me how to defend myself, and the woman in front of me was shouting for Caleb. The second I looked at her, I knew I didn't want that little boy anywhere near her.

She smelled like cigarettes and cheap Vodka.

If this was Caleb's mother...

"Cathy!"

Both of our heads snapped to the tall, dark, broad-shouldered cowboy in the black hat stalking toward the house. It didn't take him long to reach us, but Cathy met him halfway, putting her hands on her hips as she yelled at him. I sucked in a breath as Denver's body went tight, from his shoulders to his jaw, all the way to his boots.

She just said something that put my cowboy on alert.

He stepped closer to her, his nostrils flaring under the brim of his hat. His lips were moving, but I couldn't hear what he was saying. She pointed a finger in his face, yapping at him like a dog. Anger ignited inside me, and I found myself grinding my teeth.

Did she just put her finger in his face?

My feet were moving again, and once I got close, I heard, "If you don't do this, I'll go to the police."

Denver huffed a harsh laugh. It was menacing and sent a chill down my back. "You are the biggest whore in the county, Cathy. You've sucked off half the police department and tried to fuck the other half. When Sheriff Bowan caught a whiff of your rancid cunt, he chased you off. So, you tell me, *sweetheart*, who in the hell is gonna believe that pile of bullshit?"

In a flash, she shot her palm out, ready to slap him. He caught her wrist with a snarl. Slowly, he turned his head to look at her hand and then turned it again to look at her face. "You're done, Cathy."

All at once, her façade dropped, and her body sagged. "No, Denver, please. Denver—"

"Get the fuck off my property. I'll see you in court," he barked.

"Denver—"

"OFF OF MY FUCKING PROPERTY!" he screamed in her face, causing me to jump. His voice echoed all around us, lingering in the air.

She ran. The woman ran away from him, trembling in fear. I watched as her car sped down the drive. A hand gripped my jaw, and my head was twisted. Angry gray eyes met mine and his presence overwhelmed me.

"She say what she was here for?" he clipped.

"She was calling for Caleb."

He turned his head, his eyes on the pasture. "Denver?"

"Moonie got to her."

What?

What did he just say?

"What?"

"Moonie couldn't get you to convince me, so he found Cathy," he hissed. He was still holding my jaw in his big hand. I wrapped a hand around his wrist, just in case he was about to go to the place he went yesterday.

"Hon—"

His lips were on mine in the next second and his arms were around me, caging me to him. By the time he pulled away, I was breathless and clinging to him. "Tim Moonie is playing dirty, City Girl," he growled.

City Girl.

He hadn't called me that in what seemed like forever. My stomach twisted. "Denver, what do you mean?"

"He's using Cathy to get to me. The only thing that bitch can use against me is—"

"—Caleb," I gasped. My fingers wrapped around the back of his neck. "Denver, what did she say?"

A shadow fell over his features as he said, "She is going to accuse me of rape."

My brow furrowed and I felt my spine straighten again. "That fucking bitch," I snapped.

His eyebrows lifted in surprise. "You aren't going to ask—"

"You saved me from being assaulted, Smoke. You aren't that kind of man," I said, my voice getting softer with each word. He stared at me for a beat.

"My momma would've loved you," he said, his voice gentle now.

My heart leaped. My stomach sank.

Where was his mom? I knew his father passed away, but I knew nothing about his mother.

"Valerie," he called. I shook my head, clearing the fog as I looked up at him.

"Yes?"

"I'm going to need your help."

My hand dropped to his chest, directly over his heart. "You have it."

Chapter Twenty-Six

Denver

Two days after my son's mother tried to slap me, I was standing at her door, pounding on it with my fist. "Open this fucking door, Cathy!" I boomed.

No answer. Just before I was about to kick the door in, a person approached me from behind.

"Mr. Langston."

I turned to find Cathy's landlord coming to me with a set of keys. I nodded to him. "Thank you so much. Caleb needs his backpack for his summer studies," I lied through my teeth.

The old man nodded. "That boy is a smart one, bless him. Sorry it took me a second to find my keys," he grumbled, stepping past me to open her door. "You know, I was worried about the old girl. She hasn't been home for the last few days."

I sighed through my nose.

Probably sucking Moonie's cock.

That woman was always after something when it came to men. Took me half a second after Mason busted open my door with her in my bed over a decade ago, to see she never loved him. She was using my brother for his potential fame, but I knew he loved her. I saw it in his eyes.

He loved that woman with everything he had.

"Appreciate it," I muttered as I stepped through her door. The first thing I noticed was the smell. Stale smoke, alcohol, and sex. My upper lip curled. The second thing I noticed was the mess.

Her apartment was small. There was a large open concept living room/kitchen area that went straight back. There was the master bedroom to the left and then Caleb's room on the right. At one point, this place was actually decent. Now it was littered with empty bottles, trash, cigarette buds, and clothes.

I shook my head, taking everything in.

"Oh my," the old man breathed, stepping in beside me. I adjusted my hat and turned to him.

"If you could give me just a moment, I need to document this for my lawyer."

He nodded. "Keep that boy out of here."

Fucking Christ, what was I thinking sending him to his mom's? Court custody agreements be damned. This was no place for a child to grow up.

After he shut the door behind me, I took a few photos of the space. My gut turned at the thought of what I was going to find in her room, so I went to Caleb's first. The door was closed, and when I pushed it open, I wasn't surprised.

It was tidy. His bed was made, the few toys he had here put away, and it even smelled alright. I snapped a photo and made my way to the closet. Pulling out the duffle on the top shelf, I threw things inside. After a few minutes, his belongings were packed.

Never again, bud. Never again.

I knew Cathy had a problem with alcohol, but it had never been this bad. Caleb probably didn't say anything because she manipulated his young mind. A part of me wanted to get her some help, but the monster inside of me didn't give a damn. She wasn't the mother Caleb deserved.

My mind drifted to the enchanting woman on my ranch.

For the last two days, Valerie had been digging up old dirt on Moonie. However, there wasn't much. She showed me an article of him hazing a kid in high school. The kid ended up in the hospital and Moonie got away with it because of the cash in his father's wallet. There was nothing we could go on, but one thing was certain…Moonie had damn good lawyers. If he was using Cathy and trying to play the "rape" card, there wasn't a doubt in my mind he had cops in his pocket.

Just because Hayden PD wouldn't believe Cathy doesn't mean that a more…*willing* department would. Chase told me that he put a man on Moonie so he could keep an eye on him. He told me that the fucker was staying in the hotel, he rarely leaves. When he does, it's to go to Tinkles.

He was playing with fire, and I feared we were the ones about to get burned.

Valerie also told me Moonie doesn't skimp when it comes to obtaining land. He will pay what he promised, and he does it *quickly*. She told me that the sooner the owners were off the land the better. Currently, there was one pipeline being worked on in Texas. There was another project that starting in September in Nevada, one that he wants to run under my land.

I crossed the apartment and pushed open Cathy's bedroom door. To my surprise, there was a man in the bed. Passed out. My hand went to my gun as I walked up to the low set bed. The man was alive—thank fuck for that. His arm was hanging off the side and he was buck ass naked. I looked to the ceiling, pinching the bridge of my nose.

I should pray for patience, but I'm not patient enough for that shit.

"Yo!" I kicked the mattress. The fucker didn't wake up. Biting off a curse, I scanned the bed and tables beside it. My eyes landed on a bottle of melatonin—an empty bottle of melatonin. I took a picture of that, too, before sending it over to Diana.

She responded immediately. **Got it.**

Forgetting about the fucker in her bed, I made my way through her room, looking for anything—*something*. My eyes caught a blue folder sticking out underneath a pile of laundry on her desk.

Don't even know why she has a fucking desk. The bitch doesn't do shit.

I yanked the folder out and scanned the contents. My spine stiffened as my brain soaked in the words. My father's words echoed in my head, the promise that Mason and I made him ringing in my ears. There was a pain in my chest, sharp and precise. That fucking bitch.

That.

Fucking.

Bitch.

This was a contract. Without looking back, I grabbed Caleb's stuff and left the apartment.

On the way back to the ranch, I made a phone call.

Two more days passed.

Valerie and I were on the couch, watching a movie with Caleb when it happened. There was a knock on the door. I heard the car driving up, but I didn't want to disturb my boy, who was currently resting his head on my thigh.

The last two days had been a dream, aside from the Moonie bullshit.

My enchantress was in my bed and even though we hadn't done anything since she came apart on my jeans, she was still in my arms at night. I was trying to keep my distance from her—*sexually*. I didn't want to move too fast, because I was already spinning out of control when it came to her. I needed to show some restraint, and right now, I couldn't be more thankful for my cockblock of a son. Sex would push me over the edge of insanity. I never knew it could be like this. When I was younger, I'd hoped. I hoped that someday there would be a woman as beautiful, kind, and fierce as Valerie in my bed.

That hope died years ago.

This woman, who currently had her hand on my chest, her fingers curled into my t-shirt as Frodo ran through the woods on the screen, had reinstalled that hope inside of me. She told me she would give me a week. We both knew that was bullshit. She was going to give me more than that.

She was going to give me her life and that scared the shit out of me.

knock, knock

"Who's that, Dad?" Caleb asked, sounding sleepy.

I ruffled his dark hair. "Your old man has to do some work, okay? It's getting late; why don't you get ready for bed?"

He sat up, rubbing his eye with his fist. "Okay," he grumbled. Valerie stood and opened her arms.

My heart damn near stopped at the sight. She was dressed in jeans and one of my old t-shirts—it looked damn good on her. She could go out tomorrow, buy the most expensive dress on the rack and it still wouldn't compare to my shirt on her body.

"Goodnight, sweetheart," she whispered, pulling him in for a hug. Her hand was on the back of his head, her thumb swiping back and forth over his hair. I watched as my son tightened his arms around her waist.

"Goodnight, Val."

There was a lump forming in my throat, and my skin felt tight.

My boy ran upstairs, and my woman stared up after him. After a moment, she cleared her throat and said, "Okay, I'll give you two a minute." She turned away and, in a flash, my hand was around her wrist, guiding her back to face me.

"You're a part of this now, Val. I want you with me," I declared softly, my thumb stroking her skin.

Her green eyes bounced back and forth between mine as her lips parted at my declaration. I gave her a gentle tug, pulling her to my body. Her breasts were pressed against me, her arms snaked around my waist. I brushed the lock of her hair back. "You good with that?" I murmured, my eyes dropping to her lips.

She nodded. I pressed a kiss to her lips and then spun her to face the door. "Let's get this shit over with." Valerie headed into the dining room, and I went to the door. After putting my hat on and checking my pistol, I opened the door, shoving the gun in the waistband of my jeans.

Joseph Grayson was standing on my porch, his back to me as he leaned against the post, staring out into the night.

"Evening," I greeted.

He didn't move as he replied, "Mr. Langston."

I hired the man two days ago after leaving Cathy's apartment.

Diana, my lawyer, had come over immediately to look over at the contract I'd found. It was a binding and valid contract, no bullshit, which meant that since Cathy's dumb ass decided to sign it, she has no choice but to do everything Mr. Moonie tells her to. If she didn't, he would collect all of her assets. Not that there was much left anyways.

My lawyer proceeded to tell me that normal people wouldn't get away with contracts like this, but Mr. Moonie is far from normal. Things were heating up and I need Hallow Ranch to be defended—by everyone.

Which led me to calling the bounty hunter standing on my porch.

Mags recommended me to him a long time ago. A few years back, there was a harsh winter, and I needed my brother. As usual, he never answered or cared. My friend told me that he knew a guy who would bring him home, if need be. I never made the call. Until two days ago.

"Come on in."

The man turned then, and I got a good look at him. There was a scar on the right side of his face, starting at his temple and disappearing into his scruff. He was dressed in back cargo pants, and a T-shirt. There was a gun strapped to his waist and a bag sitting by his black combat boots.

I stuck my hand out. "Thank you for coming out."

He picked up his bag and swung it over his shoulder. "I was in the neighborhood," he mused, shaking my hand. "Good to meet you."

Three minutes later, we were walking into the dining room. Valerie was cradling a cup of coffee in her hands, staring out the window.

"Valerie," I called softly. "This is Joseph Grayson."

She stood to greet us, stopping to set her cup on the table first. My woman held out her hand to Mr. Grayson. "Hi, I'm Valerie. Thank you so much for coming," she greeted.

I looked to the man, who was staring at her. Tension settled over us. Mags had warned me about this. Grayson had a past, like all men do, but his involved a woman. A woman nastier and meaner than Cathy. A woman who fucked him up so badly, that after getting out of the military, he never went home.

After a moment, he blinked and took her hand. "Yes, of course."

My eyes swung to hers and I saw the hesitancy in them. She cleared her throat, hoping to break his stare. He did, muttering an apology to her. I gestured for him to take a seat and put my hand on the small of Val's back. My lips found her ear as I walked her to her seat around the table. "You alright?"

She nodded, giving me a slight smile.

After taking my seat at the head of table, in my father's chair, I turned to Mr. Grayson. "I wanted to thank you again—" Mr. Langston, you are paying me. There is no need to thank me. You just give me the target and I'll do my job," he said, cutting the bullshit. I felt a smirk wanting to form on my lips, but I suppressed it. We were going to get along just fine.

"I need you to find my brother," I stated.

He stared at me, his left brow slowly raising. "Mason Langston?"

"Yes."

He braced his tattooed forearms on the table, and I took a moment to look at them. They were two snakes starting at his wrists and wrapping up each arm, disappearing under his sleeves. The one on his left was black and the one on his right was dark red. My eyes snapped up to his eyes.

"I wasn't aware he was missing," he said incredulously.

"He isn't," I sighed, sitting back in my father's chair. Memories of happier times-simpler times flashed before my eyes. Memories of Mason and I fighting, throwing food at each other while Pop listened to Momma. Memories of Christmas dinner and birthdays. Laughter once filled this room and bounced off these walls. Now this room was rarely used.

I planned on changing that.

"Your brother is in Little Rock this weekend," the bounty hunter deadpanned, his lips turning down. I knew the schedule. I knew where he would be, but that wasn't the issue.

I felt the muscle in my cheek tick. This was going to be harder than I thought. Even though Valerie told me about her past, I had yet to tell her about mine.

"Mason is a free spirit. He doesn't travel with the rodeo. He just shows up when it's his time to ride," I explained truthfully. Mason was never one to follow orders. For the longest time, he couldn't keep a fucking manager. Now, after *years*, he had a decent manager and a PR team. However, none of those fuckers keep tabs on him when he wasn't on the back of a bull.

Grayson nodded and pulled out his laptop. "So, you want me to find him and bring him back here?"

I shook my head. "No. I want you find him and give him a message."

The bounty hunter froze and shot his gaze to me. I could feel my Enchantress' eyes on me too, but I couldn't look at her right now. If I did, I would give in to her. I would tell her everything right here and now, Joseph Grayson be damned.

I couldn't.

I feared that when I did, when I told her about the monster inside of me, she would run. I would have to see her back again as she walked away from me. I would be alone again.

She isn't leaving you, my sweet boy. She will understand.

My jaw tightened at the sound of Momma's voice in my head. She had been speaking to me more in the last few weeks than she had since her passing, and I knew deep in my gut that it was because of the woman next to me.

"What message?" he pressed.

"Tell him to come home," I growled, not meaning to.

Grayson sighed, clearly frustrated. "You aren't telling me everything."

"Nope."

He stood up and walked to the window, his brown eyes looking at one of the most precious things in my life. The one thing I vowed to protect. I couldn't lose it. Mason signed over his rights to the ranch, telling his lawyer he didn't want or need Hallow Ranch's money. He was still getting it, whether he liked it or not. There was a bank account waiting for him. Even his sponsor was Hallow Ranch.

"Smoke," Valerie whispered. She reached over and put her hand on my thigh under the table. My head slowly turned to hers to find her eyes pleading. Without a second thought, my hand enclosed around hers, giving it a squeeze.

Before I could say something, the man by the window cut me off. "Before I take on new clients, I like to have all the facts, Mr. Langston. I don't like being left in the dark," he said, an edge to his voice now. "You're paying me a shit ton of money to find your brother and give him *a message.* That's not what I do. I am not a messenger." Joseph's voice was angry now, and I could see the glint of distrust in his eyes.

"My brother and I aren't on speaking terms," I explained, through clenched teeth.

"Why is that?" he inquired, coming to take his seat again. This time, he leaned back, pushing the chair out a bit so he could cross an ankle over his knee.

Great, it's fucking therapy.

"We had a falling out years ago," I admitted, turning Valerie's hand up so I could entwine my fingers with hers. "I haven't spoken one word to my brother in over a decade, Mr. Grayson. Could I get his phone number? Yes. Would he answer? Hell, no. He didn't answer me years ago, and he sure as fuck ain't gonna answer me now. I don't blame him, but I need him to come home."

He studied us for a moment, his brown eyes looking to Valerie for another moment. I get she was stunning, but if he kept his eyes on her for a second longer than I'm comfortable with, his ass would be on the ground.

"Because of Moonie Pipelines," he guessed. My body went on alert as a cocky smirk formed on his lips. "I did some digging of my own."

"If you did, then why in the hell did you just throw a hissy fit?" Valerie spat.

Hissy fit?

Did this woman just say hissy fit?

He smiled at her, chuckling a bit. "Never go into a man's home without knowing his enemies, Ms. Cross." *He knew her fucking last name.*

"You looked into her?" I hissed.

"I look into everyone. I gathered all the facts I could. Just because I have the facts doesn't mean they passed my test," he explained. "You need your brother home to take down Moonie. I just needed to know why you couldn't do it yourself and I need to know why a former employee is in your house, holding your hand under the table." He jerked his thumb at her.

"I'm here in this house because I want to be. You're correct, Mr. Grayson, I am a former employee of Moonie Pipelines. I was hired, I did the work, and he fired me."

"Why did he fire you?" he asked coolly, his eyes never leaving hers.

"I refused to sell," I said, my voice low.

"And you worked for him because of the outstanding medical bills," he returned to Valerie.

She flinched. "That is none of your god damn business," she snapped.

Slowly, he unfolded his legs and leaned against the table. "Babe, I'm the best for reason," he implied. "You want to know why that is? I do my homework. Your mom has lung cancer, you work to pay the bills. There is no shame in that, but if you want me to find Mason, then don't keep shit from me."

"Call her that again, and your ashes will be on my mountain," I threatened, standing up slowly.

His smile grew. "I think I'm going to like you."

"The feeling isn't mutual."

Valerie was still staring at the man, tears shining in her eyes. I swear to fuck, if he makes her cry—

"Can you do it or not, Mr. Grayson?" she asked, keeping her sweet voice level.

"Yes."

"Then get it done," I ordered.

Chapter Twenty-Seven

Valerie

I woke with a start, sitting up and gasping for air.

"It was just a dream. Just a dream," I whispered, running my hands through my hair. My body was slick with sweat, but I was shivering. I took a moment, closing my eyes and taking a deep breath.

You are fine.
Mom is fine.
You are at Hallow Ranch with Denver.
Everything is fine.
Breathe, Val.

When I opened my eyes, I looked to my side, expecting to find my cowboy. The bed was empty, the sheets thrown back, the light in the bathroom off. Had he already gone for the day? My eyes drifted to the clock on his table.

It was only one in the morning; he shouldn't be up this early. Swinging my legs over, I made my way to the window. The bunkhouse was dark, but there was a light on coming from the loft in the barn. Denver's truck was still here, too. The cowboys had their own trucks, of course, but they parked on the other side of the bunkhouse.

Without a second thought, I slipped on the slippers Den brought home from the store the other day. I'd mentioned to him that his floors were cold, and he showed up with those. His thoughtfulness gave me whiplash sometimes. I headed downstairs, pausing by Caleb's rooms first. I could hear his light snoring on the other side, and I smiled to myself.

Once I was out of the house, I shut the front door quietly behind me and headed towards the barn. The night sky was bright with stars, and the moon was high, the eerie light shining down on the barn. The air was warm, a lot warmer than it had been the night I witnessed Denver's dark side. I felt comfortable in the nightie I chose for the night. I was hoping he would touch me again tonight. He hadn't touched me or initiated anything in days. He would kiss me until I was dizzy and then pull away. It worried me.

Once I made it to the barn, I slipped inside quietly, not wanting to disturb the horses. The light was still on in the loft. There was a small staircase to my left that led up, and I swallowed my fear and moved.

I was halfway up when I heard the low rumble. "Enchantress."

My skin prickled and my nipples hardened at the sound. I climbed up the rest of the way, and my body froze at the sight before me. The breath in my lungs stuck, and my heart pounded quicker in my chest. It was borderline erratic.

In the corner of the loft was my dark cowboy, his smoke eyes pinning me in my spot. He was sitting in a wooden chair, his boots crossed at the ankles resting on top of the horse saddle, which was perched on a stool in front of him. Wranglers covered his thick, long legs, a dark Henley stretched across his abdomen and chest. His black hat was pulled down low, only his mouth and bearded jaw visible to me. There was a bottle of whiskey in his right hand, his long fingers wrapped around the neck.

I wasn't scared coming in here, but there was something making its slow climb up my spine, something that teetered the line between fear and excitement.

"What are you doing here?" he asked gruffly.

"Just came to make sure you were okay," I uttered, breathless at the sight of him and the sound of his voice.

A dark chuckle came from him at my words, causing the hairs on the back of my neck to rise. I wanted desperately to move, but I couldn't. My body was frozen—in a trance—as I stared at the man across from me, the man who murdered two people in front of me. No doubt there were more. There had to be.

He threatened that bounty hunter on my behalf tonight.

Call her that again, and your ashes will be on my mountain.

He was killer, a ruthless, unthinking killer who would kill again, without hesitation. I knew this down to my bones. He was dangerous. He was vicious to me during our first few encounters. Nasty. Heartless.

He isn't heartless, Val. He was protecting his home.

My heart and sense of logic seemed to always be butting head these days, more so when it came to Denver Langston.

"You came up here to make sure I was okay," he repeated, his words coming off harsher than I expected. My eyes moved, dropping down to the bottle of whiskey in his lap. "This is the second time you've ventured down here at night, Valerie."

I didn't want to think of that. I wanted to know if he was okay. There were a lot of things said tonight about him and his brother. Ever since that conversation with Lance the other day, I'd been trying to figure out why Mason would've left this place. His home. What kind of man turned his back on his brother?

"Look at me," he ordered. My eyes snapped up to his shadow covered face, and I could see the *smoke*. His intoxicating smoke surrounded me and suddenly the air in the room was stifling. "Why did you run to the barn that night?"

The night of the first murder.

"I—well, I—" I stammered, unsure of how to answer. I knew the answer, my heart knew the answer, but my mind wasn't willing to give it.

"Answer me," he demanded, his voice quiet now. It wasn't a gentle quiet. It was like the calm before the storm, before everything gets obliterated and washed away.

"Denver..." I pleaded. My heart had been in his hands since the second he kissed me. Wasn't that enough proof? He was going to make me say it, expose myself to him in the most intimate way. I couldn't, because once the words were out of my mouth, it was real. It was no longer thoughts or feelings I could shove back down. No, once those words were out in the open, I would be exposed—defenseless.

The clank of a glass bottle brought me out of my thoughts, and I saw he had set it on the floor beside him. The seal wasn't even broken.

He hadn't taken a sip.

My chest moved in time with my short breaths as I watched him drop his legs and lean forward, bracing his huge, tanned forearms on his knees. His hat was still shielding those smoke gray eyes from me, and I wanted, needed, to see them. I needed to see if he had the same emotions taking over my logic coursing through him as well.

"Baby, I need you to tell me why you ran down here—*across gravel, barefoot*—when you heard those gunshots."

"I had to," I croaked, my fingers grabbing for the bottom of my nightie at my thighs, needing something to hold on to. My heart was slamming inside my chest, crying out for him.

"Why?" he pressed more firmly.

Seconds passed as I decided if I could do this, if I had the strength to admit it. Swallowing, I gathered the courage. "I was afraid you were in danger or hurt."

If you asked me what happened next was humanly possible, I couldn't give you an answer. All I knew was that one second, I was at the stairs and he was in the chair, and then the next, my back was against the loft wall and his hand was around my throat as he towered over me. He lifted his hat up and I saw the emotion circling in his eyes.

Rage.

"Smoke," I rasped, the heat of his body surrounding me.

His nostrils flared and he leaned down, getting in my face. "Gutted me, baby. That's what you've done to me," he growled. I stared at him while slowly putting my hands on his arm, the contact going directly to my core. He wasn't squeezing me. My cowboy just had me in a possessive hold. His eyes dropped to my lips.

"Should've never kissed you," he murmured, his voice gravelly.

Pain zinged through my chest at his words. Did he regret it? Is that why he'd been holding back? Because he regrets us—*me?*

"Should've called the sheriff the second you showed up on my property," he continued, studying my face.

I didn't respond. I couldn't.

"Should've left you in the fucking rain, Valerie."

My heart cried out in agony. My chest collapsed and my mind braced for the final blow that he was about to give. This was it. *He ruined me with his kiss, but he would massacre me with his words.*

"Need you to get away from me now, baby," he said with an Earth-shattering gentleness.

"Denver," I rasped, my voice trembling.

"Go back to the house," he ordered, dropping his hand from me and taking a step back. His broad chest heaved as he kept his eyes on me.

"Please, we—"

"You don't get back in that fucking house, I'm going to fuck that gorgeous body until your throat is raw from screaming my name," he growled.

My nipples pebbled again as wetness pooled between my thighs. I didn't move.

Denver shook his head, chuckling again. "This isn't a game, Val. I had to get away from you. I was one second away from pinning you down, spreading your legs, and ruining that sweet cunt."

I whimpered.

"You can't handle a man like me, baby," he sneered, turning his head away from me. "Too delicate. Too wonderful for a man like me."

"Ruin me," I begged as if he hadn't already. He had. Denver Langston ruined me for everyone else.

His head snapped back to me.

He didn't give me a chance to think about it.

He didn't ask me if I was sure.

Those two words set him *off*.

The barrier collapsed, the chains broke, and he was *on me*.

I was against the wall again, his hand at my neck once more and his other hand was snaking under my nightie.

"I'm going to make you regret those words. You're about to see the monster inside of me, Enchantress," he promised, yanking the fabric of my undies. With two vicious tugs they were ripped from me. Keeping eye contact, he shoved them in the pocket of his jeans. I reached to kiss him, but he quickly grabbed my wrists with a single hand.

Then he turned me to face the wall, my hands behind my back.

Yes, *yes*.

He was going to fuck me here. *Finally*.

My cowboy made a clicking noise with his tongue, letting go of my wrists, and then I spun back around to face him. "Keep your eyes on me," he clipped. I did as he asked, panting lightly. He grabbed my wrists together again with one hand and then reached above me. Heavy, thick rope fell down my shoulder, trailing down to my feet. My eyes dropped to look—his hand was at my jaw, gripping it tightly.

"Did I say you could look?" he clipped; his voice hard. His eyes were dilated with frustration and anger, something I should've feared but I didn't. It just turned me on even more. I shook my head as much as he would allow.

"I should shove you down to your knees and fuck your throat for that," he growled. "Eyes. On. Me." I held his eyes as his hands worked between us, binding my wrists together.

"Denver..." I breathed as he tightened the knot.

"Shut the fuck up and be a good girl," he hissed. Another moment passed, and then my hands were bound, and I was at his mercy. Before I could utter a word, I was pulled from the wall and guided to the saddle. He lifted me up with shocking ease and planted me on it, my bare pussy against the cool leather, my toes on floor. Then, he lifted my arms, and I saw the knot of rope at my wrists. The ropes looked like makeshift handcuffs. He lifted my arms high and then when his hands dropped, I was hanging.

Tilting my head back, I let out a small gasp. *I was hanging from a hook.*

Denver's heat was close now, and I dropped my head to find him in my space. My eyes met his, and the second they did, the sound of ripping fabric filled my ears once more. Denver maneuvered the baby blue silk off my body and I was naked before him—*on a saddle, hanging from a hook*. My breasts felt heavier than normal as they rose and fell with each breath. My body was tingling with anticipation.

Gray eyes raked over my body, and heat rose in my cheeks. I watched him as he moved, his boots hitting the wood of the floor, echoing across the space, circling me. His finger touched the tip of my spine, and as he dragged it down slowly, he whispered into my ear, "You going to be a good girl for me tonight?"

I nodded, twisting my wrists in the ropes. His hand snaked into my hair then, yanking my head to the side. I cried out from the force of it and stiffened when his lips found my ear.

"You are going to do exactly as I say, or you will be punished. Am I clear?"

"Yes."

"Yes, what?" he growled.

"Yes, sir."

His free hand came around me then and cupped my breast. My back arched at the feel of his rough skin against mine. "So eager," he purred as he pinched my nipple. A zap of pleasure zinged through my body. I was desperate for more. Anything. I needed *more.*

Damn him for tying my hands. I wanted to touch him.

I wanted to touch the man I was falling in love with.

Shoving that thought out of my mind, I arched into his touch. "Denver, please," I begged as he alternated from one breast to the other.

"No," he answered simply. With one last pinch, he pulled away. He took a seat in his original chair and looked up at me expectantly. "You want to come?"

I nodded, my hair falling around my shoulders.

He tipped his chin to the saddle. "Ride it," he ordered.

"What?" I tried to pull my arms down a bit, but it was no use. I was stuck—*trapped.*

Fear should've been eating me alive, but I wasn't scared.

You trust him.

He stood up again and gripped my chin firmly. "You are going to rub that needy pussy on my saddle until you come, understand?" he growled. "Move those fucking hips. *Now.*"

My body did as he commanded, my hips slowly moving back and forth on the saddle, my clit grinding against the leather. There wasn't much room for me to move, but I wanted to please him.

I wanted to be Denver Langston's good girl.

After a moment, he hummed in approval before taking his seat again. He sat back, spreading his legs to get settled in. My eyes dropped to his crotch, noting the huge erection he was sporting. My mind drifted back to days ago, when I was humping his crotch, the rough fabric of his jeans hitting my clit with every move of my hips. A whimper left me, and I thrust down harder, my clit buzzing with appreciation. I bit my lip, working my hips faster, my eyes never leaving his crotch.

"Keep staring at my dick, baby," he murmured. "Work that cunt for me."

His words seeped into my skin, and more wetness pooled on the leather, the sounds of my pussy echoing throughout the loft. I struggled against the bindings, but I never slowed my hips. If he wanted a show, I would give him a show.

"Filthy girl," he murmured, his voice rough.

I let my head fall back as my eyes closed, imagining I was in his lap right now. "Denver," I mewed.

A growl came from him.

That's it. *I was going to tease him.*

I lifted myself up a bit, arching my back, pressing up on my toes, angling my pussy to rub against the horn. This position wasn't easy, but it felt so *good*. I pretended that the hard length of the saddle horn was Denver's cock. Those smoke grey eyes were on me. I could feel them. I felt powerful in this position. Yes, I was at his mercy, but I was the one giving him a show.

"Fucking hell."

"Yes, yes. Oh, God," I moaned, moving faster. My eyes were still closed but I heard a crash and then I felt him beside me.

"My name isn't God, Enchantress," he growled low in my ear. "You are at *my* mercy. Do you understand?"

"Yes," I panted, my clit humming as my climax began to build. Denver's rough hand cupped one of my breasts again, squeezing it so tight that it hurt. "Ah!"

"You thinking that horn is my dick?"

"Yes, sir," I rasped. He gripped my jaw and twisted my head to face him. My eyes fluttered open, and I was lost in a sea of gray smoke and lust.

"Needy little slut," he hissed as he slapped my breast. Hard.

I cried out as the pain morphed into a form of pleasure that coursed through my body. He slapped the other one with the same force and my hips slowed a bit. "Did I tell you to stop?" he barked.

I shook my head, biting my lip. He glared at me until I began moving again. "That pussy is so desperate to come that you had to angle yourself, because my saddle wasn't good enough for her."

I moaned again, his dirty words urging me on.

"The first time I saw you, I wanted to fuck you. I wanted to scare you, make you run from me," he growled, his teeth nipping at my jaw. "An enchantress running through my forest, desperate for my cock. I wanted to tackle you to the ground, push that tight skirt up and fuck you in the dirt like the little dirty slut you are."

"Smoke!"

"You'd like that wouldn't you? Your cowboy fucking you like an animal and filling that sweet pussy."

Oh, God. My orgasm was nearly there, my pussy soaking the saddle, his dirty words driving me crazy. "Denver, please!"

He slapped my breast again. "Please what?"

"I want to come—*please*!"

"You gonna come on my saddle, Valerie?" he taunted.

"Yes! Please!"

He bent down, his lips grazing over my abused nipple. "Do it," he said, right before taking my nipple into his hot mouth. That was all I needed to be sent over the edge. My back arched, and as I started to cry out, his free hand covered my mouth. My body was moving in a frenzy now, jerking against the saddle, and my eyes closed. I was having an out of body experience, because I didn't notice my arms being brought down.

Then Denver's lips crashed down to mine, his tongue forcing my lips open with a growl. One hand was in my hair and the other was on my ass, kneading my right cheek.

When did I get off the saddle?

I tried to lift my arms but all too soon, he broke the kiss and spun me. My body was bent over the saddle stool, my hands still tied together, hanging in front of me. He kicked my legs open with his boot and I heard him undoing his jeans.

"Denver," I whimpered, knowing what was coming next.

"You want my cock?" he growled.

"More than anything," I rasped.

I felt his fingers rub gently against my clit, then sink down into my entrance. I was soaking wet, I knew. "You aren't ready, baby," he murmured.

"Smoke, fuck me, please," I cried. "You haven't touched me in days. I was going crazy without— Aah!"

The tip of his cock was pushing into me. He was thick—*huge*. I didn't know how big he was or if my body could take him—and I didn't care. I just wanted him inside of me as close as we could be. He worked me slowly, moving in and out bit by bit.

Denver was still being gentle with me, but right now, that's not what I wanted.

I wanted the monster.

With a frustrated growl, I pushed back against him, forcing his cock further.

"Valerie," he growled.

"Fuck me like an animal," I pleaded, my voice hoarse.

Silence.

Then his large hands pinned me down to the saddle by my waist, and he thrusted inside me—*to the hilt*. He was so...*big*. I cried out at the feel of his balls against my clit. My legs began to shake as my body struggled to accommodate him. He pulled out and slammed back into me again, over and over, as he set a steady, *unbearable* pace.

"That's it," he said gruffly as he began to fuck me harder. "Take my cock like the good little slut you are."

"Yes!" I moaned, squeezing my hands together. His hands dropped to my hips so he could hold on and bring me back to meet his thrusts. His power and smoke surrounded us, cloaking us in lust and pleasure. My pussy clenched around him as my ass slammed against his hips with force.

"Fuck," he growled, his fingers digging into my skin. I scrambled and pulled my elbows underneath me, rising up so my nipples could scrape against the wet leather.

I whimpered.

"Your little pussy is squeezing my cock so tight. It's like she wants me to stay," he hummed, his voice rough with lust.

"Don't ever leave," I breathed.

"You want this dick inside you forever, baby? Is that what you want?" He slowed his thrusts as his rough hand reached under me so his fingers could stroke my clit.

"Yes!" My eyes rolled back from pleasure as he played with me, and his cock hit just the right spot inside me with every single thrust. His big body was over me then as he picked up the pace. His beard scraped against my temple as his other hand wrapped around my throat.

"You feel so *fucking* good," he groaned, sending tingles down my spine. He squeezed my throat. "Enchantress, *my enchantress*, and her sweet little pussy."

My heart fluttered. "Denver," I moaned, arching into him.

"You like being at my mercy, don't you?"

I nodded and twisted my head up, our faces inches apart. My eyes held his as his body claimed mine with his forceful, powerful thrusts. He dropped his forehead to mine, his upper lip curled. "Words," he snarled.

"I'm yours, Denver."

He froze, hovering above me, his broad chest pressing into my back. Our labored breaths were the only sounds in the loft as he stayed inside me, the connection searing straight into my soul.

Chapter Twenty-Eight

Denver

I promised that I would show her the monster inside of me, but I found myself struggling. Struggling to be rough with her. A woman like her deserved gentle. Her pussy wasn't ready for me, but she took my cock anyways, begging for it as she bent over my saddle. Hell, I didn't even put on a rubber.

I needed to take her bare. *Nothing between us.*

My spine tingled, needing to come, to fill her up and walk away. That's how this usually went. Fuck 'em and leave. No attachments. I haven't fucked with emotion, ever.

This enchantress' pussy was gripping my cock so tightly, wanting me to stay inside of her. Her cunt was the best I'd ever had. She didn't complain when I tied her up and hung her from the ceiling. She didn't mind me watching her, in fact, it turned her on even more. She put on a show for me and drove me wild, seeing her curvy body hump my saddle while she stared at my crotch.

"I'm yours," she repeated, her soft voice washing over me.

Something snapped inside of me then. Something possessive—*controlling*—that scared the shit out of me. With a growl, I pulled her head back by her hair, my lips finding her ear. "You have no idea what you've just done."

She whimpered, grinding her hips back against me. My cock wept inside of her, wanting to ruin her. I pulled her up, her naked body flush against my fully clothed one. "Finally caught my enchantress," I hissed, walking her backwards, still inside her. In the corner of the loft, there was a pile of hay. I would fuck her there. I pulled out of her cunt, and she whined at the loss of contact. I came around to her front and gripped the back of her neck, forcing her to look up at me.

She was a fucking vision.

Too beautiful for this world.

Her dark hair was a mess, falling in waves around her face. Her green eyes were wide with need, her lips swollen. My cock jumped. "Touch me," I ordered. Her eyes dropped, and then she sucked in a breath. I looked down with her, our eyes on my thick, swollen, cock between us. The tip was an angry red, with pre-cum leaking out, ready to bust.

Valerie's delicate hands wrapped around me, her touch like fucking fire. I brought her forehead to mine, my nostrils flaring. "You see what you to do me?"

She didn't answer. No, she tilted her head up and kissed me. Our lips melded together, tongues clashing as she jerked my cock with her bound hands. My hips moved on their own, thrusting up into her hands. She smiled against me, squeezing the tip of my dick. My hands found her shoulders and I gave her a gentle push. "On your back."

As soon as she was down, I was on her like a mad man, starved for affection. Her thighs were spread as I landed over her. Without wasting another second, I fisted my cock and eased back inside her. She lifted her bound hands and wrapped them around the back of my neck. My lips found hers in the tangle of ecstasy as I slid all the way inside her.

Fucking Valerie Cross was a dream that I never wanted to wake up from.

"Denver!" she cried, pulling away from me. With a growl, I twisted her face away from me to drag my tongue up the column of her neck, picking up speed.

"You're going to take my cock like a good little slut, you hear me?" My voice was gruff, and I was barely hanging on. She was tight, hot, and so fucking *wet*.

"Yes, Smoke. Yes!"

I loved it when she called me that. *Smoke.* I loved the way her pussy spasmed around me when I talked dirty to her even more. "Look at you, spread out on a pile of hay with the sweetest pussy I've ever had," I rasped, leaning up a bit. She was fucking work of art, and I knew I would be under her spell forever. "So, God damn beautiful. It should be a fucking sin."

Her fingers gripped the hair at the base of my neck. Her eyes were hooded as she looked up at me and whispered, "You are beautiful, Denver."

I pulled all the way out and slammed into her. "Was trying to stay away from you, baby. I didn't want to you ruin you."

She shook her head, snaking her hands up the back of my shirt. "Ruin me, Denver."

Fucking hell.

With that, I buried my face in her neck and *fucked*. She hung on, her hands in my hair as she moaned and pleaded for mercy. My hands dropped down to her hips, lifting them so I could fuck her deeper—*harder*. "Fuck, yeah," I grunted, pounding into her harder. "Take it, Val."

"Den," she moaned. Our skin slapped together savagely as I grunted into hers, fucking her like an animal in the hay. Her body started to shake around me and I knew she was close.

"Milk my dick, Enchantress. Make it yours," I growled before biting down on her neck. At my words, her body arched as her nails clawed at my back. A cry left her throat, and I pressed my lips over hers, swallowing it. Her pussy milked my cock so good that my balls tightened, and white spots dotted my vision. My hips moved faster, harder, ruining her for any other man.

"Valerie," I groaned, the sound guttural as I released inside of her. Fear clawed its way deep into my gut and I knew one thing.

I wasn't the one who ruined her.

She ruined me.

"Why Denver?"

"Hm?" I rumbled, my hand on her back pausing.

We were back in bed. Her head was on my chest, her silky hair spread over my shoulder, her breasts pressed against my side, and her long, luscious leg thrown over mine. After the most mind-blowing orgasm of my life, I carried Valerie back to the house, my shirt over her naked body. After getting into the bedroom, I took her into the shower and washed her. Part of the reason was to take care of her, the other part was to make sure that my marks were there.

The fucked-up monster in me enjoyed seeing my bruises on her hips. I wanted to mark every inch of her to let every person know she belonged to me.

There was no going back after tonight.

"Do you know why your parents named you Denver?" she asked softly, her fingers playing with my chest hair.

A surprised and unexpected chuckle left me. My hand resumed trailing up and down her back, the moonlight hitting her skin. "My mom. She was the one who named me. She and Pops had a deal. She would get to name their first child, boy or girl, and he would name all the rest. She wanted the first," I explained.

"Why just the first?"

My brow furrowed in the darkness.

Tell her. Tell her the truth. Let her in.

"My momma struggled to get pregnant. They had two miscarriages before me."

"Oh, that's awful," she whispered, pain in her voice. My throat bobbed.

"She told Pop she wanted the honor of naming the first child who survived. He gave her that. When she named me Denver, according to Pop, the nurses thought she was crazy…"

Valerie remained silent, waiting for me to continue.

"Before my growth spurt in the second grade, I used to get teased a lot about it. Kids thought it was a stupid name. Hell, I even hated it. One day, I was so mad at her over it, I came home and demanded we get it changed to something normal. Like John or Matthew."

The woman in my arms made a sound of distaste. "Absolutely not."

I chuckled again, my body shaking against her slightly.

"I found her in the kitchen, cooking dinner, as usual. That's where she would always be after school and she used to always greet me with a bright smile, like I was greatest thing on Earth…" I trailed off as my chest got tighter.

"My mom looks at me like that," she whispered, her voice shaking slightly.

I nodded. "I told her I wanted to change my name. She told me she would never do it. When I asked her why she gave me an answer I would never forget."

"What's that?"

"The city of Denver is where she met Pop. She said when they met, she was in the darkest part of her life. She didn't go into detail, just told me Denver was the place where she discovered love wasn't a myth. It was real. Denver was her happy place."

"Honey, that's beautiful." I pulled her closer to me.

"I think so, too. Took me a few years to realize it, but when I did, it was too late for me to apologize."

I felt her stiffen beside me. "What happened to them? Your parents?"

A long, unsteady sigh left me. "They're gone, baby. Have been for a long time."

"I'm sorry, Denver." My name on her lips would be a blessing I would always cherish, and it killed me to know that Momma would never get to hear it. She would never get to meet the woman who made me *feel* after being dead inside for so long.

"I'm sorry, too. I'm sorry about your mom, Val."

She was quiet for a moment, and then I heard a sniffle. *Ah, hell.* I rolled us so I was on top and caged her in with my arms. "Fuck, baby. I'm sorry."

"It's okay. I—I promise," she sobbed, bringing her face to her hands. "I just—I'm not ready to lose her."

"No child is ever ready to lose their mother, Val," I softly said. The thought of Cathy came to my mind. I still haven't had the chance to sit down with Caleb to tell him he wouldn't be seeing his mother much anymore. Dread settled on my shoulders. "I was only a couple of years older than Caleb when my mom passed."

Why in the hell did I just say that?

She wiped her cheeks and put her hands on my biceps. Fuck her touch was everything. "Smoke," she whispered.

Part of me knew shouldn't keep talking but here I was yapping like a fucking dog for this woman. I felt like I could tell her anything, confide in her. Something changed between us tonight—aside from the sex. She and I both knew that wasn't just sex.

It was my life finally starting.

My son was a gift from God. I knew this, but eventually, he would have his own life to live. He was my son, but he couldn't be my life. One day, he would be his own man, making his own way in the world, and I would be here.

I wanted this woman with me.

In order for that to happen, she needed to know me, to see me for who I truly was, monster or not. "My mom was murdered, Val."

"Denver," she gasped, her hands cupping either side of my face, her thumbs stroking my rough cheeks. I rolled again, taking her with me. I needed to look up at her while I did this. She read my eyes and straddled me.

Valerie leaned down, her breasts against my chest as she braced her hands on my pillow. My hands went to her waist, holding her close, my thumbs stroking her soft, cherry-scented skin. The moonlight gave me just enough light to see the curves and dips of her face, along with the mesmerizing green of her eyes.

My forest enchantress.

"Momma had her spot on Hallow Ranch. When Pop brought her here for the first time, he gave her a tour of the grounds and took her to a steam about halfway up the mountain. That was her spot. When she was pregnant with Mason, Pop made me go up there with her. He didn't want her alone while she was pregnant. Over the years, she marked the trail, but eventually, Pops and Jigs made a little pathway for her," I explained. "She went there every single day, in the mornings mainly. That's where she liked to pray and thank God for everything we had."

Valerie nodded, her fingers moving through my hair. I needed her touch right now more than I expected. I hadn't talked about this in years. The last time was about five years ago, when I needed my brother to come home and he refused. I ended up drinking a fifth of whiskey and hiking up to Momma's spot. The boys found me a few hours later. The twins were fairly new to the ranch at this point and Beau had only been here about a year. Mags and I were close, but not that close. Jigs was the only one who knew about Momma. I told the boys everything that night. That's when they made a vow to protect Hallow Ranch with everything they had.

"One morning, she left a little earlier than normal. I was twelve at the time and Mason was only eight. She told us she wanted to watch the sunrise. Pops was fine with her going by herself, and she knew the land well..." I trailed off, my voice getting thick as anxiety swarmed over me.

"Honey, look at me."

I found my baby's green eyes and stayed locked in her gaze. "You don't have to tell me if you don't want to," she whispered.

"You need to know what kind of man you just fucked, Valerie," I vowed. Before she could argue, I began again. "Momma was usually back around lunch time, except that day, she wasn't. We didn't think anything of it because—because Momma was a photographer. If something caught her eye, it wasn't unusual for her to photograph it. Pops made her darkroom studio in the room that's now my office."

"That's amazing," she added.

I nodded. The love Pop had for Momma was unlike any other. "Pops and I were in pasture three with the boys, managing the herd. Mason was back at the house, doing chores in the barn. It wasn't until we saw the smoke that we knew something was wrong." My woman grew tense above me, her hand frozen in place on my head. I gave her a squeeze and continued. "There was a forest fire. Normally, we don't mess with them. Mother Nature has a way of cleansing her land and she does that by fire, but only in a drought. It had been raining for a week straight beforehand."

"No," she whispered.

"I don't know all the details. Pop and his men charged up the mountain. A chopper was brought in to dump water on the fire. It was a small one, contained...forest fires are not contained. Ever. Not natural occurring ones anyway. Took a day to find her body—"

"Denver," she rasped, sitting up and covering her mouth. I sat up with her, wrapping my arms around her. I buried my head in her neck.

"It was bison hunters, Valerie. Fucking bison hunters. Bison are a protected species in this part of the country. They roam freely. Momma must've seen the hunters, and they killed her. They wanted it to look like an accident. She was wearing a Hallow Ranch t-shirt. They knew she would report them to the authorities, so they burned her." My body shook as emotions I hadn't felt in years came rushing forth, crashing into me like a wave.

Valerie's arms were around me, holding me. "Honey, oh, honey."

She was trying to comfort me. I didn't deserve her comfort, her touch, her sweetness. I didn't deserve any of it, because I was about to tell her about that day.

The day that I became a monster.

Chapter Twenty-Nine

Valerie

My heart was racing as I held onto my cowboy. This man—*this broken man*—was trembling in my arms. I was in his lap, both of us naked, and his arms were wrapped around me tightly, like if he let go, I wouldn't be here anymore. His beard scratched the skin on my neck as he spoke, his voice gruff and thick with emotion.

"I don't deserve your kindness, Enchantress," he confessed. I put my hand on the back of his head and shook mine.

"Denver, of course you do. I couldn't imagine—"

"Pop got his revenge," he said darkly, his hold on me tightening. "We aren't normal men, baby. We protect our own. We avenge our own. That's just who we are. No law is going to force that."

"You were a child..."

"Two days after they found her body, Pop was mad. Mason was scared shitless, because Mason looks like Momma. Same hair. Same smile. Mase was scared Pop was going to hate him for it. I tried to be...I don't know what I tried to be. Pop and Jigs came to the house one night and said they'd found the hunters. They were still hunting on our land on the other side of the mountain."

I held onto him, my soul tensing in fear waiting for his next words.

"Took us two more days to find them, but we did." His voice was dark now, void of any emotion that he was just showing me. "Pop made me bring Mason."

My stomach twisted and I shut my eyes, leaning my cheek against his head. *No, please God...*

"Jigs and Pop did the work, but Pop wanted us there. Told us to close our eyes, to cover Mase's ears. I closed my eyes, but there was no one to cover my ears..."

"Oh my god," I choked, my body jerking a bit. He pulled back to look at me, his eyes dark.

"Learned how loud a man can scream that night," he murmured.

There were no words. I felt angry. How could a man make his children watch that? How could he—

"I see the judgement in your eyes, Valerie," he rumbled.

I cupped his cheek. "It's not for you. I promise, but your father—"

"He made Mase, and I swear we would protect his ranch with our lives, that Hallow Ranch would always be owned by Langston blood."

I looked out the window, focusing on the tree that stood tall just outside. "Moonie Pipelines never stood a chance, did they?"

"I'm sorry for calling you a bitch," he whispered.

I looked back at him, regret painting his handsome features. My head tilted, wondering why he was thinking about this right now.

"I saw you crying that day. After you left, in that rental car. I watched you through my security system that night," he revealed, pushing my hair back, his gray eyes scanning my face. "Should've hunted you down and apologized." The last part was barely a whisper, meant to stay between us and not to linger in the walls.

"I forgive you."

"I don't deserve your forgiveness, but I am a selfish bastard, so I'm taking it anyways," he growled, wrapping his large hand around the back of my head and pulling me down for kiss.

My lips danced with his slowly and the rest of the world faded away. The past didn't matter, and the future was ours.

Until it wasn't.

"Draco is so stupid," Caleb complained as we sat on the porch together. It was midafternoon, the summer sun giving us a taste of what's to come as it shined down on Hallow Ranch. It was nearly ninety degrees out.

I looked up from my laptop to focus on the dark-haired boy in front of me as I raised a brow. "Hey! Don't talk about Draco like that!"

He gaped at me. "He's the bad guy!"

I lifted my shoulder. "You'll see, but don't talk about my childhood fictional crush like that," I blurted. Caleb's mouth dropped to the ground.

"Draco! Are you serious?"

I nodded and took a sip of my iced coffee. "I had a crush on Batman, too."

He stared at me and then mumbled something about girls being weird as he hopped down from the swing. "I'm going to see if the guys are back." A giggle escaped me as I replied, "Okay, sweetheart. Be safe and drink water. It's hot out today!"

Currently, I was looking up land preservation laws to see if there was a way for Denver to ensure no one could ever build or buy his land from him. However, I was at a dead end.

Mr. Grayson, the bounty hunter who Denver hired said he would be in St. Louis by Friday. That's where the next stop on the PBR tour was taking place. There was nothing nice or light about Joseph Grayson. The man could eat you alive if he wanted to. Curiosity got the best of me, and I looked up Mason Langston. Denver hadn't lied; Mason was the best. Those eight seconds were nothing for him. He would get on the back of the biggest beast there was and hop off it with a charming smile on his handsome face.

His mother's smile.

Part of me wondered if, when Mason closed his eyes that night, if he saw the horrors Denver heard. There was a line crossed last night. Denver shared something painful with me, trusted me with it. Last night, I shared my body with him, gave into him, and he gave into me. Both of us had been through so much, somehow, in the middle of our trials, we found each other.

It felt like fate.

A smile formed on my lips at the thought of my dark cowboy kissing me until I was breathless this morning before he left, how my stomach flipped, my heart fluttered. The sound of tires crunching gravel pulled my eyes away from the screen.

The butterflies swarming in my stomach died quickly at the sight in front of me.

A black SUV was pulling up the drive. I looked to the barn and field to see if there were any cowboys lurking about, and when I found none, I pulled out my phone and shot a text to Denver. I didn't know if he would get it or not. The SUV came to stop at the back of the Denver's truck. I stood slowly, setting my laptop aside. I knew who was in the back seat of that vehicle.

It was Moonie.

The driver came around and opened the door, laughter spilling from the other inside of the cab. Tim Moonie stepped out, wearing his signature navy tailored suit, despite the heat. There was a sinister smile on his face as he stared up at me from behind his shades. "Ms. Cross, how lovely it is to see you again. Though, this is the last place I expected to see you," he drawled.

I stood on the top brick step of the porch and crossed my arms. "He isn't going to sell to you," I called, keeping my voice level. Thank goodness Caleb went down to the barn.

He clicked his tongue. "Let me ask you this, Valerie. Did you start taking his cock while on my payroll? Because if so, I wouldn't have fired you. Never knew a woman like you would…use her talents in that way."

I sneered, "You're a sick son of a bitch, Tim."

He smiled again. "What happened to calling me Mr. Moonie? I rather enjoyed that."

"Get the fuck off this property," I spat, dropping my arms.

The air around us shifted, and Tim Moonie's cold, dead blue eyes were revealed to me as he pulled his shades off. That sinister smile returned. "Talk to me like that again, Valerie. I dare you."

I smirked and took two steps down. "Fuck. You."

He lifted his foot to move towards me, but a voice from the side of the house cut him off. "Move an inch, Moonie. *One inch. I dare you.*"

Denver.

I turned to find my cowboy emerging from the side of the house, Mags and Beau in tow. I looked back to Moonie, who was plastering on a fake smile for the man of the hour. My eyes dropped to Denver's hand, and my stomach tightened. He had a pickaxe in his fist.

My heart fluttered as the dark cowboy charged towards me. He didn't pull me behind him like I thought he would. No, he was the *one who got behind me*, pulling my body flush against his. His scent wrapped around me as I met my ex-employer's eyes. He studied up for a moment, his eyes dropping to the weapon by my thigh and then dismissed it by adjusting his sleeves.

"Mr. Langston, you and I have business to discuss."

"Pretty sure you discussed everything you needed to with Cathy," Denver replied coolly. Beau chewed a piece of gum loudly and put his foot on the front tire of the SUV, leaning over his knee to pull his aviators down a fraction. Mags was standing a few feet from us, his jaw tight. He wasn't wearing sunglasses, but his eyes were shadowed by the brim of his hat.

Tim Moonie's eyes flashed with something that could make a grown man cry. "She's just doing what's best for her son," he assured, dropping his arm.

"Sucking your limp dick ain't doing shit for him," Beau snorted.

Moonie turned to face him. "I'm sorry, how are you relevant to this conversation?" he asked.

Beau's face split into a dazzling smile, his white teeth stark against his tanned skin. "Give me a second and I'll be the man breaking your spine. Then we'll see how relevant I am."

A dark chuckle came from Mags as Denver growled, "That's enough."

"Mr. Langston, I suggest you get your dogs under control—"

He was silenced by Denver's pickaxe flying through the air and piercing the car door an inch away from his thigh. My cowboy didn't wait for a response. "Insult my boys again, Moonie."

Though he tried to conceal it, Tim was scared. His hands were shaking, and his skin seemed a shade paler than before. He looked up from the weapon to the man standing behind me, his eyes wild. "Congratulations, Mr. Langston. You just gave me the fuel I needed."

A chuckle came from the men around me. "I have cameras all over this property, and there isn't a doubt in my mind that you intended to lay a hand on Ms. Cross before I came around that corner," Denver snapped.

"You know nothing! I was just explaining to—"

"Get your slimly, greasy ass off Hallow Ranch. My lawyer will be in touch," my cowboy quipped, shutting Tim up. Mags moved then, walking slowly, power oozing from him as he closed the distance between him and Moonie. Without breaking eye contact, he pulled the axe out of the car door and stepped back. "You folks have a nice day now," Mags said, dismissing them both.

Tim Moonie's dead eyes swept back to me. As he slid his shades back on, a chill went down my spine. "I'll be seeing you real soon."

I didn't know if he was addressing Denver...*or me.*

He was about to shut the door when he called, "Valerie, be sure to tell your mom hello for me."

Mom.

My knees gave out. Strong arms banded around my waist, holding me against a strong chest as a bearded jaw scraped against the side of my face. "I've got you, baby," Smoke said in my ear as the car drove away.

I've got you, baby.

No one has had me in a long time.

I broke then, my face crumbling as I let out strangled, broken cry. My hands braced against Denver's arm as I doubled over, tears streaming down my face as the revelation hit me like a swinging baseball bat to the gut.

"Jesus, Valerie," Denver cursed, his other hand coming up to my front. He spun me in his arms, and immediately, I fisted his T-shirt, burying my face in it. My body shook violently as it let out more emotions I bottled up. My toes curled in the dirt as my body tried folding in on itself, bracing for impact.

The impact was the man holding me.

The impact was the unwavering, staggering, harsh love.

I was in love with Denver Langston.

Strong arms kept me upright as a silent scream came out of me, the ache in my chest intensifying as fear overcame me, perching itself on my shoulders. The tears were never ending, and I held on tighter to the man I loved. Fear would eat away at me for the rest of my days, because of this love.

This was a love I couldn't lose.

If I did, I wouldn't survive it.

Before Denver, there was only my mother. She was all I needed, but over the last few weeks, she's been teaching me to let go. Let go of her. Death is inevitable, and I knew I would lose her. Like everything else, I would bottle it up and go with the motions. That was the plan.

That plan was officially derailed because of my heart. My stupid, stupid heart.

"Valerie."

Smoke.

I lifted my head and was surrounded by him again. Much like last night, he invaded my presence, stealing my ability to breathe. His dark brows were pinched together in concern, his jaw tight under his dark scuff. His rough hand cupped the side of my face, pushing my hair back, taking some tears with it. His gray eyes bounced between mine. "Talk to me," he whispered.

I love you.

I'll always love you, even if you don't love me.

There will never be anyone else for me.

My bottom lip trembled again, and his thumb dropped to it as his throat bobbed. "Your tears have the power to bring me to my knees, Enchantress. Talk to me."

I inhaled an unsteady breath, focusing on the other problem. "He mentioned my mom."

He nodded once, his jaw tightening again. "I know."

I looked down. "I need to go home," I whispered. Maybe that's why my body reacted like that, because I had to go.

"You aren't leaving," he growled, his breath hitting my ear.

"Denver..."

He gripped my chin, forcing me to look up at him when I wanted to look anywhere else. My eyes held his fierce gaze.

"She comes here," he declared.

I flattened my hands on his chest. "Denver, she can't."

"Yes, she can."

"Where will she go for her treatments?" I asked in a panic.

He looked up and over my shoulder. Tipping his chin, he ordered, "Round up the boys. It's time for a meeting."

"On it," Beau replied, and I heard him walk away. I looked to my side. Mags was still standing there, eyes on me.

"Mags."

The man ignored Denver and made his way to us. With each step he took, my stomach dropped a bit more. He stopped two feet from us, his eyes never leaving mine.

"You're family."

My lips parted.

He walked away, brushing past us to head down to the barn. When I looked up at Denver, something flashed in his eyes as he stared at Mags' back. Then, he looked down at me. "Tim Moonie will not harm anyone on Hallow Ranch, and that includes your mother."

Chapter Thirty

Denver

"Now, what's all this about, Denver?"

I was in my office, staring at the painting of Hallow Ranch, holding my phone to my ear. A sigh left me. "Doc, I just need to know if you can do it or not?"

"Son, of course I can."

"I'll have a schedule for you when she arrives," I said into the phone.

"I'll need to verify her insurance and get—"

"The Hallow Ranch will be covering Mrs. Cross' medical bills from here on out."

"Denver..."

"Do it, Doc," I ordered.

A few moments of silence passed between us. Doctor Clide Martin was the resident doctor in Hayden, had been for over thirty years. When Pop went downhill, Doc started coming out to the ranch instead of us driving into town.

"I'll contact her clinic to have her records sent over," he concluded.

"Much appreciated," I muttered, looking away from the painting. After hanging up the phone, I sat there for a moment, processing the afternoon. Diana was on her way. Chase was on his way. The boys were heading back from the barn. Caleb was going to his buddy's tonight for a sleepover. Valerie was on the phone with her mom downstairs.

Tim Moonie crossed a line today, and it took everything in me not to reap his greedy soul right then and there for the way he was looking at Val. I've seen that look in a man's eyes before. That's the same look that was in those two rapists' eyes they night I killed them. Men like that think that they own the Earth. Nothing can own the Earth, not when Mother Nature rules it.

How easy it would've been to kill Moonie and the driver. Their ashes would've been on my mountain and our problems would be over. Unfortunately, Tim Moonie was too big of a man to not be overlooked. He wasn't a small chess piece. He was the fucking king of his pipeline kingdom.

"Denver?"

A sweet voice broke my thoughts, and I looked up to find Val standing at the door, holding her phone to her chest. I took a moment to look at her, trying to process once again how we got here, how this enchantress turned my life upside down. Now, there wasn't anything I wouldn't do for her. If she wanted the moon, I wouldn't stop working until I had it in my hands to give her.

She didn't want the moon, though. My sweet woman just wanted the cure to cancer. I couldn't give that to her, no matter how much it killed me not to have that power.

I could give her the next best thing.

"Plane tickets have been purchased," I informed her, sitting back in my chair, keeping my eyes on her, taking note of how she tried to not let her bottom lip tremble. She was trying to be strong for me. I knew the next words to come out of her mouth before she said them.

"You don't have to—"

"I'll take you over my knee, baby. Stop while you're ahead," I warned, my voice low. This woman had been taking care of everyone around her for so long that she forgot how to be taken care of. I was going to change that.

Her green eyes held mine, a hint of challenge in them. That was fine with me. I didn't mind spanking that perfect ass until she submitted. She looked away for a moment, her eyes drifting to the painting. Appreciation washed over her features. "That's beautiful," she breathed.

My eyes never left her as I whispered, "Yes, you are."

Her eyes darted to me again, flush crawling up her delicate skin. Slowly, I rose from my seat and crossed the room. Grabbing her arm, I pulled her all the way inside, shut the door, and pressed her against it. My hands braced against the wood on either side of her head, caging her in as I dipped and ran my nose along the edge of her jaw. "Gonna take care of you, Val. You're going to learn how to be a good girl and accept that." My voice was lower—rougher.

"But—"

I pressed my body to hers with a growl. "No fucking buts. You are mine. Do you understand me?" My head came up and I gripped her chin. "I take care of what's mine, yeah?"

She didn't say anything, and she didn't have to. Because when she rose on her toes, wrapped her arms around me, and pressed those sweet lips to mine, I knew we were on the same page. I kissed her back, my hand diving into her hair, gripping it at the base of her skull. My tongue touched hers, and fire spread all around us, my skin burning as she let me consume her.

She was all I needed, she was all I ever wanted.

I would kick myself every day for turning her away for weeks. You don't turn away this kind of woman. She was beautiful, strong, and so damn loving. A whimper came from her, and my cock hardened, ready to take her addictive cunt again.

Fuck, but it was all I could think about this morning. When I got out of bed, I left something in there with her, something I was terrified to admit. When this was all over—when the dust settled—I would tell her.

I would tell her every fucking day for the rest of my life.

A knock on the door had me pulling away from her with a low, frustrated growl. She looked up at me in a lust filled daze, her lips swollen and red. My beard had scratched against her skin, leaving a pinkish tint in its wake. *Fuck.*

There was a second bang, but I ignored it as I rubbed my thumb over those lips, my dick begging for mercy in my jeans. "I'm going to fuck that mouth," I growled. "That mouth, that pussy, and that ass is mine."

"Oh," she breathed, her hands coming to my shoulders. My hand dropped to her throat as I leaned down to whisper in her ear.

"Good little sluts get all of their holes fucked," I rumbled, licking the shell of her ear. Her knees buckled and a dark smile spread across my face against her skin. I loved that my filthy mouth turned her on. I loved that she liked being degraded and praised.

"Your cowboys are downstairs," she reminded me, trying to escape.

I dropped my lips to her neck, thrusting my hips to press my erection against her. "Gonna need to have that cunt again soon, baby. Going crazy thinking about it."

"Denver. Your cowboys—"

"I wonder if you would be quiet enough for me to fuck you while they're downstairs…"

She froze.

My hand trailed down and up underneath her dress. She was wearing the blue one today, my favorite. I skimmed my fingers over the apex of her thighs and relished the sound of her breath hitching "My sweet, slutty pussy wet for me right now, Enchantress? Hm?"

"Y-yes," she uttered, breathless.

"You want my cock?"

Her fingers gripped my shoulders tightly, and I could hear her heartbeat. A chuckle left me. She did.

I removed myself from her, adjusting my jeans in the process. Valerie remained plastered against the door, her knees bent, and thighs pushed together. Her nipples were pebbled underneath the fabric of my favorite dress. Her green eyes were dilated—wild. *Fuck.*

I wanted to ruin her. I wanted the mascara she wore running down her face, mixed with her tears as she looked up at me, my cock in her throat. I wanted to spread her ass cheeks and watch while I fucked that little hole, stretching it to fit me and only me.

Jerking my chin to the door, I said gruffly, "Get downstairs before I fuck you against the door."

"Has anyone seen Cathy?"

Chase shook his head. "I'm sending a deputy out to the hotel now. He's going to question Bart."

I looked at Diana, sitting at the other end of the table. She had her tablet and a few files spread out around her, twirling her Apple Pen in her fingers while reading over something.

"Anything?" I pressed. That contract I found in Cathy's apartment had been nagging me.

She looked at me, pushing her black glasses higher on her nose. "He's dirty, Denver. Real dirty. However, Caleb will be protected no matter what. Caleb wasn't a part of that contract. I've spoken to Judge Harway, and we can press charges against Cathy for child neglect. We have the proof—those pictures were more than enough evidence."

A round of grunts came from the boys.

"Can we know what Cathy's contract said?" Lawson asked, tipping his cowboy hat up a bit before crossing his arms. She looked at me for approval. These boys knew the worst parts and the very few good parts. They were family. I gave her a single nod.

"Cathy signed a very *weird* contract, to say the least," Diana began. "My team and I have never seen anything like it. In short, it states Cathy is employed by Tim Moonie, to do whatever he so wishes. Once her duties have been fulfilled, she will receive a one-time payment of one hundred thousand dollars."

Lance, who was sitting across from his brother, scratched his jaw. "Sounds like an escort contract to me."

All eyes went to him.

"What? I watch a show on HBO," he blurted, looking at each of us.

"*Fifty Shades of Grey* bullshit," his brother muttered shaking his head.

"Actually, that makes sense," Valerie stated from my side.

All eyes glued to her.

"When I worked for Moonie pipelines, there wasn't a lot of time I spent in the office. When I did, I tried not to pay attention to the gossip. I was just there to work. But now that I'm hearing this, there is something..." She trailed off for a moment. "Tim Moonie hired escorts often. He was never with the same woman at company events and that's how the rumors started."

Valerie began to tell them about the article she found about him hazing that boy in high school. Diana grimaced; Chase looked pissed.

"My brother is a detective in New York," Chase noted. "Guys like Moonie can get away with anything."

"Isn't he involved with a Mafia case?" Beau asked the sheriff.

"Yeah, the Romano Family. The case was handed over to the FBI a few months back, but Chris still keeps tabs on it. My point is, Moonie is a powerful man, and the green in his pockets makes him that way. He is untouchable when it comes to the law," Chase explained.

"Not to mention his army of company lawyers," Valerie added with a sigh.

"So, the mother of my child signed a free-for-all contract?" I deadpanned, looking at my lawyer. She nodded, disappointment in her eyes. She had been with me since the beginning. The second Cathy had shown me the positive pregnancy test, I went in search for a lawyer. At the time, I didn't trust women, but Diana proved herself to me and Hallow Ranch.

Beau leaned back in his seat, his eyes on Chase. "Moonie was going to raise a hand to Valerie today. Could see it in his eyes."

Chase's gaze swung to Valerie, who was standing beside my chair. I offered her a seat and then my lap. She refused both. She was nervous, and I could hear her counting underneath her breath from time to time.

"That true?" the sheriff asked.

"Well, I—"

"He was a second away from losing his shit on you," I hissed, looking up at her. Had he touched Valerie, we would be burning a body tonight instead of sitting at this table.

She looked down at me with fire in her eyes. "I would've handled him if he'd touched me," she returned with confidence.

"No offense, darlin'," Lance drawled from his spot. "But a man touches a woman like that, men like the ones in front of you would've taken care of it. In a fucking heartbeat."

His twin grunted in agreement. Mags was standing in the corner, the same spot where Joseph Grayson stood a few nights ago, staring at the back of Diana's blonde head. He had nothing to say.

"All in favor of burning the son of bitch," Lawson called, raising this hand.

Chase looked to the ceiling, sighing through his nose. Diana plugged her ears and returned her attention to the paperwork in front of her. Jigs slapped Lawson upside the head. "Dammit, boy. In front of a lawyer *and* the sheriff?"

Valerie stifled a giggle, covering her mouth. I shook my head. "While I love where your head's at, we have a bigger issue."

Everyone looked to me, the bullshit done with. "Valerie's mom was threatened by Moonie today in not so many words," I said, my voice hard.

"That bastard," Beau and Lawson snapped.

"We aren't taking any chances, whether he meant it or not," I continued. The boys nodded. "I'm flying her and her nurse here the day after tomorrow. I need one of you to fly to Dallas to bring them back here," I directed, resting my forearms on the table, my eyes scanning over their faces. Nancy and Jackie were going to have protection.

"Or I can go," my woman suggested from beside me. I could feel her emerald eyes on me.

Absolutely fucking not.

"You aren't going anywhere," I said, not looking at her.

Beau raised his finger. "I'll go."

Jigs nodded. "Good man."

For the next hour, we discussed a game plan, the slim possibility of Mason coming home, and what to do if Cathy shows up. Chase ordered us to detain her. Whether or not she was involved with Tim Moonie, she would be facing the charges I was pressing against her. There would be a court date set soon and if she failed to show, I would have a hundred percent custody of Caleb. Mason likely wouldn't be coming home; I knew that much.

When it came to my brother, I didn't have high hopes.

A part of me stopped hoping all together.

Tinkles Bar. Hayden, Co.

Tim Moonie had lost his patience with Cathy. She wasn't doing what needed to be done. His hand connected with her cheek again, the force of his slap sending her flying back against the wall. She came to him days ago, saying that Denver wasn't going to budge and that her story didn't scare him.

She also clung to Tim like a lost puppy. He had made her sign a contract before shoving his cock down her throat during their first meeting. When he walked into Tinkles for the first time, he had high hopes. Now? He just wanted to kill the woman.

"Should've known you didn't have it in you!" he yelled.

"Tim—"

His hand shot out, gripping the back of her hair tightly, yanking at the skin on her scalp. "Enough!" he roared.

He threw her across the room, her used, ragged, half naked body landing on the floor with a loud thud. Tim's chest heaved violently as he stared down at her. She had crashed into the filing cabinet before collapsing on the dirty carpet. The two of them were in the back office of the bar. Tim had just gotten back from Hallow Ranch, where he was shocked to find Valerie Cross standing on Denver's front porch.

She was fucking him.

Tim Moonie cursed under his breath as he ran a hand through his hair. He should've kept her on. He had no idea Denver Langston would be attracted to a woman like that. Cathy was nothing like Valerie. Tim could've used Valerie.

It would have been dirty, but men like him didn't stray from dirty.

"I'm sorry," the woman wheezed out from her spot on the floor. Her eye was bruised from his strikes. There was a drop of blood hanging from her trembling bottom lip. He squatted down in front of her, seething.

"You are nothing but a fucking failure. A rotten whore!" he spat. The woman flinched. There were tears in her eyes now.

Tim could care less. He rose to his full height, pinching the bridge of his nose. A lighthearted laugh came from him as his anger took control of his senses. "I just—I don't understand it, Cathy. You tell me you're going to be faithful to me. That you're going to do everything I told you to do. Yet, you failed."

"Tim, please! I went to the police station in the next county today. I filed a report!" she cried. "They're going to call me! I know it!"

It was no use.

Ms. Cross was siding with Hallow Ranch, and she knew too much. She had been on the inside; she knew how his company functioned. It was too late for Cathy. Tim knew that approaching her had been a risk—a long shot—but he'd been desperate. The local governments weren't working with him, even though he promised this community jobs. The town of Hayden didn't want the pipeline.

Hallow Ranch was all Tim wanted. Truthfully, he couldn't care less if his pipeline destroyed the town. He had investors and materials waiting for the green light.

Before, he was willing to do this while keeping his hands clean.

Now?

Now, he longer gave a fuck. Anyone who stood in his way would fall. Hallow Ranch would be his, and in a year's time, his pipeline would dominate that land.

Slowly, he looked down at Cathy, putting the tip of his shoe underneath her chin. "Sweetheart, I'm giving you one more chance," he said coldly. His hands itched to beat her. He wanted to hear her screams of pain as he took control of her body. He wanted to watch the life drain from her eyes.

These thoughts made him miss his perfect girl. One day, he would find her again, but for now, he would settle with Cathy. Without a second thought, he kicked the woman in the stomach, a snarl leaving his lips.

He wrote out instructions for her and left it on the floor beside her.

Tim had other business to attend to.

As he walked out of Tinkles, the man pulled out his phone and called Valerie Cross' former supervisor. "Good evening, Charlotte. I hope I'm not bothering you after hours," he said sweetly. He got into the back of the SUV, and the driver pulled out immediately.

"No, sir. How can I help you?"

"I know it hasn't been that long since we terminated Valerie Cross' employment, but I require her file."

"Of course, sir. I'll get that sent over to your assistant—"

He cut the woman off, loosening his tie. "Send it to me, please."

"Yes, sir."

After Tim Moonie hung up, he studied the town of Hayden as he rode through it. It was a quiet, boring town. Towns like this were easy for men to control. He'd been here a little under two weeks, took one look at the sheriff, and knew he wouldn't be of any help.

Men like Denver Langston and Chase Bowen are cut from the same, stupid cloth.

Once in his hotel room, he went to his luggage and pulled out a burner phone. The number he needed was on speed dial. He walked to the window as the line rang in his ear. The man he needed answered on the third ring.

"Sir."

"Hallow Ranch," Tim stated.

"Hayden, Colorado," the deep voice replied a few seconds later.

"The very one."

"How many targets?"

Years ago, Tim would've taken this moment to think about the outcome of his actions. Now, the only outcome he would accept is the deed to that fucking land. So, when he answered, he knew he would sleep like a fucking baby.

"All of them."

Chapter Thirty-One

Valerie

Mom was going to be here in less than five hours.

She was going to be near me again.

After a month and a half.

My heart was bursting with anxiety and a strange sense of happiness. Every day since meeting over FaceTime, Denver would show Mom something new on the ranch. Whether it be through FaceTime or through texts, he would make sure that she got to see a piece of this beauty. I was happy she got to see it, but I was overjoyed she could see it in person.

Strangely enough, it had been quiet since Moonie's visit the other day, except for the final termination process email I got from Moonie Pipelines yesterday, which was a PDF document of my tax information, more exit paperwork, and a farewell letter from Mr. Moonie himself. *How kind of the bastard.* When I opened the email, I immediately called Denver, who had been down at the barn with the vet. One of the horses, Lawson's, was pregnant.

The letter from Moonie was signed and dated the day I was fired. Still, it made me uneasy. I didn't like knowing he knew I was still here. There was something about the look in his eyes when he saw me on the porch that made a chill crawl up my spine.

He looked *unhinged.*

Denver and the men assured me that nothing would happen to me or my mom, and, I trusted them.

Denver also told me that for right now, he didn't want me going anywhere alone. If I left the ranch to go into town, one of them would follow. Caleb would remain at the ranch, not that he seemed to mind. He'd been spending most nights in the bunkhouse with the cowboys anyways, swapping stories and playing games.

Last night, Denver took me down there for dinner. He was too tired to cook and said Mags was cooking. I learned quickly that Mags was a better cook than Denver, which I didn't think was possible.

We ate, we talked, we laughed, and they even taught me poker. Well, they tried anyways. I felt like I was finally a part of something—*a family*—Denver's family. Lawson and Lance teased me about being a city girl from Texas. Beau had gone to Dallas. Jigs told me stories about when Denver was a boy, running circles around him and his father. Mags was quiet most of the night, only answering if he was directly spoken to. He cooked the meal, served it, ate in silence while sitting in his chair, which was in the corner away from everyone, and then he observed everyone from afar. When Denver and I were heading back up to the house last night, I asked him about Mags.

"A man like Mags has demons, Val. He served in the Marines, like me, but what he saw was different from what I did."

My throat tightened as I thought about Denver's childhood, what he shared with me the other night. "What about your demons?" *I asked softly.*

He stopped and turned to me, his gray eyes scanning my face. *"I have my ways of fighting them. Everyone has demons, baby, and everyone must make the choice."*

"*What choice?*" I whispered.

"*To either fight them or let them consume you.*"

It was mid-morning now, and I was in the laundry room. A beautiful laundry room, I might add. It had the same color scheme as the kitchen, the cabinets above the washer and dryer painted sage green. One half was for laundry and the other half could be considered a mudroom. As I was putting in the last load, I heard the low rumble of Denver's truck outside.

I had been cleaning all morning, trying to familiarize myself with the house...

Trying to make it into a home.

Mom would be here soon; she would be taking the guest bedroom and Jackie would only be staying two days. She would be staying downstairs. I wanted to make sure the laundry was done, the kitchen cleaned, and the new sheets were on the beds...

"Baby?"

My stomach flipped at the sound and my heart jumped for joy.

Denver was home, calling for me.

He had a meeting with Diana, his lawyer, and Judge Harway this morning. Cathy was still nowhere to be found. Sheriff Bowen had Tinkles, the stripper club on the outside of town where Cathy worked as a bartender, searched. There was a squad car parked outside of her apartment and the Hayden hotel. Bart was questioned and he said Cathy had only been to the hotel twice since Mr. Moonie had been staying there.

Cathy was nowhere to be found, same with Mr. Moonie. According to Bart, he hadn't checked out of his hotel room, but he hadn't been there in days.

I came down the hall, swinging by the kitchen to drop off the freshly folded dish towels. Denver came in behind me, causing me to yelp before he wrapped me up in his strong arms.

"*Fuck*," he groaned deeply into my hair.

"What's—"

"Coming home to *you*, the house smelling good, and the washer going..." he trailed off, nestling his face in my neck. "Feels like a dream, and I'm terrified."

At that, I turned around to face him. He didn't move his arms. I cupped his face in my hands, my brow furrowing. "Terrified of what?"

His throat worked as he stared down at me. "I'll wake up and the dream will be over. You'll be gone." His gray eyes looked behind me then, but his smoke lingered around me.

"Sometimes, I find myself struggling to wrap my head around this," I added.

He looked at me again and pressed a soft kiss to my lips. I knew he was feeling the same.

When he pulled away, I asked, "How did it go this morning?"

Denver walked away from me, pulling his hat off and hanging it on the hook by the fridge before heading to the coffeemaker. A deep sigh left him. "Caleb deserves better," he muttered, pouring himself a cup. He turned to face me, leaning his hips against the counter.

I gave him a sympathetic smile. Caleb did deserve better, but I didn't think that I was my place to comment. Not yet, anyways. Maybe someday, but not today. My dark cowboy saw right through me.

"Val, you can agree with me," he stated, setting his mug down.

I took a seat on a stool. "It's not my place," I admitted. He stared at me for a beat before his boots moved again, his spurs clicking with every step.

"You my woman?" he quipped, bracing his palms on the island.

I nodded.

"Say it," he ordered, his voice low. His jaw was tight, his eyes flared.

"I'm your woman," I breathed.

"Then you have a right to agree that my son deserves a better mother. Cathy is a fucking snake."

The hatred in his voice sent goosebumps across my arms. How could he hate the mother of his child so much? Then again, I didn't know much about his ex. I didn't know how they met. Where did they meet? How long they were together? Why did they break up? Had they been high school sweethearts? Were they divorced?

My stomach turned at the thought of another woman being Denver's wife, of another woman being in this house, doing the things I was doing...feeling the things that this man was making me feel. Another woman in his bed...

How could a woman like Cathy walk away from a man like him? Couldn't she see? Couldn't she see he was broken?

"Can I ask why you and her split?"

He blinked, and I shook my head quickly. "That's none of my business. That was rude of me to—"

"Valerie, Cathy and I were never a couple."

My head tilted as he continued. "What happened between Cathy and I..." he sighed as he ran a hand through his black hair. He looked away, focusing on his hat on the wall. "Mason bought me that hat."

I followed his gaze and then looked back to him. His throat bobbed as he backed up to lean against that counter again. He braced his hands on either side of his hips and looked at his boots. "Told myself you would have to know the truth, but fuck, I didn't want to do it this soon."

Fear crawled up my spine and I tried to ignore it, but my body froze. "Why?"

He raised his eyes to me. "Because our dream might end when I'm done telling you what I have to tell you, baby." His rough voice was painfully soft now, and that scared me even more.

I swallowed the lump in my throat. "Honey..."

Denver held my eyes as he delivered the truth to me. "Cathy was Mason's fiancée."

I stared. There was nothing else I could do. There were red alarms going off in my head, my heart was terrified, but my soul remained calm.

Listen to him, Valerie.

You love him. Remember that.

I nodded for him to continue. A confused look washed over his face, but it was gone in a flash.

"I've told you before that I was in the Marines. I enlisted when I was eighteen. That wasn't the plan, and when Pop found out...fuck, he was so mad." He looked away and continued. "Hallow Ranch was always going to be passed down to me. I was the first-born son. Pop raised me to be a rancher. He taught me everything I know. He was grooming me to take over at the age of twenty. That was the deal, and I was fine with that. Hallow Ranch was my dream, it was the most beautiful place in the world."

I smiled. He was right about that.

"But," he sighed, "when I was seventeen, I got this desire to see the world. I knew my slice of heaven would be waiting for me when I got back. The only way for a boy like me to see the world was to enlist. I also wanted to serve, like my grandfather did. I enlisted in secret on my eighteenth birthday. There was a recruitment office a county over, and I took the truck keys and went. Pop was so pissed, like I said, that he didn't speak to me for a month. Didn't even tell me goodbye when I left for basic."

"Denver, that's terrible," I objected. How could a father do that to his son?

Your father left you in the dust completely.

The corner of his lips turned up. "Like it when you get mad for me," he murmured. I was glad, because apparently, I would be doing it a lot.

"So, you left and served your country. How long were you gone?" I asked, wanting to hear the rest.

"I was gone for a little over five years. I came home after basic, but I wasn't welcome here. Pop was still mad and Mason—he was pissed too. I never understood why. He would get to chase his dream. Mase had dreams of being in the PBR since we were kids, and because he was the second son, the responsibility of the ranch didn't fall to him. Not that I minded, because there was nothing else I would rather do with my life. I just wanted a chance to—"

"You served your country, Denver. You sacrificed yourself for this!" I snapped, gesturing around me. I stood from my stool and began to pace. "You could've died! Did your father not get that? That there was a possibly of you coming home in a box?" My voice was raised now, and I was on a roll. This man chose to defend millions of innocent people. He risked his safety, his relationships, his mental health, his life!

How could his family be mad at that? "Valerie," he called. I looked at him. His tanned, muscular arms were crossed over his broad chest.

"What?" I spouted, glaring at him.

"I don't fucking deserve you," he whispered. Before I could tell him otherwise, he continued, "Let me finish the story, and then you can decide if you want to keep that anger for me...or direct it at me." There was a hint of sadness at the end of his statement.

How bad was the ending of this story?

Reluctantly, I nodded.

"Anyways, I came home five years later. Hadn't spoken a word to Pop or Mase in all that time. I wrote letters, of course, but I never got a response back. Which was fine with me, because I knew that whatever shit we needed to hash out, we could do it when I was back. Except when I got home, Mase was nowhere to be found, and Pop—he was acting differently. He wouldn't talk to me, only stare. Later, after everything went down, I found out that Pop had dementia." He looked down at his boots again.

I could only stare at him; he was trying to bury this pain. I could see it happening before my eyes, and he didn't need to. He needed to let it out.

"At the time, I didn't know. I just assumed he was still pissed. So, not wanting to deal with that, I went out to the bar. I needed a fucking drink and there was no whiskey in the house. I tried reaching out to Mason, to let him know I was home. He didn't answer, but Jigs told me he was a town over. He was bull riding that night. Went to the bar, sat down with the intention of drinking until I was numb. Then, this woman pressed up against me. She was laying it on thick, and if I hadn't just gotten home, I would've told her to fuck off. But I gotta be honest, baby, after the shit I'd seen...I needed the distraction."

Oh, God.

He looked away from me as he delivered the final blow. "Fucked her. Used rubbers and told her I would buy her a Plan B when we were done, and that I would watch her take it. I didn't need a kid, not with a woman like her. She was just a fuck. Mason came home, found her in my bed as I was trying to get her out of it, and that's when it happened. That woman was Cathy, and she was his fiancée of six months. They had been together for two years and he promised her the world."

Silence filled the room.

He wasn't done. "She spat out her venomous lies, telling my brother I knew she was engaged. I didn't even know her fucking *name*, Valerie. There wasn't a ring on her finger, but my brother believed her. He believed I would pursue *his woman*. He kicked her out, called her a whore, and took his ring back. She had it in her fucking pocket. *Her pocket.* Then, he turned to me and told me how much he hated me. How I was a piece of shit brother, even though I explained I didn't know who she was. Hell, I hadn't talked to the guy in *five fucking years*. I didn't know he was dating, let alone engaged."

"Denver," I rasped, my heart aching for him.

He was innocent in all of this, but he was taking the brunt of everything.

My broken cowboy.

"Two months later, Mason was gone, Pops was off the deep end, and she came back to Hallow Ranch with an ultrasound. She expected me to marry her, and to give her the life Mase promised her. After she had Caleb, she left town for three months. She was chasing after Mason."

I was shaking my head, disgusted at that vile woman.

"There you have it," he finished, his jaw jumping. His shoulders were tense, his feet were planted apart, like he was bracing for something.

Wrath.

Anger.

Judgment.

Hatred.

Denver Langston would receive none of that from me. Wordlessly, I made my way around the island, my eyes never leaving his gray ones. There was one more step between us and I lunged for him, jumping up to wrap my arms around his neck. My lips collided against his.

I kissed him with the forgiveness he needed.

I kissed him with the gentleness he craved.

I kissed him with the love we both desired.

A groan left his throat as he unfolded his arms and set his hands on my waist. His tongue worked against mine, and nibbled and sucked his bottom lip before fluttering my tongue against his again. His fingers flexed against me, squeezing me tighter as I angled my head to kiss him deeper, my fingers diving into his hair.

The world went on around us as I gave him everything I had with a single kiss.

My dark cowboy was broken, and in turn, that broke me.

I wanted to put him back together again. I wanted him to be *loved*.

When I pulled away, breathless, I met his lust-filled gaze. "Mason was wrong," I said firmly. His jaw tightened. He needed to hear this. "He should have listened to you. You're his brother."

"Baby, he's a cowboy," he defended softly.

My head shook against his forehead. "No, no, that's not—"

"Cowboys aren't like other men."

"You're the best man I've ever met," I countered, my voice a weak whisper as tears stinged my eyes.

"You're standing there defending me when I was the one—"

"She wasn't wearing a ring, Denver. She played you. She *used* you. She played your brother, and instead of you two leaning on each other—he—he just left!" I stammered, anger rising in me.

Though his jaw was tight, and his shoulders tense, his eyes were warm as he assessed me, and when he spoke his voice was soft. "He's my brother, baby. If I were in his shoes, I would've beat the shit out of him."

"No—"

"Cowboys aren't like other men. Cowboys live simply, fuck hard, and love with everything they got. Cowboys also don't fucking share," he said firmly.

"You aren't at fault for this, and your brother is missing out because of his stubbornness."

"He's living with his pain in the only way he knows how."

"By avoiding it," I told him.

He nodded. "That's exactly right. Someday, when he's ready, I'll be here. I won't stop trying to get him home, and the door will always be open to him."

I refrained from telling him that Lance said he would kill Mason if he ever stepped on Hallow Ranch again. I also refrained from telling him that Mason would be getting a swift kick in the nuts from me if he ever came home. Then my mind focused on Denver's words. He still had *hope*. Whether he wanted to admit it or not, he still had hope his brother would come home.

Hope was something I'd lost a long time ago and seeing a man like Denver still hold out for something that might not happen…it warmed my soul. He was strong. So strong and he didn't realize it.

I nodded, and then he gave me a piece of information that made me weak in the knees.

"His biggest sponsor is Evergreen. That's just a cover up, a false name."

A tear fell from my eye as my heart pounded loudly in my chest. My fingers linked together at the back of his neck, anchoring myself to him. "It's you, isn't it?" I whispered.

My cowboy nodded. "Gotta make sure he gets his dream, baby."

Denver Langston was a good man and a wonderful brother.

"You deserve so much more than me," I rasped. He was wonderful and I…I had nothing to offer him. Nothing but baggage.

He looked pained as he said, "You're all I want."

"I'm not going anywhere," I promised.

Silence stretched between us, and I could hear his beating heart in his massive, hard chest. I was sure he could hear mine, too.

"I—"

"Hey, dad!"

Denver's forehead met mine as he let out a growl of frustration.

I giggled.

"Not funny," he hissed, his hands squeezing my waist.

"It's always going to be funny, Smoke," I returned softly. The door opened and I heard little footsteps.

"Dad, Beau called Jigs and said—what are you doing to Valerie?" Caleb asked from behind me. I tried to move but Denver kept me in place. He looked over my shoulder.

"Kissing her, son," he stated.

"Why are you kissing her?" he yelled in shock. *Oh, the mind of little boys.*

A chuckle came rumbling from Denver's huge body. "Because I like her, bud."

"Can I kiss her?" Caleb asked.

"Oh, goodness," I hummed, burying my face in Denver's chest, heat rising in my cheeks.

"Only on the cheek, bud, and only if she's comfortable with it."

My heart swelled.

"Is she comfortable with you kissing her?" he laughed.

Denver's chuckle only got deeper, making my toes curl. "You have no idea," he muttered under his breath before saying, "Yes, she is. You always have to make sure the other person is comfortable with you touching them."

Of course, he had to get more perfect. He valued consent.

This man—this *cowboy*.

My cowboy.

Caleb asked us to join him outside. He wanted to show his us that he finally figured out how to saddle his horse. I stood on the porch while Lance and Denver watched him saddle his young steed.

Heat crawled up my cheeks as Caleb told me he had to learn on a saddle stool first. He went on to explain there were two saddle stools in the barn, one upstairs and one in the storage room on the ground floor. I cleared my throat and noticed a cocky grin poking out from under Denver's hat.

Thankfully, Lance didn't notice *that*.

After a few minutes, Denver told them he would be down after lunch as he ushered me up the porch steps. He pushed me inside, barking at Lance to keep an eye on Caleb. I was standing in the foyer when he stepped inside, something radiating off his large body that I couldn't quite pick up on. I held my hands up and opened my mouth to say something, but he didn't let me. He dipped his shoulder, put it to my stomach, and lifted me.

"Denver!" I cried.

I was upside down, watching his ass as he walked us into the kitchen. Denver set me down on the island, swiping all the stuff behind me onto the floor with a growl. I gaped at him. "Den—"

"Shut up," he hissed, shoving my legs open. I didn't wear underwear today, and he sucked in a breath at the sight of my damp pussy. He took off his hat and set it on my head.

"Fucking *starving* for that cunt," he clipped, dropping to his knees.

Before I could utter a word, his mouth was on me. My back arched as my mouth fell open, a breathy moan leaving me. His tongue flicked against my clit roughly before he bent lower and impaled me with it.

"Denver," I gasped, lifting my knees higher and gripping his hair with one hand. He groaned against me, the vibration sending pleasure zapping through my body, straight to my nipples. His hands slid under my legs and, one by one, he hooked them over his shoulders.

Denver lifted his head and the second his eyes met mine, his smoke surrounded me, closing off the world around us. "Lie back," he ordered, his voice gravelly and thick with desire.

"You didn't lock the door," I rasped, my body tense with anticipation.

"Lance knows to tell everyone not to come up here," he informed casually as he kissed my inner thighs.

"Wha—"

"Told him was going to eat lunch," he stated, his gray eyes on my entrance.

"Honey—"

His hand shot up and he pushed me back. "Lie back, spread your legs, and let me fucking eat my meal," he growled.

I nodded and spread my thighs further. Without delay, he was back on me again, holding my thighs against his broad shoulders. He went at me like a man starved, growling and groaning against me. His beard only added to the sensations, as he tongue-fucked me, his moustache rubbing against my clit in the most intoxicating way.

It was too much.

When my hips started moving against his face, he pulled away slightly. "Slutty little pussy, fucking my face," he whispered. His words shot up my spine and I let out a moan, arching for him. His cowboy hat fell forward, covering my face.

"Please," I begged, pulling his hat away from my face.

"Again," he taunted, dragging the tip of his tongue over the tip of my clit. It wasn't enough. I needed more.

"Smoke, please!"

"Please, what? Tell me what you want," he demanded, his voice gravelly and deeper than before.

"I-I—"

"This needy cunt wants to come on my face, doesn't she? Is that it?" he asked softly, inhaling my scent.

"Yes!" I cried.

"Anything for you, Enchantress." He licked me again, but this time, he shoved a finger into me.

"Yes! More!" I pleaded, moving my hips against him, setting the hat on my chest, and sinking both hands into his hair. A moan left him, and I swear, Heaven's gates opened for a fraction of a second. I would never tire of hearing that sound. He finger-fucked me harder, adding a second finger as he sucked on my clit. My climax was peaking, and hips moved faster and harder against his face, my body chasing the high. "Oh, oh! Denver, right there!"

He pulled away, and I whined in protest. "Come on my face. Give that to me," he ordered before he latched onto my clit. He sucked it in between his teeth, pain and pleasure swirling together within me.

I was *gone*.

As my orgasm took over, my mouth shouted for him, and my body began to shake. I felt him move, and then his presence was above me. When I came back down to Earth and my eyes focused, I found him unbuckling his jeans, frantically.

He shook his head with a snarl on his. "Shouldn't fucking need you this bad. Should be satisfied with you coming on my face, but no. I need you to come on my cock for me, baby," he hissed. I watched as he fisted his thick cock and licked my lips at the sight of it leaking. When he lined the head up to my pussy, I pushed up on my elbows. He reached for his hat and put it back on my head.

"Don't take it off," he clipped, dropping his eyes down my body.

"Fuck me, please," I whimpered.

"So God damn beautiful," he growled, slamming into me in a single thrust. I cried out, but he didn't show me mercy. He grabbed my hips, lifting them to an angle that should be a sin and began fucking me savagely. My hands flew out, trying to find something to hold on to as he used the bottom half of my body. His balls slapped against my ass over and over as he stretched me.

My cowboy jerked his chin to me. "Pull that dress down, Val. Wanna see those tits bounce while you take this dick," he ordered gruffly. I whimpered but obeyed. His eyes flicked from my breasts to my face, then back down to where he was entering my body, claiming me.

"Who does this pussy belong to?"

"You," I breathed, bringing my hands to my nipples.

"You're nothing but a dirty little slut, aren't you?" He slammed in and pulled all the way out, leaving me empty and panting. I nodded, pinching my nipples. I thought he would slide back inside of me, but he didn't. He was teasing me again.

"Denver," I begged again. He stared down at me, a lock of his hair hanging in the middle of his forehead.

"Say it," he ordered. "Tell your cowboy what you are, City Girl."

"I-I'm nothing but a dirty little slut," I whispered, spreading my legs as much as he would allow. His hands snaked underneath me, cupping my ass.

"You're *my slut*, Valerie. Only for me, do you understand?"

I nodded. "Yes, sir."

"Good girl," he praised. Then, he slammed his cock back into me and resumed fucking me, harder and faster than before. The sounds of our bodies meeting filled the house, along with my moans and his grunts.

"Smoke—I—I—" I sucked in a harsh breath as the tip of his cock hit just the right spot over and over.

"Give me that," he commanded harshly, his fingers gripping me harder. I knew I would have bruises tomorrow. I loved it. I loved his marks on me.

"Honey—" My back arched, and my thighs clung to him. He didn't let up; he keep pounding into my pussy relentlessly.

"Give it to me or I will fucking take it," he snarled.

"Take it! Take it!" I cried, putting a hand on the top of his hat to hold it in place as he fucked me.

He shifted me, and then his rough thumb was on my clit, circling slow. The contrast sent me over the edge.

"Denver," I moaned, my eyes rolling back. My pussy tightened around him, and I saw the Heavens again.

"*Enchantress*—fuck! Jesus Christ!" he growled, setting my hips down. He pulled me up to him. My legs wrapped around his waist as his hands shifted to my ass again, holding me in place. As I came back down, my body sighing, I found him staring down in between us.

"Look at that," he clipped, still moving. I dipped my chin and focused on the erotic sight before me, his thick cock going in and out of me at a steady pace, claiming me.

"Look at how well you take me, Valerie. You were fucking *made* for me."

I looked up. He was staring at my face now, his eyes holding me captive. I couldn't look away and neither could he. Wet sounds echoed between us as he slowed his thrusts, taking his time. My walls fluttered, and I could feel my second climax coming.

I was made for him, and he was made for me.

He was perfect to me, broken pieces and all. He was all I needed.

"D—Denver," I stuttered, sucking in a breath as my arms shot up to wrap around his neck. His dark brows furrowed, not stopping his movements. We continued to hold each other's eyes as he spoke.

"When will you stop?" he asked gruffly, snaking a hand around to my front to stroke my swollen clit. His forehead rested against mine, pushing his hat further back on my head.

"Stop—stop what?" I moaned.

"Enchanting me."

Never.

I yanked him down to my lips and kissed him hard. My thighs began to shake again, and his thumb moved against my bundle of nerves faster, but his thrusts remained steady. His tongue teased mine. The taste of myself on him was intoxicating. After a few moments, a growl left him, and he fucked me faster.

"I want to mark you," he growled against my lips. "I want your body covered in my bruises and bite marks."

I whimpered, wanting that too. I wanted the whole world to know I was his and he was mine.

"I want this little pussy filled with my seed every day."

My core clenched around him. "Yes!" I cried.

"You gonna be a good girl and let me fill that cunt?"

I nodded as my head fell back, my breasts bouncing with each thrust.

"Say it," he spat, pinching my clit.

"Ah! Please!"

He grabbed the back of my head and yanked me upright. The look on his face was downright feral. "Say the words."

I love you.

"Fill me, Denver. That's what I want," I gasped.

I love you. I love you. I love you.

"Valerie," he moaned, and that set off my third climax. He said my name like a prayer. His movements became erratic, and with two more thrusts, I felt him swell inside me as I squeezed him. We held onto to each other, neither of us speaking. The kitchen filled with the sounds of our breathing, and it was music to my ears.

He was music to my ears.

I love you, Smoke.

I couldn't tell him, not yet. There was too much going on. Once the dust settled and nothing surrounded us but his smoke...then I would tell him. I would tell him he owned me. I would tell him my heart was his, that I never wanted to part from him or Hallow Ranch again.

Until then, I would love him in silence.

Chapter Thirty-Two

Denver

"Holy, Mary."

A smile tugged at the corner of my lips as I stared down at the two women before me. I found myself smiling a lot more since Valerie came into my life, dragging the women in front of me in it with her. One was Valerie's mother, Nancy, and the other was Jackie, her nurse. Both were gaping at me as they craned their necks to look at my face.

"Good afternoon, ladies," I drawled. Beau had just pulled up about two minutes ago in his truck. After helping Nancy down from the cab, Jackie joined her, and they've been staring at me since.

"It's great to finally meet you in person," I said, holding my hand to Nancy. She took it just as I heard Valerie burst through the front door. I turned to look at her. Tears were in her green eyes. She had been upstairs when they arrived, fussing about the spare bedroom, making sure it was perfect for her mother. It was. It was because Valerie made it so. She was making this old house feel like a home again, and fuck, that made me feel good.

"Mom," she breathed before darting down the stairs. My chest ached at the sight of her nearly crashing into her mother. My baby stopped just before she did and wrapped her up in a gentle hug. Nancy was wearing her oxygen today, and I knew that she was weak from travelling.

That didn't stop her from wrapping her daughter up in a hug so tight, it made me envious. Suddenly, the absence of my mother was heavier than before. When the women parted, the heartfelt moment came to an abrupt stop when Jackie spoke.

"That's all fine and good, but—" she paused to gesture to Beau and me, "If all the cowboys look like this, I'm pitching a tent in the backyard."

A low chuckle came from Beau, who was unloading the bags. When he was done, he shut the tailgate. He came around to us, a cocky *son-of-a-bitch* grin on his face.

"Ms. Jackie, you are good for my ego," he noted, putting on his sunglasses.

"Those abs I saw this morning are good for your ego," she deadpanned.

I shot Beau a look as he winced, putting his hand on the back of his neck. "Jackie!" Nancy and Valerie scolded.

The woman turned to them, her dark skin glowing in the sun. She pointed at Valerie. "You already got a panty-melting cowboy, so, you don't get to judge. And you," she said, pointing at Nancy, "need some rest. Let's get her inside."

At her words, everyone moved.

Ten minutes later, Nancy was on the couch, drinking a protein shake that Jackie made. Jackie excused herself and went upstairs to unpack Nancy's things. Valerie was talking quietly to Beau in the foyer.

I studied them from my place on the wall.

Beau's hat was off, and his features were soft as he looked down at my enchantress, listening to every hushed word she spoke. She reached out and put her hand on his arm, and an unfamiliar jealousy sparked inside me. This was different from the time he made her laugh.

"My daughter is in love with you, you know?"

My train of thought was derailed at her mother's soft-spoken statement.

I looked down to the couch and found the woman staring at me, her pale green eyes filled with something that looked a lot like acceptance. She had a pink satin wrap on top of her head and a chunky white sweater hung from her too thin body. Her eyes were sunk in, her cheekbones too sharp, her skin too pale.

Despite all that, and the pain I knew she was in, she smiled up at me brightly.

"I can see why," she said softly in a tone that reminded me of Momma's.

My heart flinched.

I shook my head, ready to deny it. Nancy's drawn on brows came together as she studied me. Her eyes dropped, taking in my dirty boots, worn out Wranglers, dirty T-shirt and old flannel. When her eyes rose past my face to focus on my hat, she spoke. "You know, when you're on death's doorstep, you think about the things you missed. The things you could've done differently...and I have to tell you, Mr. Langston..." she trailed off to look behind her, where Val and Beau were standing in the foyer.

When she looked back to me, she whispered, "I'm glad that I got sick, because it led my daughter to you."

My jaw tightened to the point of fucking pain and *at this point*, I wanted it to *shatter*. I remained silent, unable to speak from the raw emotion burning in my throat.

I wanted to scream.

I wanted to fall to my knees.

I couldn't. Valerie's footsteps filled my ears, and I heard Beau call, "See y'all in a bit!"

"Mom, the guys want to come up here for dinner and meet you both, is that alright?" she asked her mother softly, taking a seat at the far end of the couch.

Nancy tore her eyes from me, her smile growing wider by the second. "I would love nothing more, Vallie."

"Faster, Ranger!" I commanded, kicking my boots. My horse's hooves thundered against the rich earth below as the wind whipped all around us.

I needed to get away. I needed to think.

I needed to be out of that house with the dying woman who just told me she was happy about it.

Because of me.

After mumbling an excuse, I headed down to the barn, grabbed my emergency pack, mounted Ranger bare back, and took off. I didn't have time to saddle him, I just needed to get away. My grip tightened in his mane as he charged forward into the nest of trees. The sun was setting, reminding me that darkness would soon cover this beautiful land as we flew through the field.

The herd was gazing in pastures two and four today. The work was done, and the boys were cooking dinner in the bunkhouse for us. My dining table would be full tonight, and an *actual meal* would be shared, not some take out bullshit. The person Valerie cared most about in this world would be sitting next to her tonight as they talked to my son.

My house, empty and lonely for so long, wouldn't be anymore. Who was I kidding?

It hadn't felt empty since the day I carried Valerie through my front door, both of us soaked from the cold rain.

Everything changed the day of that storm.

I should have left her in the rain.

I'm glad I got sick, because it led my daughter to you.

Those words echoed in my head over and over at the same tempo of Ranger's hooves. I shook my head with a growl, trying to shove it away, but they were still there, chanting in my ears.

Minutes later, I was easing Ranger to stop.

We were at the base of the mountain, on Momma's trail. I tied him off and pulled an apple from my Carhart jacket.

"Be back in bit, boy," I whispered, petting his neck and giving him his treat. I didn't have much time. It would be dark soon, and Ranger would be a sitting duck to predators nearby.

The hike was short, one I'd taken countless times during my life. The leaves above me blocked out the remaining rays of sunlight, cooling the forest as it prepared for the night. An owl was calling out in the distance, waking up in time to hunt. Twigs and leaves rustled, but I learned not to look a long time ago. Never look into the trees at night, because you don't know what you might find staring back at you. Instead, I kept my gaze ahead and focused on the sounds of nature.

Five minutes later, I came to the stream.

This wasn't mom's favorite spot; I didn't have the guts to go up there, not since the day she died.

I found other spots over time and the one in front of me was Caleb's favorite.

I shoved my hands in my pockets as I stared down at the water, my jaw jumping. There was a rule on my mountain and the Hallow Ranch boys knew it well. Never spread ashes on this side of the mountain. This side was to remain pure and untouched.

The only sin committed on this side was my mother's murder.

Pop set that rule decades ago, and I have managed to enforce it.

Sighing, I adjusted my hat. "Don't know what the fuck I'm doing," I whispered.

Nothing answered back. No one ever did.

"Never intended to fall in love with her. I was supposed to hate her..."

A flock of birds shuffled in the distance. My eyes didn't stray from the stream.

"She was the *enemy*, and now I'm afraid she's becoming my whole world."

Good, my sweet boy.

My eyes closed at the sound of Momma's voice, and I swallowed hard. "What am I going to do when she loses her mom?"

You continue to love her.

An overwhelming guilt washed over me, like acid rain, burning my body, seeping into my skin and tainting my blood. It was immediately followed by anger, a fury so intense that I found my composure crumbling and then I started screaming into the forest, letting it out.

I screamed for Nancy's life, for Valerie's pain.

I screamed for my son.

I screamed for the lost years between my brother, for Hallow Ranch.

I screamed for everyone trying to take it from me.

I screamed for my unforgiving father.

I screamed for Momma.

My knees buckled, and when they hit the soft, cool grass below me, my chest caved in as the pain I'd been burying for years came rushing to the surface. I felt my hat fall off as I looked up to the sky. My body shook with emotion as I struggled to breathe.

I failed them.

I failed Mason. I should have been a better brother.

I failed my son for not giving him a decent mother.

I failed Hallow Ranch because it was becoming harder to protect it with each passing day.

I failed Valerie. I won't be able to stop the pain. One look at her mother, and I knew—*she didn't have long.* That was another reason why she agreed to come out here, why I kept showing her pictures. I would FaceTime her to show her the herd and the land around it. The way she looked at me today...I knew.

Valerie wanted to go home weeks ago, but I couldn't—I couldn't watch her go, so I held on. My selfishness resulted in time she could've had with her mom. Precious, precious time. Nancy would be gone soon and there was nothing I could do to protect Valerie from that pain.

I've felt that pain. It was rooted deep within me, and you can never escape it.

I wasn't going to be able to protect her from it. Valerie was happy. I could see it. I saw it in her eyes when I was buried inside of her this afternoon. She was happy and now that her mom was here...

I was foolish for keeping her here. I should've let her walk away.

Love is truly blind, shielding you from the pain that is to come.

Chapter Thirty-Three

Valerie

Denver was gone.

Shortly after we got Mom settled, he excused himself and left without giving me a second glance. Dinner had come and gone. Now everyone was being served the apple pie I made this afternoon.

The house was filled with comfortable conversation and laughter, and Denver was missing all of it. The boys didn't seem too worried about it, and Jackie was surrounded by men, so I don't think she noticed, but Mom... Mom had a look in her eye, one that I'd only seen a few times in my life. I couldn't figure out what it meant.

My fingers tingled and my stomach churned as I stared out into the darkness from the front porch. I heard the screen door open and shut behind me, laughter flowing from the house. My eyes never left the darkness, hoping to see any sign of movement.

Smoke, where are you?

It had been hours since he stormed out.

A presence stood by my side—*a shadow* loomed over me.

"He'll be back," a deep voice rumbled. I flinched in surprise. *Mags.*

I wrapped my arms around myself as a chill coursed through me.

"Is he alright?" I asked. The sad truth was that I was in love with a man who was still a mystery to me. There were things about him I had yet to learn, despite him sharing his deepest, darkest memories with me. I had a gut feeling there were more.

"Kings always will be alright. That's just who he is," he said, leaning against the opposite post. I gathered the courage to look at the quiet man. He was wearing dark Wranglers, a black t-shirt, his cowboy hat, and boots. His tattooed arms were crossed over his chest. I could see some of his dark hair poking out around his ear. He had a strong jaw, dusted with dark stubble. He had a beard when I first arrived. Everything about Mags was dark.

"I wonder if this is too much for him," I murmured, more so to myself, but Mags heard it. His eyes met mine and my mouth decided to ramble. There wasn't much else I could do. "I know he lost his mom in a tragic way...and having my mom here when she's this sick..."

Mags cursed under his breath causing my head to snap to him, my eyes wide with shock. He pushed off the post and got into my space. I backed up, holding my hand up. The cowboy didn't stop, not until my palm was pressed against his hard chest. His nostrils flared as he stared down at me under the brim of his hat. My breaths were shallow and for once, I found myself being afraid of one of Denver's cowboys.

"You're in love with him," he stated.

Oh.

My mouth opened and closed again, unsure of what to say. *Was it that obvious?*

"Fucking hell," he muttered. "Come on."

"Come on?" I parroted.

He stepped away from me and held his hand out. "I have a feeling of where he might be. I'll take you to him."

My arms fell to my sides. "Is it that obvious?"

If it weren't for the night around him, I could've sworn I saw his lips twitch. He made his way down the steps and when he looked over his shoulder, he replied, "It wasn't until you opened your mouth about your mom being here, knowing that the ghost of his Momma haunts him every day. So yeah, darlin', it's obvious."

Minutes later, I was looking up at Mags as he got settled on his beautiful black mare. He looked down at me, the moonlight shining behind him as he held his hand out. "Up," he demanded.

I was scared shitless. My fear was clawing at my body, telling me that I was a nothing but a coward. I couldn't do this.

My love for Denver was stronger than my fear.

I grabbed Mags' hand, and he hauled me up. I was in front of him, his front pressed against my back. He grabbed the reins on either side of me and I heard his voice next to my ear.

"Gonna ride fast to get to your cowboy, got me?"

I nodded.

"Brace yourself."

The beautiful beast underneath me broke off into a trot and then quickly—*more quickly than I would've liked*—she broke into a run. I reached for the horn of the saddle and held on for dear life. Her hooves pounded against the steady ground as the moonlight provided us with the light we needed. It was a full moon tonight—thank God. My hair whipped behind me, and I tried to contain it by pulling it around the side of my neck. My heart was racing, matching the horse's pace. She was having a great time.

"That's it, girl! Faster!" Mags called from behind me.

We were halfway through the field in front of the barn when Mags got close to my ear again, his voice louder now due to the wind. "Keep your eyes straight ahead when we come around this bend. Don't look anywhere else."

I did as he instructed, keeping my eyes on the base of the mountain before me. It stood strong and tall, unwavering as it had been for the last thousand years. No amount of wind could move it, no matter how hard it blew. Tall dark trees were scattered across it, promising you miles of pure, untouched land, a sanctuary for hundreds—maybe thousands of creatures. As Mags eased his horse to a slow trot, I heard another horse.

There, directly in front of us, was Ranger—Denver's horse. He was tied to a low hanging branch at the opening of a trail, grazing on some grass, appearing unbothered. My eyes drifted to the trail opening beside him.

Was this Denver's mother's trail?

"Whoa, whoa—easy, girl. It's just Ranger," Mags cooed. He directed us over and shortly after, he dismounted. I moved to do the same and he held his hand up, his eyes on the woods. "Look at the saddle, Val."

Val.

My heart warmed at his acceptance.

Last week, he looked like he wanted to kill me. I liked that fact he called me that. I liked that they all did. They accepted me into their fold the second Denver claimed me, no questions.

"Gonna tie Midnight next to Ranger, and then I'll help you down," he informed. He clicked his tongue and Midnight was moving again. My body moved with her. The ride was hard, and I knew I would be sore tomorrow.

I didn't care how sore I was; I just needed Denver to be okay. After Mags helped me down, he handed me a lighter. I looked up at him, raising a brow.

"Never go out into the wilderness without a fire starter. That thing could save your life."

I nodded.

"Hold onto the back of my shirt and keep your head down. Don't let go of me until I tell you to, we clear?" he asked in a stern hushed tone.

"Why can't I look?" I whispered.

"You don't wanna see what might be looking back. The forest is a different kind of monster at night."

Alrighty, then.

That's all that I needed to know.

I got behind him and we entered the woods. There were sounds all around us, and the moonlight had dimmed thanks to the lush trees above. I focused on my shoes, matching Mags' pace. Thank God I'd changed before dinner. I had rushed upstairs to put on a pair of jeans, tennis shoes, and snagged Denver's Marines shirt.

Minutes passed, and I'd grown comfortable with the sound of our shoes and owls in the distance. That changed when I heard a steady stream of water.

That's when my stomach dropped.

This was the place Denver told me about. *His mother's spot.* I opened my mouth to say something when I heard a familiar, eerie click of a gun being loaded.

Mags came to a fast halt, and I slammed into his back. "Oof."

"Kings, it's me," Mags called.

"Fucking hell, Mags," a deep voice grumbled.

Denver.

I poked my head around Mags' frame, my eyes landing on the dark, mountain of a man in front of standing a few feet away. There was a small fire going a few feet behind him, next to the stream. I was so focused on the sound of the water that, I didn't smell the campfire.

The wilderness should explored, but not by me. I would die out here alone.

"The fuck?" Denver growled, his head turning slightly in my direction. I couldn't see his face due to the shadows, but I could feel his smoke.

"She was worried about you," Mags replied coolly, amusement lacing in his voice.

"Valerie," Denver called, his voice lethal.

"Yes?" I breathed.

"Get your hands off him."

Oh.

I released my hold from Mags and stepped out from behind him. Then I heard something, something so faint that it had me twisting my neck to look up at the mysterious cowboy. *He was smirking.*

Did Mags just laugh? His dark eyes flicked from me to his friend.

"I'm going back. Taking Ranger with me," he informed us, his eyes on Denver, who nodded. Mags looked at me. "Have fun," he whispered, turning on his heel.

Have fun?

"What're you doing out here?"

I turned around to face my dark, broken man. My feet moved, not stopping until I was directly in front of him. "Are you okay?" I asked.

"Val, what in the fuck—"

I reached up and grabbed his face. "I'm out here because I was worried about you," I admitted softly, stroking his rough, warm cheeks. He remained silent, not touching me. It was still too dark. I wanted to look into his eyes. I wanted to see the smoke that danced within them.

"Come this way, let me see you." Dropping my hands, I walked around to the other side of him. He spun slowly, his eyes never leaving me. When the glow of the fire hit his face, a heaviness settled over me. Devastation lingered in his eyes.

"Smoke, I—"

With a growl, he cut me off, his lips crushing against mine painfully. I whimpered and clung to him as he bent us over, my hair falling off my shoulder when his arms banded around my back as he kissed me with abandon. He ripped his lips away from mine a few moments later, and our eyes met.

"Fucking selfless," he hissed, bringing us back up. My arms snapped up to band around his neck, that he was going to push me away.

"I just needed to know you were okay," I whispered, studying him.

"Like the night I killed a man in front of you?" he snapped, his jaw tight. Something was going on. Something happened this afternoon after Mom and Jackie arrived.

"Talk to me, please," I begged. "Don't push me away. Not now."

"Should've let you walk away from Hallow Ranch—from *me*," he muttered.

No, I should've never walked away in the first place.

I shook my head, standing on my toes to get closer to him. "If you did that, I would've never gotten to live."

Tears formed in my eyes as my soul chanted the words.

I love you. I love you. I love you.

Tell him.

Tell him.

Tell him, Valerie.

His forehead landed against mine as he grabbed my upper arms. "God dammit, Val." He shook me gently. "You shouldn't be out here with me! You—"

"You make me feel alive," I wept, tears coming down my face now.

Guilt washed over his features. "Never chase a cowboy, baby."

"You chased me, remember?" I reminded him, my voice cracking.

He had no response. He didn't need one.

"Do you want me to leave?" I whispered. I hated that question, but I would, if he wanted me too.

He shook his head.

Relief washed over me. I tightened my hold on him. "Did you come up here because of my mom?"

A harsh breath left him, and he rose to his full height. He turned his head focusing on the stream instead of me. "The day I chased after you and found you in the road, you told me your mom was all you had," he said, his voice rough.

It hit me like a harsh, cold, unforgiving wind.

When I saw my mother today, I knew. I didn't want to believe it, but the proof was right there. Right in front of me. Jackie pulled me aside earlier and handed me Mom's last doctor's note.

She didn't have much time.

Denver knew it, too.

A lump formed in my throat and my hands began to shake.

My cowboy felt guilty because my mom was dying and there was nothing he could do about it. He didn't need to feel that way. She wasn't all that I had—not anymore.

Say it.

The words left my lips before I could stop them.

"That was before I fell in love with you, Denver."

Time stopped.

The sounds of the forest quieted as I focused on man before me, the man who, only weeks ago, was just another payday to me. The man who scolded me and sent me away. The man who came for me in the rain. The man who held me to keep me, his enemy, warm. The man who was a killer and slept soundly at night. The man who saved me. The man who chased me. The man who scared me. The man who sheltered me. The man who fed me. The man who pleasured me. The man who called me Enchantress. The man who made me *feel*.

The man who showed me that life could be beautiful. I just had to live it.

I studied his profile, saving each detail to my memory, so someday I would have something to look back on. Something to remind myself of what it felt like to *live*.

His beard was a little longer now, thick and black, but it failed to hide his strong jaw. His tanned skin looked even warmer as the flames danced against it. His messy dark hair was poking out from under his hat, and my fingers itched to run through it. The bridge of his nose was crooked from a break he had yet to tell me about, but I hoped that someday, he would.

I hoped he would share everything with me.

It felt like hours had passed when he finally looked back down at me. I sucked in a quiet breath as his smoke reached out, surrounding me in a familiar embrace, much like the first time I saw him. His lips were set into a small frown and his dark brows were slightly furrowed.

"You love me?" His question was filled with disbelief, proving to me that he didn't think he was worthy of love.

He was worthy of everything, and I would gladly spend the rest of my life proving that to him.

I nodded as I rasped, "Yes, Smoke. I love you so much."

My cowboy moved then. In a flash, his lips were on mine again, and his rough, large hands were in my hair. Our lips worked against one another for a moment before he shoved his tongue between mine, demanding access. I granted it with a loud whimper. One of his hands left my hair to drop down to my behind, where he grabbed a handful and pulled my body flush against his. My hands slid under his Carhart and up around his shoulders.

Denver yanked my head back with a vicious tug of my hair, breaking our kiss. The gray of his eyes was barely visible now. His dark, wild, dilated eyes scanned my face, lingering on my lips. "Do you know what it takes to love a man like me?"

Before I could utter a word, he was on me again, kissing me as he backed us up to the fire. His hands pulled my shirt up and over my head as I pushed his jacket off. Piece by piece, we shredded our clothes, desperate for connection as thick need spread between us. I was on my back, the cool grass beneath me, sending shivers down my body. Denver stood above me, his massive chest heaving as he fisted his cock.

He was fucking glorious. Dark hair dusted his chest and abs, trailing down to a mass of dark hair that surrounded the base of his cock. His thick legs were corded with muscles, just like his arms. Locks of his hair were hanging down, close to those smoke gray eyes I loved so much.

My gaze dropped down to his cock, the tip of it leaking already. I wanted that. I moved, needing to taste it, but his harsh command stopped me. "Don't move."

I licked my lips and looked up at him. "I want to taste you," I begged, my nipples hardening at the thought of him in my mouth. The thought of him losing control.

A dark chuckle left him, and he pulled his hand away. "Alright, Val. Come taste my cock." I scrambled up to my knees. He came to me, and before I could touch him, he fisted my hair, yanking my head back again.

"Gonna fuck your throat first, then your cunt, Enchantress. Hands behind your back." I did as he demanded, keeping my eyes on him. "Open."

I opened my mouth for him, my core getting wetter by the second. He wasn't going to be gentle with me. We both knew this. I didn't want gentle.

I wanted unhinged.

I wanted passion.

I wanted to scream for him.

I wanted to choke on his cock as he lost control.

Just as I expected, he shoved my head down and thrusted into my mouth. He didn't go far, though.

"Suck," he ground out, his teeth bared.

I closed my mouth around him, my tongue underneath his shaft as I sucked. A harsh, guttural groan left him as I began to work his length, moving my head back and forth, his hand guiding me. He didn't thrust again, just watched with a slack jaw. A drop of him landed against my tongue, and I moaned at the salty taste. His hand tightened in my hair as his head fell back.

"That's it, baby," he groaned, moving my head faster, back and forth. There were still inches of him left untouched. He told me to keep my hands behind my back, but I ached to touch him.

Fuck it.

I brought my hands up to him, one cupping his balls and the other fisting the rest of him. His head snapped forward, and he yanked me away with a growl. He bent down, his upper lip curling. "Did I say you could do that?"

"I wanted to—"

"Are you not my good girl?" he hissed.

I nodded, biting my lip. "Yes."

"Put your hands on my thighs. Tap me if it gets to be too much," he ordered.

I did as he said.

"Your throat will take my cock until you agree to be good," he warned before thrusting back into me. He held my head with his hands and pulled out, the tip of his cock hovering against my lips.

Then, he *fucked* my mouth, thrusting in and out as his groans filled the air around us. Spit dripped down my chin and tears stung my eyes, but I kept my mouth open for him.

"That's a good girl," he praised, thrusting into my mouth slowly, not stopping until my nose was against his abdomen. My nails dug into his thighs, and I choked around him. "Such a *good girl*," he groaned.

Then he was gone, and I was gasping for air. I watched as he moved to a bag on the other side of the fire. My core throbbed as he pulled out rope. Denver made his way back to me, his cock bobbing up and down with each step.

"Get up," he ordered.

Once I was on my feet, he shuffled me to the nearest tree before he spun me to face it. My breasts scraped against the bark as he yanked his hands above me again, just like the night in the barn. My core clenched, needing him, and I felt wetness pooled between my thighs. Within seconds, my hands were tied together, the end of the rope was thrown over a branch above us, the other in his hand. He tugged on it causing my arms to raise higher.

"Honey," I gasped.

"Fuck, I love tying you up," he growled.

I heard him move behind me, and then I felt his tongue on my clit. I cried out, yanking on the rope. He chuckled against my pussy and pulled on his end, yanking my arms back straight. Then his tongue was back on me, stroking, flicking, fucking me. His beard scraped against my sensitive skin, but he didn't let up. His teeth nibbled on my clit, sending pulsing pleasure throughout my body. My nipples pressed against the rough bark of the tree, giving me just the right amount of pain. I dug my heels into the dirt, pressing my ass against his face while moving my hips. I needed more.

He fucked me with his tongue until I was on the edge, before he pulled away, leaving me trembling tied up to a tree. His large body was behind me now, caging me in. The warmth of his skin surrounded me, and I knew we were safe. Denver would protect me here.

He would protect me anywhere.

"Spread your legs," he clipped, his wet beard closing to my ear. I shivered, but I did as I was told. He praised me, his rough hand running down the length of my spine. I looked back and found him stroking his cock shamelessly as he stared down at my ass, a primal hunger in his eyes.

"Fuck me," I pleaded, tugging on my binds.

Gray eyes snapped up meet to my face. "Say it again."

I knew what he needed to hear.

"I love you," I whispered.

Denver put his hand, the rope wrapped around it, on my hip. I was at his mercy once more. His cock lined up with my entrance. "Again."

"I love yo—*Oh, God!*" I moaned as he filled me to the hilt.

He didn't hesitate. He pulled out and slammed back into me again, not giving me time to adjust.

"Yes," he growled, doing it again and again.

With each powerful thrust, I was shoved further into the bark. My breasts and stomach would be covered in scrapes by the time this was over, but I didn't care. We needed this. I pushed back against him, wiggling my ass as his cock throbbed inside me. He allowed it, rooted deep in me as I ground against him. His huge thighs surrounded mine, his chest shielded me, his forehead pressed against the back of my head.

"Look at you, Valerie," he rasped. He snapped his hips, pulling out and slamming back into my quivering, soaked pussy. "Look at you, filthy girl. You came here to take my land, and now you're taking my cock."

"Yes!" I cried. The hand on my hip came up and fisted my hair. He yanked my head back and I was looking into his eyes. "Oh God, Denver!"

At the sound of his name, he began fucking me. *Hard.* His powerful, punishing thrusts didn't let up, and we didn't break eye contact. Our sounds echoed throughout the forest, and it was the most natural thing in the world to me.

Here, in the middle of nature, he was claiming me in the way I needed to be claimed. He was fucking me in the way he needed to fuck me.

I was his good girl.

As my climax began to peak, my legs shook. With a growl, he kissed me, and when he pulled away, he pressed my head against the tree. His lips found my ear, his teeth grazing against my skin as his animalistic grunts filled it.

"Maybe I should leave you here, tied to this tree, ready for me to fuck you whenever I want," he growled. His words and the picture they painted in my mind caused me to let out a guttural moan.

"Yes!"

"Mmm. You like that, don't you? You like the idea of being my little cum slut."

My pussy began to tighten around him, and I whimpered. His other hand sank between my legs to flick my clit. My entire body twitched but his steady thrusts didn't let up. We were slick with sweat, but I never wanted to stop.

"Say it," he ordered gruffly, his finger circling my clit.

My head fell back against his shoulder, and I turned to face the column of his neck. "I love you."

"Again!"

Thrust.

"I love you," I wept, my body ready for release.

Thrust.

He stayed planted in me, his voice rough as he said, "Scream for me, Enchantress. Let every single soul, dead or alive, on this mountain know that you belong to me."

With that his fingers worked faster as he fucked me again. My cowboy didn't stop thrusting as I clamped around his length and my orgasm took over. He didn't stop when my eyes closed, and I saw stars. He didn't stop when I screamed his name. He didn't stop when his hand fell away from my clit and his arm banded around my waist. He didn't stop when my legs gave out. Instead, he pressed my limp body against the tree, held me up, and fucked me like a madman.

"Denver!" I cried.

"Never stopping, baby," he hissed.

"Smoke, please! Please!"

"You begging for my cum, baby?" he taunted. A second later, my arms were dropped, tingles spreading throughout them as feeling returned. I was hauled away from the tree, breathless and sated.

He wasn't done with me, not by a long shot.

I was on my back again. He yanked my legs apart, hooking one of them over the crook of his arm before he thrusted into me. I gasped at the new position, my hands going to his biceps. My eyes closed, my pussy quivering around his length, ready to give in to him again. Ready to submit to him again.

"Look at me," he ordered gruffly.

When I did, I saw it. I sucked in a breath as the smoke in his eyes cleared, revealing his broken, tired soul. My soul called to his, and something flashed in his eyes. I knew it then.

He loved me too.

"Denver," I whispered.

"Valerie," he whispered back, his deep voice trembling for me.

He pulled out and snapped his hips, filling me again. He moved slowly, taking his time. The world around us fell away, and nothing else mattered besides him. Our damp bodies were pressed together, and I wrapped my tied hands around his neck. There was a bond between us, and perhaps it had been there from that first moment. We were drawn to each other. I could lie to myself and say I wasn't coming back to his ranch every day *for weeks,* not caring whether or not I saw him.

The truth was that every single morning I woke up in that hotel, I hoped I would get to see Denver Langston again, that I would get a glimpse of the eye I was currently staring into. I wrapped my other leg around him and moved my hips up to meet his thrusts. My body was spent, but I wasn't done with him either.

"There she is," he rasped. "There's my good girl."

A zap of pleasure went through me, and I let out a moan. My arms slid up his neck, my fingers diving into his hair. "Harder," I begged.

He shook his head. "Need you to feel every single inch of me, baby. Feel what you do to me. Feel how well you take me. Feel how wet your sweet little pussy is for me. Feel how you tremble around me. Feel what's happening right now. Feel me, Valerie, feel me. Just me."

"I do, I feel you," I breathed, clinging to him.

"Take me, Enchantress. All of me," he grunted, moving slightly faster now. His cock began hitting that spot inside of me over and over. It was building again, and I knew in my heart that when I reached this peak, it would be the most beautiful thing I'd ever felt.

"Yes! Yes!"

His head dropped and his lips found my ear. "You are going to take every last drop of me on this forest floor. Do you understand?"

I nodded, my nails digging into his shoulders now, bracing myself.

"My perfect fucking woman, taking my cock so well as I fuck her into the dirt," he growled. He rose back up again, focusing on my face. Only my face.

"Fill me. Please, fill me, Denver."

His eyes flashed and his jaw went slack. He came with a guttural roar that triggered my own climax. My back arched, and I gasped his name over and over. A hand caressed my cheek, and I opened my eyes to find him right there. In the middle of a sea of pleasure, he was there with me, drowning in it too.

Right where I needed him.

"I love you, Valerie."

Here, on the forest floor, a dark cowboy declared his love for an enchantress.

Nothing would ever be the same.

Chapter Thirty-Four

Joseph Grayson

St. Louis, MO.

A loud, sensual beat pumped through the sound system in the space before me. Colorful lights illuminated the old, brick walls. The sound of power tools and someone barking orders echoed from the other side of the large building, providing a stark contrast to the side I currently occupied. Easy conversation and mingling took place a few feet from me at the bar.

Engines revved outside.

People cheered.

The countdown began on the loudspeakers above.

"Well, well, well, looks like we have a few cowboys at Oasis tonight," a deep voice drawled.

My eyes snapped to my target, Mason Langston, as people clapped around me.

Oasis was an underground street racing organization on the outskirts of St. Louis. A man by the name of Jeremy Jones was the ringleader, along with his partners, Leon Torrance and Dontell Michealson. This building, an old, huge brick factory, abandoned during the Great Depression, was now the hub of the street racing operation. There was an auto shop on the far end of the building and a bar on the other side. Cars of all makes, models, and years were scattered across the glistening concrete floors. A grey 2018 Dodge Challenger with black pin strips and a 1969 grey Mustang—an Eleanor—were among the collection, owned by two men who didn't give a single fuck about the law. My contact at the local FBI field office told me there would be big players here tonight, and that I needed to keep my head down.

I wasn't here for the Italian Mafia or the baseball player. Sullivan Jones' street crew and Jeremey Jones' street racing empire were of no interest to me. I didn't give a shit about the two Bratva men lingering in the parking lot outside. I was here for the bull riding cowboy who decided that Oasis was the place to be tonight. The PBR event ended about two hours ago. Mason and a few of the other cowboys came out here to let off steam or to chase the adrenaline high.

I'd been watching Mason for the last few days. I told Denver I had just gotten to St. Louis this morning, but I'd been here for the last three days. *Studying.*

Here's what I learned about the younger Langston brother—he was a wild card. He didn't follow orders. He rarely listened to his manager or his PR manager. He didn't travel with the rest of the cowboys. He didn't show up until it was time for him to mount a beast who only wanted to throw him off. He didn't stay for autographs. His only friend, it seemed, was the rodeo clown. The cowboys here tonight weren't his friends, but he smiled and laughed to keep up appearances.

Anyone could come to Oasis, but if you wanted to race?

That was by invitation only, from a private number.

Racers would get a random text stating a time and location. There were smaller races going on outside. There was an old track behind the building, but those races were minor, new, young drivers trying to prove themselves to the bigger dogs. A new race began outside, and people inside slowly began to shuffle to the large bay doors. My feet moved, my eyes never leaving the target.

It had been less than a week since I left Hallow Ranch with Denver Langston's instructions, and I knew he was expecting an update by now.

However, something wasn't sitting right with me about the green-eyed woman in his bed. She was employed by Moonie Pipelines no less than a month ago and now, she was fucking Langston.

Something in my gut twisted.

I had my contact run an extensive background check on her. Sure enough, she was clean—on paper. Before getting that phone call from Denver, Tim Moonie wasn't even on my radar. Now he was, and men like him pissed me off. I did some digging of my own before taking this job. Denver wanted me to be his messenger and nothing more.

There was something about that woman...

Or it's your own fucking issues.

A growl formed in my throat at the thought. There was another background check running right now in my hotel room on Valerie Cross.

Leave no stone unturned.

Mason was a few feet from me when a hand clamped down on my shoulder. Everything in my body tightened and instinct wanted to kick in, but I stopped it. *Not here, don't make a scene and blow your cover.*

I turned to find a tall, African-American man staring at me. His black hair was shaved and faded on the sides. He was darker than his partners, leaner, but that didn't mean he was weak. His black eyes held mine as his jaw jumped.

Dontell Michealson.

"I suggest you take your hand off me," I said calmly.

The man smiled widely, a chuckle rumbling from his throat. "And I suggest you get your ass out of my fucking building, Agent."

Agent? I opened my mouth to speak, but he cut me off, pointing a finger in my face.

"We already have this place crawling with the FBI. We don't need the CIA here. You're drawing too much attention to yourself," he explained, his voice lower than before.

Realization dawned.

I shrugged his hand off my shoulder. "I'm not CIA or FBI."

He studied me for a moment. "Who are you?"

"A bounty hunter."

Dontell looked to the ceiling. "*Son of a fucking*—follow me."

He turned and walked away from me. My eyes darted back to where Mason was. The cowboy was a few feet away, talking with a small group of people. There was a smile on his face that didn't reach his gray eyes.

He was putting on a show for everyone.

I knew that fake smile would drop when I gave him the message from his brother. From the looks of it, Mason wasn't going anywhere for a while.

With a short sigh, I turned and followed the owner. He led me to the other side of Oasis, away from the crowd, towards the auto shop. He ducked into one of the bays, where an old Honda Civic was lifted. I followed him through and to the back. There was a small table, car part boxes scattered all around, toolboxes lining the wall. Oil stains were littered across the concrete, and the smell of burning metal lingered in the air. He led me through a door that opened into an office.

An impressive office.

A large black desk sat in the middle of the room with an Apple Mac on top. This space was clean and well put together. There was also man sitting behind the desk, wearing all black, reading a book.

Dontell whistled. "Aye! Got a problem."

No, you don't.

The man looked up from the worn book he was reading, his brows coming together. This man was Leon Torrance, an Asian-African American man with light skin and dark braids. He was also built like me—ready to fight at a moment's notice. Anyone could see that there was a monster underneath his black hoodie. His neck and wrists were covered in tattoos, including the teardrops by his eye.

"The fuck, Don?" he growled.

Dontell shook his head and gestured to me. "Bounty hunter."

Leon looked at me. "Who is it and how much?"

They thought I was after one of their people.

"He's a visitor here tonight. Not a racer or crew member," I stated.

"You here to start shit?" he clipped, setting the book on the table.

I shook my head once.

He cursed under his breath and clicked a few keys on the keyboard in front of him. Then, the wall behind lifted to reveal about twenty screens, giving us a full view on everything happening in and outside of Oasis. Mason Langston was on the third screen.

"Where?" Dontell asked, leaning against the wall, looking bored.

"Third screen."

"Mason Langston?" That was Leon. He walked around the desk to lean against it. "What do you want with a bull rider?" he asked, tilting his head.

"His brother wants him home. Family business," I said firmly, not giving them anymore.

The men shared a look. "Fair enough. Lead the way."

Two hours later, I entered my hotel room.

Two minutes after that, the second background check on Valerie Cross was complete.

Thirty seconds after that, I was kicking myself for being right.
Tomorrow, I would make a phone call.
As for tonight, I needed to ice my hand.

Chapter Thirty-Five

Denver

"I wanted to apologize for missing dinner last night."

Nancy looked up from the E-reader in her hand. She was sitting on the porch swing with a blanket wrapped around her legs, despite the summer heat. Today, a yellow silk scarf was wrapped around her head, making her pale green eyes seem brighter than yesterday.

She smiled at me. "No, I should be the one apologizing to you. I feel like what I said to you might have had something to do with that."

My jaw tightened.

Last night, Valerie and I shared something special.

Love.

Something I never thought I would have, something that scared the shit out of me. After making love to her, we packed up and left the forest. When we came out, the four-wheeler was waiting for us in Ranger's place. By the time we arrived back at the house, everyone was asleep. The kitchen was cleaned, and Jackie was snoring on the couch.

This morning, Valerie went into town with the twins to get some groceries. Caleb wanted to go, but until this shit with Moonie was handled, I couldn't let him leave the ranch. He was down in the barn with Mags and Jigs. I would be heading down there in a moment to have a talk with him about his mother.

My boy deserved better.

My thoughts drifted to the woman who woke up beside me this morning. The woman who kissed me like I was the air she needed to breathe after I repeated those three little words. The woman who looked at my boy like he was a treasure. The woman with the breathtaking smile and enchanting eyes.

"Denver?"

Shaking off those thoughts, I made my way across the porch to Nancy and got down on my haunches in front of her. There was a conversation that needed to happen here, too. As I adjusted my hat and looked out to Hallow Ranch, I spoke, "Lost my momma when I was just a boy."

"Oh, my goodness," she breathed. I looked back up to the mother of the woman I loved.

"I need you to know I'm going to take care of her," I promised, my voice rougher than I intended it to be. I needed her to know that after she was gone and in heaven, because there was no doubt in my mind that a sweet soul like her wouldn't be anywhere else, I would be there for Valerie.

Her eyes warmed and filled with tears. "Sweetheart, I knew that from the moment I saw you on my phone screen."

"But I can't protect her from the pain, Nancy."

It hurt like hell to say that. I wanted to protect Valerie from everything. We held each other's eyes, the shadow of death looming over us. For a moment, I saw fear in her eyes, but she blinked it away quickly, replacing it with a sad smile.

"Pain is just a part of life. Without pain, how does one grow?"

I smirked at her. "Didn't know I was talking to fucking Hallmark card."

"I didn't know I was talking to such a fucking potty mouth," she scolded playfully.

I blinked, then found myself chuckling. "Jesus, you and Val are just alike. I wanted to let you know Doc is going to be stopping by this afternoon, is that alright?"

"Doc?" she questioned, surprised.

I nodded. "I'm in love with your daughter, Nancy. That makes you family." I paused for a moment, looking at the ranch. When I looked back to her, I said, "I take care of my family."

She didn't say anything for a long time, and she didn't have to. When she did, the pain in my chest almost became unbearable.

"I'm just sorry I'm not going to be a part of it for long."

***

"Caleb, I'm not mad at you," I said to my boy gently as we looked out to the herd. The sun was high, the sky blue, and white clouds drifted over us. Both of us were mounted on Ranger as I guided him to the outer field, close to the fence.

"I didn't want her to get into trouble," he said, keeping his head straight.

A deep sigh left me, and I put my hand on his shoulder. "The most important person in my life is you, son, do you understand? Your mother put you in a dangerous situation."

"How was that dangerous, Dad? She's just messy."

My jaw tightened, frustrated with his innocence, but grateful for it at the same time. It wasn't his fault. Most children raised in toxic homes don't know any better. "Did your mother tell you she would get in trouble if you told me about everything?" I asked, keeping my voice even.

"She said she has to drink that adult stuff to deal with her adult problems and that you didn't like it."

Fucking Christ.

"Bud, do you like staying at your mom's?"

"No," he answered, sadness in his voice. "I love it here, Dad. I love the ranch."

Me too, kid.

"This is your home," I reminded him. "Do you feel safe here?"

He nodded, the back rim of his cowboy hat brushing against my abdomen. I swallowed the lump in my throat. "Did you feel safe at your mom's?"

His little shoulders dropped a bit. "Only when I was in my room."

Rage coursed through me, and I squeezed my eyes shut. "I'm so sorry, bud," I whispered, my voice thick.

Caleb twisted his torso then, turning to face me. His hat tilted up and his matching gray eyes met mine as his brows came together. "Why are you sorry? It's not your fault Mom has issues."

I tugged on the reigns gently, urging Ranger to come to a stop. "I'm your father. It's my job to protect you."

"You're doing it now," he said plainly.

"I'm supposed to do it always."

"Even when I'm a man like you?" he questioned. I gave him a nod.

Until I'm six feet under, son. I will always protect you.

A few minutes later, we were coming into pasture three, which came up to one of roads that lead directly to the city of Denver. There was a black Ram truck parked on the side of it, close to my fence. My body went on alert, my eyes scanning the field in front of me. When they landed on two bison on the far side of the field, near the trees, my stomach tightened. My eyes swung back to the truck and to the man leaning against it, his head turned in the direction of the animals.

"What the fuck?" I growled, reaching into my saddle bag to pull out my walkie-talkie. Switching to the right channel, I pressed the button and said, "Barn one, this is Kings. Got a truck parked outside pasture three. Over."

"Who's that, Dad?" Caleb asked, looking back and forth between us. The man hadn't noticed us yet.

It wasn't Moonie. Tim Moonie had blonde hair. The man before us had a shaved head. He was wearing jeans, a white T-shirt, and shades were on his face. He hadn't looked in our direction yet.

But I knew that he knew we were here.

"This is Jigs. Mags and Beau are heading to you. Over."

I kept the device on but put it back into the saddle bag. "Come on. Let's get you back to the barn," I rumbled, turning Ranger around. Snapping the reins, Ranger started running. "Hold on, Caleb."

Three minutes later, Ranger's hooves were pounding against the Earth, Caleb was holding onto his hat, leaning over the horn, and I leaned over him as he we came around the bend. The herd came into view, and I reduced our speed. Mags and Beau were charging towards us.

"Beau, take Caleb back to the barn. Tell Jigs to keep an eye on him," I called. The cowboys reached us, and I helped Caleb off Ranger. My son turned to me, his cheeks tinted red from the wind, his eyes wide with concern.

"Who's that, Dad?" he asked in a panic.

I adjusted my hat before grabbing the reins again. Beau was swinging Caleb up on his horse when I said, "Son, this your land. You have to protect your land and the animals on it, whether they belong to you or not."

He nodded. "He's a bison hunter, isn't he?"

The men and I shared a look. The torment of history was creeping up on me, but I would do everything in my power to stop it from repeating itself. "I don't know, bud. I'm going to talk to him."

He nodded. "Okay, Dad"

I lifted my chin to Beau. "Go. Hurry."

As soon as they were off, I turned Ranger back in the direction of pasture three and looked at Mags.

He shook his head, bringing his horse up to mine. "Don't feel like burning anyone today."

"Then let's hope that he's just a fucking tourist."

Once back in pasture three, I didn't slow down until I was about twenty feet from the stranger. The bison had moved closer to the trees, in the shade.

"You lost?" I yelled to the man, easing Ranger to a stop. Mags guided Midnight, his black mare, to a stop beside me. He leaned forward crossing his forearms on the saddle horn, appearing laid back.

We both knew he could blow a fuse at a moment's notice.

The stranger turned to us, the lenses of his shades shining under the high afternoon sun. A smile spread across his face, and I knew instantly that he was a threat. Whatever came out of his mouth was a lie.

"Holy hell, real cowboys!" he exclaimed, appearing to be excited. He jerked his thumb back to his truck. "I was just driving through, trying to get to California for my niece's birthday party. Saw the bison over there and just had to stop to take a look."

Mags grunted.

"This is private property," I replied, not buying a single word of his story.

He held up his hands in surrender, and under his right arm, across his bicep there was a tattoo a rifle and a skull. Mags sat up, pretending to stretch.

"You see that shit?" he whispered.

"I'm so sorry, gentlemen! I'll be on my way now," the man said, back away.

"Smart," I grumbled. Mags and I both watched him climb into his vehicle. As the truck pulled off the road, Mags read out the plate.

"Zero, two, alpha, bravo, six, six, nine. Texas plates. What a coincidence," he deadpanned. He had the plate number memorized, and we would give that information to Chase.

"Yes, I saw the tattoo," I said, looking at my friend.

Mags' shades faced me. "Wanna know why it looks so familiar?"

I already knew the answer. When Valerie was doing research on Moonie, the article about the boy being hazed also included photos of the high school football team. There was a boy in the back of the photo flexing his arms, and on his right bicep was a rifle tattoo. He must've added the skull later.

"Looks like we might be burning someone after all," Mags deadpanned.

"Not today, but soon."

On the ride back to the house, I felt my phone buzzing in my pocket.

I didn't answer it with the intention of calling the person back. I knew it had to be Joseph Grayson. I was expecting an update today on my brother. When we got back to the barn, I heard Valerie's laughter coming from inside the bunkhouse. Jigs and Nancy were in the middle of a card game. Jackie was standing behind Jigs, giving signals to Nancy, and Valerie was leaning up against the kitchen counter with her head thrown back.

My woman.

My Valerie.

My enchantress.

I never called Grayson back.

Instead, I enjoyed a night with my family.

Chapter Thirty-Six

Valerie

"Denver."

"It's done, baby," he said firmly, folding his arms over his bare, damp, perfectly sculpted chest. Damn me for confronting him about this when he was fresh out of the shower.

Jackie left for Texas three days ago. Beau had driven her to the airport. She swore to up and down she was going to get that man to fall in love with her. Mom reminded her that Beau was twenty years younger than her, and that earned Mom a glare. After saying our goodbyes, we went inside and played a boardgame with Caleb. Denver didn't participate, but he watched from his spot on the couch. It had been a good night. Three blissful days later, the local doctor returned to Hallow Ranch for the second time.

Three days ago, I had been in town with the twins, buying groceries and clothes when he came. Apparently, Mom asked if he could return on a different day, one where I would be present.

He took her upstairs into her room this morning and a few minutes later, they asked me to join them. After signing some paperwork, my mom granted him permission to discuss her health with me. He explained to me that he would be performing her chemo treatments here, once a week, to save her to the trouble of travelling into town. I could see the cost and the numbers rising in my head.

Then I asked him about a payment plan...

Dr. Martin was sweet man. You could see that just by his warm, brown eyes.

"Doctor, forgive me for interrupting, but I need to discuss a payment plan with you," I said, pulling out my planner and pen. "Do I need to discuss that with you personally or your billing specialist at your office?"

When I looked back up at him, there was a kind smile plastered on his face. "Sweet girl, let's talk in the hall," he said, standing up. I shot a look at my mother. She was reading again, unbothered by everything going around her. I followed him out into the hall. Dr. Martin was down by Caleb's room, looking inside when I shut the door behind me.

A chuckle left him. "You know, I've been the doctor in this town for over thirty years and I will never forget the day Caleb was born," he remarked. "I took one look at him and knew he would be a life changer."

I leaned against the wall. "He's something," I whispered, my voice filled with love.

Love for that boy.

Love for his father.

The doctor sighed and looked at me. "When I saw you downstairs, I understood. Didn't understand it at first, not after everything that Denver went through with Cathy, but I understand it now."

A lock of my hair came out of my braid, and I tucked it behind my ear. "What are you saying, doctor?"

Dr. Martin smiled again, giving me a glimpse of his youth. "There will be no payment plan, Ms. Cross."

My stomach flipped and my knees buckled. Thank God, I was leaning against the wall. "What do you mean?"

I already knew the answer.

"The Hallow Ranch account will be covering your mother's medical bills for the foreseeable future."

Denver's gray eyes were on my face as he shook his head. "It's done."

It was too much.

It was everything.

I couldn't let him do this. It was way too much for me to accept.

Turning on my heel, I crossed the bedroom to where my purse sat on the corner chair. As I got my wallet out to write a check, I turned to face him. "How much was today's—"

My back was against the wall and his hand was around my throat. With a growl, he yanked my wallet out of my hands and tossed it on the bed. His scent and smoke surrounded me. He looked down at my face, his eyes flaring with rage, and pointed at my wallet. His jaw tightened as his nostrils flared.

"You *ever* pull that shit again, Valerie Cross—"

"It's too much," I blurted.

His hand slowly dropped away from my face, and he blinked. My cowboy looked away from me, giving me his handsome profile again. Memories of that night in the woods came flooding in and heat rose in my cheeks.

Then I remembered he was still in a towel.

I put my hands on his chest, the hairs underneath my palms sending a shiver down my spine. Denver was all *man*, and he was all *mine*, but what he was doing was still too much.

"If I were a businessman, and we were in a skyrise that overlooked some fucking city, would you still say it was too much?" he asked, his voice low.

"What? What are you—"

"Valerie, just because I drive a shitbox for a truck and don't wear suits doesn't mean I don't have money." His fingers flexed against my throat. Again, he wasn't choking me. He was just holding me in place.

I shook my head. "That's not what I meant, Denver."

He tilted his head, studying me. "I don't flash my wealth around, baby. I never had the desire too, but if you want something, it's yours. If you want a flashy car, it's yours. If you want fancy clothes, take my card and go shopping. If you want luxury, you'll have it. I don't need much. Never have. I'm a simple man, but that doesn't mean I wouldn't empty my bank account in a fucking heartbeat to make sure you were taken care of."

This man. This cowboy.

"What are you—Ah!"

My dark cowboy lifted me into his arms, pinning me against the wall with his big body. His hands were under me, holding me up by my ass as my legs wrapped around him. "You feel this?" he clipped, shoving my nightie up.

He was all I felt. Everywhere. All the time. For weeks, he was all I felt, and I wanted to forever.

"Denver, you don't understand..." I trailed off as one of his hands moved to my underwear.

"No," he grunted, giving the fabric a forceful tug. When my shredded panties were on the floor and his towel was in a heap by his feet, he spoke again. "You don't understand, and that's on me. So, I'm going to explain it to you in way you will understand." With that, he entered me with a powerful thrust that had my head snapping back. The hand that yanked my panties off snapped up to my mouth, covering it to muffle the cry that escaped me.

I was still so sore from last night's lovemaking, but he didn't care. He thrust into me again with a growl. "You feel it now?"

Nodding, my limbs tightened around him, and my eyes wanted to close.

"Look at me," he grunted.

My eyes met his and I could see it. *Love.* "Denver..."

"You are mine, Valerie. You belong to *me*. Your body is *mine*. Your heart is *mine*. Your soul belongs to *my soul*. Do you understand?" he asked, moving in and out of me slowly now. He ducked his head and began kissing my neck.

I nodded, breathless. "Yes."

"I take care of what's mine, Enchantress," he whispered against my skin.

"I can't let you—Ah!"

His hand was in my hair, yanking it back painfully. "I don't give a fuck who's in this house and who can hear. You don't accept the fact that I'm going to take care of you for the rest of your life, I will punish you, and you won't be able to leave the fucking bed tomorrow," he warned harshly into my ear, slamming his hips into me.

"Den—"

"I love you. Fuck, I love you. *Dammit*, baby, let me take care of you." He let go of my hair and brought my lips to his, kissing me roughly. He fucked me faster, not breaking the kiss. My body hummed as I clung to him. When I was close, he broke away from me, halting his movements.

"You gonna let me take care of my family, or do I need to punish you?" Denver whispered, resting his forehead against mine.

"Family?" I breathed.

"Yes."

Tears stung my eyes. "I love you."

"That's all fine and good. I love you and I love hearing you say that, but I need you to let me—"

"Okay," I said, kissing him again. I pulled away, "But I get to cook you dinner."

He shook his head. "Gotta feed my woman and fuck her every night."

"Do you just expect me to lounge around the house all day and do nothing?" I asked, raising an eyebrow. He pulled out and slammed back into me again, forcing me to moan.

"You can do whatever the fuck you want," he growled. "You can write, draw, paint, start a business. I don't care. If you make money, that's your money."

"Denver," I whimpered, trying my best to protest but he felt too good. This felt too good. We felt too good.

Thrust.

"I."
Thrust.
"Take."
Thrust.
"Care."
Thrust.
"Of."
Thrust and hold.
"You."

"Then—then I want to cook dinner," I stammered, not giving up even though my body was about to give in, trembling around him.

He smiled and dropped his face back into my neck. Dragging his tongue up the column of my neck, he whispered, "Three nights. That's all you get. Now shut up and take this dick like the good, sweet, little, slut you are."

Three orgasms later, my head was on his chest as I listened to him sleep. The moonlight shined through the windows and the room was filled with Denver's breathing. There was a smile on my face as I fell asleep.

He might take care of me, but I knew I was taking care of him too.

"Sweetheart, will you grab that blanket out of the dryer?" I called out to Caleb in the living room. Mom was upstairs taking a nap, Denver was working, and Caleb said this morning he wanted to stay inside today and read *Harry Potter*.

I couldn't blame the kid. He was on the fourth book, my favorite. I read that book in one setting when I was kid.

"Caleb?" I called, wiping my hand with a towel. I was making a blueberry lemon cake for the guys. No answer. Did he go outside?

The living room was empty. I turned and went upstairs. Mom's bedroom door was closed, the office was empty, and his room was empty. Panic set in as the hairs on the back of my neck stood up. I never heard the front door open and if he was going to go outside, he would have said something. I hurried downstairs and went to the laundry room.

The back door was open.

"Caleb! Come here!" a woman's voice called.

"No!"

Cathy.

I was running out the back door to the backyard before my brain could alert me of the potential danger. My eyes scanned the area quickly, and I saw a flash of bleached blonde hair around the corner of the house. My heart was hammering in my chest as I ran through the small picket fence gate. When I got to the front of the house, I saw Cathy trying to drag Caleb by the arm to her car. He looked back as saw me, tears in his eyes.

She was traumatizing him.

"Let him go!" I screamed. The insane woman whipped around, and I was close enough now to see her fake nails digging into Caleb's skin. He was holding on to her wrist, trying to break free.

"You," she sneered.

I came to a stop about three feet from them. Denver and the men were out at the second barn, fixing the roof. He was too far away to hear the commotion.

"Cathy, let him go," I snapped, taking a step forward. I took a second to look at her. She had a black eye and busted lip. There was no doubt that Tim did that to her. Her hair was knotted, and there was dried blood across her right temple. She looked dirty, like she hadn't showered in days. The makeup on her face was smeared and worn. I could smell the alcohol on her from here, and along with the faint scent of urine.

Cathy shook her head violently. "This is my boy, you understand me, bitch? He will never be your son," she cried. Caleb was looking at me now, fear in his gray eyes as well as tears.

"Val, help me! She just showed up and called my name. I don't want to go with her! I want to stay here!" he cried, yanking against his mother's hold. Her nails were piercing his skin now, and I saw a trickle of blood run down his little arm.

"You have two seconds to release him, Cathy. I'm warning you," I said calmly.

She scoffed. "What are you going to do?"

My hands came up to my hair and I tied it into a knot on the top of my head as I hissed, "Last chance."

A cruel, ugly laugh came from her. "You think you can take me?" She shook her head and then looked down at her son, the one person she was supposed to love unconditionally and treat with care. With a swift push, she shoved him into the dirt.

I was moving in a blind rage before she could make one more snarky comment. My fist connected with her face in an instant, and pain radiated up my arm. She staggered back, her dull brown eyes wide, palm to her jaw. "You fucking—"

I bared my teeth. "Cathy, shut up." Putting my hands on her shoulders, I shoved her back against her car. She slammed into it and slumped against the door, breathing heavily. Her head rolled and she tried to push herself up, but I put my hand on her chest, holding her in place.

"Stay down, Cathy."

She screamed at me. I ignored it and twisted my head to see Caleb running away. I looked back at his mother, shaking my head.

"That little boy will never forget the pain you caused him today, the fear you instilled in him, and the confusion he will feel when he looks back on this. Moms are supposed to love, Cathy. Love."

She stared up at me with hatred in her eyes. "Fuck you."

I took a step back from her. "Hallow Ranch has cameras everywhere. Sheriff Bowen is looking for you. The whole town is looking for you. You have a choice to make. Right now."

When I turned to head to the barn, she hissed, "He'll never love you. Denver Langston has a heart of ice."

"Goodbye, Cathy."

I didn't bother looking back as I ran down to the barn.

"Caleb!" I called, once I entered the building. The horses were gone for the day and silence filled the space. I ran upstairs to find the loft empty. I ran to the bunkhouse, fear clawing at my soul.

"Sweetheart," I called. The small kitchen was empty, and the muffins I made last night were gone, an empty plate remained on the counter. The cowboys' bunks lined the walls, all of them empty. I heard water running in the bathroom. Slowly, I made my way to the ajar door.

"Caleb, it's me," I said gently, leaning my forehead against the door.

"Go away," he cried, his voice shaking.

Pushing the door open, I was greeted with the heartbreaking sight of the little boy sitting on the counter, holding a damp paper towel to his arm. His cheeks were red, his dark hair windblown, and his eyes were shining with tears. I took a step inside.

"Go away!"

"I can't do that, sweetheart," I whispered.

He shook his head. "You have to," he cried.

"Why?"

He sniffled and looked away from me. "Because cowboys don't bleed."

I closed the distance between us, cupped his handsome, little face in my hands, and my thumbs wiped away his tears. "Look at me. You are so brave, do you know that?"

"She hurt me," he whimpered, holding up his arm. "I'm trying not to cry, because Dad never cries."

I gently lifted his arm so I could take a better look. Sure enough, his horrid mother's nails left bloody half-moon marks on his forearm. The sight made me want to punch her again and again, but I shouldn't have punched her, Caleb didn't need to see that violence.

"I'm sorry she hurt you. I'm also sorry I punched her."

"She deserved it," he grumbled. I tilted his head up so I could look him in the eyes.

"You didn't deserve to see that," I declared. "I didn't think, and that's on me."

He raised a dark brow. "You apologize for weird stuff."

"Maybe," I agreed. "Let's get you cleaned up."

After wrapping his arm, we walked back up to the house. Cathy's car was gone and my mother was on the porch, dressed in overalls and a blue paisley scarf was wrapped around her head. There was a look of concern painted on her face as we approached.

"Is everything alright?"

Caleb went inside, and my eyes met Mom's.

It was time to tell her the truth.

Chapter Thirty-Seven

Denver

"Yeah, that's good," Beau said, walking away from me, taking Ranger with him.

In was the end of the day—*a long day*. The storm from a few weeks ago caused some damage to the secondary barn that went unnoticed until Lawson went out on a ride last night. The boys and I have been working on it since the crack of dawn, and the sun granted us no mercy.

Now, the work was done, the herd was managed, the livestock exchange was around the corner, and I had two women and a little boy at the house waiting for me, along with a cold shower.

"Have a goodnight," I hollered, putting my hat back on. I turned to head out of the barn when my cellphone rang.

It was Grayson.

"This is Denver."

"Took you long enough," he deadpanned.

"Did you get in touch with my brother?" I asked, cutting straight through the bullshit.

"I did."

I remained silent waiting for him to continue, and when he didn't, I growled, "Don't have all night, Grayson."

"He isn't coming home, but you and I both knew he wouldn't."

I ignored the burning in my chest, shoving it down where it belonged. "I appreciate the time," I clipped, ready to hang up.

"Denver, there's something else."

My feet moved to the corral, and I leaned against the metal fence, my eyes on the sunlight setting behind my mountain. "There always is," I grumbled.

"Your girl is playing you."

I stiffened, my blood running cold. "The fuck you just say to me?"

"You heard me. One thing to note; I never ignore my gut, and my gut was telling me that Valerie Cross was a fucking—"

"Careful, bounty hunter. Choose your next words wisely," I warned, my voice low.

"Ran an extensive background check on her, Langston. Didn't like what I found," he quipped.

"And what did you find?" I snarled.

How dare he? Valerie was clean—*good*. She was everything to me.

She cared about me.

She cared about my son.

She cared about Hallow Ranch.

Whatever Grayson found was—

"She's still on the Moonie Pipelines Incorporated payroll," he informed, his voice tight.

I scoffed, pushing off the fence. "You do realize he fired her less than a month ago and that your data is—"

"She was removed from it the day she was fired, company policy. She was added back to the payroll a week after Tim Moonie fired her."

The world around me stilled.

The beauty of the sunset dulled and faded away, along with the lush green covering the valley before me. In its place was a construction site and a Moonie Pipelines semi-truck parked where the bunk house should be.

I took a slow turn, watching everything that my grandfather, my father, and me built and protected. The bunk house, the barn, and my home vanished before my eyes. Piles of dirt stood in their places, and standing in the center of it all was the woman I'd fallen in love with. The woman I'd bared my broken soul to.

My enchantress.

The woman sent by the enemy to seduce me.

The woman with the gorgeous green eyes and dark hair.

The woman who smelled of cherries and happiness.

That woman was now standing beside Tim Moonie dressed in the same outfit from that first day. Tim wore a snarky smile as he ripped a check from his checkbook.

"Pleasure doing business with you, Ms. Cross."

Her green eyes shone, and when she smiled, it reminded me of the smile Cathy wore when my brother found her in my bed. My gut twisted violently, like there was a knife being shoved into to it, along with the one in my back. I blinked, but the image didn't go away.

Now, there was the man from the other day. The bald man. He came up behind Valerie and put his hand on her shoulder.

"Aren't you going to say something, Val?" he asked, jerking his chin to me.

She looked at me, and the love I'd seen in her eyes the last few weeks was gone, replaced by pride. "Checkmate, cowboy." She gave me a wink and my chest cracked open.

"Denver!"

I blinked and Hallow Ranch returned to normal, but the woman was still in front of me. She was closer now, her hair braided, hanging over one shoulder, and she was wearing a red sundress with little white polka dots. Her cherry scent took over my senses, as her green eyes bounced back and forth, scanning my face.

"Honey, you are you okay?" she asked, her voice soft, like an angel.

I pulled the phone away from my ear, hanging up on Grayson as I stared down at her. There was a pain inside my chest I hadn't felt in a long time. The first time I felt it was the day Momma was murdered. Today was the second.

The second time that my heart would be broken—shattered into jagged pieces so small that it would take *decades* to put back together. I've done it before. I could do it again.

"So, all that bullshit about money last night...it was guilt, wasn't it?" I asked, keeping it short and to the point.

Valerie jerked back slightly. Clearly, she wasn't expecting my question. Then again, she wasn't expecting me to find out. *Right?*

"Smoke, what are—"

"Don't you dare," I seethed, stepping to her, closing the distance between us. I looked down at her like she was the shit underneath my boot, and she was. "Don't you dare call me that."

Her head shook, and she brought her hand up to her chest. "What's going on? Did something happen?"

A harsh, dark laugh escaped me, and I adjusted my hat, looking away from her. "How long were you going to take my dick before you tried to convince me to sell the ranch?"

Her skin paled, and her eyes grew wide. "Denver, what are you talking about?"

God damn, she was a good fucking actress. There were tears forming in her eyes. She got me good.

"That's why you were nervous when that bounty hunter came by the house. You knew t he would look into you. He looks into everyone."

"Joseph? Did he call you? What did he—"

"Did you think I wouldn't have found out? That somehow with your kind eyes, breathtaking smile, and your sweet pussy would convince me to sell my home to a greedy bastard like Moonie? How did you think that was going to work?"

She stared at me.

Another laugh left me. "Fucking Christ, I am such a fucking idiot. Told you that first day my dick wasn't a leash, and yet here we are..."

"Denver," she croaked, tears slowly falling down her cheeks now.

God, I wanted to wipe them away and I hated that. Fuck, her claws were in deep.

"Fuck, but I fell in love with you, ya know?" I bellowed, backing away from her and holding my arms out wide. "You were going to leave me and my son in the dust, weren't you? After Moonie signed your check?" My voice was getting louder as my anger grew. I needed to be angry. I needed to hate her. It would numb the earth-shattering pain in my chest. I heard the bunkhouse door open behind me. Good. They needed to hear this, too.

"Denver, I really have no idea what you're talking about!" she cried, trying to reach for me.

"Put that fucking hand down," I growled, my voice stilling her movements. "You will never get to fucking touch me again."

She was shaking now, her arms wrapped around her middle. "W-what—I don't understand."

"Neither do I, baby. That's what love does to you!" I shouted. "It blinds you and sucks the air out of your fucking lungs, leaving you desperate and defenseless. Let me tell you something, Valerie Cross, you will never have my fucking ranch!"

She flinched and backed away from me.

"Kings."

That was Mags. He was somewhere behind me, but I didn't care. I wasn't done. I knew this woman didn't love me, but fuck, I wanted her to hurt like she hurt me. I wanted her to cry like she did on the first day I met her. Hell, those tears were probably fake, too. She probably knew about the cameras. She played me for a god-damn fool.

"Denver, please. Listen to me, let me—"

"Get the fuck off my land, Valerie."

The air between us was thick.

"Denver, please—"

I took a step towards her, ready to hit her where it hurts, but something stopped me. Maybe it was the love I had for her, the love that would haunt me for the rest of my miserable life, because I knew I wouldn't be able to get over her. There was no getting over Valerie.

My Enchantress had marked my soul, branded it.

I was hers, even when I didn't want to be.

She would never know it.

"Leave!"

My anger and volume made her flinch. That alone damn near killed me, but someday, I would learn not to care. I watched as she ran away from me, but I didn't get to see what direction she was moving in because I was spun around.

Mags was in my face, studying me with a frown on his face. "What happened?"

"I need whiskey," I croaked as the pain washed over me like acid rain. Mags held my eyes for a second longer before nodding.

"Done, brother."

"Kings, get up."

I groaned.

"Your boy is outside looking for you. Beau is distracting him. You and I both know he doesn't need to see you like this," Mags said.

Hungover and heartbroken?

I opened my eyes and sat up. My body ached and my throat was dry. I hadn't drunk that much in years. Last night, I'd fallen asleep in the bunkhouse after drowning out all thoughts of tear-filled green eyes with a fifth of Jack Daniels. Reaching for my hat, I put it on my head as I stood.

"You good?" Lawson asked. I looked to where he and his brother were. Both of them wore unreadable expressions, same as last night. Then again, that woman played all of us. I gave them a single nod.

"Dad!" My boy pushed past Beau, and my eyes dropped to the bandage on his arm.

"What happened?" I asked, harsher than intended, gently grabbing his arm.

Caleb yanked it away. "I ain't here for that. Where's Valerie?"

My jaw tightened and the knife in my back twisted once more, burying itself a little deeper than before.

"What's this all about, Caleb?" Jigs asked from his place at the table. He was sipping on a cup of joe, the steam covering his face.

Caleb looked around. "Valerie didn't come home last night!"

This was never her home, son. Not to her.

"Caleb—"

"No, Beau!" The boy whirled, pointing at the man in the doorway. "She came down here to get Dad for dinner last night—"

"Enough," I barked. He looked up at me, shock on his face. Confusion followed.

"Where is she, Dad?"

I shook my head. "That woman is gone."

He stepped back, shaking his head in disbelief. "No, she can't be. Not after..."

"Not after what?" Mags pressed.

Caleb held up his arm. "Mom did this to me yesterday."

A cold, deadly silence, filled the room. I stared at the little boy who kept me from putting a bullet in my mouth ten years ago, trying to comprehend what he was telling me.

"What did you say?"

"Mom came up to the house yesterday while you were working on the other barn. She tried to take me, but Val stopped her. Mom's nails here cutting me, Dad. Val told Mom to let me go. Then Val punched Mom in the jaw!" he explained.

I flinched.

She still defended my boy.

While Moonie was dropping money into her bank account.

"I ran down here to get help, but no one was here. I went into the bathroom to clean up the blood, but Valerie found me, and I didn't want her to."

"Why?" I found myself asking.

Caleb met my eyes. "Because cowboys don't cry, and I wanted to cry then."

Oh, bud, how wrong you are.

Cowboys cry.

They just don't let anyone see the tears.

He continued. "She can't be gone. Miss Nancy is getting worried. Val promised me something yesterday! So, I know she can't be gone."

"What did she promise you?"

She promised me things, too...

His bottom lip trembled. "She promised she would try to love me like a momma should."

Fucking hell.

My knees gave out, and I fell onto the cot again. Elbows on my knees, my head fell, and I gave the room the top of my hat.

Cowboys don't cry, they mourn.

A single tear pooled in my left eye, and I watched it fall. I watched as it landed on the tip of my boot. I watched as it glistened against the worn leather. I watched it slide down to the floor as my heart pounded in my ears. She was gone and it was for the best.

Protect Hallow Ranch, boys, with everything you have and then some. Give your blood, sweat, and tears to this land and no one else.

For the first time in years, my father's voice filled my head. Momma was silent. She had been since I declared my love for Valerie in the forest.

It had been the best night of my life.

Who knew that only days later, I would be living a nightmare.

"Kings."

I raised my head, evidence of that single tear long gone. Dried up. That would be the only tear shed for Valerie Cross. She took my heart with her last night; she didn't need my tears, too. "What?"

"Dad, she never came back to the house last night," Caleb said, fear in his voice.

She ran away from me, but I didn't see where she ran to.

Dread pulled in my gut, along with something else.

Fear.

Fear for her not being okay.

Fuck.

Chapter Thirty-Eight

Denver, CO. Tim Moonie's penthouse hotel room.
"What?" Tim barked into the phone, getting up from the couch.

"I have her," a voice said on the other end of the line.

A sinister smile spread across the man's face as he stared out of the window, the city of Denver bustling below. It was a sunny day, and the temperature was set to reach a record high. After leaving Cathy bleeding in the floor with instructions to kill herself, he came back to the city, needing to attend some meetings with investors and construction crews.

Moonie Pipelines was set to break ground on the Hallow Ranch project on January first. That meant he had six months to get the Langston family off that land.

He didn't care if it was in body bags or not.

However, today...today, Tim was feeling a bit nostalgic. "Did you know, old friend, that years ago, a woman was burned to death on Hallow Ranch?"

The man stayed silent.

Tim continued, chuckling a bit as he made his way back to the couch, "It was the owner's wife, actually. After doing some digging, I found an old article. Believe it or not, it wasn't the fire killed her. No, no, old friend, it was the bison hunters."

The man grunted.

"Unfortunately, the fire that the hunters had set for her killed them, too," Tim sighed.

"Is that what you want me to do with her, sir?"

Curiosity got the best of him. "Have you fucked her yet?"

"No."

"Do you want to?" he pressed, his mind going back to his perfect girl and how he used to fuck her until she cried.

"Maybe her mouth, but I don't need her biting my dick off."

The owner of Moonie Pipelines threw his head back and laughed, the sound echoing throughout the entire space. The woman on the bed stirred. "Best avoid that at all costs, old friend. She's a fierce one."

The line was silent again as the man waited for instructions. Tim would give it to him, of course, but he liked how powerful he felt when men waited for him.

"I do love how history seems to repeat itself," he murmured, looking at the redhead in the bed. She was covered in bruises from her beating. Tim liked that, beating them into submission.

"Consider it done, sir."

The phone call ended, and Tim walked to the bed, staring down at the naked woman. Red hair. Not like hers. Never like hers.

There was no other woman like his perfect girl.

No other woman who cried like her. Begged like her. Screamed like her.

She had gotten away from him, but yesterday, he found her. After six years, he found his perfect girl again. She would be his again soon.

Until then, the woman in front of him would have to suffice.

Valerie

The man stepped up to me again. He palmed the front of his jeans, making me want to vomit. I looked up, the rag in my mouth stretching around the back of my neck, causing resistance. He was wearing a ski mask—*how typical was that?*

"Boss said I could fuck you," he drawled.

I stiffened.

"I don't like fat bitches...but you do have a pretty mouth," he said, leaning down to yank the rag out of my mouth.

"You put your cock near me, I'll bite it off," I hissed, breathing hard.

He chuckled. "Relax, fatty. Not gonna do that."

I didn't relax. I didn't believe him.

I clenched my teeth and twisted my bound wrists together. This wasn't rope; it was plastic—a zip tie. I was on my knees, the hard, wooden planks beneath me digging into my skin. The man had been sitting in a chair in the corner, on the phone. Now he was in front of me, rubbing his jeans like a sick fuck.

If he wanted to fuck my mouth, he would have to break my fucking jaw. If he wanted to rape me, he would have to knock me out. There was no way I was going down without a fucking fight. I would not break for any man.

"Mr. Moonie said you were a fierce one."

I rolled my eyes. "How lovely."

No surprise that Moonie was behind this. He was becoming desperate.

The man stared at me for a beat, and I held his stare. He wasn't going to see a shred of weakness from me. Not today. I wouldn't let give him that fucking power, no matter how scared I was, no matter what.

Grey smoke filled my vision.

Enchantress.

Denver.

Tears stung my eyes at the thought of my dark cowboy.

My cowboy, who, for some reason hated me. That thought alone was enough to break me. *Get the fuck off my land, Valerie.*

Last night, after he pushed me away, I ran. I ran from him. I ran from Hallow Ranch. I was trying to run away from the agony that pierced my heart. Then, I ran to my mom.

I never made it back to the house.

I didn't know if it was hours, days, or weeks later, when I woke up an hour ago. I had been counting the minutes in my head. The room I was in was small, hot, and dark. There were holes in the ceilings and walls, sunlight seeping through them. Outside, I heard the rustling of trees and the occasional bird. I knew in my gut I was far away from any civilization.

My dress and panties were still on, thank God. I wasn't sore down *there*, but I don't remember getting here. All I remembered was that I was running, felt a burst of pain, and then nothing.

That's what scared me the most, the nothing. The time in between.

"Aw, you crying for me?" my kidnapper drawled.

I blinked my tears away, cursing myself for it. "Never."

The man chuckled. "We'll see about that."

Before I could stop it, I felt a prick in my neck, and everything faded away. Memories of smoke gray eyes under a black cowboy hat were left behind, along with my mom's smile and the sound of a little boy's laughter.

As I slipped away, I heard Denver's deep, sultry voice whispering in my ear, his beard tickling the shell of it.

"I love you."

Chapter Thirty-Nine

Denver

"Denver, where is my daughter?"

My eyes lifted from my security monitors to the sick woman standing in the doorway of my office. Mags was leaning against the wall by the window looking out. Beau was standing by the painting of Hallow Ranch. The twins were standing by the desk and Jigs was sitting in the chair in front of it.

The old man twisted at the sound of her voice and hopped out of the chair. Nancy looked worn down today. She was still recovering from the chemo treatment. Dressed in pajamas, a robe, and carrying her oxygen bag, she looked miserable.

"Nancy," Beau said, going to her. He held out his elbow and she took it immediately.

It was late afternoon. Valerie had been missing for over seventeen hours.

Because you chased her away.

"We're trying to find her," I said, my voice void of emotion.

Pale green eyes met mine and I watched as she straightened her back. "Boys, I would like to talk to your boss alone."

The twins shared a look, both their faces hard.

"The sheriff has dispatched his deputies and we—"

The woman cut me off. "Denver, so help me God! You and I will hash this out alone, or we can do it in front of your boys."

"Leave us," I clipped.

Beau helped her get to the chair Jigs vacated, and then they were gone. Once the door shut behind Lawson, she unleashed her fury.

"What did you do to her?" she snapped.

"I'm going to find her. Then, you two are on the first plane back to Texas," I promised.

She shook her head, her face twisting in confusion. "I don't understand. I thought you loved my Vallie."

Oh, I do.

I had a feeling that was something that would never change. Even if I cut my own heart out from my fucking chest. Loving Valerie was now a curse instead of a blessing.

"Let's not play dumb, Mrs. Cross," I drawled, my upper lip curled.

"How about you cut the shit and tell me what the hell happened last night?" she demanded, her voice rising. She was out of breath, her chest rising and falling rapidly.

Concern hit me. "Do you really not know how she played me?"

"Played you?"

With a growl, I stood from my chair, bracing my hands on the desk. I leaned over the woman. "She's still working for Moonie!" I yelled. "She's still on his fucking payroll, Nancy! Are you really going to sit there, in my house, and act like you didn't know?"

Hell, Valerie probably agreed to have her mom come out here to see her latest conquest. Then, they would run off into the sunset together, Moonie's check in hand. My skin grew tight, and I felt a drop of sweat trickle down the side of my temple. The second chair beside Nancy had been empty, but now it wasn't.

I blinked, but the man in the chair didn't disappear.

The man in the chair was my dead father. He was old, worn, and had white hair. His gray eyes assessed me as his head slowly tilted. He crossed his ankle over the opposite knee and sat back. Then, he pointed to the woman beside him.

"This is a wolf in sheep's clothing, son. I thought I taught you better than that," he said, his old voice shaking slightly, but it was hard to miss the disappointment in it.

I brought my hands to my hair, pushing my hat off. It was happening again, and I couldn't stop it. In the distance, I heard bullets flying and bombs exploding. Pop didn't seem to be bothered.

"You know, I always was proud of you. Then you had to go and become something you aren't," he continued. "A hero."

"Stop," I ordered, blinking and shaking my head. It's not real.

I was back in the war zone, the Marine beside me firing his gun, yelling out something as I ducked to reload. When I looked back up not even half a second later, blood splattered across my face. The soldier fell, his face in the dirt.

Never leave a man behind.

I sprang into action, my ears still ringing from the bomb. Crouching low, I called out his name and pushed him over. That wasn't soldier. With a cry, I jumped back, landing on my ass. That wasn't a Marine.

It was Valerie.

"Baby," I croaked, crawling back to her.

The light in her enchanting green eyes was gone, her mouth open, her jaw slack. Blood covered her forehead, oozing from the bullet hole, tainting her soft, flawless skin. "No, Val. Fuck, baby," I whimpered, hauling her to me. I shook her. Once. Twice.

She was gone.

My arms wrapped around her, holding her body to mine. I twisted, shielding her from the incoming bullets. Even in death, I wanted to protect her. Even in death, my love for her still lived. The gunshots ceased and a low, cruel chuckle filled my ears.

I lifted my head to find Tim Moonie standing a few feet away from me, dressed in a navy suit and gold tie. He was holding a bottle of champagne. The smile he wore was so sinister, it could've given nuns nightmares. He raised the bottle in victory, and suddenly, everything around me changed.

Valerie's dead weight vanished. She was no longer in my arms. I scrambled, putting my hands on the green grass—*grass*. I looked at Moonie again and realized we were home. We were back at Hallow Ranch. There was a red ribbon that stretched between two poles, sticking out from the ground. Moonie tossed the bottle to me, and I caught it just in time.

"Go ahead and pour a glass, Langston! It's time to celebrate!"

The bottle disappeared from my hand and was replaced with a glass.

A glass filled with blood.

"You know, I liked that girl. She did such a good job. Made me a lot of fucking money," Moonie sighed. He lifted a pair of scissors, lining the blades up with the red ribbon. "Shame I had to kill her because of your stubbornness."

The glass in my hand bubbled up and over flowed, the blood covering my skin.

"Denver..."

It was a whisper in the wind. A plea. A cry for help. My head snapped to the right. There she was. My enchantress. She was running to me, wearing her blue dress, her shiny, wavy, dark hair flowing behind her. There were tears running down her face, ruining her mascara. I don't know why she was wearing makeup. She looked beautiful without it. I'd told her that a thousand times...*hadn't I?*

Tim laughed again. "Oh, no you don't, Ms. Cross. Sacrifices don't get to run."

My eyes didn't leave her as her body jerked back from the force of the bullets. One. Two. Three. I shouted and tried to run, but I couldn't. I was being held back by someone.

"Damn, bro. Another one bites the dust, huh? First my fiancée and now her?" Mason's deep voice filled my ear, his light laughter making my stomach turn.

I fell to my knees, fighting against his hold. Valerie was on the ground now, on her stomach with her hand stretched out to me, in the dirt.

"Beau! Get Nancy out of here!" Mags yelled.

Nancy?

Fuck, what was I going to tell her? I killed her daughter.

I was a worthless—

"You got two seconds to get a fucking grip before I break your fucking nose—again," a growl came from in front of me.

My eyes opened and Mags was standing above me, his hat off. His long dark hair hung down on either side of his face, his dark eyes flashing with panic. Beau was across from him, chewing his gum slower than normal, his blue eyes on me.

I was on the ground.

No, I was on the floor of my office.

Nancy. I had been talking with Nancy about Valerie—

I sat up quickly and Mags' hands landed on my shoulders. "*Steady*, Kings."

My head shook and I pressed the balls of my palms into my eyes. "What the fuck is wrong with me?"

"Nothing," he answered. "Just got some demons still trying to haunt you, that's all."

"She's dead," I croaked.

"Who?" Beau and Mags barked.

Pain crashed into me like a thousand-pound weight. "Valerie. I killed her." I brought my knees up and put my arms on them before hanging my head.

"This is all Moonie, brother. We're going to find her. We're going to bring her home," Beau promised.

She would never forgive me.

I wouldn't blame her.

"I saw Pop," I admitted, my eyes on the floorboards.

Mags bit out a low curse. "When this is all over, promise me something, Kings."

I lifted my head. He was in front of me now, on his haunches. His eyes held mine as he spoke. "Promise me you'll talk to someone about what you saw over there."

I nodded.

They told me that Nancy called for them when I mentioned Pop. I didn't try to hurt her; I was lost in my own nightmare.

Once I got back in my chair, I got back to work, scanning the security footage from last night. The cameras from the barn and bunkhouse recorded Valerie running up to me. My eyes never left the screen as I watched myself step up to her. I could see the anger pulsing and radiating off my body. I could see the confusion and hurt on her gorgeous face. I could see the fallout. I could see the moment my heart shattered.

When she ran away, I focused on the other cameras. The sun had been setting when we'd started fighting. She didn't head to the house. She ran through the field, cutting through it to head to the driveway. I zoomed in on the frame when she stopped. She was just on the other side of the tree in front of the house, her head buried in her hands, her shoulders shaking. It reminded me of the first day we met. She cried in her car on the edge of my property for twenty minutes.

Guilt cut deep, deeper than the pain I was feeling.

Then, I saw movement in the corner of the screen.

"What the fuck?" Beau hissed. Mags and he leaned in closer to the screen.

"I don't know," I said to no one in particular.

The three of us watched as a masked man crept up behind Valerie. His arm shot out, sticking something into her neck. My blood boiled. She fell limp against the man, and he threw her over his shoulder.

I was about to stand up when a shrill cry of terror cut through the house. A chill brushed over my body, leaving fear in its wake. I was on my feet and moving, the boys charging behind me. Our boots thundered down the stairs and I yanked open the front door. Caleb was at the bottom, his back to us.

"Bud, what's—"

"FIRE! DAD! THE MOUNTAIN IS ON FIRE!" he screamed, pointing.

My eyes jumped up. Dark, thick smoke ascended into the blue sky from the side of the mountain, angry orange flames engulfing the trees, destroying everything in its path.

"Mags?" I said quietly, my eyes not leaving the burning mountain. He knew what I was asking. I didn't have to say the words. My mind was playing tricks on me. I'd seen that fire before, in that same spot, twenty-five years ago.

The day Momma died.

"It's real."

It was hushed confirmation from a brother who understood.

I was moving again, pulling Caleb back and tossing him over my shoulder. I went back into the house, directly up the stairs to the spare bedroom. Nancy had her face buried in her hands, sitting on the bed. Jigs was beside her, his arm on her shoulder. Both of their heads snapped up to me.

"Jigs," I clipped, setting my son down. "Watch the house. Protect my boy. Protect Nancy."

He stood, nodding. "With everything I have."

Beau stepped in beside me, handing his father a pistol. "Just in case."

They shared a moment, and I looked to Nancy.

"I don't have much time. There's a fire on the mountain."

"She's up there, isn't she?" she whispered, her voice trembling.

I hoped God wasn't that cruel.

"You bring her back home," she demanded.

Home.

This was her home.

She belonged with me, and I'd been a fool to chase her away.

Never again.

Chapter Forty

Denver

Sirens filled the air.

Squad cars surrounded the barn.

Sheriff Bowen's men were everywhere.

Someone driving on the main road saw the fire before Caleb did and called it in. The chaos was here by the time I got to the barn. The fire department was here, but there was nothing they could really do.

There was nothing anyone could do, not when it came to a fire of that size.

"Denver, don't even fucking think about it," Chase warned as he got out of his truck. He was in uniform this time. I hated that he was in uniform this time.

I mounted Ranger and pulled my hat down. "This is my ranch, Sheriff. I do what I want."

He charged towards me, but Lawson's horse stepped in front of him. Lance came up beside me on his.

"Let's ride, boys," I yelled, snapping Ranger's reins and kicking my feet. Seconds later, five cowboys and their horses were charging across the field towards the fires of hell, searching for an enchantress lost in the woods.

My enchantress.

My baby.

My Valerie.

The pounding of hooves should have provided me with comfort, but dread was the only thing I could feel. That and fear.

I leaned forward, gaining speed. Mags was beside me, keeping the same speed atop Midnight. Beau was on the other side of me, not far behind, the twins behind him. The beauty of Hallow Ranch faded away, and all I could focus on was my precious Valerie.

The woman who'd given up everything and made a deal with the devil to save her mother. The woman who held everything in until the dam broke. The woman who looked at me with love in her eyes when I told her of my sins, instead of judgement. The woman who'd given me her body and trusted me with it. The woman who smiled into my chest at night when I kissed the top of her head before sleep took over. The woman who wanted to cook for me and my boy. The woman who was making my empty, cold house a home.

The woman who made me feel something other than anger for the first time in my adult life.

The ranch didn't matter anymore, not if she wasn't going to be a part of it. Not if she wasn't going to be in my house, on the porch, on my saddle, in my bed.

We rounded the bend, coming up to the trail entrance. I eased up on Ranger's reins, urging him to stop. My cowboys did the same as I turned my steed around to face them. The smell of smoke and burning wood filled my nose, seeping into my lungs.

Taking as much time as I could, I met each one of their eyes. "You don't have to do this."

Lawson shook his head. "Don't start that bullshit."

Lance looked up at the sun and back to me. "Would ride with you anywhere, Den. You know that."

"We stand by you, but we also stand by Val. Whatever shit went down last night, it's in the past," Beau said.

"She's family," Mags declared, shifting on his saddle. "Let's get her home."

"The second any of you fuckers can't breathe, get out as fast as you can," I ordered.

"That goes for you too, boss," Beau reminded me.

I wasn't coming out of those woods until Valerie was in my arms.

Each of us had a walkie talkie strapped to our hips, along with a pistol. We entered through the trail opening. The fire hadn't gotten down to this part of the woods yet, but smoke lingered in the air, a warning sign of what's to come. All around us, we heard the cries and wails of animals, the shuffling of hooves and paws. Panic was in the trees as birds flew overhead, escaping the nightmare easily. The herd was still in pasture three, away from the mountain, thank God.

Ranger was tense underneath me; he could sense the danger. I rubbed his neck. "Stay with me, bud. Can't bring her home without you." It killed me to put him in danger like this, but there wasn't enough time for me track Valerie on foot.

I needed him.

"Break off at the stream," I ordered, snapping the reins, commanding Ranger to go faster. We were coming up on the spot where I made love to Valerie the other night. My chest tightened.

Do you know what it takes to love a man like me?

The smoke was thicker now as I came up to the stream. We spread out, and I began calling out for her.

"Valerie!"

I tried not to panic. I tried not to let the demons of my past take over. I needed to be here, for her.

Chaos continued around me, and I heard the voices of my cowboys in the distance, calling out for the lost enchantress. Ranger was cutting through the trees now, the ground beneath us slowly inclining. In another half mile, the soft ground would transition into rocks, trees standing tall between them. I looked up, taking in the lush green and the orange glow lurking behind the trees. I could feel the heat of the fire against my skin, and Ranger was neighing in protest. He got on his back legs, and I tightened my hold on him.

"Easy, boy! Easy! Yah!"

He landed back on his front legs with a thud, and we took off. I knew this trail like the back of my hand, better than the others. There were things about this trail that never changed, not since my childhood. There were carvings in the trees, put there by my mother. She hiked this trail every day.

My heart was pounding in my chest as my eyes scanned the burning forest. The flames were near me now, less than twenty feet away, showing no mercy as it spread, incinerating the green grass and climbing the tall trees, ready to burn it to the ground. I knew this land. I knew these trees.

They would still be standing long after I was buried in the ground.

Ranger made a noise again, but I couldn't take my eyes off the other side of the wall of flames. My woman was on the other side of it.

I knew it.

I backed Ranger up and leaned forward. "Gotta get her, bud."

My fists tightened on the reins, and I tightened my thighs around the beast—my friend.

To my right, I heard Mags call out to me. I turned my head and found him staring at me atop his mare. He was shaking his head.

"No! Denver, the fire is out of control!" he screamed, bringing Midnight closer to me.

Don't be stupid, sweet boy.

Momma's voice echoed in my head, but then another voice followed. A voice that I wanted to hear for the rest of my life.

Smoke, please.

I turned to my best friend; he was closer to me now. "Don't," he warned. "They're calling for a chopper. Let's head back."

I adjusted my hat, pushing it down. "Been a cowboy all my life, Mags." I shook my head and looked up at the smoke rising from the trees around us.

"I get it now, ya know?" I tightened my hold on the reins again, and patted Ranger, giving him the reassurance he needed.

"Kings," he snapped.

"Love ain't meant for cowboys. Because when a cowboy falls in love, not even the fires of hell could stop him from being with her."

He didn't have time to respond, because Ranger was already charging for the flames with me on his back.

My steed jumped into the flames, sending us both into hell.

Valerie

Air.

I needed air.

I was surrounded by thick, dark smoke.

It wasn't like my cowboy's smoke, intoxicating and full of promise.

No, this smoke was filled with death and pain.

I yanked on my binds again, praying this would be the time I would break free. It didn't work. I banged my head against the bark of the tree. My kidnapper had drugged me again and when I woke, I was on the ground, chained to a tree by my ankle.

The man didn't speak or look at me when I woke. He turned on his heel and left. Minutes later, the fire ignited. It had been far away from me, further down the mountain, but the fire didn't care about direction. It spread across everything and anything, leaving a path of scorched land behind. However, smoke cared about direction. It rose.

Perhaps that was Moonie's goal, for me to die of suffocation. How fitting, considering I'd fallen in love with a man with smoke in his eyes and darkness in his heart.

I was surrounded by the smoke now, and I could barely see anything in front of me. There had been a stream to my right, but it faded away as the fire grew. The sound of flowing water faded too, due to the panic of the forest.

My head felt funny, and it hurt to swallow.

The end was here.

There was no stopping it.

I was going to burn on Denver's mountain.

I was going to die knowing he hated me. He hated me for bringing Moonie Pipelines into his world. He hated me for being the enemy. He hated me because he loved me.

My mouth opened, and I gasped for air. I coughed and looked at the cuff around my ankle. It was barely visible. I didn't have the energy to break my ankle, and that was the only way I would get free.

It didn't matter anyways.

Fire was all around me; smoke was above me.

Coughing again, I scooted back to lean against the tree. My eyelids felt heavy, and I just wanted to rest...

Perhaps just a minute, I could rest...

"What do you mean?" Denver's body shook beneath mine from laughter.

I shot him a glare. "I'm serious, Smoke."

His handsome smile faded, and his eyes darkened. The next thing I knew, I was under him, his massive body pinning me into the mattress.

"Say it again?" he asked, his voice low. A dark lock of his hair hung down in front of his forehead.

I shrugged, trying to appear nonchalant. It wasn't working.

"Would the baby sleep in Caleb's room or would we have to redo—"

"You tellin' me my baby is inside of you?"

Tears formed in eyes as my arms snaked around his neck. I nodded, the diamond on my wedding band flashing in the moonlight beside his head. Life was good, Mom was healed, the cancer was gone, and I was going to give my lonely, dark cowboy a baby.

Heaven.

I was in heaven.

Chapter Forty-One

Denver

"VALERIE!"

Fuck.

I was in the middle of an inferno, lost in the thick endless smoke.

Ranger had been in the smoke for too long. There was no way out for me, not without her. But for him? I couldn't—I couldn't keep him with me any longer. I hopped off my stallion, coming around his front. He was scared, and guilt was eating at me. Coughing, I pressed my forehead against his, looking him in the eyes. We had been searching for longer than I intended, and I needed him to get off this mountain. He needed fresh air and clear skies. His instincts would kick in. I trusted that.

"Thank you, old friend. Go home, you hear? You get home and I'll be there soon," I promised, uncertainty seeping in my bones. The sound of cracking wood drew my attention from him, and about twenty yards from us, a large, burning tree branch crashed to the forest floor. Ranger freaked out, neighing and jumping. I let go of his reigns. "Go! Get out of here!"

He turned and ran, jumping over a smaller flame before disappearing into the smoke.

"VALERIE!" I cried out, spinning in a circle. Flames were all around me, ash and embers floating in the air. I was coughing furiously, but I had to go on.

For her.

I broke into a run, dodging the fire by ducking and squeezing between trees. There was an old hunting shack not far from here, built by my grandfather in the fifties. It was to the west of me and to the east...was Hallow Point.

That was Momma's spot.

The spot I had been too much of a coward to go back to. The place I avoided for the last twenty-five years of my life.

"Baby, where are you? Tell me where you are," I croaked out, coughing. My eyes closed in defeat as the weight of failure and sorrow settled on my shoulders. My body was tired. The air in my lungs was toxic. My head was killing me. "Valerie," I whispered, my eyes closing as I tilted my face to the sky.

For a moment, the world around me quieted, the smoke wasn't burning my throat, the heat of the flames around me cooled.

For a moment, I wasn't the monster who hurt people and chased them away.

Go east, sweet boy.

My eyes snapped open and with all the energy I had left, I ran.

Through the fire, I ran to her.

For the rest of my life, I vowed I would run through fire to protect her.

Whether she forgave me or not, I would always protect her. I would always love her. I was a fool to think she betrayed me; Grayson's data be damned. I was a fool to think she didn't love me. I was a fool to push her away.

My eyes spotted one of Momma's carvings in a tree up ahead. It was an H with three hearts around it. One for Pop. One for me. One for Mase. I was close. Tears stung my eyes as the smoke became thicker, the air thinner due to the elevation. I hauled myself over a boulder, the same one I used to perch myself on while Momma would take her pictures for the day.

Coughing, I rose to my full height and called out Valerie's name again. My voice was hoarse, weak, and I knew it wouldn't carry far. Everything seemed to be closing in on me.

Death was near. My soul could feel it.

I looked up to the sky.

"I'm not a good man. You and I both know that, but she's a good woman. She's everything I didn't know I needed. Please, please," I begged, falling to my knees as slight pain shot up my thighs from the hard stone beneath me. I coughed again, but that didn't stop me from holding my arms out wide.

"You can take me," I wept to the God I'd stopped believing in. "Let me save her and take me!" The smoke was getting to me, and I fell forward, landing on my palms. My head hung and tears fell from my eyes.

"Take the broken cowboy, spare his enchantress." My voice was cracking, and my head was spinning. There was no air.

Not for me.

Not for Valerie.

I was too late.

Before my eyes, images flashed before me. A funeral, the town dressed in black. Mason's hand squeezing mine as the casket was lowered into the ground. Mason riding a bull for the first time. My first kiss. The homecoming game. My dog tags hanging around my neck as my rifle was being issued to me. The letters I wrote to Mason. The American flag burning, sticking out of a tank that had just exploded. My sergeant being shot eleven times beside me. Me trying to drag his body away. Me coming home, my bags thrown over my shoulder. A dark house with Pop sitting in Momma's rocking chair. Cathy. The hate in Mason's eyes the night he left. The love in Caleb's when he saw me for the first time, his tiny fingers wrapping around the tip of mine. Endless nights with my cowboys. Whiskey-laced laughter. My lonely bed.

Green.

Green eyes and the smell of cherries. Dark hair and curves. An enchanting beauty. A thunderstorm and a red rental car in a ditch. Hearing her name for the first time and tasting it on my lips. Kissing her, feeling her against me. Holding her. Listening to her pain and her accepting mine. Hearing her tell me she loved me for the first time, only days ago.

It wasn't enough time.

A lifetime of loneliness.

Only weeks of happiness.

It wasn't enough.

Hell, forever wasn't even enough. Not with a woman like her.

I needed more than forever when it came to my Valerie.

I wasn't going get forever.

I was only given *days.*

My heart would stop beating soon, and as the flames burned my body, erasing my existence from this planet, I would still be grateful.

Grateful for the short time I got to have my enchantress. Grateful for falling in love. Death would take me, leaving me in ashes, and my soul still wouldn't belong to the Grim Reaper.

No, it belonged to a green-eyed miracle named Valerie.

My soul was hers, and not even death could take it from her.

Denver.

My eyes opened, and I knew I had been sentenced to hell.

That's where most cowboys ended up, anyways.

With a groan, I sat up, coughing into the crook of my elbow. The forest was still burning around me, and I heard the sounds of a helicopter in the distance.

Holy shit.

I wasn't dead.

Pushing to my feet, I scanned the area around me. I was still on top of the boulder, a crowd of flames surrounding the base of it. Something glistened to the right of me, catching my eye.

The stream.

The water was still flowing, defying the will of the harsh flames. There was a fallen tree ten feet away, but the water still pushed underneath it. I followed the line of the tree trunk, my stomach in knots. Then—then, something else caught my eye.

My enchantress.

Her red dress was like a beacon in a sea of darkness, calling out to me. She was on the ground at the base of a tree. A guttural cry left my body.

"VALERIE! BABY!"

Coughing, I reached for the walkie. "This is Denver! I got her! She's at Momma's spot, Hallow point," I yelled, breathless.

"The chopper is coming! Hold on, Denver!" That was Jigs.

I was heading to my love, too busy to respond. I backed up to the opposite edge of the boulder. "I'm coming, baby. Hold on," I murmured before I broke into a run. I leaped off the boulder and over flames. The ground greeted me with resentment as I crashed and rolled. Pain shot through my shoulder, but I ignored that. Pushing to my feet with a grunt and a curse, I was running again.

As I got closer, I saw she was face down in the dirt, her dark hair spread around her shoulders and back.

"No, no, I'll have none of that, baby. Ya hear?" I rasped, coughing through the thick smoke. I dropped to my knees and rolled her over.

Fuck.

My beauty.

My enchanting Valerie.

Frantically, I bent, putting my ear to her chest, and my fingers on her neck. There was a pulse, but it was fading.

She was fading away from me.

No, no, no.

I couldn't lose her. Not now. Not when I just got her back.

Coughing again, I hauled her up against the tree, using my body as shield from the fire. I gripped her face with one hand, bracing the other on the trunk.

I was dizzy—lightheaded—and I just wanted to sleep, but my heart and soul wanted to see her green eyes open again.

"Open your eyes, Val. Let me see that green. Give me my green," I begged, my voice shaking with desperation and sorrow.

Nothing.

My head fell and my shoulders began to shake.

Denver, focus.

I lifted my head, coughing some more, and squinted. I scanned her body for any other injuries. My hands followed my eyes. She was okay.

Fuck, but she was okay.

No bruises or blood I could see. My hands and eyes went further down. She wasn't wearing any shoes, and she had been last night.

I couldn't wait to kill him.

I couldn't wait to hang him up like a hog and make him scream.

I couldn't wait to hear his cries and pleas for mercy.

Until then, I needed to get Valerie home—where she belonged.

I made sure she would stay leaning back against the tree before I moved, trying to find the other end of the chain. "Where the fuck is it?" I growled. There was no way I was getting that cuff off her ankle—not without breaking it. That was a last resort. I found the other end; it was lodged into the other side of the tree by a spike.

Yanking it out with a grunt, I began wrapping the chain around my arm. I came back to her, kneeling and scooping her up. I didn't know where this energy came from, but I was grateful, so fucking grateful. I twisted and leaned my back against trunk, holding my woman close to me. I pressed a firm kiss to her temple.

"Hold on, Val. Hold on for me, baby," I chanted as I heard the chopper get closer. The tops of the flaming trees fanned, and the flames grew higher—angrier. There was no time for anything else.

Before my eyes, a thick cord fell from the heavens, and a forest firefighter landed in front of me. He turned to me, running over to us. He pulled his mask down to tell me his name and the game plan. I didn't hear a word.

The only thing that I could focus on was the precious human in my arms. When he tried to take her from me, I growled, baring my teeth and getting his face. There was no time to argue, and he didn't. He strapped us up and a second later, we were being lifted into the air. The seal of smoke broke, and blue filled my vision. The sky. I inhaled a deep breath, my body thanking me for the fresh air.

Everything was a blur, but when we were set back on the ground, in the field in front of the barn, I dropped to my knees and laid Valerie on the lush grass. People were running to us, and the firefighter was trying to pull me away from her. I shoved him back and turned back to my love.

My hand, which was covered in soot, cupped the side of her dirty face, my fingers tangling in her soft hair. I leaned down and studied with her. A set of knees appeared on the other side of my baby, and a paramedic started barking orders.

"Mr. Langston, can you lift your arm?"

I gave them an inch, my eyes never leaving her face. They checked her pulse and put an oxygen mask on her.

Everyone around us stilled, waiting for her chest to rise and inhale the air, but nothing happened.

Nothing happened.

She didn't move.

"Baby?" I called, not understanding why she wasn't breathing. She had fresh air now. That's all she needed.

"Mr. Langston, we need you to move—can someone get him out of the way, please?"

I shook my head. "I'm not fucking moving."

Hands landed on me, and I was being hauled away from her—*my love*. My Valerie. With a growl, I tried to fight, but my body was too weak.

"Denver, let them work!"

"Brother, it's okay!"

"Kings—Kings, calm down!"

"Let me go!" I shouted, surging forward. The paramedics were ripping open her dress, exposing her skin to the sun above. A defibrillator was being passed to the main paramedic, and then the pads were pressed to her body. I didn't understand it. My baby just needed to breathe. Why wasn't she breathing?

"Clear!"

Silence.

No movement. Nothing.

"Try again!" I demanded.

They were trying again.

"She's okay, Den. She's gonna be okay," Lance said next to my ear. I don't know if he was trying to convince me—or himself.

"Clear!"

Valerie's limp body arched and fell back down to the ground.

Nothing.

Tears clouded my vision and the ache I'd been feeling for the last twenty-four hours morphed into something else. Something stronger.

Despair.

It slammed into me like the force of a falling tree. It shattered me like an earthquake, breaking the ground beneath me and swallowing me whole.

"Valerie!"

The hands on me loosened and I broke free, running and crashing to my knees beside her again. I cupped her face, lifting her head gently.

"Baby, don't you fucking leave me," I pleaded, my voice cracking. The people around us were fading away, and it was just her and me. I studied her face, her clear fair skin, dark lashes and brows, her perfect lips, her cute nose. Everything was perfect, designed for me to love. Those perfect lips were set into a small frown, unmoving—*lifeless.*

My body shook as anguish took over and my tears landed on her chest. Cowboys cried, all right. I reached down and pulled her dress closed. Her body was for my eyes only.

"You need to come back to me, ya hear? I need you. Is that what you want to hear, Enchantress?" My thumbs stroked her cheeks. "If that's what you want to hear, then I'll tell you every second of every day, baby. Morning, noon, and night. Dammit, I'll never stop telling you how much I need you—how much I love you. But you gotta come back to me—come *home* to me, Valerie."

Nothing.

My head dropped and I hauled her body up into my lap, my arms banding around her. I began rocking, holding her head against my heart. "You hear that? You hear that, baby? That's for you. That's yours. It beats for you and Caleb. No one else."

Nothing.

A broken sob escaped me, the force of it shaking me and her. My hand sunk into her hair, holding her close. I looked up, my eyes taking in the ranch, the land, the mountain, the smoke in the sky, and the sun above us. When I looked down at her, I pressed my trembling lips against her forehead.

"You can have my land! Take it, baby! As long as I get to keep you. Do you hear me? Hallow Ranch isn't home if you aren't here. Valerie, please—*please*," I sucked in an unsteady breath. I pressed my forehead to hers and closed my eyes.

"Breathe for me, Valerie. Breathe for me and never stop," I cried, shaking her body. "Breathe for me because I'm breathing for you."

Chapter Forty-Two

Valerie

"You found my spot."

I twisted and looked up behind me. The sun was in my eyes, so I brought my hand to my forehead.

"I'm sorry?" I called.

There was no one behind me, just the tall, proud, sturdy trees. The sun wasn't out today, but that was alright with me. Overcast days were my favorite. With a shrug, I turned back to my book. Pride and Prejudice. A first edition, believe it or not, that I snagged at the bookstore that recently opened beside my mom's flower shop.

The stream in front of me was flowing, the birds were chirping, and wildflowers were blooming all around me. I don't remember how got to this place. All I remember is coming around a large boulder and stumbling on this sanctuary.

Upon seeing it, I decided this was a lovely place to indulge in Mr. Darcy. He was a guilty pleasure of mine. Tall, broad, handsome, and grumpy. His dry humor made me laugh time and time again—it never got old. My brow furrowed as my eyes scanned the delicate pages and patterns of worn ink.

When was the last time I sat down to read? When was the last time I painted?

"You paint?"

I let out a yelp and clutched the book to my chest.

There was a woman in front of me on the other side of the stream. She was wearing light washed jeans, a navy T-shirt with an "H" over the pocket on the left side. Her dirty blonde hair was tied behind her in a messy knot at the base of her skull. She had a pink bandana over her head, along with an old camera hanging from her neck.

The woman lifted a finger and pointed to the flat rock I was sitting on. "You found my spot," she stated. Her voice was soft, but strong.

I scrambled to my feet, brushing off the back of my blue dress. Funny, I thought I picked out the red one this morning... I shook my head and focused on the beautiful woman. "I'm so sorry. I had no idea. Honestly, I was just..." I trailed off and I could feel my brows coming together.

What had I been doing before I got here?

The woman smiled. "I'm Jane."

I found myself smiling back. "I'm Valerie."

She tilted her head to the trees. "What a pretty name."

"Thank you. My mom picked it."

I felt something tug on my heart at the mention of my mother. She was working at the flower shop, right? Did I need to pick her up?

"What are you doing here, Valerie?" Jane asked, her blue eyes coming back to my face.

I held up my book. "This spot—your spot—looked like a lovely place to read," I explained, laughing a bit. "In fact, I can't remember the last time I actually sat down to read something that wasn't court papers."

Another tug. I was a lawyer. I owned a small firm.

Didn't I?

"Mr. Darcy is a stubborn one," she noted, hopping over the small stream to stand beside me. I hummed in agreement.

"He is, but I think that's a loveable quality."

Jane looked to her feet, a small smile playing on her lips. *"I have a stubborn boy—two, actually."*

I smiled. "Just two?"

Sadness drifted over her face. *"The Lord only let me keep two of them. The rest...the rest had to go home."*

Silence stretched between us, and a sense of longing snuck into my chest. I had children, didn't I? The law firm, a husband...was he stubborn? Was he broad and tall enough to make me feel small? Were the kids okay?

"What are you doing in my spot, Valerie?" Jane asked, repeating her question. I watched as she held her camera to her face, pointing it to a bushel of wildflowers in front of us, the wind commanding the bright yellows, pinks, and dark purples to dance. She snapped a few photos before looking at me, smiling again.

"You don't have to tell me if you don't want to. I'm just surprised to see you here."

Confusion resurfaced. *"I'm not supposed to be here, am I?"* I asked, looking at the book again.

A deep sigh left her, and she dropped the camera from her face, letting it hang down from her neck again. *"You paint?"* she asked, changing the subject.

I nodded, a melancholy feeling hitting me now.

What was wrong with me today?

"I liked painting as a kid. Then, when I went to college, I promised myself I would pick it up again after I got my degree," I explained, dipping my toe in the stream.

"Did you? Pick it up again?"

I paused, trying to remember. A soft, sad laugh left her. *"What are you doing here, Valerie?"*

"Why do you keep asking me that?" I snapped, backing away from her now.

She shook her head. "I don't mean to scare you, sweet girl, but you aren't supposed to be here."

"Where am I supposed to be, Jane?" I was scared now. I didn't know how I got here. I didn't remember anything. My past was fuzzy, and I all knew was that this looked like a good place to read. Jane didn't answer me. Instead, she took a seat on the flat rock, looking up to the trees and the clouds above them.

"You know, every ten years or so, Mother Nature will throw this valley for a loop. When I was pregnant with my first, it had been a hot day in the dead of winter..." She trailed off and looked at me. "Recently, it had been a storm. It brought in a cold front at the beginning of summer, believe it or not. The rain was freezing, and it shocked the town."

"Get in the God damn truck!"

My body jerked at the sound of the deep voice. I looked around.

Who said that?

When I looked to Jane again, she was staring into the forest, smiling brightly. The sound of children laughing filled my ears, and my heart warmed. I smiled, my eyes following hers, but I couldn't see the children. It looked like Jane could.

"Those your boys?" I asked softly.

She shook her head. "Not my stubborn ones." She sighed again. "No, I had to leave them behind..."

"Where are they?" I asked.

"Discovering themselves, I suppose. Everyone does at some point."

I nodded, shifting on my feet.

"You know what I miss the most?"

My eyes met hers. "What?"

"My green kitchen."

"Valerie."

Another body jerk, but this time, I felt warm all over. Excited. The deep voice said my name and made it sound like a song. I wanted to hear it again, but I wasn't sure if was going to.

"Then, of course, my porch swing," Jane continued.

A deep, raspy, velvet laughter filled my ears, followed by a familiar feminine one. Mom. That was Mom's laughter.

"Is my mom here?" I breathed, looking around.

"Not yet, sweet girl. She won't be here for a while," Jane replied, picking up her camera again.

"What am I supposed to be doing, Jane?"

Everything around us shifted and suddenly, we were in a field. There was a man, a tall man, with a black cowboy hat on. I watched as he fell to his knees, his body rocking back and forth. He was crying.

I turned my head to Jane, struggling to peel my eyes from him. "Why is that cowboy crying?"

Tears shined in Jane's eyes, and I could see only one thing in them. Love.

"Who is that?" I asked, needing to know. I needed to know everything about him.

She blinked and wiped away her tears. "He's so stubborn, sweet girl. You are going to have to be patient with him, you know? The past hasn't been kind to that cowboy."

I looked back and forth between the broken man and her. "I don't understand."

"You will," she promised. "Now, take my hand."

My book was gone, and I took her hand. She wrapped her other over the top of mine. "Here's what you need to do, Valerie..."

Jane started fading before my eyes, as well as the scene around me, fading into a warm, white sea. Her touch was gone, and she was nearly gone, too.

"What, Jane?" I cried out. "What do I need to do?"

I was floating—drifting in an endless space of white now, alone.

I felt the tug again.

Then, I was dropped on my feet, back in the forest. Now, it was on fire. I looked down at my body. My skin was covered in dirt and my dress. It was red now, torn down the middle. Frantically, I looked around, and then I realized...

I was back at the stream, except it wasn't green and thriving. It was charred and smoke lingered in the air. No, it wasn't lingering. It was reaching out to me from the forest, stretching and surrounding me.

This was gray smoke.

A familiar gray.

A comforting gray.

I looked up and sucked in a breath. Jane was here again, except now, her dirty blonde hair was down, surrounding her face. She was wearing a cream dress and a blue jean jacket.

"Jane?"

"You have to go back, do you understand? You can't stay here," she said gently.

"I don't know what I'm supposed to do if I leave," I admitted.

She gave me another small smile and lifted her chin. "Breathe, sweet girl. That's all you have to do. Breathe for him. Trust him. Be patient with him. Love him. That's all, sweet girl."

"I don't...I don't know how."

"Breathe for him."

"Breathe for me, Valerie. Breathe for me and never stop."

Air. Burning. Gasping. Gripping. Light, sunlight. A shadow.

A man. A man's face.

Eyes.

Gray eyes.

"Smoke," I whispered.

Denver's face crumbled above me, his handsome features twisting in disbelief. "There she is. There's my enchantress."

He pulled me up right into his lap, and his arms wrapped around me. I felt his hand on the back of my head, and he stared at me. "Fuck, I thought I lost you," he rasped, pressing his lips to mine.

Everything snapped into place.

The last memory I had of him. The anger and hurt that masked his features as he sent me away. The kidnapping. The fire. None of that mattered now. The only thing that mattered was this.

Us.

Our hearts were beating as we breathed.

We breathed for each other.

My lips danced with his, my hands sliding into his hair. His hat fell forward slanting over both of us, but we didn't care. I whimpered, savoring his taste as his tongue touched mine. He kissed me harshly, with a desperation that went beyond words. There were no words to describe this kiss. His head slanted as he kissed me deeper. My fingers gripped his hair, and I pressed my body further against him. I could feel his heartbeat against me, and that had me gasping.

I pulled away and looked into his eyes.

"Denver?"

"Yes, my love."

"What's your mother's name?" I asked, bringing my hands to his face. His beard felt like home—he felt like home. His dark brows came together, and his throat bobbed.

"Jane. Her name was Jane."

Tears filled my eyes as I nodded. I didn't give him a response. I couldn't. So, I kissed him again.

Okay, Jane. I'll do it.

I'll breathe for him.

He'll breathe for Caleb, and he'll breathe for me, too...

Epilogue

Denver

August

"Baby," I growled, pulling her back to me.

"Denver," she protested.

My hands slid up her wet, naked body. "Not starting my fucking day without being inside of you." My hands cupped her breasts, squeezing them. She arched against me, her perfect ass rubbing against my hardness.

"We woke up late..."

With another short growl, I pressed her against the shower wall, my hand on the back of her neck. Then, I lifted her leg, placed her foot on the ledge as I lined my dick up with her soaking entrance. With a slow, powerful thrust, I sunk into her tight, magnificent heat. Our bodies connected, and I felt like I could breathe easier again. The fire was nearly two months ago. The forest was healing, and so were we.

Every morning, I made love to Valerie. Slow and sensual or hard and fast, it didn't matter to me. I just needed to be inside of her. I needed to feel her body against mine, needed her to hear her cries of pleasure. Most of all, I needed to tell her I loved her while we were connected.

"Honey," she gasped, reaching back and gripping my wrist.

"I know, baby," I whispered in her ear, pulling out and thrusting inside her, to the hilt this time. She quivered around me. Fuck, I would never tire of her.

"D-Denver, move," she begged, grinding back against me. My hand came to her front, gripping her throat and pulling her flush against me. Her head rested on my shoulder, her mouth close to my ear, just the way I liked it. I moved slowly at first so I could savor her.

I was supposed to be down at the barn an hour ago. We were sending some cattle to the livestock exchange today, and then we would begin to prep for the next season. But since the fire, I couldn't leave the house without showing her how much I loved her, with my tongue, hands, and my cock.

I pulled out and slammed into her again, her gasps playing like a symphony to me, over and over, until her nails were digging into my skin. Her cunt tightened around me, fluttering, and I knew she was close.

"Already, Val?" I taunted, loving the way her body responded to mine. My hips were slamming into her ass now, giving her everything I had, forcing her to take it as I held her captive in my arms. Her breath against my skin sent tingles down my spine. Fuck, I loved it.

I loved the sound of her breathing.

I loved the sight of her green eyes.

I loved the smile she gave me first thing in the morning.

I loved her.

My soul was tethered to hers, and there would be no parting from it. She was mine and I was hers. She made me a better man. She accepted my demons, and the pain of my past. She was patient with me and I her. There were days when it would hit her—the pain of watching her mother suffer—and I would have to give her space. Sometimes, she would want me to hold her and while other times, she wanted to be alone.

Nancy's cancer was progressing, faster than Dr. Martin expected. However, we were making her comfortable, so that when the time did come for her to leave us, she would be surrounded by family. Yes, there were good days and bad. Valerie and I leaned on each other through it all. I was falling in love with her a little more with each passing day, which seemed impossible because I loved her more than the air in my lungs.

"Yes," she panted, her hand leaving my wrist to play with her clit. I slowed my movements, relishing the way her body shook around me. She was so fucking close, and I knew the second her climax peaked, it would send me over the edge.

"Such a good girl," I purred, my voice gravelly. My hands dropped to her hips so I could pull her back to meet me thrust for thrust. She whimpered, working her fingers faster. "Play with that little pussy, Enchantress. Fuck, you take me so well." I pulled out all the way, the head of my cock hovering over her entrance.

Valerie whined, "Please, please. Please, Denver."

"You gonna come on my cock like the good little slut you are? Hm?"

She nodded against me. "Yes, yes!"

Slowly, I pressed back inside her, loving her. When I was balls deep, I pressed a kiss to her temple. Then, I fucked her hard, not stopping, even as she came apart on my cock, her cries bouncing off the shower walls.

"*Fuck*," I ground out, thrusting my hips into her. "Fuck, that's good. Take it, Valerie. Take it and tell me what I need to hear."

"I-I love you!" she moaned. "I love you, Denver."

White dots scattered my vision as I filled her, a guttural roar coming from my lips. "Valerie—*fuck*—*Valerie!*"

When we were both sated, leaning against the wall for support, my arms around her, I whispered in her ear, "I love you more than air."

Now, I could start my day.

Valerie

"First of all, get fucked," Lawson grumbled, causing the whole table to erupt in laughter. His brother threw his head back. Mags shook his head and looked at the ceiling. Beau put a hand on his flat stomach and the other on Lawson's shoulder. Denver's body shook under mine, his face in the back of my hair. Jigs' shoulders shook as he raised his glass of whiskey to his lips.

Caleb was back at the house, his friend Adam, Dan's son, staying the night. Jackie had flown back in for the week. She and Mom were on the porch swing under a blanket, talking about life, I'm sure.

The rest of us were at the bunkhouse, playing cards. It was Friday night, and we were celebrating the end of the season. The livestock exchange had gone well, and Denver sold a quarter of the herd, meeting his goal. The payout was done, and the sun had set. The whiskey had been poured, bellies were full of dinner I made, and laughter filled my ears.

Things were good.

For now.

Tim Moonie had disappeared, along with the man who kidnapped me. Cathy was still missing, the last time anyone had seen her was when she tried to take Caleb. Sheriff Bowen suspected that she cut ties and skipped town. He brought me in for questioning a week after the fire, and when I told him Cathy had a black eye, he had the same thoughts that I did. Moonie. Moonie beat her because she couldn't convince Denver to sell.

After the fire, my dark cowboy hovered over me for days. He apologized a thousand times. Yes, I counted, even though I'd already forgiven him. He explained to me that Joseph Grayson, the bounty hunter, did an extensive background check on me. According to the Moonie Pipeline database, I had been added to the payroll again. It made sense to me, then, why Denver looked so betrayed.

"I shouldn't have pushed you away," he whispered, his voice cracking.

I looked up from my lap. He was sitting on the edge of his bed, leaning forward over his knees. His hat was beside him on the bed, and his dark hair was still damp from the shower. It was five in the morning. There was work that needed to be done, but Denver woke me up and told me that he couldn't hold it in any longer.

"Nearly killed me, seeing you on the ground like that," he croaked. His throat bobbed, and he tore his gray eyes away from mine.

My bottom lip trembled as I rasped, "I understand why you lashed out, honey."

He shook his head, ready to dismiss my forgiveness. He didn't think he deserved it. I stood from the chair, letting the blanket pool at my feet before stepping in between his legs. My hands went into his hair, and I tipped his head up so I could get lost in his smoke as I poured my heart out to him.

"You are a good man, Denver Langston," I whispered. "Your past doesn't define who you are now. The mistakes of your father and brother haunt you. Your mistakes are still haunting you. The promise you made your father weighs down on you every single day. Hallow Ranch is yours. It's all you've ever known. Hallow Ranch has branded you, my dark cowboy."

"Val..."

I cupped his scruffy cheeks and leaned down an inch away from him. "You. Are. Good. You. Are. Worthy. Of. Happiness."

"Stop."

"*I understand. I understand why you did it. I understand you were hurt and felt betrayed. You lashed out, Denver. You did the same thing that any other human would do,*" I explained, stoking his skin.

"*I hurt you.*"

"*I hurt you, too.*"

His eyes closed and his arms wrapped around my middle. "*You did nothing wrong.*"

"*Accept my forgiveness, Denver,*" I pleaded. "*Accept it so we can move on.*"

He hadn't—not yet, but he was working on it.

He was also seeing a professional about his PTSD, provided by the Corps. Once a month, he goes to Denver for therapy. He completed his second session on Monday. My cowboy doesn't talk about it, and I don't push him. He was fighting his demons in a healthy way, and I couldn't be prouder.

As for me, the smoke from the fire could've done severe damage to my throat and lungs, but after several visits to Dr. Martin's office, I was cleared. My lungs were healthy and clear. I should have rejoiced, but there was another set of lungs on my mind.

Mom's.

The cancer was getting more aggressive. Dr. Martin told me it was best we make her comfortable for the time being, that he would still do her chemo treatments, if she wishes.

Her last treatment was yesterday.

That was her decision, and I was trying my best to accept it. Every night, aside from tonight, Mom and I would sit on the porch swing together. Sometimes we would talk, and sometimes, we would just sit in silence.

Because sometimes, you didn't need words.

Sometimes you just needed the person.

"You alright?" Denver's deep voice rumbled from behind me. I was sitting in his lap. I twisted my head and gave him a small smile as I nodded.

He studied me for a moment, his gray eyes searching mine. His smoke surrounded me, and my heart fluttered. I could breathe easier with his smoke. "You ready to leave?"

I looked at the boys, who were currently arguing about the cards Beau just played, and then went back to Denver. "I think I'm going to sit with Mom." His hands slid over my thighs, squeezing them gently.

"You want me to walk you up?" he asked softly.

I leaned into him, pressing my lips to his. "I'll be okay, cowboy."

He grunted.

The boys said their goodbyes, and as soon as the bunkhouse door shut behind me, I heard Denver say, "Beau, you know that hand is bullshit."

Smiling to myself, I put my hands in my jean pockets and started up the hill. The warm, welcoming light of Denver's house—*our house*—guided me home. Mom and Jackie weren't on the porch swing, but I could see their silhouettes in the front window. They were on the couch, watching a movie. My eyes lifted to the second story front window to the little boys running around and playing with swords. Or they could be lightsabers. Or wands. The possibilities were endless with that kid.

Once I was close to the house, I heard a throat clear.

I let out a scream, jumping and spinning around. There, parked back up behind Denver's old red Chevy was a new, all black, Z71 Chevy Silverado, but my eyes weren't focusing on the truck. They were on the cowboy sitting on the tailgate. His long legs stretched for miles, hands hanging between his knees. He was wearing a black cowboy hat, a dark Henley, jeans, and boots.

Gray eyes assessed me, trailing up my body slowly, drinking me in. The five o'clock shadow that dusted his jaw couldn't conceal the tension. My eyes snapped up to his.

Only, when I looked into these gray eyes, there was no smoke.

There was a storm inside of them, raging, destroying everything in its path.

"Mason," I greeted.

A ghost of a smirk teased his lips, and that's when I knew. Mason Langston, gorgeous like his older brother, was trouble.

"Denver around?" he clipped, his voice deep.

Bite your tongue, Val. Don't say anything.

I stared, not saying a word.

He sighed and hopped down from the tailgate. Goodness, he was tall, too, towering over my tall frame, making me feel small. He slammed the tailgate shut and stalked towards me. The sleeves of his Henley were pushed up, revealing warm, tan, toned, forearms. There was a tattoo peeking out from the inside of his left arm, but I couldn't make it out.

"I asked you a question, darlin'," he said, softer this time.

"And she won't answer it."

Oh, no.

Denver.

Mason's eyes snapped up, looking over my head. I saw pain flash in his raging storm like a lightning strike. Just as quickly as it came, it was gone. His jaw ticked. "Denver," he bit out.

"Mason." Denver's voice wasn't angry, but it was stern—cautious. "Valerie, come here," my cowboy ordered. Mason looked back down to me, and I backed away from him. When my back hit Denver's front, he pulled me to his side.

"What are you—"

"You son of a bitch!"

Oh, shit. That was Lance.

Before I knew it, a body rushed to Mason and a fist connected with his jaw. Denver moved immediately, yanking his man off away from his brother. To my right, I saw movement; the rest of the boys were here, clearly enjoying the show.

Jigs was shaking his head.

Mags, Beau, and Lawson were smirking.

Heaven, grant me the strength.

Mason rubbed his jaw, glaring at Lance. "The fuck?"

Lance was fuming, his eyes wild. Denver pulled him back and released him, standing between the two men. "Lance," my cowboy warned.

Lance shook his head. "No. No. Told myself if this sorry son of a bitch ever stepped foot on this ranch again, I'll—"

"I'm not here to cause trouble," Mason deadpanned, walking back to his truck. For a second, panic shot through me, worried he was leaving. No, he went for the passenger door. He looked back at all of us.

"That bounty hunter you sent after me told me about Moonie," he explained, his eyes on Denver. I stepped up to my cowboy, wrapping my arm around his waist, hating how tense he was. When I looked at his face, his stone-cold mask was on, the one he used to give me.

"What's it to you?" Mags asked, his voice hard.

Mason looked to the five cowboys behind Denver, the ones who showed up, put in the work, and kept Denver from falling apart for the last decade. When his stormy eyes met Denver's again, there was no mistaking the pain within them.

My heart ached.

They didn't hate each other.

They were broken and they didn't know how to mend it.

"Found a way to take Moonie down," Mason said.

Everyone stiffened and the air around us shifted. He pulled the truck door open to reveal a sleeping woman.

A beautiful woman.

Her hair was reminiscent of the fire that nearly killed Denver and me. She was tucked under a fuzzy tan blanket, her light pink lips parted. She was also clutching a teal metal water bottle to her blanket-covered chest with both hands.

"Who the hell is that?" Denver questioned.

Mason looked to me and back to his brother.

"My wife."

To be continued...

Author's Note

Babes,

What. A. Ride.

First, I want to thank you, new and returning readers, for taking a chance on my dark cowboys. This was the most emotional story I've ever written, and I am so grateful for each and every single one of you.

When Denver first came to me, I was in the middle of writing **Grand Slam**, the fourth book of the **Batter Up Series**, and he took me by surprise. A dark cowboy? How was I going to swing that? Then he told me about his brother, Mason, and their broken bond. I knew I had to write their stories—*soon*. The cowboy romance that I'd planned on creating was intended to be short, hot, and extra spicy. Instead, it transformed into this beautiful, dark, gut-wrenching romance about love and lost. Of course, we couldn't forget the spice. ;) I hope that you enjoyed Valerie and Denver, and also hope that you'll stick around for book two! Mason's story, **Sing for Me**, is up next and it's going to hurt....then again, everything I write hurts...

Returning readers, welcome back! I'm sure that you noticed some little easter eggs that I hid in this book...hinting at what is to come.

A note to my new readers: Hi, I am so happy you are here. FYI, all of my books take place in the same universe. There were characters mentioned in reference to the **Batter Up Series** and the upcoming **Burn Out Trilogy,** a dark street racing romance series. If you're in the mood for a dark baseball romance that involves that mafia and the FBI—check it out! Start with Dean and Gwen's story, **Batter Up**!

Acknowledgements: To Alexa *(The Fiction Fix)*, thank you for everything. You are amazing and so special to me. I love you. To Sam, thanks for listening to all my voice messages without complaint. I love you so much. To my team, you already know that I love you to the moon and back. Thank you for supporting me, making me laugh, cry, and being the *best* team a little author like me could have. To my family, thank you for supporting my dreams. To Dean Connors, none of this would be possible without you popping into my head seven years ago, thank you.

Don't forget to leave your review for **Breathe for Me**! Reviews help authors out so much!

Leave your review here: Breathe for Me (The Langston Brothers Duet Book 1) - Kindle edition by Ann, Brittany. Romance Kindle eBooks @ Amazon.com.

For more updates check out:

Home | Brittany Ann (brittanywitte1495.wixsite.com)

Follow Brittany Ann on Instagram!

@authorbrittanyann_

Follow Brittany Ann on TikTok!

@authorbrittanyann

Titles

The Batter Up Series
Batter Up
Swing Batter, Swing
Strike Zone
Grand Slam
Slugger (a Batter Up Novella)

The Langston Brothers duet
Breathe for Me (Denver and Valerie)
Sing for Me (Mason and Harmony)

The Burnout Series
St. Louis isn't done with you yet, babes. Buckle up.
Breakneck (Dontell and Mina)
Clutch and Shift (Leon and Amara)
Full Throttle (Cain and Dominque) – Spring 2024

About the Author

Brittany Ann is an indie author.
Batter Up *was her debut novel, published 09/2021.*
Brittany's dream has come true, and she has her readers to thank for that.
She has been writing since she was eight years old, creating worlds in composition notebooks underneath her math homework.
The story of BU came to her years ago in a dream and it changed her life.
Writing romance makes her soul feel whole.
Her favorite meal is mac n' cheese and her first crush was Batman.
Brittany Ann is working on multiple projects and she cannot wait to share them with you!

Milton Keynes UK
Ingram Content Group UK Ltd.
UKHW011609050624
443786UK00024B/202